WOODS
ON
FIRE

WOODS
ON
FIRE

SOMETIMES, THE BEST NEWS STORY IS BURIED IN A SHALLOW GRAVE

BRIAN LEE WEAKLAND

Word Association Publishers
www.wordassociation.com

Printed in the United States of America

ISBN: 978-1-59571-430-5
Library of Congress Control Number: 2009931821

Word Association Publishers
205 Fifth Avenue
Tarentum, Pennsylvania 15084
www.wordassociation.com

To Louann,
my joy, my heart,
and my love.
Always.

When we were fleeing the burning city
and looked back from the first field path,
I said: "Let the grass grow over our footprints,
Let the harsh prophets fall silent in the fire,
Let the dead explain to the dead what happened.
We are fated to beget a new and violent tribe
Free from the evil and the happiness that drowsed there.
Let us go" – and the earth was opened for us by a sword of flames.

— Czeslaw Milosz, "Flight"
The Collected Poems, Ecco Press (1988)

Prologue

December 1965

Twelve miles into his journey, Brother John began to doubt his stamina.

The path along Kinzua Creek was overgrown with brambles, and his canvas moccasins accumulated mud and silt from a late November storm. Each step was twice as heavy as it should be, he thought. Only five slogging miles to go. Then he could rest before his return trip.

Sharp moonlight shot through the pines, dotting the narrow path with specks of white. As midnight approached, colder wind shifted from the northwest. Within hours, freezing rain would begin.

Brother John did not choose this night for his journey; the council did. The whole idea seemed both ludicrous and glorious – a 71-year-old man traipsing miles along a creek bed in the rugged Allegheny National Forest.

Alone.

At night.

Towing a canoe upstream.

Floating $5 million worth of pure silver.

Brother John Brontzman was, perhaps, the most distinguished elder of the Senecas of Pennsylvania. He avoided high office in Seneca Nation. He preferred to work quietly. His life was the Indian life – respect for the land, respect for his heritage, respect for God and family.

He was a retired lumberman and owner of the Quaker Bridge general store. It was destroyed by the United States Government a few months ago. Brontzman had watched helplessly as federal officers removed his store inventory and loaded it on a northbound truck. Then the officers laid a torch to his store.

Brontzman always stood at attention, never conceding any curvature of age. His silky white hair always grew a bit longer than it should. When hair reached his collar, he cut it himself. He resisted the urge to braid it or, God forbid, gather it in a ponytail.

Two other features were striking: his high protruding cheekbones and searing deep brown eyes.

Brother John was every inch the Indian. A descendant of two pure Iroquois bloodlines, he was received into the Nation as "Towanda Scribe."

As a teenager, he adopted his family's English name solely to get a job. Brontzman was one of few Senecas who could claim purity in a sea of European contamination. He never lorded that fact over his contemporaries, however.

One look at Brother John confirmed his authenticity. He commanded respect, not by his tongue but by his physical aura.

So it came to pass that this final task devolved to Brother John.

By unanimous vote of the tribal council, Brontzman was chosen. He alone could be trusted to return the silver bars to their burial site. He alone was virtuous enough not to be corrupted by greed or avarice of the white man. And he alone was strong enough to survive the solo eastern voyage in bitter cold while tribal councillors and their families fled north into New York State.

At least, that was the plan.

Like everything else in his life, Brontzman approached the challenge with equal parts courage and allegiance to Indian tradition. Because he was honoring a command of the Seneca president, Brontzman dressed in native fur and headdress. He adorned his face with crude paint, not as a warrior but as a hunter in the forest. He carried a simple knife and wire.

His canvas canoe bore precious cargo.

Brother John charted a route along the centuries-old Indian path that crisscrossed the westward flowing Kinzua Creek. His journey began fifteen miles east of Warren before it continued upstream into the more desolate Allegheny Forest.

It was a path Brontzman recalled from his youth. He often camped along the creek with his older brother on summer nights, sometimes venturing as far as the railroad bridge at Mount Jewett.

About equal in size, the boys could portage their canoe in Seneca style, using a leather tumpline over their foreheads and supporting the canoe's weight directly by their backs. The return trip floating downstream was their reward.

Brother John had no assistant tonight. He alone pulled the floating canoe upstream by rope. Fortunately, November's rains swelled the creek and the canoe easily traversed the rocky bed.

Brontzman paused to examine his cargo. Hundreds of heavy silver bars lining the canoe floor seemed unshaken by the journey. He had carefully placed the bars in two layers from fore to aft. A stiff canvas covered the treasure.

Gathering clouds obscured the moonlight as he neared the headwaters of Kinzua Creek. He tugged his canoe past a series of bends. Through the trees he could see a silhouette of the Kinzua Viaduct Bridge. Its steel trestles seemingly glimmered with ice as he pulled the canoe up a bank and onto a grassy knoll. His shoulders ached.

The precise location for reburial was important. According to his Tribal Peacemaker, the silver treasure was poisonous. Its source was Spain, and Spanish explorers spread terror to Native Americans, the Peacemaker said. The silver must be returned to the spot where Seneca scouts discovered it years ago.

Now, in moonlit shadows of the great Kinzua railroad bridge, John Brontzman double-checked his tattered map and drove a shovel into the damp earth.

By 2 a.m., as a light rain began to fall, he had completed a three-foot-deep trench. One by one, he lowered the shiny bars into their muddy grave.

John surveyed the submerged fortune. It was of no use to his wandering people, he thought. The silver was cursed.

Shovelfuls of dirt then filled the trench. Brother John laid topsoil and grasses over the site. On his map, he indicated a burial spot about 50 feet from the third bridge trestle. He folded the yellowed paper and returned it to his tackle box.

As he pushed off the canoe, Brontzman remembered the acrimony that led to this moment. The tribe's forced relocation by federal officials triggered overwhelming emotion among the Senecas. Some younger men vowed to hold their ground and fight. Older men, resigned to a history of broken government promises and forced assimilation into white culture, advocated a peaceful move to Seneca land in upstate New York.

Brontzman was too old to fight, but not too old to forfeit his heritage. He asked the Peacemaker for an incantation. The wise man replied that Spanish fingerprints on the silver would provide "enough of a curse" to its finder. But Brontzman insisted that the treasure should not be extracted "without consequences."

The Peacemaker recalled legends passed down from warriors of old. Then he recommended an incantation uttered by TI-OOH-QUOT-TA-KAU-NA at the moment the Senecas secured their treaty for the land in 1794.

"Bury the silver with your bare hands," the Peacemaker had told Brother John. "Tamp the soil with your feet and raise your eyes to those who passed before. Then, in a loud voice, you must proclaim to all within hearing that *harm will befall any white man who disturbs the peace of this land – for all eternity.*' Then quietly withdraw, with your head high and your heart in good spirit. For your life's work is done."

Brontzman did as he was told.

In haste, he returned to the canoe, slid it into the chilly water and paddled away.

Kinzua Creek became comfortably wider and quicker within a few miles, but a cold rain soaked the old man. A few hours later, as dawn began to break in the forest, Brother John's canoe passed the mouth of Kinzua Creek and glided westward into Allegheny River.

Brontzman ached. Exhaustion set in. He opened his tackle box and retrieved a bottle of Blackbeard's Rum. He swallowed a shot. Warmth oozed down his throat, and he relaxed for the first time in months. He took several more drinks before pulling the canvas tightly around him.

The canoe glided in open water.

Brontzman was content. He closed his weary eyes and lay back. His work was done.

He fell asleep.

Swift water veered the canoe into a deep channel. Cross-currents from an emptying tributary pushed Brontzman toward the southern bank, wedging the now-pilotless canoe under a fallen tree trunk near shore.

And there it stayed for an hour, while intensifying sounds of rushing water advanced up the valley.

Soon the water level rose one foot, then two feet. Haphazard currents extracted the tackle box. It fell from the craft.

The last Indian of Pennsylvania, intoxicated and unconscious, flipped into warmer water – water that was flowing upstream.

Soon the old man's body was submerged by ten feet, then twelve feet, then more.

Brother John's canoe dislodged after the tree trunk gashed its hull.

Silently, it disappeared into the deepening reservoir of Kinzua Dam.

Chapter One
The Interview

February 2008

Tom Zachary finally had his interview date with the governor.

Zachary, editor of the Kane News Leader, had kept his part of the bargain for nearly four years. If the weekly newspaper withheld publishing its exposé about Governor Jimmie Bailey's activities on a certain night in Pittsburgh, Zachary was promised exclusive access to the full sordid story of the Bailey family.

The editor never understood why he had to wait so long. Perhaps, he thought, the story was so sensational that the young governor wanted to secure his re-election first. The "gag order" worked; Jimmie won in a landslide.

Before he would sit for an interview, Jimmie insisted that Zachary agree to certain ground rules.

First, the interview would be conducted at Leigh-Rose Mansion, the Pennsylvania governor's McKean County estate. Second, no sound-recording equipment of any kind could be used.

Third, the interview was one-on-one; only the two of them would be in the room.

And, fourth, the most troubling condition to Zachary, the governor could review and edit his quotes before any story would be published. Zachary only acquiesced to the last condition after Jimmie reminded the editor of his well-known reputation to print first and ask questions later.

Shortly before 2 p.m., Zachary turned his old station-wagon

off Sowers Road and onto the rugged driveway. He was met by dazzling sunshine and then by a hassling state trooper. After showing his credentials and pressing a News Leader business card into the officer's palm, Zachary was waved through.

Leigh-Rose Mansion stood on the hill like a proud grand dame. Ancestral home of the Bailey family, the sprawling mansion withstood an 80-year history of triumph and tragedy. Jimmie Bailey's grandmother commissioned the home in 1920. Expert craftsmen from the secluded northwest corner of Pennsylvania gathered on the site to build a masterpiece. Mahogany and other hard woods, hand selected from the Allegheny Forest, adorned the first floor library and greeting room. Local stone was cut and incorporated into the dining room fireplace and the spacious kitchen. Best of all, the mansion came with stunning views of the unspoiled, forested Kinzua Valley.

But the important historical value of Leigh-Rose accrued from its occupants, Zachary believed.

It was here that Jimmie's rascal father, Brock Bailey, was born. It was here that Jimmie's mother was brutally kidnapped. And it was here that the new governor and his bride, Ann Negley, were married. In fact, Zachary recalled, the new governor's wedding day was the last time he was invited here.

"You may wait in the study, Mr. Zachary," the housekeeper told him as she removed papers from a wingback chair. "Governor Bailey knows you are here and will be with you shortly."

Zachary unbuttoned his winter topcoat and hung it on the chair. Without a word, the housekeeper folded his coat over her arm and left the room.

The editor opened his briefcase and removed a dog-eared legal pad. For the past four years, Zachary added new questions on the pad for this interview. He anticipated a private meeting with the governor at any time, so preparation was key. His questions were sharply worded. He wanted as much information as possible before Jimmie tossed him into the cold.

The legal pad's first entry was dated July 21, 2003. How well Zachary remembered that day. Everyone in McKean County remembered that day.

Zachary was an invited member of the press corps at the morning funeral of Jimmie's mother, Sallie Bailey. Her funeral procession involved a ride in the open-air Knox-Kane steam train from Kane to the overlook cemetery. For years, Zachary had covered the political rise and fall of the Bailey family.

Buffeted by high winds, the passenger cars swayed dangerously as the train crossed the historic Kinzua railroad bridge on its way to Bailey's family cemetery plot. During the crossing, Jimmie Bailey summoned Zachary to his car. Jimmie told the editor that, someday, they would have an interview and that the entire story of Bailey's family, good and bad, would be revealed.

Later that afternoon, an unexpected storm raced up Kinzua Valley. Within minutes, the 100-year-old, 300-foot-high railroad bridge was blown apart by an F-1 tornado. Yes, Zachary remembered that day.

"It's been a while, Tom." Governor Bailey entered the study and broke Zachary's trance.

"Just thinking of things, Governor." Zachary stood and smiled.

"Please sit," Jimmie directed him. "You remember Bill Pennoyer, my chief of staff?" A balding man, with a band of reddish hair encircling his head, followed and sat to one side.

"Yes, but our rules...." Zachary felt betrayed.

"Yes, yes the rules," the Governor replied. "Rules are for mules, at least that's what the General Assembly tells me. This is not unusual, Tom. Bill goes where I go. He's an extra set of ears. Maybe he can fill in some blanks if I don't remember."

"Well, I thought we had an agreement that just the two of us would...."

Pennoyer loosened a rung on his belt and pulled a steno pad from his coat pocket. "Let's get going, Jimmie. Get this over with."

Zachary addressed the governor. "Is Bill taking notes?"

"Yes, just for my records," Jimmie said. "Is something wrong?"

"Oh, no. Not at all." Zachary pretended to scratch his shoulder under his suit jacket. His hand slid to an interior pocket and found his Dictaphone. A simple flick set the machine on "Record." Two can play this game, Zachary thought.

The governor cleared his throat and crossed his legs. "Let's see. Where should I begin?"

Zachary laughed. "I probably know more about your family than you do. The News Leader has been following the Baileys for about 100 years."

"You know a lot about me." Jimmie suspected that Zachary knew more details than the Pennsylvania State Police.

"Can I talk in front of Mr. Pennoyer?"

"He knows everything. Go ahead."

Zachary cleared his throat and flipped to page two of his legal pad. "This is what I know. Correct me if I'm wrong. You became governor after your father died. In March 2003, while he was Governor of Pennsylvania, his limousine was involved in a crash on the Fort Pitt Bridge in Pittsburgh. He was **not** in the limousine at the time."

Pennoyer was scribbling furiously.

"You're not correcting me, Governor," Zachary observed.

"Continue," Jimmie replied.

"Somehow, your father escaped searches made by the state police, Pittsburgh police and federal authorities," Zachary continued. "What happened in the next four months is unclear to me, but your dad flew his helicopter to the landing pad here at Leigh-Rose on the afternoon of July 21, 2003. He used a walking cane and started to cross Kinzua Bridge. This was minutes before the tornado struck. And you, Jimmie, followed him onto the bridge."

Zachary looked up from his notes and saw a blank expression on Jimmie's face. "Do you dispute that, sir?" Zachary asked.

"Listen, Tom. This is an interview, not an interrogation. Just ask me questions."

"I just did, Governor." Zachary placed his pad on the floor. "Here's my next question: When you saw the man on the bridge, did you know it was Brock Bailey?"

"Not at first." Jimmie felt Pennoyer's hand on his back, and he shrugged it off. "The man on the bridge was a mystery. I saw him land the helicopter and watched him through the mansion windows. He used a stick or a cane and was limping onto the bridge. I followed at a distance and, when he turned to face me, he had a full beard. And the light, well, it was really dark because of the storm."

Zachary pressed forward. "When did you first realize the man was your father?"

"When he told me to get the hell off the bridge," Jimmie answered. "God, it was all so unreal. He was supposed to be dead. They were looking for his body in the Monongahela River. And there he was, cursing at me in this horrible storm."

"He took a shot at you, right?"

Jimmie recalled answering this question twice before. The first was to his then-fiancée, Ann, as he tried to explain the weird happenings of that day. The second was to state police commissioner Josh Gibson as the cop was waving handcuffs in his face. Jimmie hadn't yet revealed the details to Pennoyer, who poised his pen for more notes.

"Yeah. He shot at me. The bullet glanced off the deck near my feet. And then he raised the gun again," Jimmie told Zachary.

"There was a second shot, at the same time Brock Bailey fell backwards," Zachary said. "I saw that on the state park surveillance tape."

Jimmie turned to his aide. He noticed a look of shock on Pennoyer's face. Maybe, Jimmie thought, the rules should be followed after all. "Bill, you're excused. We'll be another hour or so."

Dolores Gibson was remarkably composed for a woman who lost a $2 million insurance claim. Moments after McKean County Judge Horace Van Lear issued his ruling in the three-year-old case, Mrs. Gibson bounced to her feet and hugged her attorney.

She chatted easily with the bailiff as he returned her trial papers. With a wink to the judge and a wave to his secretary, Mrs. Gibson pushed upon a swinging courtroom door and met reporters waiting outside.

"How do you feel, Mrs. Gibson?" was the first dumb question posed.

"Disappointed, for sure." Her attorney grabbed the attractive widow under her arm and directed her toward the stairs. Two staffers from the Bradford Era followed.

"Are you going to appeal?" one asked.

Gibson dug her heels into the marble floor and pivoted around. With a smile that could thaw the courthouse roof, she answered: "An appeal? Yes, yes, let's do an appeal young man."

Her attorney had already secured a hefty retainer for such a contingency.

"So Judge Van Lear is wrong?" another reporter asked.

"He's such a sweet man. Very charming, and he tries so hard to be a good judge," Mrs. Gibson answered in measured tones. "But nobody is correct all of the time. On this case, he simply didn't know my husband. Josh would never do such a thing."

The attorney waved off any more questions and ushered his now-famous client and her chinchilla stole into a waiting limousine.

Meanwhile, the 14-page opinion from Judge Van Lear was copied and distributed throughout the McKean courthouse.

Grisly details of the death of Frank "Josh" Gibson, former state police commissioner, were found on pages 4 through 8, to the delight of courthouse mavens.

According to the judge, Gibson's fall from the ruins of Kinzua Bridge's southern terminus was roughly 250 feet. His head struck a concrete support pier and splashed into two pieces. The area of his "brain distribution" near the fall site was measured and dutifully recorded by the county medical examiner. Assuming they could put Humpty-Dumpty Gibson back together again, his weight was estimated at 280 pounds.

As Judge Van Lear noted, no one was present in late May 2004 when Gibson leaped into immortality. He likely entered the Kinzua State Park after midnight, used his master key to unlock chain-link security fencing and then inched onto the southern bridge deck, the judge surmised.

There was no investigative reason for the portly commissioner to visit the doomed bridge at that hour, according to the opinion. His autopsy reported no intoxication.

Dozens of witnesses testified that, in his last few weeks, Gibson was gloomy. He told friends that shadows were chasing him and that he felt cold. While Dolores maintained that Josh was as "cheery as ever," his associates said he began smoking again and spent hours alone in his office.

One state trooper recalled Gibson standing alone on the bridge a month earlier during Governor Bailey's wedding reception, but testified that the Commissioner returned to safe land with a smile and a remark about the beautiful Kinzua Valley. "He had every opportunity to jump right then and there," the trooper said. "But he would have spoiled the governor's party."

Months later, on the fateful May night, Gibson approached the missing center span of the half-mile long bridge and "made a conscious decision to step off the edge," Van Lear wrote. "A suicide note was not found, but that fact is not critical for this ruling. The man simply wanted to say goodbye in quick fashion.

"Our sympathy for Commissioner Gibson and his wife does not permit this Honorable Court to void the plain language of his life insurance policy. Commissioner Gibson's suicide excuses payment of the $2 million in policy proceeds to his wife, the plaintiff, Dolores Gibson. SO ORDERED."

Tom Zachary and Governor Jimmie Bailey, the only two men who knew Brock Bailey's final chapters, stared at each other in uncomfortable silence.

Each knew that Jimmie abandoned his father on Kinzua Bridge seconds before a tornado ripped through the center span. Each knew that Jimmie, wanting to cover up his moment of cowardice, found his father's body in the valley, drove it to Pittsburgh and dumped it into the Ohio River – fooling police into believing that Brock Bailey actually perished in the Fort Pitt Bridge accident months earlier.

Zachary, too, covered up Jimmie's misdeed by agreeing to withhold the story until he interviewed the young governor. As days stretched to months, and months to years, Zachary's delay in the story became harder to justify. Now, more than four years since the tornado, the News Leader editor would appear unethical, or at least foolish, if he printed a story.

Jimmie knew that fact, so he delayed the interview as long as possible. But, after his re-election, Jimmie could postpone Zachary no longer.

"When I saw you on the train, Tom, none of this stuff had happened," Jimmie began. "It's true that I took my father's dead body from the bridge debris and put it back in the Pittsburgh rivers..."

"But it never was in the Pittsburgh rivers before," Zachary interrupted.

"Yeah. That's true. But everyone was looking for him in that river, so he was easier to find in Pittsburgh. He was dead, Tom. What's the difference?"

"Gibson knew what happened," Zachary said. "We talked before Josh died."

"Gibson never arrested me, Tom. He had every opportunity. Are you suggesting that I had something to do with Josh jumping from the bridge?"

"No, I didn't say that." Zachary could sense Jimmie had

inherited the rage of his father.

"Well, I don't know why the hell Josh did that. For Heaven's sake, I had offered him the commissioner job for another term. He was delighted and then, six months later, he did something really stupid."

Zachary's interview hit dry land. Jimmie was providing no news, and Zachary wondered whether he made a mistake not printing his exposé four years ago. But there was something intriguing about the Baileys; he couldn't resist Jimmie's tease about more family secrets.

"You've stalled me for four years, Jimmie. I haven't printed anything about you and Brock and the night in Pittsburgh. Why talk now?"

Jimmie checked the closed door and paced before the window. "I have a friend, not a close one. He celebrated his 18th birthday yesterday; he's not a child anymore. You need to talk to him."

"I don't understand, Jimmie. What does this have to do with you and Brock?"

Jimmie scratched a name and telephone number on Zachary's legal pad. "What I'm about to tell you is the scoop of your life, Tom. But before I do, you must promise not to print a word about what happened that night in Pittsburgh."

"Ever?"

"Yes, ever."

Zachary felt as though he were trading a decent "Let's Make a Deal" prize for whatever was behind Curtain No. 2. The newspaperman read the name on his legal pad – Mike Devlin.

"Devlin?" Zachary asked. "He's not 18. If you're talking about Van Lear's bailiff, he's older than either of us."

"You've got the right guy," Jimmie said. "Devlin will lead you to the young man. But first, give me your word about the Brock Bailey story and I'll give you a better one."

"OK." Tom relented. "I'll throw my journalistic integrity on the ash pile. You've got your deal, but you better have a good story,

Governor."

"Let's take a walk," Jimmie suggested. "The sun and cold air will do us some good."

The governor informed his staff of his plans, and the two men stepped down from the Leigh-Rose porch and onto a mulch trail leading away from Sowers Road. Winds from the previous evening had cleared snow from the trail. The expansive side yard was spotted with deer tracks and rock outcroppings.

Wet snow clung from the pines as they approached the north gate. Jimmie unlatched the hasp and motioned for Zachary to follow along a state park road.

"I don't quite know where to begin," Jimmie said. "My father was a great politician but he had his faults."

Zachary knew of Brock's greed for power and money, but the former governor's personal life was well guarded from the press.

"I don't know how to tell you this, Tom," Jimmie said. "Brock had a mistress for nearly 20 years."

"That means …"

"Yes, my father had a mistress for years before my mother was kidnapped. I think my mother knew because there was always tension in the house, and a lot of fighting. My dad would be missing for days at a time."

"Where was he?" Zachary asked.

"He arranged for this woman to live in a farmhouse in Virginia. He would fly his helicopter there most weekends."

"So he was in Virginia…"

"When my mother was kidnapped," Jimmie finished the thought.

"I'm so sorry." Pieces of the Bailey puzzle were falling into place for Zachary. Brock's unfaithfulness and Jimmie's reaction to it probably caused the juvenile incident where Jimmie fired a handgun at his father. That crime was not reported in the News Leader either.

"On the day of the tornado, Brock returned to Leigh-Rose by

helicopter and I saw him walking across the bridge toward my mother's grave. I couldn't let that happen, Tom. So I tried to stop him."

"But the tornado stopped him."

"He fell to the tracks. The tornado finished him off," Jimmie said.

"That's why you drove him to Pittsburgh, to dispose of the body in the river?" The Dictaphone machine in Zachary's pocket clicked. The tape ended.

"Yeah, but here's the story I want you to print, Tom. The woman in Virginia was my father's housekeeper. She is a black woman, now about 45 years old. Devlin, the bailiff, has her name and address."

Zachary looked puzzled. "What do you want me to do, Jimmie? Call her up and accuse her of adultery? Splash her photo on the front page of Wednesday's edition? What's the point of that? So you can exact some revenge? I'm not going to do that!"

"Hold on, Tom. You have to hear the whole story. While my father was governor, this woman had his child. A boy, a black boy."

Zachary stopped in his tracks. "Holy crap, Jimmie! You mean there's another Bailey out there?"

"I never met him, Tom. I don't even know his name. Apparently Brock and his girlfriend gave him up for adoption and kept Brock's name off the boy's birth certificate. But during the probate of my father's estate, this child surfaced."

"That explains why Judge Van Lear was so secretive about your father's will and trust," Zachary said.

"Van Lear, that son of a bitch ... Don't quote me on that, Tom ... he ordered DNA testing from the remains of my father in the Pittsburgh morgue. He had the DNA sample sent to a doctor friend of his for analysis. It was a precise match with this kid's DNA. So Van Lear split the estate."

"How much ...."

"I'm getting to that, Tom. My attorney, Pennoyer, was sitting in the judge's chambers, and he's dumbfounded that Van Lear found this missing heir, a fourteen-year old from the projects in East Liberty. Can you imagine?"

Zachary imagined all right. He imagined the headlines, as well as a Keystone Press Award, an invitation to the Penn State Journalism School Honors Banquet and, perhaps, an infinite string of sell-outs for the struggling News Leader.

But this story required a lot more legwork than one stroll with Jimmie Bailey through the snowy woods, he realized.

Suddenly, Jimmie threw his arm in front of Zachary's chest and put an index finger to his lips. About 100 feet before them, a black bear was rummaging through a state park dumpster. The bear's head popped up and a fast food wrapper fell from his teeth.

"Hold still, Tom," Jimmie cautioned. "Let me scare him."

"What? Are you nuts?"

"No, I used to sneak up on these bears all the time," Jimmie said as he picked up a rock from the trail. "Just watch."

Jimmie hurled the rock toward the startled animal. With a loud bang, the rock careened off the metal dumpster about a foot from the bear's ear. Jimmie let out a whoop and began to run toward the animal with arms flailing. Zachary stood in disbelief. The bear catapulted itself from the trash heap and bounded out of sight. Jimmie walked back while rotating his shoulder.

"You missed him," Zachary called.

"Oh, I never hit a bear," Jimmie answered. "See, in politics, just like in baseball, you want to throw the ball as close to your opponent as possible – just close enough to scare the shit out of them and earn their respect."

"Will you be throwing any baseballs at me?" Zachary asked warily.

"I don't see you as an opponent," Jimmie replied. " I see you as a friend, somebody who can help me get through my problem. Maybe the only person who can."

"What problem is that, Governor?"

Jimmie turned to face his interviewer. Zachary hadn't seen such a serious expression from Jimmie since his meeting on the funeral train.

"I'm messed up," Jimmie began. "I have a beautiful wife, lots of money and a very satisfying political career. But there's a part of me that's incomplete. You see, Tom, I've waited four years like you. Now is the time to find out who he is – to finally meet my half-brother. You are the man who can make it happen. And when you do..."

Zachary detected watering in Jimmie's eye, perhaps from the moment or from their exposure to the February chill.

"... you will have your story." Jimmie put his arm around his friend's shoulders.

"But why me?" Zachary asked. "You could do this all yourself – get the name from the bailiff and make a visit to East Liberty or wherever this teenager lives."

"No, Tom. I've thought this all out. I simply can't take the state limousine into the slums of Pittsburgh and intrude in this kid's life. You need to find him, get his confidence, learn all about him and figure out how he can be part of the Bailey family."

"And my story ..."

Jimmie reassured him. "You'll have your story, an exclusive story. The reunion of two lost brothers – one descended from wealth and power, and the other raised up from poverty and depression. But first, talk to Devlin. He knows you'll be visiting the courthouse. Keep it confidential."

"Why?"

"I don't want any direct contact with my half-brother until you talk to him. I'm the governor, for Heaven's sake. This could all blow up in my face if we don't handle it right. Devlin understands that. He's doing this as a personal favor to me."

"And the judge?"

"Van Lear knows nothing about this," Jimmie replied. "Keep that old man in the dark, Tom. Otherwise, we might be violating one of his freaking orders. OK?"

Zachary nodded in agreement. The governor turned to the side trail to Leigh-Rose Mansion. The newspaperman followed, pondering his new task. They reached the front porch as light snow flurries began to sparkle in the waning afternoon sun.

"One more thing," Jimmie said. "I don't have any animosity to this kid, even though he took a lot of money from the estate."

"How much, Governor?"

"This is between us, Tom. Van Lear would have my head if he found out I told you."

Zachary cast him a mean look. "With all due respect, Governor, you're asking me to do a Dr. Livingstone search in the wilds of Pittsburgh, for free, no less. I think I'm entitled to some background information to get started."

"More than $25 million." Jimmie appeared to be pained by this admission.

It's a safe bet, Zachary thought, this mystery half-brother was not living in the wilds anymore.

Chapter Two
The Gossip

Patrons at the Golden Wheel Restaurant expected limited menu choices. "Today's Daily Specials" blackboard, therefore, never disappointed. Wednesday's surprise was the change from Tuesday's Boston bean soup. Overnight, a cook discovered some aging sausage in a left-over container. He christened his new concoction, "Spanish bean soup." According to early diners, Wednesday's broth was slightly more flavorful.

Since 1935, Golden Wheel occupied the ground floor of General Thomas Kane Hotel and Boarding House in downtown Kane, Pennsylvania.

Nothing much had changed over the years, except its window blinds were a bit yellower and the air, a bit mustier. Elmer the Elk, at least the animal's head, still graced a wall above the restrooms. Near the emergency exit, a plaque marked the spot where Elmer was shot in 1954. The confused animal had been looking for food outside the kitchen.

As always, Golden Wheel offered two sittings for hungry masses of McKean County – the first sitting from 11 a.m. to 6 p.m. featured fine foods, the second sitting from 6 p.m. to 2 a.m. featured fine liquors. Floors were scrubbed at 3 a.m.

Gladys Toolie lived at the Golden Wheel. In fact, nobody could recall seeing her anywhere else. Northward of ninety years old, Gladys waited tables, brewed coffee and dished gossip.

She began her culinary career sometime between the Bataan Death March and MacArthur's return to the Philippines. "It's been hell ever since that awful war," she reportedly told a table of Japanese diners last fall, shortly before she was stiffed on the gratuity.

Her name tag, always pinned at an annoying slant, identified the energetic, but annoying waitress as "Toolie." That's the name she gave on her job application in 1942. "Toolie" stuck; only the most astute Kane diners knew her first name.

No happening or nuance occurred in McKean County without word passing Toolie's ears.

She lingered for hours at the cash register absorbing nuggets of information. The more animated the conversation at one table, the slower she bussed an adjoining one.

If she saw a new face in the crowd, Toolie engaged in a little chit-chat. Before lunch was through, she would learn enough from the stranger to write a short biography.

And if Toolie didn't recognize you, she would bother every other customer until your name and vital statistics were revealed.

Business was brisk for this wintry Wednesday's lunch hour, but not as brisk as the conversation. Dolores Gibson's courtroom loss was Topic A, and Toolie was leading the invective discussion.

"Now, Clete, don't call that woman a witch," Toolie pretended to scold the town drunk. "She's a widow, for the love of Josie. She's in a grieving way."

"For the 'love of Josie?' What the hell does that mean?"

"Just an expression. We say that all the time, least I do," the waitress answered. "I think that wicked insurance company should pay."

"Toolie, dear," Mayor Byrnes interjected. "You can't jump off a bridge and expect that an insurance company is gonna pay your spouse millions of dollars. That's crazy."

"By my stars and garters!" Toolie tossed in her favorite saying. "Josh didn't jump. He was pushed! Angels hold him close."

Of course, Toolie knew exactly what to say – whatever most people were thinking. There had to be foul play. After all, a legend like Gibson would not be such a coward. The same thought had crossed everyone's mind, but only Toolie could say it with impunity.

"Well, they found no suicide note," said the town's only plumber. "People don't jump without a suicide note, do they?"

Toolie was making progress with the lunch crowd. "That's right," she said, serving up another round of Spanish bean soup to a table of postal workers. "He wouldn't leave that pretty little thing behind without explaining why. Unless, of course …"

"Now, Toolie, don't you be smacking that widow," Clete scolded. "She's in a grieving way."

"Saints preserve us, young man! Josh Gibson had a $2 million life insurance policy. Why, Dolores probably stuffed the suicide note down her brassiere."

"Her what?"

Several older customers chuckled at the drunk's ignorance.

"Brassiere, brassiere," Toolie replied. "Ask your mental health therapist next time you're in rehab."

Immediately, a forensic study of Dolores Gibson's brassiere became the fantasy of Golden Wheel's male diners. Unless Josh's suicide note was longer than the national average, chances were that it could neatly fit within the folds of Dolores's Maidenform. And what man, with two good hands and a healthy curiosity, wouldn't be motivated to conduct a legal Fourth Amendment search of such evidence, preferably in private?

Imaginations ran wild.

Golden Wheel customers were not alone in their thoughts. Josh's death from the Kinzua Bridge spawned a cottage industry of gossip in western Pennsylvania.

Rumor mills ground stories of conspiracy, murder and a forbidden love triangle. Other than the Mafia rumor, most innuendo pointed to Dolores Gibson as the responsible party.

The attractive, youngish socialite seemed to be an unusual match to the corpulent police commissioner's "back country ways" when they married six years ago.

More than once, she fought with him at public events, once grabbing his necktie so viciously that Josh called for back-up from a trooper at an adjacent table.

Two weeks later, she tried to serve Josh with divorce papers, but he had the complaint dismissed due to her dalliance with the only two divorce attorneys in Oil City – reportedly at the same time.

After the commissioner's demise, Mrs. Gibson frequented clubs on Pittsburgh's South Side. She never wore the same jewelry twice, and she never ended the evenings alone. Grief has a way of bringing people together.

Sam, morning teller for Mid-State Bank, tossed his napkin on a half-eaten plate of hash browns and asked Toolie for his check. She pulled a pen from behind her ear, licked her index finger and ripped a page from her pad.

"What do you think, Sam? Was he pushed?" Toolie asked.

"Judge Van Lear said that Josh jumped. That's good enough for me."

"Well, I suppose so. If I were married to that harlot, I'd jump too, for the sake of Methuselah." Toolie tallied up the bill.

He opened his wallet. "Here, keep the change, for the sake of Toolie."

Tom Zachary locked up his News Leader building in Kane before driving east to Smethport, the County Seat.

Route 6 was largely clear of snow, except for an occasional drift from open fields. Fortuitously, he found a parking space outside Jackie's Front Porch store. One apple Danish and a brewed coffee later, Zachary crossed Main Street and climbed the McKean courthouse steps. The courthouse clock tower directly above its impressive Greek columns showed 8:55 a.m. He shook wet rock salt from his shoes as he entered the marble foyer.

Zachary had covered the courthouse beat for years, but this time he prowled the halls as an agent for Governor Bailey.

This was familiar territory for the journalist. On the ground floor, he passed offices for the Recorder of Deeds, Prothonotary and Register of Wills. Zachary detected a rare emptiness in the courthouse. The row offices were lighted, but doors were closed. Even though the courthouse opened at 9 a.m., clerks usually were handling public business at 8:30.

Taking the private back stairs, Zachary reached the long, second floor hallway. On this floor were court personnel, judge chambers and the ceremonial courtroom.

Mike Devlin, the bailiff, had a small, interior office, just large enough for a desk, credenza and a monitor with a live closed circuit video of the courtroom. Devlin's office was around the U-shaped hall from Judge Van Lear's chambers – remote enough to require a sprint by the bailiff when summoned by His Honor.

First door on the left, the one with no sign, was Devlin's, Zachary remembered. Nine o'clock was the best time to find the bailiff, after 8 a.m. daily Mass at St. Elizabeth's and before his 10 a.m. daily dressing down by Judge Van Lear.

Zachary saw no light in the office but heard rustling sounds; Devlin was probably expecting him. His visit had to be quick. He could not be seen by anyone else, just in case Van Lear would later suspect that his bailiff was leaking confidential court information.

As Zachary turned the doorknob, the rustling sounds stopped. He slowly pushed it open and saw a dozen shadows jump from the darkness.

"SURPRISE! HAPPY BIRTHDAY, MIKE!!" The lights flashed on. Zachary, who had instinctively jumped backward, was pummeled with cuss words. The saltiest were from the old judge.

"Zachary, you son-of-a-bitch. What are you doing here?" Van Lear practically charged at the stunned editor. A law clerk blocked his tackle.

"I'm sorry, I had no idea." An embarrassed Zachary turned to leave when the Register of Wills grabbed his collar and threw him into the bailiff's office. "You're part of the party now, Tom," she pronounced.

"What the …"

"Shut up, you stupid fart," Van Lear whispered in Zachary's ear, to the concealed amusement of most. "I'll deal with you later. Just keep your head down and we'll pretend you were an invited guest."

Zachary crouched behind the desk, reasonably sure that a joint appearance with His Honor would surprise the birthday boy. When Devlin arrived in a few minutes, Zachary and Van Lear popped up like turkey thermometers. Devlin's surprise turned to horror when he saw Van Lear's arm around Zachary, as if the two were best buddies. Devlin pulled Zachary into the hall when the fervor subsided.

"Don't expect any help from me, Tom. This little trick of yours is not going to cost me my job." Devlin was angry.

"Just give me the kid's name, Mike. And I'll be out of your hair."

"The estate file is sealed. Tell the governor to get a writ from the Superior Court. You have to go through legal channels now. Van Lear will find out if I give you any information. Got it?"

"It will take months to get the Superior Court to look at anything, Mike. And there's no guarantee the file ever will be unsealed."

"I have to get back to the party. You're on your own, Tom."

The second floor hallway was deserted as Tom turned a corner toward the elevators. At the far end, he could see an open door leading to Van Lear's chambers. Echoes of a party in full swing rattled behind him. Zachary entered the empty chambers and sat in the leather swivel chair of power. He placed a handkerchief over his hand and picked up the telephone receiver. He pressed #54 and was connected to a downstairs court clerk.

"Yes, Judge, may I help you," said a sweet young voice.

"Can you send a file up to chambers right away? It's the Estate of Thomas J. Bailey. It should be under seal."

"Do you know the year and the file number?"

"How the hell should I know!" Zachary did his best cursing under the circumstances. "The death was in 2003. What is your name?"

The flustered clerk stuttered, "Lily."

"Well, Lily. Get me that file, DAMN QUICK!"

Zachary detected the sound of lips moving but no words being uttered. "Listen, Lily. I'm working privately in my office so when you come up, two minutes from now ... and I'm watching the courtroom clock, just place the file on the secretary's desk and leave immediately. Do you understand?"

Before the clerk mouthed a response, Zachary slammed the phone. He closed himself in the judge's office and waited. In about a minute, he heard the tapping of high heels and a timid voice calling under his door: "The file is here, Judge." Zachary counted to fifty before opening the door to the secretary's office. A thin brown folder was on the desk. Taped across the folder opening was a yellow strip with the red letters: "SEALED by Court Order."

Zachary tried to pick at the tape with his fingernail when he noticed raised markings on the file's exterior. Someone had written names on the interior file jacket cover. Zachary traced the raised letters as best he could. The names Tanya Duncan and Matthew Moore were evident, along with a Pittsburgh area code and telephone number. Could they be Brock Bailey's mistress and Jimmie Bailey's half-brother?

The editor dialed extension #54. "Lily?"

"Yes, Judge?"

"I am so sorry. I made a mistake. I don't need this file. You can come back and pick it up."

"I will, Judge, as soon as I finish with this customer," the clerk answered.

"DO IT NOW, LILY! I mean, I'm fixing to lock up the office

and go to Devlin's party, so I really need for you to pick it up immediately. Is that clear?"

"Yes, Judge. Will you leave it on the desk?"

"Right where you left it, Lily. And one more thing..."

"Yes?"

"Please don't tell anyone, and I mean anyone, about this. I've been having some concentration problems with my new high blood pressure medication, and I don't want anybody to know."

"You have my word, Your Honor."

"Fine. I'll put in for a pay raise for you, dear."

"Bless you, Judge."

Traditions die hard at the Pittsburgh Forest Club. Since 1882, the legendary country club near Fox Chapel treasured its years of genteel respectability and professional, low-key service to the scions of Pittsburgh industry.

But last week, when Billy Herman keeled over during a gentlemanly game of gin rummy and paramedics burst into the men's dining room, the club suffered yet another blow to its reputation of tranquility. It was Herman's fourth medical emergency in five years as a Forest Club member – all of them dramatic and unsettling.

Efforts to resuscitate Herman while his gurney rolled across the manicured practice putting green were successful. As startled golfers looked on, Herman relaxed his hand, dropping three queens and an empty run of spades onto the cart path.

Dr. Frischetti, long-time greenskeeper and diplomate in agronomy, detected Herman's wry smile before paramedics covered his face with a breathing mask.

The sluggish patient raised his hand, acknowledging stares from fellow members. Sirens blared as the medical van blew by the bag drop. Commotion delayed the 3:20 tee-time golfers a full two minutes.

Herman was a relatively late-blooming member of the Forest Club. At age 46, he was nominated for membership by two senior board members. Art Diddle, a wealthy optician, met Billy in the late 90's and learned to respect his customer's conservatism. In the next few years, Diddle sold Billy five pairs of prescription aviator bifocals. Dave Morganthal, the other senior board member and Diddle's friend, was an investment banker who handled Herman's bulging stock portfolio.

Knowing only two facts – that Herman came from a respected Pittsburgh family, and that Herman had a lot of cash – Diddle and Morganthal pushed him through the membership process in record time. Herman's latest spectacle, however, would call their judgment into question once again.

When he joined the exclusive golfing club five years ago, Herman had recently retired with 25 years of service to the Pittsburgh City Police. His resumé was impressive: lead unit officer in interstate narcotics cases, murder scene senior officer and coordinating detective for "the multi-jurisdictional investigation of the disappearance of Governor Brock Bailey."

His retirement was sudden and quite surprising. Days after Brock Bailey's body was recovered from the Ohio River, the career police officer handed a two-sentence letter to Captain Gourley. The first sentence expressed thanks and the second simply said, "I'm out of here."

Herman then purchased a sprawling ranch house on two acres in Zelienople and punished himself with golf.

Never married, so accordingly without guilt, he planted himself in the club. He never strayed far from the dining room and the gin rummy table.

Health issues rarely concerned Herman until his club years. A man of average size and modest athletic abilities, Herman never expected to suffer a pierced lung during his inaugural round of golf at the Forest Club.

At the sixth hole, Herman slipped while climbing from a deep sand trap and fell backwards on an upturned rake. Thanks to quick action by his playing partner, who pulled the skewer from Billy's back and stuffed the bloody hole with his golf glove, Herman survived his first near-death experience.

Herman was not so lucky eleven months later when he sneaked onto the closed course on a Monday. Still undetected by maintenance workers after 16 holes, Herman ducked into a porta-toilet for relief. An unattended multi-head grass mower, parked on the wickedly sloping 18th fairway, lost its grip on friction, slid and then rolled down the hill. The huge machine came to rest atop Herman's rest stop, pinning the golfer inside until Tuesday morning.

A broken pelvis and near fatal pneumonia kept Herman in intensive care for six days. Fortunately, his injuries were serious enough to impede club members from snickering.

In his third year as a club member, Herman was standing, seemingly safe, in his fairway. He heard a loud TOCK before being plunked on the head by an errant tee shot that had careened from a tree. A course ranger, armed with the club's portable defibrillator, restarted Herman's heart.

Then, last year, during an oppressive July afternoon, Herman was knocked from his golf spikes by a lightning bolt. He suffered minor burns, only because he landed squarely on his cigar.

Now, behind a curtain at the Allegheny General emergency room, physicians tried to stabilize Billy's heartbeat and respiration.

Doctors probed with needles and scopes. Herman drifted in and out of consciousness. He listened to softly pounding monitors and sensed sharp lighting above his bed. He felt pressure on his wrist. Then he felt fingers jabbing into his chest, as though his heart was being manipulated through his ribcage.

And, like all patients behind other curtains in all emergency rooms, Herman asked the time-worn questions of the near-dead:

What did I do?

Why is this all happening to me?
And will I be able to have sex again?

Chapter Three
The Blessing

"Holy moly! 931,000 hits! Jessie!"

Tom Zachary bent over his computer keyboard in agony, as usual. "Jessie, I need help here. What do you know about search engines?"

Zachary's editorial assistant, Jessie Krone, ended a personal phone call and visited her frustrated boss in the next cubicle. "What are you trying to do?"

"I can't tell you. Just help me out."

Jessie grew tired of his journalistic secrets. "I can't help you if you don't..."

"OK, OK. This is a big story, Jessie. I don't want to blow it."

Another feeble Pulitzer attempt for the overexcited editor, she surmised. Oh well, might as well amuse the old boy, she thought.

Zachary's computer screen indicated a search for Matthew Moore. The results indicated hundreds of pages, with the most searched pages involving the Gospel of St. Matthew and the Mary Tyler Moore Show.

"I need information," she said. "Who is Matthew Moore?"

"He's a valuable source who lives in Pittsburgh."

"Then put quotation marks around his name and type in 'Pittsburgh.' We'll see what pops up." Jessie watched his index fingers peck at the keyboard.

"That's better." Zachary noticed the hits reduced to 695.

"Do you know anything else about him?" Jessie asked.

"He's 18 years old, he's black and he's got some money. If I tell you anything more, I'll have to kill you."

His threat fell on Jessie's deaf ears. "Get off the chair, Tom. I'll take it from here."

The exasperated assistant typed additional search terms and hit "return." Hits numbered 265, but the web pages were not at all helpful. The word, "black," veered into various civil rights websites and then into news reports articles about assaults to Port Authority bus riders by a youth wielding a fork.

"That's it, Tom," she said over her shoulder. "You can kill me tomorrow, but you need to tell me more today. Who is Matthew Moore?"

Zachary sorely needed his assistant's help. The telephone number he stole from Van Lear's sealed file was useless; the line was disconnected. Also, the name, Tanya Duncan, did not appear in any telephone book. His last chance to locate the governor's mystery half-brother hinged on the perspicacity of the blonde-headed sparkplug now occupying his computer terminal.

"All right, Jessie. Here's the story," he began.

Fifteen minutes later, when Jessie closed her open jaw, Zachary suggested they brainstorm a few ideas. Perhaps his creative assistant could develop a plan to confront this teenager.

"So you looked at the sealed file?" she asked him. "Van Lear probably appointed a trustee for Matthew. He wouldn't have just handed him $25 million. We could talk to the trustee."

"I couldn't unseal the file. I pulled his name from the file jacket."

Jessie Krone retrieved her well-worn Rolodex and flipped to her courthouse telephone numbers. "Why don't you grab me something at Texas Hot Lunch? Take your time. Come back in an hour. Don't you mind what I'll be doing here."

A Texas wiener sounded mighty good and a walk down the hill likely would give his able assistant ample time to work her magic.

But Zachary believed that locating Matthew Moore, as

difficult as that task appeared, probably would be the easiest part of his mission.

WLMI, Country Radio 104, pegged the noon temperature at 6 degrees, with the usual winter caveat: "colder than yesterday, but not as cold as tomorrow." Meanwhile, sensible patrons inside Friends Memorial Public Library on Chase Street huddled around warm air vents, while feigning interest in nearby periodicals.

Friends Library, long a popular gathering place in downtown Kane, hosted its "Adult Book Group" meeting on the first Tuesday of every month. Usually, the group numbered fewer than 10 – mostly senior residents of local assisted living facilities. Today's group totaled 20 shivering souls. Everyone was intrigued by the library's February calendar of events announcement: Pennsylvania's first lady was today's honored guest.

Ann Negley, a stunning Philadelphia native, married the new governor at Leigh-Rose Mansion shortly after his election four years ago. She made Kane her home and, when the General Assembly was not in session, visited freely with area merchants and civic leaders. All of her dry cleaning was dropped off at Judi's Place. A color and trim session at Karen & Betty's was not uncommon. She often stopped at Kane Chamber of Commerce offices to chat with the ladies and share stories of married life. Ann was bereft of pretentiousness, and McKean County loved everything about her.

At 1 p.m., bundled in a burgundy parka, her face partially hidden within a fur-lined hood, Ann shuffled her boots into the warm library. Susan, the librarian, quickly handed her a mug of hot tea and positioned her behind a podium. As soon as her lips thawed, the First Lady smiled, removed her winter gear and thanked her audience for overcoming the February chill.

"Before Ann Bailey makes her presentation today," the librarian began, "I want to thank the First Lady for her efforts promoting literacy.

Due to her generous donations to Friends Library, we have developed programs in our elementary schools to encourage kids to read."

Susan covered the microphone and whispered to Ann: "What is your speech about today? You never told me."

"Child development. That's my topic."

The librarian nodded and addressed the audience. "Our distinguished guest will report on the welfare of our children, always an important topic. Let's welcome her, Ann Bailey."

Ann acknowledged some polite applause and stepped from behind the podium. Her hip-length argyle sweater hid her waistline. Her face had a special glow. This was her first public appearance in more than a month.

Immediately, women in the crowd suspected something. The men didn't notice.

"Jimmie wanted to be with me today, but unfortunately he was called to Harrisburg last night," she began. "Let me assure you that he joins in my announcement today."

The audience grew silent. Finally, Mrs. Hancharsky mother of six, blurted out: "You're expecting!"

Ann smiled sheepishly. She nodded yes.

"Boy or girl? When's the date? What does the governor think? Any names yet?" The questions came in rapid fire.

"Mid-June. Hopefully before the festival. We don't know about the gender yet."

Mrs. Hancharsky looked her up and down. "It's a boy. You're carrying low. There's a shadow under your chin. And if you throw up more than three times before the second trimester ends, it's definitely a boy."

June can't come soon enough, Ann thought to herself.

Zachary clutched a white lunch bag containing three Texas hots when his cell phone vibrated. He stepped from the cash register and checked the device. A message from Jessie instructed him to make a calendar entry for next Tuesday. "His application for a booth at Stender High School in Pittsburgh was accepted. The job fair would begin at 2 p.m."

Huh?

Jessie was updating her Rolodex with three more contacts as her boss charged into the News Leader office. "What's up with the text message?"

"Did you fill the slot for our summer intern yet?" she asked smugly.

"We can't afford ink and paper, let alone another staffer. What are you thinking?"

"Seize the opportunity, Tom. We reserved the last booth at the Stender High job fair; you should be happy about that. Do you realize the caliber of students at that school? And we could always use some summer help."

"I'll smelling something, Jessie. What do you have cooking?" Zachary sensed magic.

"Matthew Moore. Black. Just turned 18 last week. "Trumpet player in the Stender High School Marching Band. Wanted to be drum major, but didn't want to sacrifice so much time…"

"Great work," Zachary exclaimed. "So much time for what?"

Jessie referred to her notes. "He told his guidance counselor that he couldn't be drum major the same year that he was…"

"Let me guess," Tom interrupted. "Editor of the student newspaper?"

"The Stender High School Echo." Jessie beamed with self-satisfaction.

"How did you learn all of this information?"

Jessie hated to reveal her sources, but Zachary was her boss, after all. "We'll just call her Extension 54."

The Kane News Leader editor marveled at his assistant's enterprise. She was able to extract nectar from Lily at the courthouse, while he was unable to scratch adhesive tape from the clerk's sealed file. Too bad he couldn't afford to pay Jessie a reporter's wage.

"Let me give you some more information before you kill me," Jessie continued, obviously enjoying her brief superior knowledge. "Matthew's mother was Tanya Duncan. She remarried and her name is Tanya Harper. Moore was Tanya's mother's married name."

"So when Matthew lived with his grandmother, he took her last name."

"Correct, boss. Matthew lives with his mother and stepfather, Steven Harper. They live in a modest condominium on Elmer Street in Shadyside. Harper is music director at Good Shepherd Church in the Hill District. Tanya sings in the choir."

Zachary remembered the church. Brock Bailey used Good Shepherd to announce his plans for re-election as Pennsylvania's governor. Shortly after his announcement, Bailey left the church and his limousine crashed and fell from the Fort Pitt Bridge. His body was recovered downstream from the crash site months later.

"I have their address and telephone number," Jessie offered. "It would be strange to call them up, don't you think?"

Zachary bit into the Texas hot. "I think you have a better idea, Jessie."

"Yep. Here it is. You and I set up a booth at the Stender High job fair next week. Hopefully, this kid will come around and we can interest him in a summer internship at the News Leader."

"Then what?"

"Should be obvious, Tom. We slowly gain his confidence, and eventually he opens up to us. We confirm the whole story with Matthew, and you win the Keystone Press Award."

Zachary gulped. "So you know the full story? How?"

"A certain female bank examiner was interested in a certain trust account held for Matthew Moore at Carnegie Bank & Trust. She called the trust department on your secure line and inquired about a quarterly accounting of Matthew's fund."

"Did said female bank examiner talk to the account trustee?" Zachary asked.

"Only for about five minutes – long enough to learn about the first distribution."

Zachary looked puzzled. "First distribution?"

"According to the terms of the trust approved by Judge Van Lear, Matthew Moore receives one-third of the trust balance on his 18th birthday, another third on his 21st birthday and the rest on his 25th. I bet they celebrated big-time last week."

Zachary's mind grasped the implications. "That's about eight million dollars. Quite a haul for the young man."

"Now, here's the best part…"

"Help me out, Jessie. Why would Matthew Moore, with cash stuffed in his pockets, want to work this summer for the Kane News Leader? We couldn't pay him more than minimum wage."

"Listen for a second," Jessie said. "I asked the bank trustee what a teenager would do with all of that money and you know what he said?"

"I can't possibly imagine what…"

"The trustee explored that question with Matthew's guidance counselor. Apparently, the young man is so excited about journalism that he's looking to buy a small Pennsylvania newspaper."

"Hallelujah!" Zachary slam-dunked his half-eaten wiener into Jessie's wastebasket.

Dolores Gibson, tired of her attorney's hour-long explanation for his courtroom failure, closed her cell phone and lowered her garage door. As she walked toward the mud room door, she heard familiar scratches from inside. Her only friend, Cuddles, yelped as the door opened, grabbed her leg and slobbered on her black pumps. The cocker spaniel, ever enthusiastic, shadowed Dolores as she walked to a downstairs powder room. She reached down to pet the dog and soon it settled. Then she studied the woman in the mirror.

How did she reach this moment in life? Thirty-five years old and a two-time widow. A high school graduate with no marketable skills. The scrawny monthly pension from the Pennsylvania state police. Mortgage payments on her *casa nuevo* sure to exhaust the Gibsons' savings account within six months. Worst of all, the insurance settlement guaranteed by her attorney was gutted by a cranky judge.

Banging against her ankle was a beating furry tail. Mrs. Gibson leaned over and pulled Cuddles up with one hand under its belly.

"What do you think girl?" Dolores and Cuddles looked together into the mirror. "Will we be all right?"

The dog licked her face and squirmed from her grip. Its toenails landed on the hardwood floor with loud clicks. Cuddles ran back to its warm mat near the refrigerator.

Dolores filled a drinking glass and opened her medicine cabinet. Instinctively, she reached for the prescription bottle with the oblong pink tablets. Two should be enough to shake these ghosts, she thought. One swallow was required per pill.

In about thirty minutes, her thoughts would be more pleasant. Until then, she thought about Josh.

Their marriage was the triumph of hope over experience. The burly cop was plucked from his detail as station chief in Oil City by Governor Brock Bailey. Months earlier, Gibson gained national prominence after solving a sensational murder case involving an 11-year-old girl. His quick promotion to police commissioner and his frequent trips to Harrisburg created friction with his first wife, who favored her tranquil life in Venango County. Their divorce was quiet.

Gibson, as divorcees are wont to do, stopped smoking and drinking. He installed weight-training equipment in his basement and exercised constantly. At age 50, he foolishly imagined himself as an attractive prize for any willing female. When Dolores, a file clerk at the Monroeville substation, tossed him a salacious look during a surprise inspection, Gibson returned a wink. They married in a fortnight.

Dolores's first marriage had ended a year earlier in the palliative care ward of St. Joseph's Hospital in Pittsburgh. Her husband, a shop worker, contracted mesothelioma from asbestos exposure. A court settlement with the asbestos insulation manufacturer yielded Dolores less than $50,000 – money she whittled away in nine months. She took the state police clerk job only to find a replacement husband. She never expected to snare the top cop.

The newlyweds settled on a ten-acre estate in Wexford, north of Pittsburgh. Josh spent an average of eight days a month at the house. His duties required lengthy stays in Harrisburg and business travel to out-of-state conferences. Dolores soon grew restless. She bought Cuddles for companionship and resented Josh's reference to the manic puppy as "Puddles." Their telephone calls often ended in arguments, with Josh making false promises to spend more time at home. Eventually, Dolores lost interest and became withdrawn.

A friend referred the unhappy wife to a mental health therapist named Dr. Theron. She wasn't sure he was actually a doctor, although he seemed pretty handy obtaining medicine to treat what he called her "anxiety disorder." Dr. Theron's course involved a combination of meds, relaxation techniques and a leather sofa. Office visits became more frequent as the therapist required "experimental adjustments" in her treatment plan. Some days, there were fewer meds and more relaxation techniques. Other days, there was just more sofa time.

One happy day, as Dolores gleefully emptied her dishwasher, she received a phone call from Dr. Theron's scheduling nurse. Dolores was told that she was "being released" from his medical care and that her condition was "cured." Unfortunately, the unexpected news rendered her particularly hot for treatment, so she drove to the strip mall where Theron's office was located. She arrived in time to see federal authorities loading the doctor's medical files into an unmarked white van.

After a year of highly enjoyable psychotropic care, Dolores Gibson's medicine cabinet overflowed with pharmaceutical samples and assorted narcotics. No doubt, she thought, one day she would stumble on the perfect drug combination to reach maximum cheerfulness. A little of this and a little of that produced varying levels of contentment.

Josh Gibson chose not to interfere with his wife's downward spin. If she was happy, so was he. Her pleasurable, clicking brain synapses were a wonderful thing, Josh thought. Her drug-induced joy reduced marital tension, allowing him freedom that was uncommon in a second marriage.

Dolores was spiraling with such velocity four years ago that she failed to notice how far her husband was falling. Shortly after Brock Bailey's body was pulled from the Ohio River and Josh closed the Commonwealth's investigation on the governor's death, Josh became angry and abusive. She observed him downing her Zoloft tablets with straight bourbon. He forced himself to stay awake by sitting in the study with a shotgun across his lap.

The drugs were now kicking in; Dolores began to release her thoughts. Josh's death was losing its sting. No, she could not blame herself. He was a miserable son of a bitch, who deserved to split his skull at the bottom of Kinzua Valley. He left no will to provide for her; there was little money in his retirement account. He was estranged from his family, so there was no expectation of help from a rich uncle.

There was just this one thing.

She never talked about it before he died. In fact, she never really understood where it came from, how he got it and why he brought it into the house. In his final weeks, he was transfixed by it, perhaps sensing its enormous value. But if it was so valuable, she wondered, why did he hide it in the study closet?

The more immediate question is whether there was any value to it and, if there was, how could she sell it? And who would buy it?

Her questions were complicated but, she thought, it was sure fun to look at.

Dolores poured a glass of Chablis and called for Cuddles. The dog hopped beside her as she stretched out on the study room recliner.

She took a sip of wine. The late afternoon sunshine angled through her study window and into an open closet. Sunshine struck what lay upon the floor.

Reflecting back was bright, happy light.

It was the joyous glow from hundreds of neatly-stacked silver bars.

Chapter Four
The Invitation

Matty Moore's shift at the Food Gallery ended at 10 p.m. If he hadn't stocked the canned goods in aisles 7 and 8 by that time, the morning help would finish the job. Part-time work was his idea, although wages were unnecessary. The 18-year-old learned from his stepfather that daily work was a virtue that would build good habits for life. But it was difficult for him to shelve cans of sliced beets while a shiny new Mustang waited for him in the parking lot.

Life held great promise for Matty Moore. He owed his life to a secret affair between his mother and a former Pennsylvania governor. When his mother, Tanya Duncan, was a teenager, she worked as a domestic for Governor Brock Bailey. After an impulsive love episode on a deserted mountain road, Brock decided to hide his black mistress for nearly 20 years. Matty was an accidental product of the affair.

Brock insisted that Tanya give up their child for adoption. Instead, she gave the infant to her mother in East Liberty. Tanya promised that, when the time was right to break from Brock's grip, she would return to raise Matty. When he reached age 14, Tanya returned. Brock's body was recovered from the Pittsburgh river, and his estate was settled. Judge Van Lear, happily following Pennsylvania intestate laws, ordered half of the $50 million estate to each of Brock's sons – Jimmie Bailey and Matty Moore. Jimmie became the new governor and Matty became, well, a favorite son of Carnegie Bank's trust department.

Last week, on his 18th birthday, Matty passed into adulthood, opening his first savings account, retirement account, stock portfolio and passive investment purchase in a string of dry cleaning stores. His favorite birthday present was a black and gold Mustang, for which he rented a dilapidated garage in a nearby alley. Otherwise, the first $8.3 million distribution he received from the trust did little to change his lifestyle.

Matty backed his Mustang into the dirt-floor garage. He wiped a smudge from the side mirror before closing the creaky garage door. At the end of the alley was Centre Avenue. He walked past several massive brick houses, converted decades ago into apartments. On the far corner was the block-long Ivy Street Condominiums building. The Harpers occupied a two-bedroom unit on the second floor. Matty swiped a security card and opened the metal entry door. Immediately, the condominium president, Ed, popped his head from his first floor unit.

"Oh, hey, Matty. Just checking who was coming in. We had a burglary last week." Ed, self-appointed security czar at the condominiums, lived directly underneath the Duncans. Whenever Matty or his stepfather raised their voices, Tanya would remind them that "Ed was listening."

"Just coming home from the Food Gallery," Matty told him. "Good specials tomorrow on rotisserie chicken. Get there before 4 o'clock."

"Thanks for the tip, kid." Ed closed his door, but Matty suspected the persnickety graphics designer was looking through his peephole.

Matty flipped through stacks of mail as he ascended the stairs. One envelope caught his eye, a letter addressed to him from the Kane News Leader.

Only a light above the stove illuminated the Duncan condominium. A note on the dining room table from his mother advised that she and Steve would be home later, after choir practice. A tuna casserole was waiting in the microwave to be warmed.

Matty instead opened the letter. It read:

Dear Matthew Moore:

As a high school senior, now is an important opportunity to consider career choices. Allow me to interest you in the exciting and rewarding field of journalism.

Many of our country's greatest leaders in politics, literature and business began their professional lives as small town newspaper reporters. Thomas Paine and Benjamin Franklin, two of our nation's founding fathers, earned their stripes in the newspaper office. Mark Twain, a leading humorist and author, started his career at the Hannibal, Mo., Journal.

Even famous African-American leaders, like author Alex Haley, had their roots in journalism!

Matty resisted an impulse to stop reading at this point.

*Mr. Moore, we sincerely invite you visit the **Kane News Leader** booth next week at the Stender High School Job Fair. Our weekly paper, in beautiful and fast-paced McKean County, is offering a fully-paid, exciting summer internship to the most qualified student newspaper editor in Pennsylvania.*

*You will gain valuable hands-on experience in reporting breaking news, in learning computer graphics and design, in making executive deadline decisions and in marketing and promoting our attractive and desired newspaper. And, best of all, you will gain unprecedented insights into the valuable investment opportunity of community newspapers, like the highly profitable **News Leader**.*

My assistant, Jessie Krone, and I look forward to meeting you. Let us together fulfill your dreams of an exhilarating summer in Kane, Pennsylvania!

The letter was signed by Thomas Zachary, owner/editor.

Matty had visited McKean County only once before. When Judge Van Lear was handling Brock Bailey's estate, Matty and his mother confronted the judge in the courthouse hall, asking him to delay probate until they could prove Matty was an heir. There was no need for him to return to the courthouse because the judge ordered a blood sample taken in Pittsburgh. Positive results were communicated to the judge by a Pittsburgh clinic.

Four years later, as Matty folded the job fair invitation and placed it in his school backpack, he tried to remember any shred of excitement in his visit to Smethport, Mount Jewett and Kane. As Matty recalled, the courthouse seemed to be a somber place, traffic was light and McKean County was mostly a bunch of trees. How much excitement and exhilaration would a summer clerkship at the News Leader offer?

Plus, he wondered whether Mr. Thomas Zachary knew his addressee was black. Perhaps his urban-ness in rural McKean County would cause all of the excitement.

Could be interesting, he thought. Matty marked the date and time in his school agenda.

Governor Jimmie Bailey waited until visiting hours ended at Allegheny General before sending Pennoyer to speak with security. Bailey waited in a black sedan near the service entrance while arrangements were being made. He hoped to accomplish his task with one late night meeting. If any followup were needed, Pennoyer would handle it.

Earlier that afternoon, Billy Herman was released from intensive care and admitted to a private room in the cardiac unit. His vital signs improved, but his treating physician was recommending bypass surgery in the morning. Tonight was Bailey's limited window of time to speak to the ailing man.

Pennoyer returned to the vehicle with a dour expression. "Security says no," he told Jimmie. "Herman's chart says no visitors until after surgery. I guess his heart is pretty fragile."

The governor stared out the passenger window. An ambulance quietly pulled up. Two paramedics unloaded a very still patient at the emergency entrance. Behind the ambulance, a sedan door opened and an old woman in distress was escorted into the waiting area.

"We drove a long way to get shutout, Jimmie," Pennoyer said.

"Is there a physician on staff at this hour? Is there someone who can countermand the treating doctor? I really want to talk to Billy tonight."

"I'll check." Pennoyer returned to the hospital tower as the ambulance pulled away. Jimmie looked at his watch. The time was 10 p.m. He turned off the ignition. Winter air began to seep into the vehicle.

Jimmie hadn't visited with Billy Herman since the detective headed the Pittsburgh police search for his missing father. Herman seemed to be very competent when he questioned Jimmie at search headquarters near Point Park. Almost from the outset, Herman expressed doubt about whether Brock was in the submerged limousine. He had told Jimmie that his father's body would have bobbed up to the surface in a few days. After a month, Herman called Jimmie, accusing the young man of hiding his father. Jimmie excused the comment, believing that Herman was simply frustrated by his failure to locate the body.

Contact with Herman ceased for a few months. However, shortly after Josh Gibson's body was found at the foot of Kinzua Bridge, Billy Herman visited Leigh-Rose. To his shock, Jimmie listened as Herman described how he and Josh had searched the Kinzua Valley to find Brock Bailey's handgun. Both knew that Brock fired a handgun at Jimmie before the tornado struck Kinzua Bridge. Then Herman revealed that he knew of Jimmie's crime in dumping Brock's body back into the Pittsburgh rivers.

Their conversation was short, but chilling. Jimmie asked, "Why are you here? What is the point of this visit?"

Herman told him point blank that he wanted to quit the police force and that he needed sufficient money to retire. So a deal was struck: Herman would forget everything he knew about the Brock Bailey case and Jimmie would pay him $1 million cash.

Unfortunately for Jimmie, Herman had trouble forgetting. The following year, he returned to Leigh-Rose and asked for an additional $500,000. In the spring, he needed money to install a pool for therapeutic purposes, another $50,000. Herman seemed to understand the code of successful extortionists: start high and keep reducing the demands. That gives the victim an expectation that his pain will be over soon.

Jimmie waited in the cold, hoping Herman's criminal ways would be over soon. But before then, Jimmie needed some answers.

Pennoyer re-emerged from the hospital lobby. He motioned for Jimmie to join him at the entrance.

"There is no physician on the floor who can help us," he told Jimmie. "But I was able to take the elevator to the cardiac care floor and walk through the halls. Nobody stopped me. What do you think? Should we just crash his room?"

Jimmie liked the idea. "Let's see how far we get."

They took an elevator to the eighth floor. The waiting area was empty. One floor nurse sitting at the station was more interested in her paperwork than in foot traffic. Pennoyer and Jimmie easily avoided contact with her and slipped into the patient hallway. Herman's room was along the far side, next to an empty solarium. They entered quietly.

A small reading lamp above the hospital bed and a muted television cast scant light on the sleeping patient. Tubes ran from his nose and right arm. His complexion was gray and his chest heaved and fell in steady rhythm. Jimmie leaned down to his ear.

"Billy, are you listening?"

There was no reaction.

"Billy, you sack of shit. It's the governor."

Pennoyer thought he saw slight movement under the eyelids. "I think he's drugged, Jimmie."

"I bet he can hear us," Jimmie whispered to Pennoyer before turning back to Herman.

"Listen, pal. It's all over for you. I know your surgeon; he's a friend of mine. So I've paid him to cut your aorta tomorrow..."

"Great bedside manner, Jimmie," Pennoyer said, watching the door. "This isn't working. You can't get any information from him tonight. Let's go."

"I suppose you're right." Jimmie slapped Herman's cheek. "We'll say a prayer for a speedy recovery, or maybe not."

When he heard the hospital room door close behind them, Billy Herman turned and pushed the nurse call button.

Tom Zachary unraveled his newspaper's rising sun banner and fastened it to the front of Jessie's card table. He placed a white ceramic mug with "I Love Kane" pencils at one corner to anchor the tablecloth. Jessie's elbow weighted the other corner. The News Leader interview table was assigned a spot beneath an upraised basketball backboard in Stender High's gymnasium. To its left was the booth for H.J. Heinz Company and to it right, Alcoa Corporation.

Jessie looked wistfully at the Heinz table. "Can I take a few of those green pickle pins?" she asked Zachary. "And, look, Alcoa is giving away aluminum mouse pads!"

"No, Jessie. Those are for the students. We're here for one purpose..."

"I know," she said, "we have to recruit the governor's half-brother."

A far door opened and about 100 senior students shuffled into the gym. Immediately, a freckled Irish-looking girl wandered over to the News Leader display. "Wow, this is cool!" She sat in the interview chair. "I've always wanted to work at a real newspaper."

Zachary, scanning the crowd for his prey, turned to the girl. "Excuse me?"

"I said it must be fun to work at a real newspaper."

"Where did you ever get a crazy idea like that?!" Zachary said sternly. "A newspaper job is about the worst career you could have. You work around the clock. Everybody hates you, the readers, the customers, the carriers. The money sucks…"

Jessie helped the stunned girl to her feet. "Why don't you try the Bayer table? There's good money selling aspirin." The girl did not look back.

For the next half hour, Zachary instructed Jessie to sweep students away from the News Leader table so that he could watch the handsome young man who was working his way around the gym. The teenager sat in every interview chair and seemingly engaged each corporate recruiter with style and charm. He shook hands, collected company brochures and exuded the confidence of a multi-millionaire.

"That's him." Jessie pointed. "I asked the job fair coordinator and she identified him. She said Matty Moore would be a fine catch for any of these corporations."

"Good Lord," Zachary said. "He's going to get snatched up before he gets to our table. Is there any way you can hustle him over here?"

Jessie gulped her bottled water. "Geez, Tom. They say he's real smart. If he read your invitation letter, he's probably already made up his mind."

"I was afraid of that." Tom doubted whether the letter would produce results. "I tried to make McKean County sound exciting, but let's be honest…"

"Wait." Jessie stopped her boss. "He's looking over this way. Give it your best, Tom."

Matty Moore waded through the swelling crowd of seniors. When he reached the News Leader display, he extended his hand. "Are you Mr. Zachary? It's a pleasure."

"And you are…"

"Matthew Moore. I received your letter and, I must say, I was intrigued."

Zachary studied the young man's face. He had short-cropped

hair, Anglo features and a darkened complexion. He could see Brock Bailey in the youth's sharp eyes. Matty carried a tall, angular frame as upright and proudly as his natural father. What he lacked was Brock's insincerity and haughtiness.

"Ah, Matthew Moore." Zachary feigned a sudden enlightenment. "I understand that you are editor of the Stender Echo. That's quite an achievement."

"Oh, I don't know. The former editor was expelled from school."

Jessie pushed the interview chair behind his legs. "I bet that editor exercised First Amendment rights and printed something that upset the school administrators," she said.

"No," he laughed. "The school exercised its Fourth Amendment rights and found drugs in her locker."

After a moment of awkward silence, Jessie spoke. "Well, the News Leader has a policy of zero tolerance ..."

"For unhappy summer clerks," Zachary interrupted. "How can we interest you in a summer internship, Mr. Moore?"

"I've done some research about the News Leader, and the newspaper is very interesting," Matty told his interviewers. "It has a stable circulation, about 10,000 readers. It is available in the Pittsburgh and Erie markets. It tends to rely on a few local advertisers and has yet to seek national advertising or to develop its classified ad department. That should be fixed. And the writing..."

Zachary braced for a critical evaluation of his reporting.

"And the writing is beyond electric."

"We try to conserve where we can," said a confused Jessie.

"No, that's a compliment," Matty explained. "You have a weekly paper that is published on Wednesdays. That gives your reporting staff more time to develop in-depth features. The writing is crisp and readable. You should be proud of this newspaper."

Wow, Zachary thought, praise from the next generation. Maybe he shouldn't regret his decision to purchase the struggling paper years ago.

"What are the terms of your summer internship?" Matty asked.

"You'll start with us as soon as you graduate." Zachary motioned for Jessie to write what he was saying. "We'll locate suitable housing for you in Kane. Your hours will be flexible, but no more than 50 per week. At the beginning, you will be a general assignment reporter and I will be your direct supervisor. You'll be doing some editing and page layout and, hopefully by the end of the summer, you'll have experience in the circulation and advertising departments."

"The business end of newspapers interests me," Matty offered. "I suppose I will be paid a reasonable wage?"

"Yes, yes," Zachary answered, turning to Jessie. "We pay reasonable wages, right?"

Jessie bit her lip. Reasonable for 1955, she thought. But she had to give a truthful answer to his question. "Nobody goes hungry."

Matty figured the salary to be the least of his demands. All he needed were a few bylines, a nicer garage and, most importantly, a very good chance to meet his half-brother, the governor. Perhaps his first interview would take place at Leigh-Rose Mansion. His mother had described the house to him years ago when she revealed the name of his real father.

Zachary was growing uneasy watching the teenager's apparent hesitation on the wage issue. "Do you have any other offers for summer jobs yet?" he asked.

"Just one. The features editor for the Pittsburgh newspaper wants me to ghost-write book reviews for local editions."

"Come to your senses, Matty. What could be more boring than writing reviews of Pittsburgh books? Make the smart decision. The News Leader is offering you the opportunity of a lifetime. This is experience you won't find anywhere else."

Mattie stood and thanked Jessie for her time. Then he turned to Zachary.

"I've already talked to my mom and dad. They said they'd be

happy with any decision I made about my summer job," Mattie told the editor.

"What day do you graduate?" Zachary asked.

"May 15," Mattie replied. "I could start Monday the 19th."

Chapter Five
The Researcher

"Cripes Hanna!" Toolie threw a dish cloth across the bar, striking Rocky Hillman squarely between his shoulders. "Get those pictures off my wall!"

Breakfast customers at Golden Wheel turned to watch the town photographer stumble from his step stool. He braced for an onslaught of epithets from the old waitress.

"Who said you could put those up on my walls, Rocky? My Lord in Heaven! You can't simply walk in here and pound nails in the plaster. This ain't no art gallery."

Mustering as much dignity as he could under the circumstances, Rocky peeled the wet towel from his back and lowered his hammer. "Toolie, relax. I got an OK from the hotel manager. Just a few photos in the dining room and I'll be finished."

"What do you call this one, Rocky?" Toolie waved a framed portrait in his face. The image was very recognizable.

"Its title is 'Elmer the Elk, a Study in Textures," Rocky replied.

Toolie aimed for the kill. "So you're hanging a photograph of Elmer the Elk directly under the real Elmer the Elk? Why would anybody look at your photograph when the real thing is right there on the wall?"

Giggles turned to laughter. The popular photographer was embarrassed.

"Elmer is part of my wildlife photography exhibit. I think he'll be a best-seller."

"Lookie, lookie Archway cookies!" Toolie blurted. "There's a price tag here of $40.00. Who in their right mind would pay forty bucks for a picture of Elmer?"

Rocky folded the stool under his arm and grabbed his portfolio bag. "Obviously someone with more sophistication than you," he muttered to himself, not wishing to rile the old gossip. He left without pause.

Toolie couldn't bring herself to admit it; Rocky's photographs were captivating. As the breakfast crowd morphed into lunchtime customers, she found herself gazing at Rocky's masterpieces. She had her eye on a blue jay that Rocky photographed at a neighbor's bird-feeder. The price was $35.00. This bird's feathers were a bit ruffled, its beak was open as though in mid-song and its eyes were dark and piercing – features that reminded Toolie of herself.

Today's Golden Wheel customers needed only light jackets or sweaters. Winter's final wet snowstorm had passed last week. Early April arrived to Kane and the Allegheny Forest with a hint of warming air and delightful scents of cherry blossoms. There was a certain relief this time each year. If you hadn't caught the flu or broken your hip on an icy sidewalk, you've survived another McKean County winter. Restaurant patrons gathered in good spirits, knowing that next winter was at least six months away.

Toolie hated this season. There was little gossip. Instead, everybody was talking about planting fields, doing home improvement work or making plans for summer trips. None of those things mattered to her. She thrived on the misfortunes of others, at least communicating those misfortunes to her customers.

She made a mental list of current topics for today's lunch. First, there was a theft of plastic cake decorating bags from Bauer's Bakery. She imagined that the bags would be used to distribute hallucinogenic drugs. Second, a juror from Smethport told her that Judge Van Lear was squirming on the bench yesterday, probably another hemorrhoidal flare-up. Then, she heard that Gates Hardware was 90 days late paying its bills ever since Thelma Gates starting running the cash register.

None of this was juicy enough for today's lunch, Toolie thought. A little eavesdropping on the customers was required.

"She doesn't look at all happy," Toolie overheard a cobb salad saying in the corner booth. "When I was pregnant with my first baby, I couldn't stop smiling."

The beef noodle soup with tuna salad on rye disagreed. "My first pregnancy was awful. There wasn't enough elastic in Pennsylvania to make my waistline comfortable. I gained more water weight than the Kinzua Reservoir."

Toolie leaned forward. She turned her hearing aid up to number 7.

"If I were the First Lady, I would force myself to smile in public," said the grilled chicken on a Kaiser roll, hold the mayo. "Did you see Ann Bailey at the charity bake-off? It was on the eleven o'clock news. Her face was red and puffy, and it looked like she was ready to cry."

Toolie could withstand no more. She refilled their water glasses before casting her line. "I don't think it's physical," she told them. "It's mental."

"What do you mean, Toolie?" the grilled chicken asked.

"Honey, all I'm saying is this: did you ever see a chicken smiling when the rooster's in the hen house next door?"

"Well, I never saw a chicken smiling, but I think I know what you mean. What do you think, girls? We haven't seen much of Govenor Bailey lately."

Toolie reapplied her mauve lipstick. With any luck, she could keep this conversation going until closing time. "I've never been in a family way, but in 50 years at the Golden Wheel, I've seen my share of expectant mothers..."

The diners braced for a heavy dose of Toolie tittle-tattle.

"... and I know it takes two to have a child."

"Tell us something we don't know." The diners laughed.

"If Ann Bailey felt the love of her husband, she would be enjoying these weeks. That's what I mean. There's nothing lonelier than carrying a child without love."

The Cobb and Kaiser nodded to each other. As usual, Toolie voiced what everyone was thinking: Jimmie Bailey was avoiding his husbandly duties.

"How about some dessert?" The waitress knew the women would keep lunch going now that their conversation was lively. "Lemon meringue pie, Death-by-Chocolate cake, or at least freshly-brewed coffee?" Toolie poised her pen.

"I never liked the Baileys," the grilled chicken proclaimed. "William, the rich grandfather, chased skirts. His son, Brock, was no different. Jimmie learned from the best, or worst, I suppose."

The tuna salad sandwich agreed. "How many girls do you think Jimmie bedded when he played baseball? I bet hundreds. You can't tell me that a skunk like Jimmie Bailey would be faithful after he got married. Oh, that poor Ann. She really is alone."

"Worst of all," Toolie added, "she's going to have a baby, and it's gonna be another Bailey. Great fire in the barn! The bloodline will continue!"

By now, the entire restaurant was tuned in to today's topic.

Toolie collected several orders for chocolate cake, turned toward the kitchen and winked at Rocky's blue jay photograph. With any luck, she thought, the Golden Wheel would be chirping about Jimmie Bailey's sex life all afternoon.

Three weeks after his heart bypass surgery, Billy Herman was released from physical therapy. Discharge instructions were simple but challenging: no more cigars, limit alcohol intake and only high fiber, low-fat foods. Billy returned to his ranch estate, where he arranged for a daily housekeeper/cook. He promised his surgeon that major lifestyle changes would take place. So the physician prescribed an exercise regimen, including thirty-minute aerobic walks and low stress sports like golf. Within a month, Billy returned to the Forest Club lounge and began pounding cheeseburgers and beer.

Life was returning to normal for Billy Herman. All he really needed was more cash.

Tom Zachary fielded the governor's call before locking the News Leader office doors.

"Any progress, Tom? Have you found the teenager?"

"Not only have I found him, Governor, I've hired him." Tom was pleased at his accomplishment.

"I know you have a plan, Tom. I don't need to know it," Jimmie said. "How do you propose a meeting between us?"

"Not too soon. We have all summer. Let's wait until he's ready."

"Good idea, Tom."

Meanwhile, twenty miles down the Kinzua Valley, where the creek emptied into the Kinzua Reservoir, an Edinboro University student was alone in the woods.

Megan Broward had been warned. The only way to find Maude Thunder's cabin in this thick forest was with a global positioning system. There was no street address, only directional coordinates.

The college sophomore had parked her Volkswagen along the flooded Allegheny River Basin. Then she hiked 425 yards south-southeast to the ridge line. Her professor had relayed an earlier message from Maude: once you reach the ridge, walk east until you find the clearing. Megan made her own path. She realized the irony of passing through the woods like a Seneca Indian to meet the Indian woman.

"Cabin" was a generous description for the lean-to directly

ahead. The wooden shanty appeared to lean beyond its center of gravity. A brick chimney anchored the far end. If that chimney ever detached, Megan figured, the cabin would fall toward the swollen river. High weeds surrounded the house. At the clearing's edge, chicken wire enclosed a collection of goats and hens. Thank goodness, Megan thought, this was the last interview. Her sociology research paper was close to completion.

As she neared the cabin, Megan observed a heavy woman in dungarees watching from the doorway. Megan waved and called. The woman, stepping into afternoon sunshine, motioned for the college student to meet near her gate.

"Afternoon, Miss Thunder," Megan called. "My professor said you wanted to talk to me."

When Megan drew closer, she could see the woman's sun-worn skin and wrinkled hands. She indeed bore the scars of a working life. For an older woman, she had remarkably black hair and perfect white teeth. Megan viewed her as a woman of the earth, the product of many generations on this rugged land.

Maude Thunder spoke only when Megan was close enough to touch the gate. "They told me at the activity center that you met with many of my people. They said you were writing a story about our relocation. I want to add to your story."

Megan extended her hand. Rather than grasping it, the woman admired it. "You are one of us," she said. "I can tell from your hands, and your face."

"You are so kind, Miss Thunder. I am not sure, but some of my family believe a Seneca woman is our ancestor, perhaps as long ago as the 1600's. We don't know her name or anything about her."

"A Seneca woman is a beautiful woman. You are lucky, Miss Megan. We are known by our mothers. Please sit down. Now what is your story about?"

The two women sat at a redwood picnic table not far from bleating goats. Megan pulled notes from her folder, and began to ask her standard interview questions.

"Do you remember how you first learned that the Kinzua Dam would flood your home?" Megan was not sure her interview subject had a recollection of events in 1965.

Maude Thunder opened a photograph album. She turned to a page of black-and-white prints under a plastic sheet.

"There." She pointed to a photo of a small frame house. Megan noticed window boxes filled with geraniums. A family of five posed for the photograph in their Sunday best. "That's me. I was 10. Here are my ma and dad. He worked with the railroad. These were my brothers, Jack and Robert."

She held the album open for a moment. She ran her index finger over the images as though she could touch them. "I'm the only one left." She paused again. "I'm the survivor, if you can call me that."

"I'm sorry." Megan didn't know what to say. She returned to her notes. "Did your family live here on the ridge?"

"Oh, no," the woman answered. "Our house was near the river bank, back when the Allegheny was a river and not a damn lake." Maude stood and pointed down the slope. "Our house was down there about 200 yards. Can't see anything now; it's all under water."

"You were 10 when the federals relocated your family, is that right?"

Maude wrung her worn hands before closing the photo album.

"That question you asked before, when did I learn that the Kinzua Dam would flood our property? Let me answer that." Maude faced her interviewer and spoke as though the pain had never vanished.

"I was eight years old in 1963. Technically, I was in third grade, but we were all crowded together in one room at the Indian School on the Cornplanter Reservation. Our teachers never talked about the Kinzua Dam in class. In fact, our parents didn't talk about it in front of the children.

"So, this one Friday afternoon in May … I remember because the school was so hot we had to keep the doors open for ventilation.

There was this earth-moving equipment that came and all of these men with picks and shovels. They opened the cemetery gates next door and went in.

"Miss Hoover, our teacher, quickly pulled the shades. One of the men had black plastic sheets and tacked it over the windows. We were told to hush and stay in our seats all afternoon. I could hear Miss Hoover whispering to the other teachers.

"My brother, Jack, was in another room of the school and he peeked under the black plastic. He told me later that men in the cemetery were digging up the Indian graves. He said wooden boxes tagged with stickers were stacked up in pick-up trucks. He said a forklift loaded the old tombstones into another truck.

"Jack said some of the men wore uniforms with badges, and they were covering their mouths with handkerchiefs. He said he counted at least 40 boxes and body-bags."

Megan stopped writing when the woman paused to gather her thoughts. "They moved the cemetery?" Megan asked. "Where?"

"New York," she answered. "They moved it all to the Allegany Reservation in New York. My grandmother, my Aunt Agnes ... we found them when we moved, but it's not right to disturb the dead."

Maude Thunder's story was not unusual. Megan's research on the Seneca relocation was filled with similar anecdotes. Children were the last to know and, in many ways, the most traumatized.

"They closed the school in June. That's when the truck came and they loaded all the desks and chairs and whatever else they could pull from that old building. Jack and I sat on the hill as the truck pulled away. We watched them torch our school. Burned like a son of a gun."

"What about your house? What happened to that?"

Maude nodded and flipped her hand in the air.

Megan understood. "So they torched your home, too?"

"We didn't stay around long enough to see it, but that's what the government did. Somewhere under that pile of water is the Thunder house. You know, when you're a child, you think your home is forever ..."

The woman excused herself and stepped into her house. A few minutes later, she returned with two soup bowls. She placed one on the picnic table before Megan.

"Have a taste. This is hominy corn soup. An old family recipe."

Megan tried a spoonful, and then another.

"You're probably wondering why I live here and not in New York." Maude interrupted her guest. "About 10 years ago, after Jack died, I needed to come back to this land, back to these mountains. So I petitioned the Seneca council for a grant to this one acre."

"But it's on the side of a hill," Megan said. "Why not something more level?"

"Our people were given this entire river valley, but when they flooded the lower valley, the steep hill was the only dry part left. So I built here."

Megan swallowed her last spoonful and stood. "Thank you Miss Thunder. You have been a wonderful source of information for my report. But it's getting dark and I have to return down the mountain."

"Wait!" The woman seemed distraught by Megan's announcement. "I have something to show you, something maybe you can explain to me after you finish your research."

Megan pondered this mystery while Maude returned to the house. About a minute later, she reappeared with a metal box. She placed it on the picnic table, covering the lid with her hands. The box was no more than a foot long, six inches wide and about five inches deep. Green paint clung to the sides where rust had not treaded. It looked like a primitive tool box.

"I've been saving this for about fifteen years. Shortly after I returned to the valley, I found this under a log in the woods."

Megan asked, "Did you open it?"

"Yes, it wasn't locked. The box looked like it had been in the reservoir for a while. I haven't shown it to anyone else."

Maude opened the lid. Inside were an empty bottle, a flashlight and a folded paper. She laid all three items on the table and set aside the box.

Megan examined the bottle. "Blackbeard's Rum. I've never seen this before. Must be pretty old. No smell to it."

"That's a strong clue that an Indian owned this," Maude said. "The Seneca men were proud warriors, but they liked their rum. I can't find a date on the bottle, but it must be about 100 years old."

"Well," Megan said. "The flashlight can't be 100 years old. And this map ..."

Maude unfolded the paper and spread it out. "The red markings look very old. I don't recognize these letters, but it could be Iroquoian. If so, the map dates back to the early 1800s. But look at this..."

Megan looked more closely. Some markings in black ink appeared to be newer. Despite a large water stain, she could see a long string of hyphenated capital letters and the year 1794 in parentheses.

"Somebody wrote this part in the 1900s," Megan said. "Have you shown this to the Seneca Nation Council?"

Maude laughed. "Look at me. I'm too old to feed the goats, let alone hitchhike to New York to see my people. Can you take these things and find out if they have any value? If they do, come back and tell me."

"Oh, no, Miss Thunder," Megan answered. "These are your Indian relics. I couldn't take them from you. Here, just stack them on the table."

Megan lined up the bottle, flashlight and metal box. She flipped open her cell phone and took a photograph. Then she stood over the outstretched map and captured it in as much focus as possible with her phone camera. She turned the map over and took another photograph.

She handed the woman a slip of paper. "Here is my telephone number. Whenever you go to town, call me. I'll tell you whatever

I can find out."

Maude again pleaded with the student to take the box and its contents. And again Megan politely refused. They hugged.

As Megan carefully retraced her steps down from the ridge to her car, Maude Thunder slowly refolded the map and returned the box to its safe place.

The woman was not totally honest that afternoon.

She did recognize the old red markings.

"Bad words, mean words," she muttered to no one.

"Please let these words never come true."

Chapter Six
The Newbie

"Not too bad. Plenty of room. But I can feel cold air around the windows."

In reality, Matty Moore was repulsed by the musty hotel room. He felt like he was stepping into the 1950's. In fact, he wondered whether his was the first human foot to step into the suite in fifty years.

It had possibilities, though.

"Would you mind if I painted something neutral over the wallpaper, and maybe replaced the carpeting?" he asked the hotel manager.

"Sure. Nobody's ever offered to do that before."

Tom Zachary stood speechless inside the door. He hesitated to inspect the rooms with his new summer intern. Earlier, when he suggested that Matty reside at General Kane Boarding House during his summer stay, the editor had no idea of the wretched condition of the third floor unit. The squeaking floors signaled structural weakness, Zachary surmised.

He took the young man aside and whispered, "Listen, we could probably find you more up-to-date accommodations…"

"No," Matty said. "This is kind of cool. I'm right in the heart of town. I can walk to your office. And I can park my Mustang in the garage across Fraley Street. There's a laundry and pizza place close by. All this apartment needs are a few simple touches."

"You could spend thousands to fix these rooms, just to make them liveable," Zachary said.

"Oh, not that much. There's a carpet and furniture store a couple blocks away. All I will need are a plumber and a painter..."

A sudden crash from the bathroom stopped Matty in mid-sentence. The hotel manager sheepishly smiled and told them about a fallen medicine cabinet. "We can fix that."

"... and maybe a carpenter," Matty continued.

"And a tile installer, and an electrician," Zachary offered. "I don't see any telephone or cable television jacks. You'll feel very isolated here."

Matty already noticed. He hesitated to tell the hotel manager of his improvement ideas involving a satellite television dish on the roof, recessed lighting and stainless steel appliances.

He could afford dozens of high-end upgrades. Being a new millionaire had its privileges.

His young eyes saw nothing but potential. The suite had two large bedrooms, one of which he could convert to his computer room. A galley kitchen was roomy, but with a new countertop and stock cabinets he actually could entertain guests there. He was given a key to a private entrance, so he could come and go without notice. And, best of all, he was only two floors above the Golden Wheel Restaurant.

"I'll take it." Matty took the keys from a happy hotel manager. "By the way, who are my neighbors in this place?"

"You're it, at least for the summer," the manager answered. "After dark, things will be pretty quiet around here, not like the city."

His words were music to Matty's ears. He could play his music and practice his trumpet at all hours of the night.

"Except for one tenant on the second floor," the manager said. "She's been here forever, but she's no trouble."

Zachary took his intern by the arm and led him to the dark hallway. He had forgotten to warn Matty that the town's notorious waitress resided somewhere in the bowels of the General Kane Boarding House. He recoiled at the thought of Matty Moore

being interrogated by Toolie. Why, she would drag information
from the young man so quickly and efficiently that her "gossip
network" would scoop his Pulitzer story, Zachary realized.

"What's wrong, Mr. Zachary? Why are you pulling me away?"
Matty was confused.

"I know the tenant and she is trouble," Zachary told him. "You
must stay away from her. And don't tell her anything."

Matty Moore reacted like any 18-year-old, who was being told
by an adult to avoid a bad influence. He was intrigued, and
suddenly was dying to meet this strange woman.

"Who is she?" Matty asked.

"Her name is Toolie. She has a one-word name. She tends
bar and works at the restaurant downstairs. She knows everybody
and their business. When she sees you, well it won't be pretty..."

"A waitress, huh? She's interested in me? Sounds like a good
thing." Matty was starting to appreciate his decision to intern at
the obscure newspaper. "Is she married? How old is she?"

Zachary laughed. "This is against my better judgment, but I
suppose you'll run into her soon anyway. Let's go downstairs for
some lunch. Toolie will be there and I'll introduce you. But please,
please don't tell her anything. It will drive her absolutely mad."

The hotel manager cleaned up most of the broken glass with
his fingers. He promised to have the apartment "broom clean" for
his new tenant's move-in day.

Matty took one last look at the sitting room near an oversized
row of windows facing Fraley Street. He imagined a late-night
tryst with the only other hotel tenant. Just him and Toolie relaxing
on that crushed velour sofa he saw in the furniture store window.
Some cool jazz, maybe John Legend, would be oozing from his
surround sound speakers. Maybe they could nibble on a midnight
calzone from opposite ends.

Yes, this is the summer of endless possibilities, Matty thought.

Ann Bailey felt queasy late in the morning. After a sleepless night alone at Leigh-Rose Mansion, she advised her housekeeper to postpone a scheduled visit with Dr. Cochran, her obstetrician. After a light breakfast, Ann sat in the front study and tried to catch up on correspondence, but a sickness grew within her.

About 11 a.m., she slowly climbed the stairs to the second floor master suite. If she rested a bit, she thought, the nausea would leave. Five months into her pregnancy, she rested comfortably only on her left side. Unfortunately, that position provided a view of the empty bed beside her; Jimmie was in Harrisburg again.

Ann dozed for almost an hour. She was awakened by a creeping moistness on her left thigh. She reached down and felt wetness. She raised her arm from under the blanket and, to her horror, saw that her hand was red with blood.

"Oh, my God!" she screamed.

The housekeeper burst into the bedroom and saw Ann trying to stand. Her pajama bottoms were stained in bright red.

"Help me! Help me! What is happening?" Ann lay back on the bed. The housekeeper grabbed a towel and wrapped her stomach and upper legs. Then she dialed 9-1-1.

Within five minutes, an ambulance arrived at Leigh-Rose, together with four state police cruisers. Paramedics rushed up the stairs and carefully placed the frantic First Lady onto a stretcher. Some blood stains were visible on the towel.

"Call Jimmie," Ann shouted to an on-looking state trooper. "He needs to be here."

Ann was transferred to a gurney and loaded into the ambulance. Two paramedics sat on either side of the woman as they sped onto Sowers Road. "Please remain calm, Mrs. Bailey," one of the said. "We're taking you to Emergency at Kane Community. Should take about 15 minutes."

"My baby! What about my baby?"

"You're hemorrhaging, Mrs. Bailey," the paramedic said. "Your vital signs are OK, but we need to stop the bleeding first. Do you understand?"

"No, I don't. Am I having a miscarriage? Oh my God! Please say no."

The paramedics looked at each other. Neither spoke for the next few miles.

Ann held the towel around her abdomen tightly, hoping that more pressure would protect the growing life within her. She felt no kicking inside. She began to cry, softly at first.

As the ambulance turned onto Route 6, paramedics removed the towel and wrapped fresh linen sheets around Ann's midsection. The bleeding had subsided, but the woman appeared to be going into shock. One paramedic snapped a smelling salts stick under her nose, sending the sharp smell of ammonia throughout the vehicle. The other paramedic tried to lower her head.

Ann did not lose consciousness. Her mind was racing, remembering all of the advice from her obstetrician, friends and dime store magazines about high risk pregnancies. Perhaps she had been too active in the past few weeks. Maybe her diet was wrong. More folic acid. Less exercise. More reading. Less worry and stress. More prayer.

None of it mattered anymore. She closed her eyes and let go.

When the ambulance stopped, Ann was jolted awake. She felt the bumps and ridges of Kane Community Hospital's asphalt driveway and sidewalk as her gurney rolled into Emergency. Having been forewarned of the First Lady's arrival, emergency room physicians wheeled her to a bed and flung a curtain around it. Ann helped doctors move her to the hospital bed. She could not erase fear from her face.

Within minutes, nurses had completed readings of her blood pressure and pulse. The linens were removed and the bloody bed clothes, discarded. An on-call OB/GYN remarked that bleeding had stopped. He ordered a nurse to clean Ann's abdomen before he applied a coating of ultrasound gel. Ann turned away from the monitor; she could not face the image from her womb.

"OK, we have a heartbeat. It appears strong and unaffected," the physician announced to the relief of all. Ann, tears welling, turned to look at the screen. The physician moved the wand toward her navel and pointed. "Look at the heart beating. This girl is one healthy baby."

A girl? Ann never knew. She wanted Jimmie to hear the news.

Ann gripped the hand of a smiling nurse. "A girl, that's so wonderful," Ann told her.

"I had three daughters," the nurse said. "They're all grown and moved away, but I remember the dolls, the make-up and all of the pretty clothes. Girls are fun."

The physician placed his hand on Ann's forehead. "Listen, young lady. Your child is strong and healthy. We won't do anything to risk your pregnancy. But we need to run a few tests, just to be sure that you're all right."

"I understand," Ann replied. "How could this have happened today?"

The physician jotted notes in her chart. He did not hear her question.

"I'm having you admitted today for observation," he told her. "I'm ordering blood work and a few other non-invasive tests. How old are you, Mrs. Bailey?"

"I just turned thirty-five. Why?"

"And this is your first child?" he asked.

"Yes."

"We may need to locate a specialist."

Professor Dulaney's sociology class numbered only eleven students. Unless you had a peculiar interest in social relationships coupled with a need for self-flagellation, Dulaney's class was to be avoided at all costs. Edinboro University tolerated the sadistic professor because he was tenured and two years from retirement. Megan Broward took Dulaney's spring semester class by a quirk of scheduling. Truth be told, she was starting to enjoy the challenge.

Megan's career aspiration was teaching. But if she ever wanted to be a school administrator her course load required a showing of behavioral sciences. So Dulaney was the diabolical *Diablo* in her path.

She tolerated his classroom ranting better than most. She forced herself to meet with him at least once weekly. Their talks were brief and increasingly cordial. Midway through the course, Megan regarded Dulaney as a helper rather than a hindrance.

Megan developed an interest in his academic interests, particularly his research in Seneca Indian culture. She read several of Dulaney's books on the topic and, to his delight, challenged several of his observations. She pointedly disputed his theory that the Seneca relocation to New York strengthened the tribe and improved Indian living conditions.

It was no surprise to Dulaney that his upstart student chose the Kinzua Dam's effect on the Seneca Nation as her term paper. In early May, with her deadline fast approaching, Megan realized that her topic was too broad and required additional research. Her last interview with Maude Thunder raised new leads. If only she had another month to check them out. Perhaps Dulaney would allow more time for her paper, an extension into the summer. She anticipated his angry response.

"Absolutely not." Dulaney glared at Megan, his steely eyes popping over half-glasses. "Your final grade depends on the punctual completion of this paper. I've never heard such a ridiculous request from a student."

"Professor, I can give you a paper, but it would be so much better with a few more weeks of research. Everything was fine until you told me to interview Maude Thunder..."

"Sit down, Megan." Dulaney rubbed his temples and slid back in his swivel chair. He turned toward his bookcase and removed four black binders stuffed with papers. He dropped them with a bang in front of Megan's nose. "Let me tell you about the Senecas, and maybe you'll come to your senses."

For the next hour, Dulaney told Megan chapter and verse of his extensive research of the Iroquois tribes. Unlike Megan, Dulaney conducted hundreds of interviews and gathered innumerable bits of Indian writings and relics. He touted himself as the "leading Irish authority" on the Seneca Nation past and present. He told her not to be "snookered" by time-worn Indian stories and myths. Senecas must be viewed, like every other culture, through the lens of the 21st Century, he said.

"It was a mistake for me to send you to Maude Thunder," Dulaney told his student. "I've talked to Maude several times for my research. Maude is typical of what I call 'the reflective Seneca.' There are two kinds of Senecas, in my opinion. The reflective and the prospective. The reflectives, and there are many, are harmful to the Tribe."

Although she regarded Dulaney's remarks as somewhat prejudicial, Megan took notes. When he paused, she asked him to explain the two "kinds" of Senecas.

"I would define a 'reflective' Indian as someone who elevates primitive culture above modern development," Dulaney explained. "This would be a person who espouses a return to the idyllic pre-European model of the Native Americans. You know, a nomadic existence, living off the land and the hunt."

"And the prospective Seneca?" Megan asked.

Dulaney laughed. "That could be an oxymoron. But I would define that as an Indian who lives in the present, who accepts social development and new technology and who…"

"Doesn't view himself as an Indian at all?" she asked.

"Well, I wouldn't go that far." Dulaney answered. "We all have cultural backgrounds. I'm proud of my Irish heritage, for example. But I don't look backward to the days of Irish farming as a model for my life."

Dulaney continued, "However, many sociologists believe that setting aside land for Native Americans led to their stagnant economic development. Many Indians have not kept pace with modern society. They have made themselves non-players in the American experience."

"Whoa, professor. That's very controversial. If that's what you're expecting in my term paper, you'll be disappointed." Megan never spoke to him so directly.

"What are your thoughts, Ms. Broward? You've interviewed Maude Thunder. Do you think her lifestyle and attitudes are advancing the Seneca Nation?"

Megan regarded his question as unfair, given the forced relocation of the Pennsylvania Senecas and Maude's traumatic separation from her family home. Before she spoke, Dulaney answered his own question.

"I like Maude. She calls me every so often. I've interviewed her several times for my research. I've even camped out on her property to understand her way of life. But truly she's not helping her people, Megan. She's too reflective. My God, this all happened 50 years ago. She's living in squalor to make her point, but today no one is listening."

"So why did she want to talk to me?" Megan asked.

"I don't know, frankly," Dulaney replied. "In my last conversation, I told her that I had a student researching the Kinzua relocation. She insisted that I send you to her."

"Is that all she said?" Megan asked.

"Only that she would tell you things she never told anyone. And, one more thing, she had something to give to you. What was that?"

Megan relayed the woman's description of the schoolhouse windows covered with black plastic, corpses removed from the Indian cemetery and the torching of her family home. Then she described how the Indian woman removed a rusted tackle box from her cabin.

"Do you have the tackle box?" Dulaney's interest was piqued.

"No. She opened it and placed its contents on an outside table. Just three things, an empty bottle of rum, a flashlight and an old map of some kind."

"A map? What kind of map?"

"A really old one, seemed to me. Parchment paper, folded into fourths. There were script markings, probably in Iroquoian, and then newer markings that were partially obscured by a water stain."

Dulaney began to take notes. "Where is the map now?"

"She wanted me to take it, but..."

"But you didn't, right?" Dulaney shook his head.

"It was hers. I couldn't just take it from her. It is an Indian relic."

"Oh, brother." Dulaney sighed. "You think there's some magic in the map, some hex or curse or something? Why didn't you just take the damn thing?"

Megan flipped open her cell phone. "Well, I sort of did. Look."

In the two-inch square screen of her phone, Megan showed Dulaney her snapshot of Maude Thunder's artifact. The professor adjusted his reading glasses and held her phone a few inches from his face. He scribbled more notes on his pad. Then he asked if she had any other photos. She advanced to the next shot and he peered more closely.

"I can read some of this," he said. "Did you write down these red letters?"

"Sorry, professor. This is the only evidence I have. Why is this so important to you? Seems like you're becoming a little 'reflective.'"

Dulaney quickly reverted to his gruff persona. "I'm terribly disappointed in you, Ms. Broward. When you do research, do a thorough job. Objects of antiquity can reveal a great deal about the development of a culture. A document like this map is probably worthless for our purposes. However, if you obtained it for the university collection, we could use it to show early Iroquoian language. Don't you agree?"

Megan was disappointed in herself.

"Now finish your term paper and have it on my desk by
Monday," Dulaney told her.

"And I will excuse your research failure if you send me a text
message with the map photographs by the end of the day. Do you
understand me, Ms. Broward?"

She understood, but didn't answer. Apparently, her final grade
from Dulaney required one more visit to Maude Thunder's cabin.

Not for an interview. For a map.

Chapter Seven
The Bombshell

Tom Zachary and his summer intern slid into a booth near the kitchen. Zachary felt stares from the Golden Wheel patrons, but Matty Moore was oblivious. People were talking in hushed tones. Zachary correctly surmised that customers were curious about the stranger. Matty was indeed a striking new figure in town. He was tall, young and athletic-looking – an unusual combination in these parts.

If only they knew the young man could buy their farms, their cattle and them, with enough left over to swallow up Lantz Corners, Mount Jewett and Smethport. Zachary smiled at the idea. He hoped that Matty's spending spree would include the Kane News Leader. The editor's days of bleeding ink may soon be over.

"Land sakes!" Golden Wheel's famous waitress screeched. "Who do we have here?" Toolie grasped Zachary's shoulder nerve as effectively as any second-grade teacher. "Or is it, 'whom do we have here,' Mr. Big-Time Editor?"

Zachary recoiled as Matty read her slanting name tag.

"Toolie? You're Toolie?"

"In the flesh, sonny. Now who are you, some basketball player who got lost?" Toolie knew that nonagenarians can say such things.

Matty's face was a snapshot of disappointment. His new apartment neighbor was hardly what he expected. His earlier plan to snuggle on a couch with "Toolie," while John Legend jazz pumped from surround sound speakers, was kaput. She was more likely turned on by Perry Como from a 78 r.p.m. victrola.

Zachary intervened. "I suppose you'll find out somehow, so let me stop the rumors right now. This is Matthew Moore. He's from Pittsburgh, a high school senior, and he'll be working as a summer intern at the News Leader."

Toolie eyed him up and down. "Stand up, Matthew."

He swiveled from the booth and stood next to her. As the couple dozen customers watched with amusement, Matty put his arm around Toolie and flashed a wide grin.

Toolie shifted weight from her bad hip. "Glory be! I haven't been squeezed like that since the Armistice."

"Sorry, ma'am. Didn't mean to hurt you," Matty replied. "It's just that you remind me of my grandmother. She was sweet and pretty, just like you."

"I gotta sit." Toolie pushed into the booth beside Zachary. She ignored calls from nearby customers. "You don't remind me of anybody, honey, but you're sweet. Now what are you doing here in Kane?"

Zachary tried to confine Toolie to her duties. He closed the menu. "Chicken noodle soup with a grilled cheese…" Zachary stopped when he noticed Toolie reading Matty's palm.

"Matthew. He was a saint, and wrote one of the gospels. You are a good writer, too. I can see that. Do you write stories? Could I read one?"

To say Toolie was excited would be an understatement. She must learn all about him; that was her job.

"I really don't, not a whole lot…" Matty stumbled for an answer. "All I've written lately is some poetry, but …"

Toolie was in full swoon now. "I looooove poetry. You must recite something for me. Just a few lines."

"I don't know. You're kind of busy here."

Toolie raised her arms to exhort the crowd. "This is Matthew Moore, not the gospel writer. He's a poet. And we'd like to hear one of his poems, do you agree?"

Soon dozens of voices were pleading for a dramatic reading.

Matty waved and cleared his throat. Zachary offered his glass of water. The young man positioned himself under the stuffed head of Elmer the Elk, and began:

"Once the child became a man,
Woe to he, is what he am.
And full of life and love and spit
To take his aim unto the pit
The pit of death and blood and gore,
The hole of Hell is at the door.
And punk his puny face, it will shatter
And grisly pulp and juice will splatter.
With horrid stain, he breathes no more.
The fire of Hell is at the door."

Before Matty began stanza two, Zachary started clapping. Polite applause trickled through the dining area. Toolie shifted hips before retreating to the kitchen.

"Good job, man," Zachary said. "I never saw Toolie turn that shade of purple before."

"Did I scare her? That was my only love poem."

"Listen, Matty. You are who you are. You have an urban edge to you that is unlike anything these people have seen. Keep it. Use it in your writing. I have a feeling we're going to shake up McKean County this summer."

Toolie returned with two plates of burgers and fries. "Ketchup and mustard are on the table. Careful you don't splatter it and make a bloody stain."

Matty took the check from her hand. "Toolie, what's your real name?"

"Nobody's asked me that for years. It's Gladys, why?"

"Let me think. Gladys. Gladys. I remember now. My Greek mythology class. Gladys was the goddess of inspiration and creativity. The great thinkers would pray to Gladys for ideas and innovations. I will pray to you, Gladys, for inspiration."

"Inspiration for what?" the flattered waitress asked.

"For story ideas, of course. I'll be writing stories for the News Leader this summer, and I want some blockbusters," Matty replied.

"You can pray, Matty, but if you hang around the Golden Wheel for a few hours you'll have all the story ideas you can handle," Zachary said. "And Toolie is the head storyteller."

The waitress ran her fingers through her blue hair. She processed decades of story ideas in a few seconds. One stood out.

"Here's one I haven't seen in the News Leader," Toolie said. "There's a widow by the name of Dolores Gibson. Her husband, Josh, threw himself off the Kinzua Bridge five years ago. Nobody knew why."

Zachary stopped her. "Now, Toolie, we don't want to rehash that story..."

"Hush, you old goat! Listen, Matthew, you want a good story, right? Well, you should talk to Mrs. Gibson. She told the judge last month that her husband was murdered, but the judge paid no mind to her. She may tell you everything."

"C'mon, Toolie." Zachary interrupted again. "Dolores Gibson is mentally unstable. Everybody knows that. No one believes her. Matty would be wasting his time talking to her."

"Sounds interesting to me." Matty put a 40 percent tip on the table. "Where can I find her?"

Zachary pulled Matty to his feet. "It's time for you to see the newspaper office. We'll introduce you to the staff and get you settled in. Thanks for lunch, Toolie."

"One second." Matty approached the bar. He handed a few bills to the bartender. Then he removed the framed photograph of Elmer the Elk. "I had my eye on this. What a great addition for my apartment."

"Jeepers Louise!" Toolie exclaimed. "You paid money for THAT! What kind of fleabag apartment did Tom get for you?"

"Upstairs, third floor."

"Jeepers Louise!"

"No Perry Como after 11 p.m., I promise."

"Jeepers…"

Ann Bailey didn't look at all like Ann Bailey. After two days in the high risk pregnancy ward, she looked like a 7 a.m. produce clerk at Safeway. No make-up, no hairstyle and no smile.

Her obstetrician made a 5 a.m. visit, mumbled some encouraging words and initialed her chart. He promised a diagnosis after blood tests were analyzed. Otherwise, all she could remember him saying during her sleepy haze was about the heartbeat. It continued to be strong. Her baby was healthy, he said.

As the morning sunlight brought her fully awake, Ann turned toward to the figure sprawled in a recliner beside her bed. Jimmie was breathing heavily. The flowers he brought last night were still fresh in a cut glass vase. A "get well" balloon, probably from the hospital gift shop, was starting to droop toward the sleeping governor.

Ann was struck by the quiet. Hospitals normally were not this quiet, she thought. Perhaps births were down, or Kane Community discharged many patients over the weekend. At least the First Lady should receive more frequent nursing visits, she figured. But the floor seemed to be empty of nurses.

The unusual quiet afforded her time to think, an opportunity that perhaps was not welcomed.

Just last month, she and Jimmie celebrated four years of marriage. Throughout that time, he served as the Commonwealth's governor. At the start, she traveled with him to Harrisburg and stayed at the rather plain governor's mansion. They attended dinners and campaign events in Philadelphia, where she visited her parents. They took almost weekly trips to Pittsburgh, Erie, Allentown, Johnstown and lesser towns, where voters had to be reminded that their governor was working for them and, coincidentally, he had a good-looking wife.

In the last year or so, however, she grew tired of incessant traveling. So, after the winter holidays, she scheduled a day for the two of them, just to talk. In the manner of two business consultants charting course for a fledgling corporation, Ann and Jimmie examined their relationship – where it was, where it is and where it would go.

Ann begged Jimmie to start a family. Reluctantly, he agreed. Four months later, she became pregnant.

She learned the good news in a telephone call from her obstetrician, a full ten weeks into the pregnancy. She reached Jimmie by text message while he was dedicating a new highway in Altoona. He quickly called her. His voice stuttered, and he seemed to be overjoyed. When he returned to Leigh-Rose, they celebrated all night.

Surprisingly to Ann, however, Jimmie did not scale back his schedule. He was absent from Leigh-Rose just as often. Government business. Campaign stops. Media interviews. Late night travel.

Now, midway into her pregnancy, with an uncertain diagnosis hours away, Ann wondered. Did Jimmie really want to be a father? And, just as importantly, did he really want to be her husband?

He would be there when she needed him, Jimmie promised. So there he was now, sharing her hospital room. Jimmie's eyes were closed and he appeared to be sleeping. But his mind was hard at work.

This baby stuff was new to him, and he feared that the pressures of parenthood soon would damage his marriage. It was a fear he lived through as a child. His parents constantly fought. Their love had evaporated as he matured. He was the stranger in their relationship, and he regretted the strain he added over time.

Jimmie never knew whether his closeness to his mother drove Brock Bailey to find love elsewhere. Jimmie assumed that Brock was weak and unable to commit time and attention to his family.

Brock's footsteps could not be followed. They could never be followed. The pain he caused to Jimmie's mother before her death was unforgiveable. When his mother learned that Brock was seeing another woman, she withdrew from everyone. Her smile was gone. Jimmie vowed not to repeat that tragedy with Ann.

He never cheated on her. He never would.

Ann's treating physician knocked twice on the hospital room door. With a resident in scrubs, he entered and pulled her chart. Ann raised up on her elbows and Jimmie slid to his feet.

"Mrs. Bailey, Governor," the doctor began. "I'm glad you're both here, so we can go over these discharge instructions together."

"Is everything OK, doctor?" Jimmie asked.

"The test results look good. The blood work was normal. The fetus is developing without problem. We had an episode that is not uncommon for a woman of your age."

Ann looked at Jimmie, as though to say what does that mean?

The physician jotted a note and handed Ann's chart to the resident. "You have a condition known as placenta previa. This is caused when the placenta, the sac carrying the baby, lies low in the uterus and partially covers the cervix."

"Is there a danger to the baby?" Ann asked.

"Not usually," the doctor replied. "But you, Ann, have to follow my instructions to the letter. You cannot exert yourself in the next few months. You need as much bed rest as possible."

"How about, ah, you know, other bed things?" Jimmie asked.

"No sex and no traveling!" The physician handed Jimmie a typewritten list of no-nos. At the top of the list was "copulative activity."

"Thanks, Doc," Jimmie said dejectedly. "Looks like I can still hold her hand."

"Not too tightly." The resident chuckled.

When the doctors left, Jimmie took his wife's hand and climbed beside her on the bed. As the mechanical back rest whirred to level, the Baileys embraced.

What the hell. Only three tablets left.

Dolores Gibson popped all three into her mouth and chased them with a warm gin and tonic.

Cuddles ducked as Dolores tossed the prescription bottle into her bathroom trash basket. The dog whimpered, as though she knew her master would be passed out for the afternoon. Again.

For Dolores, the occasion called for Percocet and White Diamonds perfume. After all, when was the last time a young man visited her house in Wexford? A young and enthusiastic newspaper reporter was only minutes away from her doorstep – a man raging with testosterone and eager to seduce her for a good story, she imagined.

Her attorney had warned her not to talk to reporters. Her appeal of Judge Van Lear's denial of insurance money was in the balance. Any side comment or bad publicity could doom their chances with the finicky appellate judges, he said.

But when Dolores received a late night called from a "Mr. Matthew Moore of the Kane News Leader," her pallid attorney's advice was ignored. In her chemically enhanced mind, she was the prime hunk of a humanoid. She approved of her increasingly blurry image in the bathroom mirror. Bring on the reporter, she thought. This body was made to talk.

Cuddles buried itself under the sofa when Matty's Mustang roared up the driveway. Dolores peered through the front door side window. He was an imposing figure, indeed. Nothing like she expected, but a pleasant surprise, nonetheless.

Matty carried a steno pad in his hand, a pen behind his ear and an ambition to write the definitive account of Josh Gibson, his horrible plunge from the Kinzua Bridge and his mysterious widow. He was flying solo on this mission; no one from the News Leader knew his whereabouts. For some reason, Tom Zachary was hostile to any suggestion of a Dolores Gibson interview.

Only his apartment neighbor, Toolie, had encouraged him.

Before Matty reached her front porch, Dolores opened the door.

Her first impression was excitement. She giggled and flung her hair from her perfumed neck.

His first impression was disbelief. If there was a soft, perfumed neck leading to a plunging neckline caressed by faux pearls, Matty didn't notice. All he saw were shapely pair of legs starting from a pair of four-inch red pumps and sensually moving thigh-ward.

"Mrs. Gibson?" Matty emphasized the "Mrs."

"Mr. Moore. I've been expecting you." Dolores wheeled from the door and shoved Cuddles away with her foot. She slinked aside and allowed Matty to step into the foyer.

"I'm so glad you're doing a story about Josh. You know, it's been five years and a lot of people are forgetting what happened. First, though, will you join me in a drink?"

Matty noticed a cocktail bar illuminated by recessed lighting. Seven bottles, probably one for each day of the week, stood in a row. Two crystal glasses on a silver tray caught his eye. Was she giving out more than just her story?

"No, thank you, ma'am."

"Oh, Matthew. Please call me Dolores. My friends call me Dee Dee. Although, after Josh died, I don't have many friends."

Matty pulled a chair from her breakfast table. "This would be a good spot for our interview." He suspected that she preferred the sofa or something more horizontal.

"You're all business, Mr. Moore." Her speech started to slur.

"I've done some research about Colonel Gibson," Matty said. "Army Reserve, expert marksman and an avid outdoorsman. His education and police experience were lacking. Why do you think he was picked as state police commissioner?"

"Me. None of the other candidates had such a good-looking wife."

Matty remembered Tom Zachary's opinion that Gibson's

widow was crazy, but he wrote her quote down *verbatim*. Maybe she was the best-looking wife.

Dolores wriggled off her wedding ring and placed it on the table. "Look at the inscription, it's from Josh."

Matty held the ring to his eye. He turned it as he read: "From Josh to My Bombshell." Matty handed it to her and said, "He must have loved you very much."

"When he bought the ring, probably. Other times, he was a shit."

Considering that comment to be off-the-record, Matty pressed on. "You told some people after the court case that Josh was not the kind of man to commit suicide. Do you think he was murdered?"

"Listen, Mr. Moore." Her "s's" were becoming "th's". "Josh was in politics. He made many enemies. When Jimmie Bailey followed his dad as governor, Josh was expected to lose his title with the state police. But he kept his job. That pi'th'ed off a lot of state troopers."

"How did he keep his job as commissioner?" Matty asked.

"I think he knew something about the governor. He had the goods on Jimmie. But he never told me anything."

"Tell me what happened on the night Josh died." Matty noticed the woman's glassy eyes as she slumped lower in her chair.

"He got a telephone call about 9 p.m. He took it in the study. I was in bed, as usual, hoping for some attention…"

"Who was on the phone?" Matty asked.

"I don't know. It was a short call. The next thing I know, Josh is pulling on his trousers and strapping on his shoulder holster. He said something about an incident on Interstate 80, and then he left."

"Did he seem upset? Was he in a bad mood?"

"I could tell something was bothering him, but if you're implying that he was depre'th'ed, I don't think…"

"What happened next, Mrs. Gibson?"

"He called from the road, about midnight. He told me not to answer the door for anyone, even if I knew the person. Then he says to lock up the closet with the 'th'ilver.'"

"The what???"

"Oh, crap, I shouldn't have told you that. Come here."

Dolores led the young reporter down the hall to a back bedroom. She staggered toward a closet door before stumbling back onto a loveseat.

"Open the door, Matthew. Take a good look."

Matty did as he was told. On the floor were stacks of silver bars. Some were pitted and ill-shaped, as though the bars were recovered antiquities.

"Where did this come from?" he asked.

"Josh brought them home, right at the end of the Brock Bailey investigation. He said he found them. That's all he said, that he found them."

"These are hundreds of years old." Matty lifted two bars and looked for any identification. "They must be worth a fortune. What was Josh going to do with them?"

"He never said. And I don't know what to do with them."

Matty had riches of his own, mostly numbers on account ledgers. This was a true fortune, one he could see and touch. But its location, here with Josh Gibson's widow, was an investigative story he must pursue.

He turned to the dozing Dolores. "Did Josh hunt for treasure? Did he poke around old mines? Was there some police investigation that would involve silver theft? Surely, he told you something."

She opened one eye.

"Ye'th' he did."

Matty poised his pen for a good quote.

Dolores sighed. "He said that after things cooled off, we'd sell this shit."

Chapter Eight

The Peacemaker

Maude Thunder's map folded nicely into a business envelope.
Megan was careful, keeping the tattered edges intact when she
tucked the envelope into her leather binder.

The map was full of mystery. What did the drawing represent?
Why was a distance of 50 feet marked from "bridge abutment"?
What were these curious red markings? Indian symbols, perhaps?

Professor Dulaney, who researched the Seneca Nation customs
from the 1600s, did not answer these questions. So Megan decided
to take a weekend drive up the Allegheny River Valley to
Steamburg, New York. She called first, to make sure the Seneca
history center was open.

Megan's car drove by the Buckhorn Inn and Casino, its gaudy
billboards and signs seemingly coaxing dollar bills from her purse.
Then she turned onto Sycamore Road. She passed an Indian
smoke shop and a countless number of liquor stores.

Seems like Steamburg had all the vices covered, she thought.

Sandwiched between these dens of iniquity was a rather plain
cement block building. A rotted sign hung from the eaves, "Seneca
Community Center." Only one automobile was parked in the
gravel lot. Megan was happy to know that at least one other visitor
was not interested in cigarettes, liquor and gambling – at least at
that moment.

"Excuse me, sir." Megan stood at the front counter. She saw
a teenage boy in a far room. MP3-player buds were lodged in his
ears. She knocked on the front desk with her fist, but he was

unmoved.

"Sir, Sir," she hollered without success. The door opened behind her and an older man entered. He unloaded advertisement flyers onto a display and walked past her to the back room. He sharply slapped the boy's back and pointed to Megan.

Struggling to his feet, the boy ambled to the counter. "May I help you?"

"I'm Megan Broward. I called earlier. Are you the person who can translate a Seneca document for me?"

"Oh, no, ma'am." He pulled the cords from his ears. "Ain't more than about a dozen Indians anymore that can do that. They teach us Spanish in school. You know, so many Mexicans around here looking for work."

"But someone told me I could get these papers translated. Who can do that?"

The boy pulled a telephone directory from under the counter. "We have a few older volunteers who work here, but there's one old guy who's probably your best bet. We call him Mr. George."

"I'm only here for the day," Megan said. "Where can I find him?"

"OK. Right here's his number. He's at the nursing center, but he still gets around and he's not crazy like some of them there. Let me call."

Megan double-checked the envelope as the boy dialed. She heard him ask the nursing center to ring Mr. George's room. After a few minutes, the boy said, "Yes, yes. What time did he leave? Is he on the center's van now? OK, thanks."

"Is Mr. George on the loose?" Megan asked.

"Actually, ma'am, he's a few doors down at Prantle's Bakery. You can catch him there."

"How will I know him?" Megan asked.

"He's tall, has a buzz haircut and he's older than crap. Should be easy." The boy laughed as he pointed her in the right direction.

Megan followed her nose to the bakery. Inside were tables for two pushed against the wall. Along the other wall were delicacies and a deli counter. An old man with a stained raincoat and all-terrain sneakers sat alone.

"Mr. George?" she asked.

"You must be the Edinboro student, what's your name?"

"Megan Broward, sir."

"Lovely eyes, Seneca eyes." In another era, it was probably his best pick-up line.

"There's a rumor, but my family can't confirm it…" Megan blushed.

"I can. Once I was director of the Seneca genealogy study. We traced all the maternal lines back generations. You may be on our list." The old man's eyes brightened.

"I would like that, but that's not why I'm here…"

"Betty, dear," he hollered to the bakery worker. "Two coffees and two Danishes, do you like cheese, Ms. Broward?"

"Megan, please, and yes, but I'm paying." She sat across from him and placed the envelope before him.

"Can you read the Seneca language?" she asked.

"Yakökwe Hatënotha'."

The words fell from his lips as smoothly as cheese oozed from her Danish. "What does that mean?" she asked.

"We speak very simply, Megan," he replied. "Very few words, but very accurate words. I made an observation about you. Your voice and your manner are like a beautiful melody. All I said was 'the woman sings.'"

Megan blushed again. "You are so sweet, Mr. George. What did you do for a living?"

"I used to be somebody," he said, slightly chuckling. "When I was young, I studied the Iroquois culture, the five nations and their cultures. I used my powers of observation to look beyond people's faces and into their souls. I communicated with others who did not, or could not communicate. Even at a young age, I was held in high honor."

"Were you leader of the Seneca Nation?" Megan asked.

"No, better than that," he answered. "Long before you were born, the Senecas honored their Medicine Man as a spiritual guide. Over the years, our culture has turned away from witchcraft and superstitions. The Medicine Man was replaced by the Peacemaker."

"You were a Peacemaker?"

"I was, for about 30 years," Mr. George said. "Best job I ever had. People would come to me for advice, and I would tell them how the Seneca Indians of old would solve their problems."

"Did you just make up stuff? How did you know what to tell them?"

"Some of it was plain common sense, but a lot was advice I learned from the old stories handed down through our history."

Megan opened her envelope. "You are a very wise man, I can tell. You should be able to help me out with this map."

Mr. George slid his breakfast to the side as Megan unfolded the grayish paper before his eyes. His hand began to tremble as he touched it.

"Great God in Heaven! Where did you find this?" He spun the map around to face him.

"A woman, an Indian woman who lives in the Kinzua Valley found it," Megan said. "She didn't know what it is or what it represents."

Mr. George was speechless. Megan noticed his fingers slowly rubbing over the red markings. He mumbled something. It was a strange language to her.

"I must go." He stood and plunked some quarters on the table.

"No, no, you can't." Megan blocked his exit. "Please sit. You are wise. There is no witchcraft or superstitions, you said. Tell me what this is."

"I am old. My time is short. I pray that no harm comes to me." The Peacemaker returned to his chair, but did not touch the map.

"Tell me, Mr. George, is this a map? You recognize it, don't you?" Megan asked.

"I've seen this, young lady. Many, many years ago. This map is about 200 years old."

"But these ink markings, they're newer right?" she asked.

"Maybe we should start at the beginning."

Megan pulled her chair closer and opened her notebook.

"The Senecas were given land in Pennsylvania by George Washington in 1794. So we settled in the Allegheny River Valley and along Kinzua Valley.

"Together with American and French soldiers, we fought against English invaders in the Revolutionary War and during the War of 1812. So the Senecas asked for this land in return for their contribution to the new country.

"In many ways, these river valleys were sacred to us. We gained this land through our blood and sacrifice. That's what many of our people believed."

Megan understood this history from Professor Dulaney's lectures. She wondered what this had to do with the map.

"Then something quite remarkable happened. One night, late in the summer of 1812, two Seneca scouts followed a wagon drawn by oxen along Kinzua Valley. They watched as several English traders pulled the wagon to the edge of Kinzua Creek. It was probably the steepest and most impassable part of the valley.

"In the pale moonlight, the Englishmen dug a trench and filled it with things they removed from their wagon. The men cursed the heat. Their sweat drenched the ground. After they retreated from the valley, elk appeared and licked salt from their sweat."

Megan looked up when he paused. "What did they bury?"

"Silver," the Peacemaker said. "Millions of dollars of pure silver."

"What did the scouts do?" she asked.

"Well, they dug it up of course," he replied. "And they conveyed it by canoe down the Allegheny River and presented it to their leaders. It was worth millions, even then."

"So this map…" Megan began to understand its significance.

"That map was drawn by the scouts to show where the silver was buried. Now, other people have drawn on the map since then … including me."

Megan was stunned. "Why you?"

"The silver was a closely guarded secret. Only the highest officers and council members knew about it. As Peacemaker in the 1960's, I had access to everything involving the Senecas. We kept the silver for about 150 years, mostly because we didn't know what to do with it."

"You could have sold it," Megan said.

"That's what I wanted to do. I was a pragmatist. But others were worried because the silver was Spanish."

"But you said that English traders buried it," Megan interjected.

"That's right, young lady. An English captain raised the treasure from a sunken Spanish galleon off the Carolina coast. At the time, there was a war between England and the United States. We sided with Americans, naturally, because the English abused our Iroquois tribes."

"But Spanish explorers were even worse." Megan recalled Professor Dulaney's last lecture.

"That's what worried our people. There were Spanish and English fingerprints on the silver. Some of our leaders believed the silver was cursed. If we sold it, they said, great harm would visit us."

Superstitions and witchcraft. Megan understood that the Seneca Indians never fully abandoned their old beliefs. In fact, she thought, the same could be said for many non-Indians she knew.

"Did the Seneca leaders ever test that theory?" she asked. "Did they ever sell any of the silver?"

The Peacemaker nodded. "Just once. In the late 1950's, the U.S. Government set aside money for the Kinzua Dam on the Allegheny River. We knew that it would flood the entire Cornplanter Reservation in Pennsylvania as well as hundreds of acres of our land in New York. We protested, wrote letters to congressmen and tried to stir up public opinion, but that didn't work. The dam was going to be built."

"So you sold some of the silver? Why?"

"That was my idea. I believed that we could get the federal courts to stop the dam. We had our treaty with George Washington. These were our lands. Surely, I thought, any federal judge would honor George Washington's word."

"So money from the silver was spent..." Megan sensed what happened.

"On the lawyers," he said. "The damn lawyers, who said our case was good. But we lost at every step, even at the Supreme Court."

"I'm sorry," Megan told him.

"Then President Kennedy was elected. He said he was a friend of the Indians. So we cashed in some more silver, hired this famous civil engineer and paid for an alternative flood protection design that would save our land. Kennedy was no friend. He owed favors to Mayor Lawrence of Pittsburgh, and Mayor Lawrence wanted the dam to protect his city."

"I know what happened, Mr. George," Megan said. "The dam was built, and the Senecas were relocated here, to Steamburg."

"Nothing good happened from that silver money, Megan. So, before Kinzua Dam was finished and while our homes were being torched by federal agents, the council voted to return the silver."

"Return it to..." Megan paused in mid-sentence.

The Peacemaker put his index finger to his lips. He looked around to see if any bakery workers were eavesdropping. Then he pointed to a mark on Megan's map – fifty feet due east of the third trestle, inside the shadows of Kinzua Bridge.

"Oh, my G..." Her lips could barely form the words. "You mean..."

"You've got the treasure map, Ms. Broward," the Peacemaker said. "It's all yours if you want it. But before you dig up the silver, you may want to know what else is written here."

Megan remembered her original purpose. Mr. George was just about the only person who could translate the Seneca language on her map. Professor Dulaney would surely be impressed when she included a translation in her term paper.

"These markings here," the Peacemaker pointed to faded strokes near a water stain, "were probably made by Chief Cornplanter himself when his Indian scouts returned. It says the bars numbered 416. These words here say 'Spanish silver.' I don't know what this means; it could be someone's name, or maybe the person who would keep the silver."

"What are these red markings, Mr. George?"

"That, Megan, is the signature or mark of the Medicine Man or Peacemaker at the time. I know of this man's reputation. He was feared."

"What was his name?" Megan pressed.

"TI-OOH-QUOT-TA-KAU-NA. That's him. He was called 'Woods on Fire.' He kept that name. I don't think he ever took an English name.

"Woods on Fire held many beliefs that were opposed by Chief Cornplanter and his half-brother Handsome Lake. As the story goes, Handsome Lake was visited by representatives of the Great Creator on three occasions. He gained understanding of Heaven and Hell, and he preached that our people had to follow rules of good conduct."

"What were the beliefs of Woods on Fire?" Megan asked.

"I'm not sure he had beliefs. It seems as if his powers were mystical. They were dark powers. He did not follow Handsome Lake and his preaching. Woods on Fire threatened others by using prophetic incantations, which often turned out to be true. He preyed on people's fear."

"What kind of threats?"

"Most were visions of what was going to happen, usually bad things. He would tell others in the tribe that their crops would fail or their hunt would be a failure. He would predict that certain people would get sick or that others, usually elderly people, would die soon.

"Some of these visions undoubtedly came true by chance. Old people usually die and, often, crops would fail with bad weather.

"Woods on Fire was the classic negative person. And, for other negative people, he became a leader. As a medicine man, he gave out plenty of bad medicine."

The Peacemaker studied the map more closely. He recalled that tribal elders guarded both the old map and their silver bars at a safe place in the Allegheny Forest for decades. Some elders regarded the silver as "mad money" or the Nation's "rainy day fund." Having an unliquidated treasure, even a Spanish one, provided much comfort in lean times.

"What do these words mean, Mr. George?" Megan pointed to more recent markings.

The Peacemaker shook his head. He seemed to be embarrassed. He recalled the last time he spoke with Brother John Brontzman, the elder tasked with returning the silver to its burial spot in 1965. Brontzman had asked for an incantation to protect the silver. The Peacemaker borrowed one from the Woods on Fire collection – an incantation the 19th Century medicine man had pronounced when the land treaty was signed by his chief.

"These are words that were uttered when we re-buried the silver bars," he told Megan. "And if you believe in witchcraft, they have some meaning. If not, they are just words from an old Seneca medicine man."

The Peacemaker pointed to the incantation as he translated.

"Harm will befall any white man who disturbs the peace of this land – for all eternity."

Megan let the words linger a bit. "Exact translation?"

"Exact," he answered.

"So if I take this map, find the silver and disturb the ground, then…"

"Nothing will happen, Megan. That is, unless you believe in this witchcraft. Personally, I don't. But then again, I'm not interested in Spanish silver."

Always a down side, Megan thought. Her parents never paid her allowance until she vacuumed the house. She was permitted to watch television only after her homework was done and her pajamas were on. Now, she couldn't dig up a treasure unless she overcame an old hex from a dead medicine man.

Mr. George finished his coffee. "Do you want my advice?" he asked her.

"I don't know what to do," Megan replied.

"Let it be. Great riches like that will only cause trouble, whether or not someone put a curse on them," he said. "Look at me. I've known where that silver's been buried for 50 years. I could have dug it up, sold it and had enough money to build my own Indian casino. But I didn't."

"And no harm came to you, Mr. George," Megan said. "You didn't disturb the land."

The Peacemaker spoke his peace. It was time to leave.

He reached across the table and shook her hand. Her smile was forced.

"Safeguard that map, young lady. Don't let it fall into the wrong hands. You haven't shared it with anyone, have you?"

"Just my professor, but he can't read your language."

The elderly man walked a few steps toward the door. He turned and whispered, "I hope not."

Chapter Nine

The Attack

Widow Gibson Searches for Answers
Five Years After Commissioner's Death
by MATTHEW MOORE
News Leader Staff Writer

(WEXFORD, PA) – Monday marks a painful anniversary for Dolores Gibson. Five years have passed since her husband, Pennsylvania's popular state police commissioner, plunged to his death from the Kinzua Railroad Bridge. So many years, she says, but so few answers.

In an exclusive interview at the Gibson estate north of Pittsburgh, Dolores Gibson recounted the final hours of Frank "Josh" Gibson's life. The burly "top cop" left his home after a mysterious, late night telephone call. The next morning, his broken body was found at the foot of Kinzua Bridge in McKean County.

"Josh packed his service revolver that night," Mrs. Gibson recalled. "He was responding to a police call. I'm sure of it. How can anybody say he committed suicide?"

McKean County Common Pleas Judge Horace Van Lear, however, ruled that Josh Gibson likely jumped from the bridge. Judge Van Lear denied $2 million in life insurance benefits to Mrs. Gibson in February. The ruling has been appealed to Superior Court.

Still weepy when she speaks of her husband, Mrs. Gibson vowed to find answers to the "bizarre sequence of events" that changed her life. Although time has softened her features and slowed her step, she promised this reporter that "no stone will be unturned" in her private investigation of Josh Gibson's death.

"My flesh will not rest until I have caressed the truth," she said.

On the night of Josh's death, Mrs. Gibson recalled, the telephone rang about 9 p.m. She did not hear her husband's conversation. He quickly got dressed, she said. He told her that he had to respond to an incident on Interstate 80. Then he left. A few hours later, Josh called her from the road and told her to lock up their house, she said.

"I could tell something was bothering him, but he wasn't depressed," she said.

Although Josh Gibson left no suicide note, Judge Van Lear found that death was likely self-inflicted. "The man simply wanted to say goodbye in quick fashion," the judge wrote, noting no evidence of foul play.

Dolores Gibson bristled at the judge's opinion. "I knew Josh. I made him happy," she said. "Obviously, that judge needs someone to make him happy, too."

Josh Gibson was lead investigator in the 2003 disappearance of Pennsylvania Governor Brock Bailey. His professional work in that case prompted Governor Jimmie Bailey, Brock's son and successor, to reappoint Gibson as state police commissioner.

Matty Moore proudly stared at his first byline. The News Leader's weekly edition landed on his desk at 3 p.m. Jessie Krone had placed a yellow smiley-face sticker beside his front-page article.

"Nice story, kid," Jessie said.

"So Mr. Zachary decided to run it? That's great."

"Tom likes you, Matty. He only changed a few words."

"Where is he?" Matty asked. "I want to thank him for the front-page display."

Jessie smirked. "Tom just got a call from Judge Van Lear's

chambers. He's on his way to the courthouse."

Uh-oh, Matty thought. Maybe Van Lear was not a happy man at all.

There are only a handful of ways to blackmail a governor. You can write a letter, but who needs a trail of evidence? You could call, but telephone lines are tapped more frequently than ever. Or you can meet face-to-face, but the chances of violence and mayhem are too great.

Billy Herman always liked working through an intermediary. Such was the usual mode of skullduggery in Pennsylvania politics. Every politician had his bag man. When klieg lights from the district attorney or big city dailies focused on shadowy public servants, the glare deftly deferred to their criminal associates. Governor Bailey was no exception.

The governor's chief of staff, William Pennoyer, a balding, chubby chunk of turpitude, held Jimmie Bailey's bag. Pennoyer was the bulbous buffer between Jimmie and his extortionist.

Pennoyer found himself figuratively and literally miles away from his law school ethics classes at Pace University in New York. After graduation, he developed a practice in sports agency. He landed Jimmie Bailey, the Arizona State pitching phenom, as his star client. When Jimmie left baseball to succeed his father as governor, Pennoyer went along to keep Jimmie out of trouble.

Pennoyer soon found himself in the thick of it.

The typical venial sins of public office – graft, patronage and petty bribery – are what Pennoyer expected to fend off for his boss. However, six months into his new role as Jimmie's right-hand man, Pennoyer was introduced to the mortal sins of Billy Herman.

Pennoyer vividly recalled his first meeting with Herman. They met at a Front Street tavern in Harrisburg on St. Patrick's Day. Pennoyer's distinctive item of dress was a Kiwanis pin. Herman's was a white carnation, dipped in green ink.

They drank two pitchers of Jägermeister. It was the only hour they were friends.

Their second meeting was more business-like. Herman invited Pennoyer to the Forest Club for a round of golf. By the ninth hole, Herman described all he knew about the night Brock Bailey died, how Jimmie struck him with a thrown baseball, how Jimmie left his father to die in the tornado, and how Jimmie tossed his father's body off Pittsburgh's West End Bridge.

Herman had told Pennoyer that Gibson knew the whole story, too, but covered it up to keep his job. Then he told Pennoyer, "I really don't want to hurt the new governor and I won't. But I just need some money. Do you think the governor can help?"

They arranged a million-dollar payment. In return, Billy Herman promised that he would never be heard from again.

Six months later, Pennoyer found a sealed envelope that was slipped under his Harrisburg office door. It was marked "Confidential."

Pennoyer opened it later at home. It read: "Dear Bill... Seems like retirement is costing me a lot more than I expected. I've been hit hard with medical bills. We should have been doctors. Ha-ha. Anyway, can you suggest any source of funds? I need to borrow $90,000 to get over this situation. Talk to your bank. I'll get with you next week. B.H."

Jimmie's reaction was fury. "I'm not a bank!" he told his chief of staff.

At that point, Pennoyer advised that Billy Herman was dangerous. They had no choice but to play ball with this "carnie," Pennoyer said. Maybe he could negotiate a lower number, he said, or at least get some assurance of finality to this extortion.

Herman did not relent. The $90,000 payment was made in cash, literally in a paper bag passing from Pennoyer's hand to Herman's in a downtown Pittsburgh parking garage.

The next note, slipped under Pennoyer's door a year later, was more bizarre. Herman wrote:

"Dear Mr. Pennoyer. Since we last met, I have learned that your boss was involved in a clever scheme with Josh Gibson. I was a partner with Gibson in the discovery of a very valuable treasure. Surely you know of this matter.

"It is my firm belief that Gibson transferred this treasure to Governor Bailey in order to keep his job. My share of this fortune is $5 million. It is disgraceful that the governor has control of my fortune. I hereby demand its return to me, or I will take appropriate action. B.H."

When Pennoyer handed the note to his boss, Jimmie erupted: "This man is a freaking crackpot. I don't know what he's talking about. What treasure? What fortune?"

So a meeting was finally planned between the governor and his tormentor. Pennoyer set it up at a rest stop off Interstate 79. They talked in an unmarked state van.

"Are you wearing a wire?" Pennoyer asked. Despite Herman's denial, Jimmie told Pennoyer to search him. Nothing was discovered.

"Now tell me about this treasure," Jimmie said.

Billy Herman was outnumbered in the van. He gave a guarded response. "It was right there, practically in your backyard, Governor. We found it, Josh and me."

Jimmie waited to speak. Surely, there was more to the story.

Herman continued. "Josh and I were in that valley for days, looking for anybody killed in that tornado. We hiked all through the bridge debris with dozens of other police officers.

"Late in the second day, Josh decides that we should all use metal detectors, so he hands them out to the other officers. After everyone quit for the day, Josh and I stayed behind. I asked him why we were looking for bodies using metal detectors."

"What did he say?" Pennoyer asked.

"He said there were no dead bodies here. He was looking for a gun. Then he swore me to secrecy, said I couldn't tell anyone about this. He said that Brock Bailey was standing on the bridge right before the tornado hit, that he fired a gun at Jimmie, and the gun fell somewhere into the valley.

"Well, sir, the bridge had been destroyed and all the metal supports were scattered in the valley like pick-up sticks. I asked him how we were ever going to find a gun in this debris. Josh had a wicked look in his eye. 'Never quit,' he said. 'We must find it.' Then he explained that the gun was evidence, the best evidence in his case against Jimmie Bailey."

Jimmie reacted coolly. He suspected that Josh Gibson wanted him in jail. When Jimmie won the election, though, Josh wanted something more personal: to keep his job.

"Before we quit for the day," Herman continued, "Josh's metal detector starts to go crazy. He's thinking he's found the gun. So we dig a little bit in this grassy area and we can't find anything.

"The metal detector gives off a stronger signal, so we know something big is there. Josh takes this shovel and he's going through this dirt like a madman. Next thing I know, the shovel gives off this loud clang.

"I bend down and start swiping away loose dirt with my hands. And then I see it. Josh called it the mother lode. All this freaking silver. Unbelievable."

"Silver? In the Kinzua Valley, well I…". Jimmie stammered.

"We're running out of daylight fast," Herman recalled. "So Josh tells me to cover it up real good and says the two of us will come back in a few days to dig it all up."

"Did you?" Pennoyer asked.

"Hell, no! Gibson wouldn't take my calls. I couldn't talk to him. So about a week later, I came back to the valley. I wasn't sure of the exact spot, but I couldn't find any silver. Nothing. Naturally, I assumed that Josh beat me to it, and stole it from under my nose."

Jimmie remembered tales of a long-lost Spanish treasure chest that was rumored to have been buried by an English captain near the village of Gardeau in McKean County. Did Josh Gibson, who stumbled through his police career, stumble upon the Spanish treasure?

"Why do you think Josh gave the silver to me? That's what your note implied?" Jimmie asked.

"I know he did," Herman replied. "Josh told me."

"When did he tell you that?" Pennoyer asked.

That was a question the extortionist could not answer, at least without incriminating himself.

"This story about Dolores Gibson in your newspaper today... I find this to be very interesting." Judge Van Lear sneered at Tom Zachary over his half-glasses. "This writer, Matthew Moore, is he new to your paper?"

Zachary had been called on the carpet of His Honor before. In the editor's experience with small town papers, Zachary believed the local judiciary can be somewhat thin-skinned.

"Mr. Moore is our summer intern from Pittsburgh," Zachary replied. "Good writer, don't you think?"

"Please tell Mr. Moore that I am happy. That my wife makes me happy. That his failure to call my chambers for a response to his insinuation that my libido is unstirred was inexcusable." Van Lear puffed his chest like a bantam rooster.

"We will run a correction about your libido, Your Honor," Zachary teased.

"You will do nothing of the sort!" Van Lear bellowed. "How did you find this young man to be your summer intern?"

Zachary, avoiding the part about impersonating a judge to look at the sealed Bailey file, told Van Lear that Matty Moore was discovered at a high school job fair. Van Lear pumped him for the details – time, place, location, dates of employment, and his working hours.

"Tell me, Zachary, when will Mr. Moore be assigned to cover

the courthouse?" the judge asked.

"I don't believe his beat will include…"

"Oh, fiddle, Tom. You must have him cover the courthouse. Please send him to visit me tomorrow. I'll be doing chamber work all morning. You do want the young man to have the complete news writing experience, don't you?"

"Certainly, judge. Tomorrow morning, it is."

Thank goodness for young idiots, Professor Dulaney thought as he hiked down through the pines. College students often lacked the focus to exploit an opportunity right in front of them. When Megan Broward texted him "the map," Dulaney seized the moment.

The Kinzua Valley path and its wet aromatic mulch stretched a few hundred feet before him. Getting around a chained state park gate was the easy part; his descent to the valley floor in midnight darkness was more challenging for the graying professor. With a flashlight in his belt and shovel in hand, Dulaney navigated the path, unseen by human eyes.

Megan's map proved to be more detailed than he first believed. Downloading her text photo to his home computer, Dulaney noticed fine specifics in the cartographer's sketch. The treasure's precise location was triangulated between the bridge trestle and a peculiar bend of the creek.

Fifty feet due east of the trestle and twenty feet due south of the creek were distances easily stepped off, he thought. The map also showed rise and fall of the terrain, indicating a mound slightly west of the burial spot.

Dulaney's only concern was the silver's weight. He could nab a dozen bars tonight and return tomorrow with a wheelbarrow or wagon. For a one-man job, the work required more than one visit, the professor decided.

Mulch blended into stone and grass at the path's end. Dulaney surveyed the peaceful valley for a moment. He imagined Kinzua Valley as it likely appeared to the Seneca Indians. Certainly Kinzua Bridge had not yet spanned the magnificent gorge when the treasure was first buried by Blackbeard and his crew. The forest likely was thicker with virgin hardwood timber. There were no power lines to the east.

When silver was returned to the spot in 1965, a Seneca Indian drew the railroad bridge and wrote "abutment," according to scribbles on Dulaney's map. The Indian's artful detail was fascinating to Dulaney. Perhaps, he thought, Seneca Nation did not foreclose its option to retrieve the treasure after its land was flooded.

Suddenly, to his right, Dulaney heard rustling in the shrubs. He ducked behind tall weeds. His shovel smacked against an exposed rock.

The rustling stopped. Dulaney felt his heart pumping. He wanted to quiet the thumping in his ears. He caught himself breathing heavily.

After a few minutes, he ventured from the weeds. All was still.

The path had ended. Dulaney moved closer to the third trestle. Burrs clung to his trousers and an occasional wet step soaked his socks. Over his right shoulder, Kinzua Creek bubbled and churned through its rocky course.

He reached the concrete abutment as a heavy cloud obstructed any moonlight. He detected little scurrying noises, perhaps mice or chipmunks darting through tall weeds.

After resting his back against a bridge support, Dulaney began taking deliberate steps to the east. Fifty feet could not be precisely stepped, he reasoned, because the direct route ran along mounds and depressions. Nonetheless, when he reached the desired distance, the ground below his feet was remarkably level and soft.

Kinzua Creek, to the north, curved precisely as diagrammed on his map. This surely was the treasure's location, Dulaney concluded.

His first shovel thrust was deep. The dirt was loose and easy to pick up. Dulaney tossed it to the side and plunged a second thrust. Then a third.

Dulaney was not a strong man, and was not known for physical stamina. But this manual labor seemed effortless. He was not disappointed that the first hole produced no silver.

Moving to a spot a few steps closer to the creek, Dulaney dug a second hole. The dirt, a little firmer, seemed to give under his determination. On his third thrust, the shovel hit a stump. Dulaney bent down and reached in the hole. He felt no metal.

Perhaps in the other direction, he thought. Maybe a few feet farther from Kinzua Creek was the spot. Dulaney laid shovel to dirt, and soon he produced a third hole. He became a bit light-headed.

Moonlight reappeared. Water had collected in the hole. Dulaney saw a reflection. It was white, maybe the outline of a container. He tossed aside his shovel.

Dulaney's mind was focused. Focused not like his students, he thought. Focused on untold riches he thought were beneath his feet. He smiled. His years studying the Indians of Pennsylvania, their culture and language were finally paying off. The mythical Seneca Indian treasure was real, and it was his.

For Dulaney, though, his focus was misdirected.

No one heard his screams.

When the claw swiped his forehead, cutting inch-deep gashes in his skull, the Kinzua Park was empty.

When Dulaney's jugular was severed, no one heard his gurgling sounds. His body slumped over the bloody dirt pile with a dull thud. No one witnessed the carnage.

When the bear's teeth grasped Dulaney's neck and fractured his cervical spine, no one was there to fend off the attack upon the greedy professor,

Who had disturbed the ground,

Who, minutes before, was so pleased with his good fortune,
And who, seconds later, would be dead.

Chapter Ten
The Overlook

Professor Dulaney's shredded remains were discovered at dawn by a state park ranger. An 8 a.m. police radio report confirmed the death by bear attack. Word spread quickly.

Governor Bailey was a first responder, having been awakened at Leigh-Rose by sirens and circling helicopters. Kinzua State Park, only a few hundred yards from the mansion, was abuzz with state police units and emergency vehicles. Jimmie made the short trip on foot. He easily passed security checkpoints and encountered the lead investigator.

"What's going on, sergeant?" the governor asked.

"An adult, white male, apparently alone in the park last night, was killed. We suspect he was mauled by a black bear. Very unusual."

Jimmie knew that black bears populated McKean County, but humans and bears usually kept their distance. "This is the first attack in these mountains that I can recall," he said.

"We don't know what prompted this. Maybe the trespasser agitated the bear, kept it from its food. This is mating season, and they're a bit more aggressive, I'm told."

From the corner of his eye, Jimmie saw Tom Zachary and his teenage intern walking toward him. This was not how the governor wanted to meet his half-brother, Matty Moore.

"Excuse me, detective," Jimmie said. "I'd like to visit the scene. Please cordon this area from the press until I return." He then ambled down the mulch path and out of sight. He overheard the trooper halting Zachary and his intern at the overlook.

When he reached the valley floor, Jimmie counted six officers beyond the bridge trestle. He picked his way around the scrub brush and weeds. He noticed a freshly trodden path created by police and paramedics.

Yellow crime scene ribbon marked the location. As Jimmie approached, paramedics covered the remains with a canvas sheet. Jimmie recognized Kinzua's state park ranger and called to him. "Jason, Jason, over here."

"Governor, I've never seen anything like this," the ranger said. "That bear must have been provoked to react with such violence. This man had no chance."

"Who is he, Jason?"

"Papers in his wallet identify him as Geoffrey Dulaney. He's a faculty member at Edinboro."

"Do police know what he was doing here at night?" Jimmie asked.

"That's quite a mystery, Governor. You see, Mr. Dulaney had two shovels and was digging around. We saw three small holes. The detectives don't know why."

Jimmie had a good idea. Dulaney was looking for buried treasure. But, given his shady deal with Josh Gibson and his shadier relationship with Billy Herman, Jimmie preferred to keep the silver story buried as well.

"Oh, and we also found this," the ranger said, handing the Indian treasure map to Jimmie. "Police detectives gave it to me. They thought it was some relic that belonged in the park. Have you ever seen this before?"

Jimmie recognized the curved line as a peculiar bend of Kinzua Creek. He assumed that the rectangular markings represented bridge abutments. Other markings appeared to be words from a strange language.

"My gosh, Jason! This is an Indian artifact. Where was it found?"

"As we approached the body, we saw a blood-stained shovel in a thicket of bushes. I'd guess it was about 20 yards over there," he said, pointing away from Kinzua Creek. "The bear must have dragged the shovel away from the body. The victim had a second shovel at the scene of the attack," the officer said. "Seems strange that one man would use two shovels."

"But this paper, where was it found?" Jimmie asked.

"About a step away from the body. Mr. Dulaney must have dropped it when he was attacked."

"Obviously this has nothing to do with a bear attack," Jimmie said, stuffing the map in his jacket pocket. "We'll donate it to the county historical society. Now, see if you can remove this unfortunate fellow and notify his family."

A state police major recognized the governor and ambled over. "Sir," he said, "for your safety, it would be best for me to accompany you from these woods. We don't want another encounter with the black bear."

Jimmie smiled. "OK, Major, but first let's talk about how much of this investigation should be public. We should keep this off-limits for a while. Otherwise, every busybody in McKean County will be hiking around here looking for a wild bear."

"What are you suggesting, Governor? Should we keep some troopers here to protect the area?" the major asked.

"No, that would be expensive," Jimmie replied. "My suggestion is simpler. When you report this incident, don't give the exact location. Just say that an attack occurred in a remote area of Kinzua Valley."

"But police reports will identify our investigation here in the state park."

"I'll issue an administrative order to classify your reports," Jimmie said. "Otherwise, until we find this dangerous bear, there will be dozens of adventure seekers combing the valley. And another thing…"

"What's that, Governor?" the major asked.

"This business about the victim having two shovels and digging up dirt should not be public information either. Your report should say the professor was taking soil samples near the creek, that's all. We don't need any wild-eyed speculation about what he was doing here. Got it?"

The now-confused major agreed. "We'll trim down the report, and we'll spare the public all of these unnecessary details."

"Fine, Major. Now remove the body and get your men out of here in ten minutes. Tell your commander that's my order."

Meanwhile, at the overlook, Zachary protested the police barricade.

"Here, here are my press credentials." He waved a business card at the trooper. "The public has a right to know. I demand to speak with your supervisor."

"Governor's orders, Mr. Zachary. No one goes down there. We don't want you and your associate to interfere with a possible crime scene. Please conduct yourself appropriately."

Zachary was more enraged. The governor was shielding the News Leader from its first hard news story in years. "It's not a stupid crime scene! The guy was killed by a bear! Are the police going to bring a case in animal court!"

"Orders are orders, Mr. Zachary. Again, I'm telling you to back off. You can wait for the press briefing like everyone else." The trooper, frustrated by the editor's insistence, stood his ground.

Zachary took two steps toward the valley path. Matty sneaked to the overlook's railing. Distracted by Zachary's attempt to pass the barricade, the investigator failed to prevent Matty's rapid-fire zoom photography of the scene below.

"You take one more step, Zachary, and you're in the county jail," the officer hollered.

Suddenly, Zachary was confronted with a teaching moment for his summer intern. Should he acquiesce to police power? Or should he advance freedom of the press? What would Matty Moore, his talented and wealthy protégé, think of him if he cowered now? More importantly, would Matty buy the struggling News Leader if the paper were merely fish wrap and not a citadel of truth and justice?

Defiantly, with malice aforethought, Zachary raised his foot and plunged it forward. The trooper leaped.

Matty focused his Nikon, capturing his boss and the cop wrestling in mulch. By the shutter's third click, Zachary's wrists were locked behind his back. By the tenth click, Zachary was being led to a squad car.

What luck for the News Leader, Matty thought. Two hard news stories in one day!

Megan Broward received a text message at mid-morning. Her sociology classmate relayed word of Professor Dulaney's unfortunate ursine episode. The text message noted that the bear's behavior "varied from acceptable social norms." The humor was lost on Megan.

Her efforts to discover more details, especially the location of Dulaney's demise, proved to be fruitless. State police referred her to a 2 p.m. press conference at the Kane Barracks. Megan had time for the two-hour drive. Certainly, her term paper for Dulaney could wait.

Megan traveled east on Rt. 6 through Pennsylvania's Allegheny National Forest. The drive did not calm her. She feared that Dulaney acted on her text message, that he downloaded the Indian map and went treasure hunting. After her meeting with the Peacemaker, Megan knew the full story: there was silver at the foot of Kinzua Bridge, but it was buried with a curse.

The town of Kane clung to the far end of Allegheny Forest. As Rt. 6 emerged from elegant stacks of pine trees, Megan felt growing warmth of May sunshine. Her car twisted properly on the winding road leading to the business district. After stopping for directions at a convenience store, Megan found the state police barracks with ten minutes to spare.

Local media outlets, comprised of two radio stations and the News Leader, sent representatives. The Bradford Era reporter was sick at home. When Megan entered the barracks conference room, eyes turned. Megan took a seat in near the exit. All eyes turned back, except for Matty Moore's.

"I have a short statement, then I'll open it for questions," the major began. "Sometime between the hours of 10 p.m. last night and 6 this morning, a black bear attacked and killed an adult male in Kinzua Creek Valley. Next of kin have been notified, so we can report the victim as Geoffrey Dulaney, age 59, of Wattsburg in Erie County. Mr. Dulaney was a tenured professor at Edinboro University. I'll take questions."

"Has the bear been found?" the radio reporter asked.

"No. That's why we're asking folks to stay away from the scene."

"Where exactly should we stay away from?"

"The entire Kinzua Valley. That bear could be anywhere."

"That's thousands of acres. Could you be more specific?"

"No."

"The police call said the man was found near Kinzua Bridge. Is that right?"

"I can't verify that."

"Wasn't the body found by the Kinzua State Park ranger?"

"I don't know."

Matty raised his hand. "What was Mr. Dulaney doing in the valley at night?"

"We believe he was taking soil samples. Next question?"

Matty again raised his hand. "What was the professor's field of study?"

"We don't know at this time," the major replied.

"Sociology." A voice from the back startled them. Megan's utterance surprised herself.

Matty turned. "Did you know the victim, miss?"

Megan began to cry and quickly left the room. Matty followed. He found her in the parking lot. She was mumbling something about Dulaney's death being her fault.

"May I talk with you a moment?" he called. "My name's Matty. I work for the local newspaper. Do you need my handkerchief?"

Megan accepted his offer. She needed kindness at the moment. She wiped her tears smiled at the handsome young man. "I'm sorry, Matty. It's just that Professor Dulaney was my teacher and advisor at Edinboro."

"This must be quite a shock to you." Matty rested on a police cruiser. "Was he a good friend?"

"No," she said. "He was probably the most arrogant, pig-headed teacher I've ever met. But he shouldn't have died like this."

Matty never understood women, but he never tired of trying. "You're crying. You know something about him, something more than the police are telling us."

"Dulaney was not taking soil samples." Megan wiped her eyes.

"I know that, too," Matty said. "And I've got digital prints in the car to prove it."

"Photographs of what?"

"Listen, Miss …"

"Megan Broward."

"…Megan Broward, we both need a bite to eat. Follow me to the best restaurant in town, and I'll tell you what I know about Professor Dulaney and his hike in the woods."

Matty's Mustang buzzed down Fraley Street, leading Megan's car into the rear lot of Golden Wheel Restaurant. They entered the restaurant, and Toolie directed them to a side booth.

"You have photos?" Megan got down to business.

"Before the police closed off the area, I took these from the park's overlook. Here."

Megan flipped through about a dozen prints, stopping at a graphic view of the victim.

"Oh, Matty. This is awful. The poor man."

"That's not the photograph I wanted you to see, Megan. Look at this one."

She took the four-by-six print from Matty. It appeared to be a close-up area view of an excavation site. She saw three mounds of dirt and, in the corner of the photo, a bloody shovel.

"Nobody takes soil samples with an old shovel," Matty said. "What do you suppose he was doing here?"

"How would I know?" Megan turned defensive. "I'm sorry, Matty. I wish I could add to your story, but I can't."

Matty sensed her strange reaction. "Maybe, if you told me everything you know about Professor Dulaney, I could figure it out."

"Give me your business card, and I'll call you in a few days. I need some time to think."

Matty watched the young co-ed take his card, slide from the booth and walk past other busy tables. Toolie sauntered over and placed a hand on his shoulder.

"You want to listen to my poem, Clark Kent?"

Matty continued to watch Megan as she entered her Volkswagen and turn west onto Route 6. "What did you say, Toolie?"

"I've written a poem, too. Here it goes:

"Roses are red. Violets are blue.

"That pretty little girl looks good beside you."

Matty never thought about that. Well, maybe a little.

Here I sit, a sly and angry journalist, with malevolently squinted eyes. And, weighing a pen in my hand, I plot revenge.

Like most writers, Zachary had dreamed about writing his memoirs from jail. As the News Leader editor stewed in a holding cell at the McKean County lock-up, he vented with paper and pen.

For since I have opened my eyes, I have seen only the glow of injustice, humiliation, and the laughable shame of tyrants. To me is given the hope of revenge on others...

No other prisoner shared the eight-foot square room. Zachary was truly alone with his thoughts. His career had come to this: a moment of civil disobedience and, likely, a night in jail.

... Imagine, me, guardian of the truth, held like a common criminal. Held without charges, and to what authority? Who dares to pass judgment on me?

Zachary shuddered at the answer. Judge Van Lear likely would advise him of the charges. Disorderly conduct? Interference with a criminal investigation? Obstruction of justice? Wrestling with a cop? Van Lear had been throwing the book at criminals for 20 years. Van Lear was not known for judicial mercy.

Beyond the cell door, Mike Devlin, the judge's bailiff, shared a laugh with a deputy sheriff. Zachary strained to hear. Devlin joked about the "notorious" criminal finally taken off the streets. The deputy mentioned something about "throwing away the key." More laughter.

They insult me. They mock me. But I have power of the pen, the power to destroy their reputations with a few well-placed strokes of ink. Vengeance is mine...

"Zachary. Thomas Cornelius Zachary," the jailer called. "You're up."

He unlatched the cell door, and Zachary saw a smiling Devlin. A yellow file folder wedged under his arm.

"Hustle up, Cornelius. Time for your initial appearance in court." Devlin pointed to the back stairway. "Where's your attorney?"

"I don't need any stinking attorney, Devlin. I'm innocent."

"Listen up, Tom. Judge Van Lear takes these criminal complaints very seriously. Here's some advice: drop the attitude and get a lawyer."

"You can't be serious. A lawyer, for this? What am I charged with?"

Devlin looked at the court papers. "So far, one count of aggravated assault on a police officer. Let's see, according to pretrial services, that carries a possible prison term of eight years. Nice knowing you, bud."

Zachary nearly swallowed his tongue.

Van Lear was seated on the bench when Devlin and the accused entered. A courtroom clock read 4:55 p.m. Zachary noticed His Honor's intense squirming. Too bad his hemorrhoids were inflamed at such a critical moment, Zachary thought.

"Call the case, bailiff," Van Lear said with a sneer.

"I call the case of the Commonwealth of Pennsylvania versus Thomas Cornelius Zachary," Devlin loudly responded.

"Mr. Zachary," the judge began. "So you're the one crowding my docket today. I was hoping to leave early for the weekend."

"This shouldn't take too long, Judge," Zachary began.

"That depends on your acceptance of responsibility, and upon your contrition, Mr. Zachary. The Court takes this matter very seriously."

Zachary was beginning to feel lonely. Perhaps an attorney would be a good idea.

"There are very few people in the Courthouse at this hour," Van Lear observed. "So we have no court reporter for your initial appearance today."

Zachary pointed to a woman seated near the witness stand.

"Oh, she's not a court reporter," Van Lear said. "Her name is Lily. She's a clerk with the Register of Wills. You know, she handles all of the *sealed* files in the Courthouse."

Zachary tried not to react outwardly. Inside, though, was a different matter. Had the judge figured out that Zachary had used his telephone to fool Lily into delivering the sealed Brock Bailey file? Did Lily rat to the judge about the mysterious phone call from chambers? This was not a pleasant situation.

"Do you know Lily?" Van Lear asked Zachary in a sweet voice.

"First time I've seen her," he answered.

"Mr. Zachary, the first step in rehabilitation is knowing that you've done a bad thing. If you don't recognize that, I can't help you be a better citizen."

"Believe me, Judge. I realize that I was wrong when I disobeyed the state trooper and got into a little wrestling match…"

"Now, Mr. Zachary, let me stop you there. Anything you say can be used against you, so I would advise you to be careful about what you say."

"I will be careful, Your Honor."

"So let's talk about something else." Van Lear rolled back his chair and crossed his arms over his chest. "Let's talk about your summer intern. What's his name?"

"Matthew Moore."

"Right," the judge said. "He seems like a bright young man. How did you find him again?"

Zachary was stepping into Van Lear's minefield. But the editor realized that he had not yet been placed under oath. Oh well, here goes, he thought.

"The Kane News Leader set up a booth at Stender High School in Pittsburgh. It was a job fair for seniors there."

"Stender High?" The judge pondered. "We have very gifted writers here in McKean County. Why would you go to Pittsburgh to interview for a summer intern?"

"Well, uh," Zachary stammered. "Didn't you hear? The News Leader is implementing its diversity action plan. We were looking for a writer of color. And this young man met all of our expectations."

"That is very noble, Mr. Zachary. Diversity is very important. I'd like to hire more minority employees at the Courthouse. Perhaps you can send me a copy of your diversity plan."

"Well, uh…" Thank goodness he wasn't hooked up to a polygraph machine. "… our plan is aspirational. Nothing in writing. We didn't want Matthew Moore to suffer the stigma of being an affirmative action hire."

"Of course not," Van Lear grumbled as he closed the Zachary case file. "Nothing we can do here until Monday. Court is adjourned."

"Your Honor," Zachary pleaded, "what about me?"

"Devlin, transport the accused to his holding cell. Schedule his detention hearing for Monday afternoon. Have a good weekend, Mr. Zachary."

Chapter Eleven
The Prisoner

"I brought you a candy bar." Matty sat across from the prisoner. Between them was a two-inch thick sheet of plexiglass.

"A Milky Way," Zachary said. "My favorite."

"I didn't realize..." Matty knocked the glass window with his knuckle.

"That's OK, Matty. My wife brought a slice of carrot cake this morning and had to give it to the deputy."

"Oh, man, that's too bad." Matty unrolled the foil wrapping and took a bite. He pulled the candy bar a few inches from his mouth to let the caramel snap off. "So how're you spending your jail time?"

Zachary pointed to a heap of scrap paper. "I'm going to write a book. I've done the outline. It's a true story about an old county judge who thinks he's above the law."

"Let me guess the title," Matty said. "King Van Lear?"

"That's good, really good." Zachary scribbled the thought on his outline. "Keep thinking. I need ideas."

"Here's one, Mr. Z. Since you're likely to be in the slammer for a few more days, and since we have a Tuesday deadline for Wednesday's weekly edition, you need someone to put out the paper. How about me?"

Zachary, repulsed by the idea of an 18-year-old replacing him at the News Leader helm, recoiled in his chair. "Matty, are you serious?"

"How difficult can it be?" Matty said. "Jessie can help me with the page layout. Most of the stories are already set in print. We'll tack on some breaking news and, wham, we've got the latest edition!"

Zachary never planned for such a contingency. His micromanagement made him the indispensible cog in his newspaper's production. Perhaps it was time to groom a successor, especially a successor with enough cash to buy the struggling newspaper.

"Come on, Mr. Z. What other option do you have? The News Leader must go on."

The more Matty talked, the more sense he made. But there was something about the way he devoured the Milky Way, licked his shiny teeth and smiled. Could he be trusted?

Zachary was running low on alternatives. "All right, Matty. The paper's yours for the next few days. But I want to see a proof of the front page before you put it to bed. Deal?"

"Deal."

Matty accepted the deadline of his life. Sunday, Monday and Tuesday – three days to solve the Josh Gibson death, to figure out what Professor Dulaney was doing with a shovel, and to unravel the mystery of Spanish silver in Dolores Gibson's closet. This will be quite a front page for Wednesday's newspaper, he thought.

His gut told him that Megan Broward was the key.

"Don't just sit there!" Zachary startled his intern. "You'd better get moving."

Matty slapped the window and gave his boss a thumbs-up.

Zachary returned to his notes. He had another thought to write:

Dark confinement, complete solitude and the uncertainty of ever tasting freedom again – all have a profound and wicked force on the mind.

A man locked up is a man without clarity of thought. He is given to foolish decisions, reckless behavior. What treasures he possessed before his unjust incarceration he dispenses negligently to others.

Because his being trembles with scorn and hatred for the robed tyrant, the king named Van Lear.

Although she was not yet fully converted, Dolores Gibson resolved to try church again this weekend. All that singing and dancing last week amused her. Maybe this week, the reverend, if he is one, may actually quote Scriptures.

The Church of Higher Science, located in a refurbished warehouse west of Pittsburgh, attracted thousands of worshippers, largely from the economically depressed Ohio River Valley. Others, who didn't buy the concept of religious entertainment, called it a "mega-church." The local newspaper ran a series implying that church leaders were fleecing the congregation.

Higher Science was not Mrs. Gibson's first choice for spiritual healing after Josh's death. But she needed someone to console her. "We're here if you need a friend," the church's radio advertisements promised. Also, a co-worker suggested that her "soul would be uplifted by all of the energy" there. Dolores decided that, if she can uplift other parts of her body, her soul should be raised as well.

Today's service was heavily promoted. Pastor Randy O'Boyd was returning from his month-long retreat in the desert. No one knew where, but the retreat house was reportedly within driving distance of Las Vegas. The crowd also buzzed with anticipation – the pastor's pretty wife, Darla, may favor the congregation with a song.

As usual, Dolores sat in the back for better air circulation. A brass collection plate circled her row twice before Pastor Randy was introduced.

The short, boyish-looking minister threw high his hand. "Halleluia!" he shouted.

"Halleluia!" the thousands cried in reply.

"Not loud enough," he whispered into the wire microphone

that curved from his ear.

"HALLELUIA!" the crowd shouted more loudly.

"Praise Be, my brothers and sisters." Pastor Randy rolled his eyes to the sheet metal ceiling. "I feel ... I feel there is sorrow. Someone here today is in pain. It is a pain that won't go away. Can I hear an Amen?"

"AMEN!" the crowd answered.

"Amen, you feel it, too. We have a sister in our midst today who has suffered a great loss. There is emptiness in her heart."

He covered his eyes with one hand and pointed with the other.

"I feel energy from above. Who is this woman? Can she call to me?" His finger pointed directly at Dolores, 26 rows away, 45 degrees right and immediately illuminated by a proscenium spotlight. The crowd hushed.

"Come forth, and be healed, young lady," Pastor Randy commanded.

Dolores felt the arms of two security guards pull her from behind. They marched her down the center aisle as congregants bowed.

"Do not hesitate. Come and feel the healing power of Higher Science." The pastor exhorted everyone to stand.

The crowd began rhythmic clapping.

Security guards abandoned Dolores at the foot of portable stairs. She pointed to her four-inch heels, so they helped her to the stage.

"You have lost someone close to you?" the pastor asked, thrusting a microphone into her face.

"Well, five years ago..."

"Halleluia," he interrupted. "Be sorrowful no more. Higher Science has saved you."

Pastor Randy thrust the microphone again to his guest.

Dolores stood dumbfounded. Finally, she said, "Thank you."

"Are you sorrowful?" the pastor asked.

"No, not really."

"Halleluia. We have witnessed a mir-a-cle. Believe and repent. Now, as my beautiful wife Darla sings, 'Trading My Sorrows,' we ask you to be generous with the collection. Remember, we cannot continue our healing ministry unless you give with your heart."

While the sanctimonious, yet sultry Darla crooned, movie screens lowered from the ceiling. The crowd watched a slide show of biblical proportions. Alternating slides depicted John the Baptist alone in the desert and Pastor Randy alone in Las Vegas.

Dolores suffered through the hour-long ceremony, feeling unremitting stares from other worshippers. After the service, one woman in a babushka taunted Dolores, saying: "I've come every week for four years and Pastor Randy never cured my diverticulitis. Who do you think you are?"

As Dolores approached an exit, a guard stopped her. "The pastor asks for a moment of your time. Please follow me."

They moved through a side hall. He keyed open a metal door, and Dolores followed him to a room behind the stage. The guard knocked on a door marked "Private."

"Just a minute," a voice said. After some rustling sounds from inside, the door opened.

Dolores saw a man dressed in jeans and a white T-shirt. The guard slipped away.

"Come in, young lady. I'm Pastor Randy. Sorry for the informality. I like to relax after the service."

He looked like a puffy college gymnast – a few years younger and a few inches shorter than the mega-pastor on stage. Dolores had no idea where this meeting was headed.

"As you see, we run a tight schedule for our service," he said. "First a song, then a reading, then a testimonial. Then the drum roll and I come on stage, et cetera, et cetera. We keep it moving to keep the customers satisfied."

"It kept my interest." Dolores tried to say something nice.

"Well, I have to apologize to you," he said. "That's kind of scary to be pulled up on stage like that. You were a good sport."

"Why did you pick me, preacher?"

"I'll tell you a secret. We have cameras all over the hall. I can sit in front of monitors and look at the faces. I saw yours and, pardon if I'm too personal, I sensed that you were troubled by something. You looked like you needed my help."

He motioned her to sit on a sofa. He sat beside her. She detected an odor of musk.

Dolores looked around nervously. "I wanted to tell Darla that I enjoyed her singing."

Pastor Randy moved closer. "Darla and I have separated. She's sung her last song at my church."

Stetson, that's the cologne he's wearing, Dolores thought.

"Anyway, I just wanted to say thank you for being such a good sport. I also wanted to find out your name," he said.

"Dolores Gibson. Most people call me Dee Dee."

He shook her hand. "I'd like to see more of you. Next Sunday, perhaps."

"How about tomorrow?" she replied. "My place?"

Megan signed papers at the nursing center. She promised to be Mr. George's caregiver for the afternoon. Actually, she thought it would be fun, driving the elderly Indian Peacemaker through the woods of his childhood.

Mr. George slept most of the way. Megan was emotionally tired as well. After badgering him for the better part of two days, Megan convinced Mr. George to visit Kinzua Park. She needed to confirm that her professor had located the treasure burial site.

When he began to snore, Megan rolled down her window. He stirred briefly, opened his eyes to a slit and coughed. In his lap rested Maude Thunder's original map. Strangely, to Megan, the map seemed to comfort the old man. Perhaps it bridged him to another time, another generation. Maybe, the Peacemaker sensed a duty to the Seneca Nation to investigate what happened at Kinzua Bridge.

Her Volkswagen sped through Kane, following the twisting Route 6 towards Lantz Corners. Megan never visited Kinzua Park before, but remembered news reports of the unexpected tornado of 2003. The remarkable 100-year-old railroad bridge toppled like a house of cards during the crushing storm. Efforts to rebuild the viaduct failed when state appropriations dried up. Even the new governor, whose ancestral home bordered Kinzua Park, could not raise enough capital to rebuild Kinzua Bridge – a failure the locals abhorred.

At Mount Jewett, Megan turned north along the park road. A few miles later, they drove into the largely deserted park. Mr. George stirred when she turned off the ignition.

"Let me help you." Megan tried to guide his legs from the passenger seat to the gravel parking lot. "We're here."

"Kinzua," he muttered. "That's a Seneca word. Do you know what it means?"

"No clue, sir."

"My ancestors were a resourceful people, Ms. Broward. They relied on the land and water to survive. This valley was their food and shelter. Running through it is a small creek that bends and falls over rock. The water is mountain water. It is clean and pure. The water was home to varieties of trout and other, if I might add, tasty fish."

"'Kinzua' means 'fish?'" she asked.

"You're partially correct. 'Kinzua' means 'fish on spear.' That's how plentiful these waters were. The Seneca fished with spears."

Megan brought the story up to date. "And then came Kinzua Dam, and the creek was flooded, and your people were relocated."

"That reminds me of an interesting story," the Peacemaker said.

"For dozens of years, we knew the dam was coming. It was just a matter of time. Many Indians chose to ignore the situation, hoping that the federals would actually, for the first time, honor an Indian treaty.

"I knew that wouldn't happen. We had to be realistic, and our children had to learn what was coming. So we went to the Seneca schools to explain to students why they would be moving to New York."

"What was their reaction?" Megan asked.

"Generally, not good. Their parents never talked to them about it. Many children had no idea about the dam. Some cried. I remember one teacher who instructed students to build a model of the dam. She also stocked the model with live goldfish."

"Did that help?" Megan asked.

"Some students got hostile. One reacted by spearing the fish with a sharp pencil. Ironic, isn't it? Fish on spear."

Taking his arm, Megan guided him toward the park overlook. They waited a minute while a young couple took photographs of the valley. Megan supported his weight as he stepped down onto the concrete observation deck. Beyond the railing were the two remaining sections of Kinzua Bridge. Rusted trestles from the missing center span were scattered in the valley.

Mr. George studied the map. Then he pointed to a spot a few hundred yards to the west.

"There, down there," he told Megan.

"Are you sure?" Megan recognized the spot from Matty's photographs.

"Yes. That's where Brother John buried the silver."

"And that's where he ..."

Mr. George stopped her. "That's where he said the incantation."

Until Professor Dulaney was mauled at the location and died after digging for treasure, Megan was not a believer in witchcraft. Now, she was not sure.

"What are you thinking, young lady?" the Peacemaker asked.
"I'm thinking that Woods on Fire knew what he was doing."

Pennsylvania State Police Investigative File No. 03-1323 was
contained in 15 banker's boxes. The Governor Brock Bailey
investigation generated thousands of written reports from a variety
of agencies. But 15 boxes?

Matty Moore's public records request was routed to the
Pittsburgh field office. Matty labeled his request as
"emergency/urgent." A clerk promptly complied and set an
appointment via the News Leader FAX machine.

Where to start? Matty flipped open a box numbered "03-
1323-1" and pulled sample file jackets. He read several state police
reports dated March 5, the day Brock Bailey's limousine drove off
the Fort Pitt Bridge. Somewhere in this mass of documents, he
thought, there is information about the lead investigator, Josh
Gibson. Something here, he hoped, will explain Gibson's
mysterious death at Kinzua Bridge.

Time was not Matty's ally. With only three days before the
deadline for Wednesday's News Leader, Matty needed to trim his
investigation time. He allocated an hour at the state police office.
So he decided to work backwards in time, pulling the 15th box.

None of the file jackets identified any reports by Gibson
himself. Matty reviewed other papers and learned that Gibson
largely signed them as supervising officer.

Matty moved on to the 14th box. He pulled a file, labeled
"Gibson/Herman Search, July-August 2003." Inside were typed
reports generated by Pittsburgh police detective William R.
Herman. What intrigued Matty at first were detailed sketches of
the Kinzua Valley near the recently destroyed bridge. Matty copied
the narrative from one report:

August 3 – 14:30 hrs. – Accompanied commissioner Gibson to

*southwestern sector of bridge debris. Task complicated by scattered pieces
of steel bridge support. Positive readings continuously unproductive.
Teams in northwestern sector also experiencing false positives with metal
detector. Will resume search in a.m.*

    *August 4 – 9:30 hrs. – Returned with commissioner Gibson to
southwestern sector. I instructed Gibson that sweep of this area yesterday
did not produce any evidence of any victim of July 21 tornado. I advised
that search by cadaver dogs would be more appropriate than use of metal
detector. Gibson reiterated that he was lead investigator and would
determine techniques to be used in search.*

    *August 4 – 14:37 hrs. – Reported to commissioner Gibson discovery
of a loaded handgun by police team approximately 75 yards north of
third trestle on southern end of Kinzua Bridge. Gibson directed that
the firearm be treated as criminal evidence and transported to Oil City
barracks for his further investigation.*

    *August 4 – 15:30 hrs. – Commmissioner Gibson ordered all
investigative teams to abandon further search. Gibson remained in
valley and continued sweep with metal detector.*

    *August 5 – 11:10 hrs. – Commissioner Gibson and I returned to
Kinzua Valley for follow-up investigation. Gibson issued order to all
state employees to vacate Kinzua State Park, and ordered state police
troopers to guard all means of access and egress from the park for the
remainder of the day. Operation of park surveillance cameras was
prohibited for 24 hours.*

    *August 6 – 6:10 hrs. — Investigation of valley continues. Gibson
returns to southwest sector.*

    *August 6 – 10:00 hrs. – Investigation closed. No additional report
to be filed.*

    Strange, Matty thought. Gibson was looking for tornado
victims with a metal detector, and found a gun. Then, after finding
the gun, Gibson had returned to the same "unproductive" location
with a metal detector. On the next day, with detective Herman at
his side, Gibson had locked down the park and posted state
troopers to keep out visitors.

Most curious to Matty were the entries for August 6. Gibson had returned to the southwest sector for four hours before, inexplicably, closing the investigation.

And where exactly is the southwest sector, Matty wondered. If it is southwest of the third trestle of Kinzua Bridge, then Gibson was treading over the spot where Professor Dulaney was slaughtered. But why was Gibson waving a metal detector back and forth there for hours?

Suddenly, Matty recalled the cache of silver in Mrs. Gibson's bedroom closet. Could it be from Kinzua Valley? What was Megan not telling him?

Box 13 of the Brock Bailey file provided Matty's next lead. It contained the complete biography of detective William "Billy" Herman, including his office address and telephone number.

"I'm calling for detective Herman," Matty told the Pittsburgh police operator. "Could you connect me?"

"Sorry, sir. Mr. Herman no longer works for the department. Can someone else help you?"

"Do you have any forwarding information?" Matty asked.

"I'm sorry. We cannot provide personal information to the public," the operator said. "Is this an emergency?"

Matty was deadline-driven. "Yes, as a matter of fact. I have information regarding a theft of silver. He would be very interested."

"Give me your contact information and I will pass this along to him."

"Please tell him that I must speak to him by tomorrow at the latest."

"I will give him the message," the operator replied.

"And be sure to tell him, this is about *silver*," Matty pleaded.

"Whatever."

Chapter Twelve
The Scandal

Jessie Krone rarely worked Sunday mornings. Usually by quitting time Friday, the Kane News Leader office manager had finished designing Wednesday's weekly edition. However, the unexpected incarceration of her editor threw everything into turmoil.

Since Tom Zachary was nabbed last week, Jessie was the only live voice who bore the brunt of irate advertisers and subscribers.

"It's all a misunderstanding" was her usual response to nasty phone calls. "Mr. Zachary respects law enforcement. He would never assault an officer," she told callers who threatened to end their subscriptions.

The newspaper's major advertiser, Gates Hardware, hinted that its full-page ad for patio block and barbecue grills might be pulled; the business did not want to associate with a "criminal enterprise."

When the phone rang early Sunday morning, Jessie was a thread away from walking out.

"News Leader, Pride of the Alleghenies, may I help you?"

"Matthew Moore, please." The caller sounded intoxicated.

"He's not working today, sir. It's Sunday. Is there a message?"

"Tell him Mr. Herman called. I want to speak with him immediately."

"Like I said, it's Sunday. He's off today. I'm working out of the goodness of my heart. So call back tomorrow after 9 o'clock." Jessie detested phone intrusions, especially while she was donating her weekend time.

"I'm sorry, honey. Seems like you don't know what you're doing. Maybe I should talk to your supervisor," Herman said menacingly.

"Listen, buddy. I am the supervisor around here. Ain't nobody else in the office today. So I'm telling you to call during business hours tomorrow. Is that clear?"

She heard a grumpy noise on the line followed by a toilet flush. Herman breathed heavily. "You're all alone there?" More heavy breathing. "Would you like a real man to ..."

Jessie slammed down the phone and leaned against a file cabinet. Was that a threat? Was this one of Matty's friends playing a prank? Suddenly, the old newspaper office seemed smaller, darker and more frightening. She imagined her chalk outline on the floor. That is, if chalk could mark the yellowed linoleum.

She checked Zachary's office phone caller identification display. The call originated from Pittsburgh. Whew, she thought. At least her attacker was three hours away. The display read "Forest Club" and gave a telephone number.

Jessie's call to Matty's apartment above the Golden Wheel Restaurant was not answered. A running shower prevented the teenager from hearing the ring in time. After toweling off, he retrieved her message. It was the break he hoped for – a contact with Billy Herman. This might be his chance to find out what happened with Josh Gibson and his metal detector. He jotted down the number from Jessie's voice mail.

"Mr. Herman, please," Matty asked the Forest Club operator.

"Let me page him. One moment."

Billy Herman took the call in the men's locker room. "Mr. Moore, I heard you have some information for me."

"Sir, I'm a reporter from Kane. I'm working on a story about Josh Gibson's death. I'd like to ask you a few questions."

Silence on the other end was unusually lengthy.

"Sir, did you hear me?" Matty asked.

"Yes," Herman answered. "I don't know anything about

Gibson's death. Why are you calling me? Are you working with the state police? What's this all about?"

"I spoke with his wife, Dolores. She doesn't think her husband committed suicide. So I'm doing a little digging into this. I looked at the state police files yesterday. You worked with Gibson on the Brock Bailey investigation."

"Listen, kid. I don't know what you're doing. Frankly, I don't give a shit. But you said something in your message about… Well, I can't talk about it here with these naked dinosaurs shuffling around the locker room, understand?"

"Sure. You can't talk about the silver now?"

"Bingo."

"You know something?"

"Bingo, bango."

"About the silver?"

"Bingo, bango, bongo."

Matty twisted open his bedroom mini-blinds. He watched Megan's Volkswagen turn into the restaurant parking lot. His sources were aligning like a celestial constellation.

"Let's meet this afternoon, say 2 o'clock at the Kinzua Bridge," Matty told Herman.

"OK. How will I recognize you?"

"I'll be the only one listening to Kayne West in a gold Mustang," Matty said.

"You're kidding? In McKean County?"

"I'm a trend-setter here."

"You should be easy to pick out."

"One more thing, Mr. Herman," Matty said. "No need to bring your shovel."

Billy Herman snorted, "Yeah, I know."

First Lady Ann Bailey was ready for motherhood.

Sitting on the Leigh-Rose front porch swing, she gave her belly a gentle ride. The kicking subsided in the past few weeks, but that was normal, her doctor said. Today, in the soft summer breeze, Ann embraced her time alone. Soon enough, she thought, there would be cries, late night feedings and disposable diapers.

Jimmie sat in an adjacent Adirondack chair. Around him were the remains of Sunday's Philadelphia Inquirer, Harrisburg Patriot and Erie Times-News. Jimmie spent the better part of the morning clipping news articles for his Monday staff meeting.

He set aside his clippings and joined Ann on the swing.

"Only a few more days," he said. "I don't know how women handle it."

Ann patted his hand. "The scary part is over. We were close to losing the baby, at least that's what I think."

"Sometimes, doctors don't tell their patients everything," Jimmie said.

Ann pushed from the porch floor and the swing moved a little higher.

"Jimmie?"

"I think I know what you're about to say."

"We need to talk about names for our daughter. What do you think?"

Ever the politician, Jimmie tried to delay the decision as long as possible. "Shouldn't we wait to see the baby before we pick out a name? I mean, we could name her 'Rosebud' and she might look like a 'Petunia.'"

Ann brushed aside his comment. "I can't seem to find the right name, but I can cross off many of them."

"For example?"

"I was watching this daytime talk show. Some psychologist was explaining about names of babies. She said many parents select names without considering how they fit with the baby's last name."

"Oh, for goodness ..."

"Listen, Jimmie. She was right. We can rule out any two-syllable name that starts with a 'B,' like Bridget, Barbie, Billie…"

"Betty, Beulah, Bambi," Jimmie added. "And, obviously, Bailey."

"Also, with us having a two-syllable last name, this psychologist recommends a three-syllable first name," Ann said. "That seems to flow better and be a little more lyrical. "For instance, Patricia Bailey or Stephanie Bailey. See how nice that sounds?"

"What did the talk show say about using relatives' names? You know, using a name from your family history as a way to link to the past?" Jimmie asked.

Ann knew what he was thinking. Jimmie never recovered from the loss of his mother. Ann inwardly struggled with the idea of naming their baby after Sallie Bailey. After all, why enter the world with the burden of upholding a family member's name?

But how could she explain that to Jimmie? Perhaps her expression alone communicated that thought.

Jimmie understood. He reached for her hand. "I just want a healthy baby. She will be beautiful no matter the name."

Ann leaned toward him. They kissed. She felt a soft kick.

Dolores Gibson could not wait for tomorrow.

She convinced the pastor to drive her home to Wexford. He pulled his two-seater convertible to the rear of the Church of Higher Science. When he tapped his horn, she emerged from an emergency exit, letting the steel door close and latch behind her.

Angling into the narrow seat, Dolores flipped down the visor and re-applied her lipstick. Pastor Randy zoomed through the abandoned warehouse district with a blast of testosterone.

A black sedan followed at a distance.

Dolores was flushed with anticipation. The young minister beside her was shifting gears like a madman. She recalled his sermon earlier that people should be filled with love, not hate. She wondered if he practiced what he preached. And she wondered if he practiced with the same enthusiasm as his driving.

"We're far enough away from McKees Rocks," he said. "Do you mind if we lift the roof?"

"Not at all, Randy." Why not get more personal?

At a stop light at the West End Bridge, he peeled back the canvas top. Noon day sunshine reflected from a combed-over bald spot at the top of his head. How cute, she thought. Maybe he's older than 20 after all.

The traffic light changed. Dolores felt her head snap against the leather headrest.

"Do you do this often?" she asked over the din of rushing air. "I mean, drive women home from church?"

He didn't hear the last part, and answered: "Every chance I get. It's exciting. I love that open feeling!"

This was too easy, Dolores thought. Usually, she had to drink others under the table first. He was different, though. This mega-preacher was a mega-turn-on.

"Dee Dee, do you have family at home? I'd like to meet them."

"I live alone," she replied. "Just me and my dog. I've been a widow for five years. My husband was with the state police. He died suddenly."

"That's too bad." Pastor Randy tried not to smile as he thought about her insurance payment, pension benefits and other possible sources of income. "You must be very lonely."

"Yes. Very, very lonely." But not at the moment, she thought.

After motoring a few more miles north of Pittsburgh, the pastor turned onto her street and stopped in her driveway. As they approached her front door, they heard a scratching from inside.

Dolores fumbled in her purse and found her house key. She opened the screen door and unlocked her front door. Cuddles darted into the front yard.

"I'll get him." Randy turned to chase the dog.

"Don't worry. I let Cuddles do her business there. She'll come back. She always does."

Randy held the door and watched Dolores move her shapely southern hemisphere into the foyer. He turned to see if anyone else was watching. Then he followed her, the screen door shutting behind him.

"You must be thirsty. May I pour you a drink?" she asked.

"None of that strong stuff," he replied, pointing to her bar table. "I can't afford another DUI ticket."

Dolores stood, expressionless.

"That was a few years ago," he explained. "Back in my days at divinity school. Not much to do there. No girls."

"Poor thing." Dolores moved closer. "I bet you were lonely, too."

He unbuttoned the top of her blouse. "Yes, very, very lonely."

Dolores held his pretty face between her hands. She closed her eyes and let her lips find their target. His lips were soft, like butter. She held him close.

His fingers worked behind her, freeing a snap. Warm air flowed through the screen door and tingled her naked back.

"The bed would be more comfortable," she whispered in his ear.

Randy nibbled on her milky white shoulder. His eye was fixed on the street. "Not yet," he whispered to her. "Help me out of my shirt first."

Dolores obliged. Five buttons later, she tossed his shirt to the floor. Neither of them noticed Cuddles pawing at the screen.

"Your skin is so soft, so light," she said. "They said you were at a religious retreat in the desert. Where is your tan?"

"We spent most of the time indoors," he replied.

"I love spending time indoors." Dolores reached to close the front door until Randy found a sweet spot on her neck with his tongue.

As she leaned back and opened her mouth in ecstacy, they heard a "click." Then another "click." Randy swung Dolores around. Her exposed buttocks glowed in the afternoon sunshine. "Click ... click, click."

Dolores pushed back his flexed bicep in time to see a black sedan parked on the street. Pointing from the passenger window was a long camera lens. The car sped off.

"Holy shit!" Pastor Randy pulled up his pants.

"Who is it? What are they doing?"

"Hell, I'm so stupid. I should have known that bitch would have me followed!"

Dolores covered herself with a forearm and closed the front door.

Randy, in stage two of undress, buckled against the wall.

"Oh, Lord, I have sinned." He appeared to be weeping.

"Your wife? Was that a private investigator?"

"Yes, yes..."

Dolores stroked his thinning hair. "You told me you were separating. So what?" She leaned over to kiss him again, but he turned away.

"Those photographs, they'll ruin me," he muttered. "Darla will clean me out, every last dime. This is the end of me!"

Dolores tucked herself into her undergarments and sat beside him. He truly seemed disheveled. He needed comfort. He needed her. She felt herself falling in love with someone she met only hours earlier.

"I'm so sorry you're in the middle of all of this," Randy told her. "They'll drag you through the mud. Your name will be splashed in the headlines. All because of me."

He struggled to his feet and collected his shirt.

"Come here," she said, pointing to the living room sofa. "I'll get you that drink. We can talk. You don't have to go."

"I suppose," he said, flinging the shirt around his broad shoulders. "They already have their photos. Why not stay?"

While she prepared his drink in the kitchen, Randy made a visual inventory of her furnishings. A walnut breakfront in the dining area housed shelves of fine crystal. Original Rockwell artwork hung on a wall leading to the billiards room. A pearl-handled revolver, probably a relic from the old West, occupied a glass display case near the marble fireplace.

He wondered what finery she had hidden in the house.

"Here, Randy, take this. Non-alcoholic, I promise." Dolores handed him a cut glass champagne goblet. Her drink included a cherry and olive.

"Thanks, Dee Dee. I'm sorry that I swore. It's just that ..."

"I know," she said. "Women are crazy."

"And vindictive and, well, some are just plain greedy."

"That's what this is all about? Darla wants money?" Dolores asked.

Randy swallowed the ice tea. She watched the gulp descend his neck and vanish into his shirtless torso.

"Darla never wanted me, just my money," he said. "We never were in love. We just put up a good show for the congregation. It worked for a while, but a man has certain needs, you know?"

Dolores well understood.

"So, at first, the Church of Higher Science collected enough money for us to buy a nice house and car. That was not enough for Darla. She wanted a big house, a new one, with a bathroom for every bedroom, and a bedroom for each of her family members."

"More than you could afford?" Dolores asked.

"Her brother was a mortgage broker. Actually, he was a lawn service technician who thought he was a mortgage broker. He cooked up the paperwork, overstated our income and shoe-horned us into a mortgage that was way over our heads."

Dolores didn't hear a word of it. She was absorbed by his lack of body hair.

"We've been fighting foreclosure for nearly eight months. All I hear from Darla is: 'where's the money gonna come from?' and 'if you loved me, you'd work harder.' Meanwhile, she's spending at Kaufmann's like the Baileys."

Wait! There was a fine line of fuzzy hair right above his navel. Dolores tilted her head for a better look.

"So we had to put the squeeze on everybody at the church. We had extra collections just to keep up with Darla's shopping sprees. For many years, we did a good business. Lately, though, people are watching their money, and the collections haven't been as lucrative. The church has plenty of expenses – electricity bills, gas bills in the winter, costs for maintenance, plus we spend a lot for security. We've had a few break-ins. The vagrants like to sleep there on cold nights."

Her dead husband, Josh, kept six-packs in the garage refrigerator, but he never had a six-pack like the abdomen on this young man, Dolores thought. It was difficult for her to believe that Josh and Randy were of the same species, let alone the same gender.

"I appreciate your listening to me like this, Dee Dee. Darla never listens to me. I could be talking for ten minutes and her mind would be elsewhere."

Dolores calculated his weight to be about 160 pounds. Three beers or two scotch and waters would do the trick, she calculated.

"I'm hurting really bad, Dee Dee. I desperately need money."

"And probably a place to stay," she added.

"You will be rewarded for your kindness." Randy kissed her softly on the cheek. "I can't go back to McKees Rocks. I promise not to be any trouble."

Be all the trouble you like, Dolores thought. She smiled at the prospect.

"I'll make up the bed in the back room," she said. "Do you need fresh clothes?"

"Just a robe. If you don't mind washing these." He emptied change from his pants pockets and placed his wallet on her coffee table. He handed her his musky-smelling shirt.

"It will take time to finish the laundry, probably overnight," she said. "You know, air drying and ironing …"

"That's all right. I'll have time to take a shower and a good sleep. Do you have a towel?"

"Right down the hall," she said, escorting her little Pillsbury doughboy to the guest bathroom. "When you're ready, toss your stuff out the door and I'll…"

"No need to wait," he said. Dolores stared in disbelief as he stripped and handed her his clothes. "No starch. My skin gets bothered."

Dolores mouthed the letters O and K. He closed the door. She heard the shower head sputter and splash water in the tub. When Dolores heard him pull the shower curtain, she pushed open the door – far enough to reach her medicine cabinet. She swallowed two tablets without water.

"My skin is really bothered now, too," she murmured.

Chapter Thirteen
The Scoundrel

When there's silver up ahead, you can easily miss blue flashing lights in your rear-view mirror.

Billy Herman's car weaved and bobbed like a wobbly prizefighter as he drove through the Allegheny Forest. The more he thought about silver treasure, the heavier his right foot became. A police siren was not close enough to slow him down.

Two beers and one scotch ago, he spoke with the rookie Kane News Leader reporter. Billy's meeting was set for 2 p.m. at the Kinzua overlook. He underestimated the travel time. A little faster or he could miss it.

The kid on the phone had a lead. All Billy needed to do was pick the reporter's brain for a bit of information, maybe a name or a contact. Someone had the silver. Billy was getting close. He could smell it.

Sliding into the berm, Billy's tires caught some tarry gravel and tossed it. He swung his steering wheel to correct the vehicle, causing it to fish-tail into the oncoming lane. Fortunately, the only other car on the road was behind him – in pursuit.

It was a minor deviation from his silver obsession.

Billy never forgot that moment in Kinzua Valley when Josh Gibson's shovel struck metal. Nor could he forget that vision of Gibson dropping to his knees and digging with his hands until the entire silver seam was exposed.

"Cover it up! Cover it up!" Gibson had ordered. Billy had kicked dirt into the hole as the two men looked about them. "No one else has to know about this, Billy," Gibson had directed. "We'll quietly close down the search and come back next week. We'll split it up then."

But the following week, the treasure was gone. Gibson didn't take Billy's calls. Gibson stayed in hiding. His underlings always told Billy that their boss was "out of the office" or "in conference and could not be disturbed."

When he tried to tail Gibson on three occasions, he was detained by state troopers. A Commonwealth attorney threatened him with a criminal stalking prosecution, and Billy backed down. Just thinking of that threat now caused Billy to accelerate through the forest.

Stretched before the speeding car were two lanes of asphalt cutting through stacks of tall pines. The speedometer eased past 85 miles per hour. Billy goosed it to 90 during a rare straightaway. He unknowingly added distance between himself and his chaser.

Billy then recalled the surprise parcel, postmarked from Oil City. The plain brown box was labeled "Personal and Confidential." It arrived at his Pittsburgh police desk a few days after Josh Gibson's death at Kinzua Bridge. Billy cut it open and removed packing material. To his shock, the box contained 10 silver bars. Apparently, Josh wanted to make peace.

But there were hundreds of silver bars under the Kinzua Valley weeds. Did Gibson give them all away? Or did he keep them? Maybe this kid reporter found them, Billy thought.

Mid-day sunshine cast a glare on a warning sign. Traffic would be merging from the right. Billy missed it.

Alcohol dulled him enough to add seconds to his reaction time. By the time he braked, Billy was close enough to read the dump truck's report-bad-driving-800-number. He turned hard to the left. The passenger door crashed into the truck's rear fender, causing the car to rotate and flip. Billy lost consciousness as his head was pummeled by air bags popping in all directions.

The truck driver pulled onto the shoulder. He met the running state trooper at Billy's door.

"Are you all right, Ray?" the trooper asked the trucker.

"Not a scratch, John."

"Do you suppose he's dead?"

"Maybe we ought to open the door and find out," the trucker replied.

"Not me," the trooper said. "This is the part of the job I hate."

"Don't matter to me. He probably deserved to die."

The trucker popped open the mangled door. Blood stains streaked the collapsing air bags. Billy's face was bruised. His nose was cracked and bleeding.

"Ooo-wee," the trucker said. "Can you smell that?"

"Smells like booze to me, Ray."

"Wait, John. He's saying something."

Billy's lips were moving. He pushed aside the bag and his hand fell to the seat.

"What's he saying?" the trooper asked.

"He wants to know the time."

"Tell him it's 1:25. And tell him not to worry. We'll get an ambulance here in a few minutes." The trooper pushed the call button on his shoulder radio and asked for back-up.

Billy stirred in his seat and tried to move his legs.

"Hold on there, cowboy." The trucker closed the car door. "You're going nowhere until the paramedics get here."

Billy started to mouth words, but blood from his nose trickled onto his tongue, sickening him. He sat back, resigned to the fact that two strange men interfered with his meeting. That sickened him more.

Kane Community Hospital's ambulance arrived within minutes. Herman was loaded on a stretcher and wheeled into the van. Cheated death again, he thought. At least this time his heart seemed strong. His ribs and right arm, however, caused him agony.

Herman estimated another six months without golf. But he vowed not to go much longer without silver.

"Where are you taking me?" Billy asked the paramedic.

"First, to the emergency room to fix you up."

"How long will that take?"

"Judging from what I see, you could be released in a few days," the paramedic replied.

"A few days! All I need are a splint and a cast. I don't want any country doctors cutting me up."

The older paramedic mentioned a "deviated septum" and placed a plastic hose over Billy's nose and mouth. The patient squirmed.

"Do you know any country doctors, Jake?"

"The City of Kane only has city doctors, I reckon." The paramedic laughed.

Billy was getting sleepy.

That oxygen sure felt good.

It made him forget all about his obsession, for an hour at least.

Sunday brunch at the Golden Wheel was in full swing when Matty arrived. A portable salad bar, stocked with pancakes, sausage and hash browns, was surrounded by the church-going crowd. Toolie's only job was refilling water glasses. No tips today.

Matty missed the 11 a.m. service at United Methodist, despite a promise made to his mother never to miss Sunday church. But today, his deadline was fast approaching. And a key witness was somewhere in the brunch crowd. He resolved to do the church thing next week, after his exposé was published and after his boss was out of jail.

A hand waved in the corner booth. Megan was sitting alone with a Danish and coffee. Matty watched her close a notebook computer and place it in its case. He angled through the feasting customers and slid into her booth.

"You didn't call," he said.

"I figured I'd visit your hang-out, and maybe you'd be here."

Matty leaned over the table. "I know why Dulaney was digging."

"Me, too." She paused, hoping he would explain first.

"What are you working on, Megan? You were typing something."

"I'm finishing my term paper. Since Professor Dulaney died, the university gave me an extension to turn it in." Actually, she finished a week earlier.

"I'd love to read it. What's the topic?"

"Nothing real exciting. It's about the Seneca Indians and how they were relocated to New York when the Kinzua Dam was built."

"Maybe I could write a story for the newspaper," he said, reaching for her computer case.

She pushed it out of his reach. "You can read it when I'm done."

Matty felt awkward. "Sorry. I didn't mean to..."

Megan spoke up. "Get yourself some breakfast, and then you can tell me what you know about Dulaney." She picked up her coffee mug and looked out the window.

Matty took her cue and walked to the breakfast buffet. Toolie, having witnessed the little spat, saddled up behind him.

"Too early in the day to be so testy," Toolie advised him. "Get back there and patch things up. I'll be over in a few minutes to check on you."

She held his shoulders and turned him around. Matty felt the waitress's hand gently push his rear. He heard Toolie giggle like a teenager. She was wise and frisky at the same time, he thought.

Megan's expression had softened when Matty returned to the table.

"It must be difficult to be a reporter," she said. "You have to get the story. You have to talk with people. But you can't be too aggressive or they'll shut up."

"Was I too aggressive with you?"

"Just a bit," she replied. "I want you to know your boundaries."

Matty wanted to explain his deadline pressures. Only two more days of legwork before the News Leader would publish his blockbuster, he wanted to say. Matty simply had no time to explore anybody's boundaries.

"Listen, Megan. I have a meeting at 2 o'clock with a key source."

"Well, we can talk some other time…"

"No." His firmness surprised her. "There is no other time. You must come with me."

"Where to?" Megan asked.

"To the Kinzua Park overlook. Have you ever been there?"

Megan and Mr. George visited the overlook yesterday. It was there that the Peacemaker confirmed the silver treasure's burial spot. She was not ready to give Matty that information. Not yet.

"I'll drive," she offered.

Matty heard Toolie clear her throat. He looked toward the waitress, expecting to see a thumbs-up. Instead, she motioned for him to leave a tip. He dropped ten dollars on the table before following Megan outside. He ignored Toolie's puckering sounds on the way.

Megan's Volkswagen turned east onto Fraley Street. Matty directed her back onto Route 6 toward Mount Jewett. They were 15 miles from the overlook at 2 p.m.

"Who are you meeting?" Megan asked.

"A former Pittsburgh cop by the name of Billy Herman," Matty replied. "I'm writing a story about the mysterious death of state police commissioner Josh Gibson. Herman spent time with Gibson in the days leading up to his death."

"What does that have to do with Professor Dulaney?"

"I don't know. Maybe nothing. Except Gibson and Dulaney died in the same spot."

Megan immediately suspected the Woods on Fire curse.

"Was Gibson digging around under the bridge?" she asked.

Matty sensed that she was making the right connections.

"That's what I need to ask Herman. I think Gibson was digging. And I think he found something very interesting."

"Like what?" she asked coyly.

Matty let the question linger. He tried to change the subject.

"This paper you're writing about the Indians, is that like a graduate thesis?"

Megan shook her head. "No, I'm an undergrad. It's just a class requirement."

"So you're a …"

"Sophomore. My major is international studies."

Wow, he thought. She's only two years older. No time to think about that now, though.

"Megan, let me be straight with you. Gibson was digging for buried silver. So was Professor Dulaney. The only difference was that Gibson got the silver first."

"How do you know that?" she asked.

"Easy. I saw it."

Megan turned at the Kinzua State Park sign. The road narrowed, as did the topic of their conversation.

"So there was buried treasure," she said. "The Peacemaker was right."

"The what?"

She pulled into Kinzua Park. They saw a young family walking down a trail toward the overlook. Matty scanned the area for Billy Herman. He realized that his interviewee would be looking for a gold Mustang and loud hip-hop music. Maybe Matty was too late.

He led Megan toward a picnic table. They could talk here while he watched for Herman.

"Is the Peacemaker an Indian friend?" he asked her.

"Yes. The Peacemaker is an old Seneca. He was the only Seneca elder who could translate this for me." She showed Matty the map Maude Thunder found.

Matty unfolded the old paper. "What does this mean?"

"It took me a few weeks. But with help from the Peacemaker

and an old Potter County history book, I have a good idea."

"Looks like I've been stood up," Matty said. "We have time."

"You may want to take notes," she said. "But don't quote me on this."

Megan began her story in the early fall of 1680. A Spanish galleon, loaded with precious cargo, was tossed in a tropical hurricane near the Bahamas, she said.

"The powerful storm tore its main and mizzen masts, causing it to capsize and sink in about 20 fathoms of water. There it rested for more than a century."

Matty was scribbling as fast as he could.

"In 1811, a British captain received a commission from his Admiralty to raise the wreckage. The captain's name was Blackbeard."

Matty looked up. "The pirate?"

"No, he was dead by that time," Megan said. "This was a well-respected British captain who used the same name."

"Did Captain Blackbeard raise the ship?"

"No problem. Blackbeard was one of the best marine salvage experts around. He raised the boat and surrounded it with pontoons. Then he towed the ship and its cargo into Baltimore harbor."

"What did Blackbeard intend to do?" Matty asked.

"He wanted to return his prize to England and get a reward. Unfortunately for him, the British were at war with Napoleon, and French warships blocked his return."

"That's interesting, Megan. But it doesn't explain why the silver was buried in this remote area of Pennsylvania," Matty said.

"Blackbeard decided to keep his Spanish ship in the American harbor until the French were defeated. But as time went on, he became very nervous. One day, he was drinking in a Baltimore tavern and struck up a conversation with Peter Abelhard Karthaus, a rogue privateer."

"How do you spell 'privateer' and what does that mean?" Matty asked.

Megan wrote the word for him. "That's another way of saying 'pirate.' Anyway, Karthaus told Blackbeard that he knew the English sailor had found silver on the Spanish galleon docked outside. Blackbeard then realized that he couldn't wait any longer."

"Did he sail for England?"

"Blackbeard was too smart for that. He realized if he set sail from Baltimore that Karthaus would follow him to the open sea. It would be easy for the pirate to overtake his ship in the ocean.

"His options were few. Stay and risk an assault in the harbor. Move out to sea and be commandeered by Karthaus. Or risk running the gauntlet with French warships.

"So Blackbeard decided to surprise everyone by taking the silver inland. He loaded his silver on a small boat and sailed up Chesapeake Bay and into the Susquehanna River. His route took him upstream to Williamsport, Pennsylvania, and onto the Sinnemahoning River."

"Spelling, please." Matty stopped her again. She complied.

"The plan was to take the silver by oxen cart over land to Conewango Creek, near Warren, and then up to Chautauqua Lake in New York. From there, he could move the silver to Lake Erie. At that time, Britain controlled Lake Erie."

Matty tried to remember geography of the Great Lakes from 11th grade. "Then where? Through the St. Lawrence River to the Atlantic?"

"Correct," Megan said. "But Blackbeard never made it that far. The rugged mountains of Pennsylvania took their toll on his wagons. At certain points, he had to build rafts to transport the silver across the Susquehanna. Oxen fell off the log rafts into the icy river. Also, Blackbeard began to suspect that some of his men were plotting to take silver from him.

"The final straw was news that war had broken out between the British and Americans."

"The War of 1812?" Matty asked.

"Right. Blackbeard was aiming for Lake Erie, but he found out that Americans blockaded Fort Niagara and controlled the lake. There was no way he could get his silver back to England."

"So they buried it," Matty said.

"Legend has it that Blackbeard and his assistant, Colonel Noah Parker, decided to bury the silver in a remote forest in McKean County. So late in the summer of 1812, they dug shallow trenches and lowered box after box of Spanish silver into them.

"Blackbeard and Parker thought only a herd of elk were watching them."

"But they were wrong?" Matty asked.

"During their portage through these mountains, Blackbeard and his party were being watched by two Seneca scouts. They could have been standing close to this spot when Blackbeard and Parker were digging their trenches."

Matty watched the young family walk from the overlook. "Let's stand over there," he said, pointing to a path close to Kinzua Bridge.

Megan locked her Volkswagen, and the pair walked through the pine needles. Matty tried to imagine that night 200 years ago when there was no park, no bridge and no overlook – only two Indians watching two desperate English sailors struggle in the wilderness.

"This map," Matty said. "Blackbeard's map?"

"No. This map was drawn by the Indian scouts. It marks a location where Blackbeard buried his silver."

"But the bridge wasn't here then." Matty pointed to a historical marker. The Kinzua Bridge was erected 90 years later.

"Let me explain. Several people have written on this map over the years. The Indian scouts identified the burial site in relationship to Kinzua Creek. They originally excavated the silver and took it to their chief.

"According to the Peacemaker, many Senecas believed the silver to be cursed. Nothing good happened to the Indians after they took the silver. Many died in fighting and the federal government took their lands.

"When the Indians learned that Kinzua Dam would flood their land in the Allegheny River Valley, the council decided to return the Spanish silver to its burial site."

"They re-buried it ... here?" Matty asked.

"The Peacemaker told me that a tribal elder used this map to find the exact location. He drew a diagram of Kinzua Bridge. He made these markings in 1965."

"Before the bridge was destroyed by tornado," Matty remarked. "But what are these markings here, the red ones?"

"These are words in Iroquoian. The Peacemaker called it an old incantation from the days of George Washington. The Indian who re-buried the silver shouted these words in Kinzua Valley: 'Harm will befall to any white man who disturbs the peace of this land for all eternity.' Mr. George said it was witchcraft."

Matty never much believed in occult. But Megan seemed to be wavering.

"Did Dulaney know about the curse?" Matty asked.

"I texted him a photo of the map. He knew enough about Indian folklore to guess it was a treasure map, but I don't believe he could read these Indian words."

Matty took her hand and guided her toward the overlook. Down and to the left was a grassy field. They saw a matted area where police and paramedics had trod only days earlier.

"That's my story, Matty." She held both of his hands.

"Now tell me yours."

Chapter Fourteen
The Climbers

Bill Pennoyer monitored his police radio Sunday afternoon. Governor Bailey's chief of staff rarely concerned himself with ordinary police work, but today was different. The governor had directed state police to keep an eye on a man named Billy Herman.

Police surveillance began when Herman's car left the Forest Club parking lot at 11 a.m. About noon, Pennoyer received a call from the district commander. "Please inform the governor that our subject appears to be intoxicated," he told Pennoyer. "Should we pull him over?"

Pennoyer had given a safe answer. "The trooper should use his best judgment to protect others on the highway."

About an hour later, Pennoyer heard police radio reports of a chase involving an impaired driver. When the trooper reported a violent crash with serious injuries, Pennoyer dropped his bagel.

"Jimmie, something's happened." Pennoyer found the governor alone in his study.

"I already know," Jimmie said. "I just fielded the call. Billy apparently got himself tanked up and went for a drive in the mountains."

"How badly was he hurt?" Pennoyer asked.

"Not bad enough. The trooper thinks he hurt some ribs, maybe broke a few bones. They clocked him going 85 through the forest."

"So he was heading this way?" Pennoyer asked.

Jimmie sighed. "That's what I thought, so I asked the trooper an important question."

"What's that?"

"Whether he had a gun in the car." Jimmie paused for effect. "He didn't."

Pennoyer wagged his finger at Jimmie. "Quit it! You're taking Billy Herman much too seriously. He's no threat to you. He's just a lonely man looking for some respect. And you're giving it to him!"

"I see him differently," Jimmie said. "He's got nothing to lose. He's desperate for money, not for respect. He can have my stinking money. I'm worried about Ann and the baby."

Pennoyer was no psychologist. But he was astute enough to understand Jimmie's perspective. The young governor's mother was kidnapped before his eyes. Fifteen years later, her body was discovered in a storage locker. Lately, Jimmie seemed to be abnormally occupied with Ann's protection.

"Maybe you should take a vacation, get away for a few days," Pennoyer suggested.

"You forgot, Ann can't travel. She's got placebo preventia, or something. She's confined here until the baby comes."

Pennoyer offered a plan. "Let's beef up protection and put a few more troopers around Leigh-Rose Mansion for the next few weeks. We'll issue a statement that the governor and First Lady are vacationing at Seven Springs Resort. That should throw him off."

Jimmie interrupted. "One more thing. Make sure Billy Herman is charged with multiple felonies. Let me think. Driving under the influence, reckless endangerment ... and didn't he drive into the back of a truck?"

"Yes, but he didn't hurt the driver," Pennoyer replied.

"Well, see if the district attorney can charge him with attempted murder anyway. That should hold him in custody for a while," Jimmie said.

"I'll call the prosecutor this afternoon. He owes you a favor or two."

Jimmie trusted Pennoyer's instincts. His right-hand man

guided Jimmie through some thorny political battles. Perhaps he could rescue the young governor from "Hermangate."

"If Billy Herman was not coming for me, then why was he driving in McKean County?" Jimmie asked. "And in such a hurry?"

"I've thought about that," Pennoyer replied. "Seems obvious to me."

"Well, not to me."

"Look, Billy told us that Josh Gibson dug up the silver in Kinzua Valley, and that he gave it to you. Billy said the silver was his."

"OK, go on." Jimmie was putting two and two together.

"Then a few days ago, this Edinboro professor is digging in the valley. Billy hears about it and, suddenly, he's driving toward Kinzua."

"So you think..."

"So I think there's silver in the valley, right now," Pennoyer said.

Jimmie pulled Professor Dulaney's Indian map from a desk drawer. "Look at this."

Pennoyer studied the old map and pointed to a spot near the bridge trestle. "Where did you find this?"

"State police had it. They found it near the professor's body."

"It's a freaking treasure map, Jimmie."

The two friends looked each other in the eye. Suddenly, they were teenagers again.

"Are you up for a little adventure?" Jimmie asked.

"What about the bear?"

"I can handle bears. It's Herman I can't handle. Call Kane Community and get his medical condition. Make sure he stays there overnight."

Pennoyer called the hospital switchboard. He was routed to a reticent floor nurse.

"I am not permitted to comment on his injuries," she said.

"Has Mr. Herman been admitted? That's all I need to know."

"Yes. If you need more information, I can take your name and number and ..."

"No, ma'am. Can you tell me his room number? I'd like to visit."

"That has not been assigned. Call back."

Jimmie checked the Sunday paper. Tonight was to be warm and clear with a waxing gibbous moon. Just the right conditions for a midnight dig, he thought.

"You'll have to tell Ann," Pennoyer said. "She's getting close."

"What should I tell her?"

"Tell her that you and I are getting a baby gift, and that your cell phone will be fully charged," Pennoyer said.

"That sounds too close to the truth," Jimmie said. "Think of something else."

Before 8 a.m., a black sedan parked at the corner. A woman in fishnet tights, short leather skirt and a long string of pearls accented by a skimpy blouse walked furtively over Dolores's front lawn. The woman reached Pastor Randy's convertible and fixed an oversized envelope under his windshield wiper. She was gone in a minute.

Dolores was awakened by screeching tires. She felt a heaviness on her chest. Pastor Randy was sleeping, his head firmly wedged in her cleavage. His knees were drawn and poked her hip. Love can be so uncomfortable.

The young man was at peace. Dolores hated to wake him. She ran her fingers over his smooth face. Her French nails traced a line to the stubble on his chin. For the moment, his anxiety was gone. When he awakes, she thought, her new friend would be terrified again.

But she owned a closet-full of silver. Everything would be OK.

Dolores had a sketchy memory of last night. She recalled putting fresh sheets on the guest bed and doing his laundry. He showered and toddled in a robe to her kitchen. They talked about their wretched lives while her medication took hold. He opened a pinot grigio.

How he ended up in her bed with two robes on the floor was a mystery.

Pastor Randy burrowed his nose a bit deeper. His musky scent was gone. She only smelled perfumed body wash. Primrose lilac became him.

Dolores stroked his shoulder. His lips pursed and then turned up slightly. He rolled his head toward the ceiling before lifting from her.

"What time is it?" he asked.

"About 8:30. It's all right. You can rest some more."

His eyes opened to slits. Dolores pulled the sheet to her shoulders.

"Oh, oh, I'm so sorry," he said, lifting his robe from the floor. "I took advantage of you. I was so distraught about Darla. And I used you."

Randy began to stand. Dolores lunged and threw an arm around his waist. "No, no. Don't be so hard on yourself." His back fell onto her face. She squeezed more tightly.

"Dee Dee, I can't stay." He tried to peel her fingers from his abdomen. "The temptation is too great."

"But you preach love," she pleaded.

Randy spun in her grasp. The two faced each other. They kissed.

"Thank you," she whispered in his ear. "That's all I wanted."

Cuddles grunted and hopped on the bed. The dog curled between them.

"She needs to go out." Dolores wrapped a sheet around herself. "Nature calls. Excuse me." She straddled him for an awkward second and slithered to her feet. Cuddles followed her down the hallway.

Randy heard her getting dressed in another room. His clean

clothes were stacked on an end table. He decided to dress later. While she was distracted with the dog, he would have time alone to explore her house. He cinched the belt on his robe and began to search.

The far bedroom contained a desk, so he thought it a likely place to start. A top desk drawer contained bank statements. The balances were paltry, he thought. Court papers from the insurance case occupied a file drawer. Nothing there. The desk top was cluttered with unpaid bills. How was this woman keeping up with expenses?

And then he opened the closet door.

Randy jumped as claws dug into his right ankle. He turned to find Cuddles grasping his robe in her teeth. He managed to close the bi-fold doors before Dolores found him.

"Cuddles, let go," she screamed at the dog. "Randy is our guest."

The dog relented as Randy re-tied his belt. He felt cold sweat breaking out on his forehead. Finally, his curiosity got the better of him.

"Dee Dee, I was looking for a towel and I opened this closet…"

Oh no, she thought. Not another voyeur of her closet. First, the young newspaper reporter and now Pastor Randy. Dolores started to think Josh Gibson's silver treasure was becoming the worst-kept secret in Pennsylvania.

"What is all of this?" Randy opened the closet and stared at the neatly stacked bars.

"This is all my husband left me when he died. Spanish silver, he said. I don't know where he got it from, and I don't know how to sell it."

"Must be worth millions," Randy muttered. He picked up one bar and marveled at its weight. "You need to protect this. It's not safe in your closet."

"I can't just walk with it into a bank. I can barely carry two or three bars. It's so heavy."

Randy knelt and began to count. She interrupted.

"I found this on your car windshield." She handed an envelope to him. It was addressed to "Randall O'Boyd, Personal."

He stood and opened it. Inside were about a dozen 8 x 10 prints. He tried to stop smiling.

"Are those the photographs your wife took yesterday?" Dolores tried to see.

"That witch did it. She caught me good."

"Is there a note inside?"

"No, nothing. Just the photos. That says it all."

Dolores stumbled for the appropriate words. "Well, we look pretty hot."

He estimated 400 silver bars in her closet of paradise. "Yes, very hot."

She thought her butt appeared to be large, but maybe it was the afternoon shadows. He looked perfect. She flipped through the other photos, unaware of his interest in her closet.

"What will your wife do next?" she asked.

"Darla will demand money, lots of it. If I don't pay quick, these photos will be published and you and I will be destroyed."

"How much will she want?"

"I don't know. More than I have."

Dolores pulled one photo from the stack. "I think this is the best one. We're kissing and your eyes, well, your eyes are closed like you're in love."

Randy placed his hands on her neck and pulled her close. He kissed her waiting lips.

"Maybe I am in love," he said.

As predetermined, Jimmie tucked Ann into bed at 9 p.m. He sat in an adjoining chair and watched his beautiful wife drift to sleep. At 10 p.m., he whispered that he and Pennoyer were taking a midnight hike and that, if her water broke, she should call his cell phone. At 11 p.m., in dark silence, Jimmie tip-toed from the room.

Pennoyer met him at the mansion's front porch. They nodded to security officers at a gate leading to Kinzua Park. The valley path began in about 200 yards. The moon was well-hidden by clouds.

"Did you tell her?" Pennoyer asked.

"Yes, she knows."

"So it's OK?"

"Yeah. It's OK. Let's not be too long."

Jimmie and Pennoyer passed a sign stating possible danger on the valley trail. Since the bear attack, the trail was closed. But funding had been cut and the park was unsupervised after sundown.

"Where did you put the shovel?" Jimmie asked.

"Over here, behind the latrine." Pennoyer pointed to a grove of pines. Jimmie could see two shovels angled from a wheelbarrow.

"Good man," Jimmie said. "I'll take the wheelbarrow."

Jimmie recalled a similar trip down the trail with a wheelbarrow five years earlier. He loaded his father's mangled body and wheeled it back to Leigh-Rose Mansion after the tornado struck. This trip was more enjoyable.

"Do you know where the silver is buried?" Pennoyer asked.

"Beyond the bridge. Just follow this matted path."

Moonlight finally appeared. Jimmie easily steered the wheelbarrow toward the southern bridge section and along Kinzua Creek. Pennoyer followed closely, looking for predators.

"This is spooky. I just stepped in some crap," Pennoyer said.

"Was it bear shit?"

"Could be."

"Well, then, he's a happy bear," Jimmie said. "Don't worry about it."

The men traveled under the bridge and along the bending creek. Jimmie looked at his map and stepped off a distance. "Right here."

Professor Dulaney's archeological work had been erased by investigating officers. Dirt was loose, though, and easy to dig.

Jimmie tossed several shovelfuls onto a pile. He tired after ten minutes, and Pennoyer took a turn. By midnight, they had dug a trench ten feet long, four feet wide and three feet deep.

"There's nothing here," Pennoyer said.

"Dig deeper." Jimmie took the second shovel and found only rock and clay.

Pennoyer stepped from the hole and grabbed Jimmie's arm. "I hear something," he whispered.

"Stay down," Jimmie said. "Don't move."

"Here, take a shovel." Pennoyer's trembling hands lost their grip.

Jimmie caught the shovel before it could make a sound. "Follow me."

The governor walked backwards from the rustling sound. Pennoyer stayed with him. Tall grasses obscured their vision. Something was there, and it wasn't a field mouse.

When they reached the bridge trestle, Jimmie motioned for Pennoyer to sit on a boulder.

"I think he's following us, but I can't say for sure," Jimmie told his frightened buddy.

"So we just stay here and get eaten?"

"No, we climb."

"Climb what?"

Jimmie pointed to the 300-foot high steel trestle above them. "That."

"You're freaking me out."

"Listen, when we were kids, we climbed up this bridge all the time. ... To prove our manhood."

"I'd rather be eaten."

"Here, let me show you." Jimmie put his foot on a low angled beam and pulled himself from the concrete foundation. "Watch that again." Jimmie pulled up to the next beam.

"Very interesting, but I can't…"

"Nonsense, Bill. You can do it. Just repeat this step over and over. You can climb it."

Pennoyer watched his friend steadily progress up the bridge trestle.

"But what happens when you get to the top?" Pennoyer asked.

"You just climb through the open railroad tracks and boost yourself up. Then it's an easy walk on the bridge to the park. Come on."

Pennoyer heard some grunting noises getting closer. He stood on the concrete and jumped to the first angled beam. Then he reached for the second, then the third. Hey, maybe this is easy after all, he thought.

Jimmie climbed like a monkey. At the halfway mark, he looked below. Pennoyer was making steady progress, but his weight was impeding him.

"Don't look down, Bill. I think the bear found us." Jimmie watched the huge creature paw at the trestle, slump to the ground and return to a hiding place.

"I don't think we should go back down, Bill," he said. "The only way to go is up."

Pennoyer reached for another beam and pulled himself to a resting spot. "Damn you, Bailey," he called.

Jimmie reached the 200-foot level and surveyed the valley. He hadn't seen this view since he was 17 years old. He remembered the last time he climbed the bridge. It was a damp April night. His best friend made a bet. Whoever got to the top first could ask Rebecca Dunmeer to the senior prom. He pretended to cramp up near the bridge deck so his friend could win. Ms. Dunmeer was a bit too experienced for Jimmie.

Below him, Pennoyer ended his rest and climbed with greater effort. Jimmie shouted encouragement. He watched his friend methodically grasp the rusty beams and pull up. Then he saw something black fall.

"What was that?" Jimmie called.

"My shitty shoe."

"Are you OK?"

"No," Pennoyer shouted. "But this is going to hurt you more than me."

"Don't threaten your governor. I could call the state police."

"Call the friggin' police, Jimmie. I'm in jail right now anyway."

Jimmie leaned forward and grabbed a higher beam. Suddenly, strains of the 1812 Overture blurted from his jeans pocket. "Oh my ..." He reached for his cell phone.

"Where are you?" an anxious voice said.

"Ann?"

"Jimmie, where are you?"

"I couldn't sleep. I'm hanging with Bill."

"With Bill?"

"Are you all right?" Jimmie asked.

"I think I'm having contractions."

"How far apart are they?"

"I just had one. I woke up and you were gone. Jimmie, I'm scared."

"Try to get to a chair. Do your breathing."

"All right. I'm moving off the bed to the chair."

"Don't forget to breathe."

"I'm breathing. I'm breathing. One-two-three-four. AAARGHH!"

Jimmie grabbed a steel post and stood. "What happened!"

"My water broke! Jimmie, the floor..."

"Hold on, Ann. I'll be there in a few minutes." Jimmie scampered up the last 25 feet and hoisted himself to the railroad tracks. He sprinted to safe ground and to a path leading to Leigh-Rose Mansion.

Kinzua Bridge was quiet except for sporadic puffing noises. Pennoyer was alone in an unfamiliar predicament. So he tugged on another beam. Another three feet higher. He looked down and shuddered. Kinzua Creek looked like a discarded piece of dental floss. The bridge deck above him seemed unreachable.

His grip was failing. His breathing was labored.

Perhaps if he rested for a few minutes, he could regain some strength.

In the distance, he heard an ambulance roaring toward the mansion.

Pennoyer reached for a higher beam. It was time, he thought, to prove his manhood.

Chapter Fifteen
The Release

About halfway through his shower, the pipes clanged. Matty Moore turned off the showerhead and listened. From the floor below, he heard Toolie.

"You're using all the hot water," she screamed. "Cripes Hanna!"

"Sorry," Matty hollered.

He set aside the body wash and took a fast rinse. He needed to hustle anyway.

The clanging below stopped. He heard the old woman's television blaring a Monday morning exercise program. Matty tried not to envision Toolie in tights doing leg circles on her bed.

About this time every morning, Matty resolved to fix up his apartment. Walls needed painting. Carpeting had to be replaced. And the floors were so creaky that Toolie could chart his every movement from her apartment downstairs. Matty had money, but not the time. His newspaper job monopolized his waking hours. Plus, Toolie was annoyed by any sound from his apartment. She would never allow hammering, sawing or ripping down walls.

On the bright side, he had a cushy sofa, the latest sound system and an urge to entertain his new friend, Megan. Hopefully, Toolie wouldn't pry.

The General Kane Boarding House was a few blocks west of the News Leader office. Matty opened the place at 7:30. Jessie likely would not arrive for another hour. The pressmen would report for work Tuesday night to print the Wednesday weekly paper. Advertising salespersons worked in the afternoons. So Matty sat alone at a computer terminal. He questioned whether he was up to the task of publishing his exposé.

He still hadn't solved Josh Gibson's death, so that story needed more work. He knew that Gibson found the silver and took it home. He knew that Dolores Gibson had it in her closet. And he knew about an Indian curse that seemed to be working.

But Matty could not write the story without one more interview, Billy Herman.

Jessie's production outline topped his in-basket. Wednesday's edition would contain 18 pages. The front page was largely open, except for an arts festival preview story. There was unused news space on page 3, so Matty's story could jump inside. The rest of the newspaper already was committed to display ads, classifieds and sports items.

Item 2 in his in-basket was an op-ed column from editor Tom Zachary about the deplorable conditions at the McKean County Jail. Zachary noted a lack of cable television, fresh vegetables and adjustable air conditioning. "This is hardening our criminals," he concluded. Jessie's memo note asked Matty to rewrite the editorial because "Tom seems delusional after three days in jail."

Item 3 was the Kane Community Hospital list of admissions for the weekend. Jessie's memo asked Matty to input the names into the weekly Hospital Roundup for page 5. That was a task he could do in five minutes. So he opened the file and began to type:

"Agnes Browner, Cindy Crandall, Francis Driscoll, William Herman, Walter Jankovitz, Kenneth Prosser ..."

Jessie pushed opened the front door. She tossed her purse on the business counter and put her wrists on her hips.

"There's the stranger," she said. "I haven't seen you since Thursday." She waved her hand over the page design boards for Wednesday's edition. "I did this myself. No help from you."

"I've been working hard on a few news stories, Jessie," he said. "I had to meet with some people, so I couldn't stay in the office."

"Let me tell you something, Matthew. We're a small paper.

We don't have the time and money to do investigative reporting. Goodness knows, Tom tries to do that and he gets nowhere. So I have to work overtime to put together a product and get it on the streets."

"I understand, Jessie." Matty tried to soften her temper.

"No, you don't. I've worked at the News Leader for nearly 20 years. I've struggled to get this newspaper out the door every week. You don't understand what that requires, Matthew. Even Tom doesn't understand. He thinks he's Mr. Journalism, always looking for a scandal, for some chance to make someone look bad."

"Isn't that what the readers want?" Matty asked.

"No," she said emphatically. "The readers want to see their names in print. They want to know who won the orchid contest, or who attended the reunion or who served as bridesmaids at a wedding. They don't want to know how much money a lobbyist paid to a campaign or who's sleeping with whom. Well, maybe ..."

"Jessie, I'll help you get the newspaper together," Matty said. "But I'm just a summer intern, I don't know how..."

"This whole situation is crap," Jessie said. "My boss is in jail writing his memoirs and I'm left here with some rich kid who doesn't know his pica stick from a hole in the ground."

"Wait." Matty stopped her.

Jessie's rant was a mistake. She knew it.

"Why do you say I'm a rich kid?"

She stumbled into this one. "Just that you have a new car and you dress nice..."

"What do you know about me, Jessie?"

She gritted her teeth and sat. "I can't tell you."

"Mr. Z picked me deliberately because of who I am," Matty said. "So this jobs fair interview and the letter he wrote to me, those were part of his fraud?"

"I didn't tell you, Matty," she said feebly.

"How could I be so naïve? Here, I thought Mr. Zachary was genuinely interested in me and wanted me to learn about newspaper work. And it was all a joke?"

"No, Matty, don't say that. Tom really likes you and respects your work."

"What's he after, Jessie? Does he want to write a blockbuster story about the governor's illegitimate black brother? Is that what your readers want to see in the News Leader?"

"Matty, you have to listen to me. Tom is a good man. The last thing he wants to do is hurt you."

"So why did he bring me up here to Kane? This is a stone's throw from Governor Bailey's house. What's the point of this, Jessie?"

"I can't answer your questions, Matty. Tom knows why he hired you. All I do around here is clean up his messes. You'll have to ask him yourself."

Matty shut down his computer. "I'm driving to the jail."

Jessie handed him an envelope. "Look, Matty, Tom has a bail hearing at 10 this morning. You won't have much time to talk with him in jail before then. Here is a blank check from the News Leader. Use it to bail him out. Got it?"

"Sure." Matty took the envelope and kept the attitude.

"And don't make a fuss in Judge Van Lear's courtroom, Matty. You know, that judge has a short fuse."

Matty smiled. Judge Van Lear was probably the only person Matty could trust at the moment. After all, Van Lear was the fair judge who split Brock Bailey's $50 million estate between Matty and Jimmie.

But wasn't Matty's inheritance order sealed in the court records? How did Mr. Zachary discover him?

After retrieving his Mustang from the boarding house lot and driving to Smethport, Matty entered the jail lobby and spoke to a desk sergeant. He was led through the concrete block halls to a visitation area. Matty sat before the thick glass and gathered his thoughts.

Cell doors in the distance banged open and shut. He heard

footsteps approaching. The door beyond the thick glass opened. Tom Zachary, wearing a bright orange jumpsuit and looking ten years older, hobbled in as the door shut behind him.

"How's the book coming?" Matty asked.

"I finished the outline. Should take about 18 months to write."

"Jessie's got the paper ready for Wednesday," Matty said.

"Did she get my editorial?"

"Yeah. I read it. Sounds like things are pretty bad in jail."

"Well, the food's bad. At least I slept last night," Zachary said.

"Make any friends?"

"No, I'm the only inmate here. I guess they don't arrest real criminals."

"Listen, Mr. Z. There's something I need to talk to you about."

"You can tell me anything, Matty. That's what I'm here for. I want you to have to full summer intern experience. I chose you because you are bright and you wanted to learn about newspaper work. Well, you've done a terrific job. So what's on your mind?"

The door behind Zachary opened and bailiff Mike Devlin appeared.

"Cornelius," Devlin said in a melodic voice. "Time for your hearing, let's go."

He grabbed Zachary's arm and escorted him from the interview room. Matty gathered his things and took the back stairs to Van Lear's courtroom.

Matty sat in the back row because it had the poorest lighting. No need to get the judge's attention, he thought. The courtroom was empty except for a woman pouring water into the judge's glass. When she turned and saw Matty, she practically ran to a side door. A minute later, the same woman entered through the courtroom's rear doors and motioned for Matty.

"Are you Matthew Moore, the Kane News Leader reporter?" she asked.

He nodded.

"Follow me please. Judge Van Lear would like to meet you."

So much for anonymity, he thought.

Matty waited while the woman knocked and entered the judge's private office. She returned and instructed Matty to enter. He peered around the doorway and saw Van Lear standing behind his mammoth desk.

"Mr. Moore, please take a seat." The judge was uncharacteristically gracious. "We've met before, haven't we?"

"Yes, sir. About five years ago, we met in the hallway. With my mother and grandmother. We were here…"

"I remember why you were here." Van Lear sat after his guest. "You claimed to be the son of Brock Bailey, the former governor. And we had a test done."

"That's correct, Your Honor."

"You passed the test. So you shared in the estate. Quite a large estate, I recall."

"Yes, sir."

"You have certainly grown up into a fine young man."

"Thank you …"

"And I see you are working at the local newspaper. That's quite a coincidence, I think. Why would such a fine young man from Pittsburgh spend his summer at the Kane News Leader? Answer me that one."

Matty wanted that answer from Zachary, but his editor was not here to help. "Coincidence. That's a good word. Coincidence."

Van Lear was disturbed by the response. "But why would you accept such a job? McKean County must feel like a foreign country to you. Do you know anybody here?"

"No, but everybody here is really friendly and …"

"Bullshit!" Van Lear lost his judicial temperament. "How did Zachary find you? Every file is sealed. I kept your name from the public records. How was my security breached?"

"I'm sorry, Your Honor. Mr. Zachary found me at my high school job fair. I interviewed fair and square. Are you suggesting that I got my summer job because Mr. Zachary did something wrong? That would really upset me."

Van Lear backed off. "I think maybe I was wrong about Mr. Zachary. Maybe he is a good judge of talent. You deserve your job, young man. I wish you well."

The judge stood. "Now, please excuse me. I have two detention hearings to conduct."

Matty returned to the hallway in time to see two deputies escorting a man into the courtroom. The man's arm was in a cast and his face was bruised. Zachary was ushered in through a side door. He sat at counsel table beside the injured man.

"All rise!" Bailiff Devlin called from the bench as His Honor entered. An assistant district attorney shuffled papers as instructed by his paralegal. Van Lear surveyed the courtroom before summoning the prosecutor to sidebar.

"I've reviewed the complaint against Zachary," he told the assistant attorney. "I want you to drop the charges."

"But, but…" The young attorney never heard such a demand.

"You've overcharged him. From what I read in the police report, Zachary and the state trooper had a disagreement and the trooper lunged at Zachary. This poor man was just defending himself."

"But he disobeyed a police order to stay off the Kinzua path."

"Listen, sonny. Mr. Zachary has spent the weekend in lock-up. He's suffered enough. We'll let him talk and maybe he'll be remorseful. But before the end of the day, your office will drop these charges. Am I understood?"

"I'll talk to the district attorney."

"Am I understood?" Van Lear needed a clear answer.

"Yes, Your Honor."

"If I could, I'd release him now. I can't because he's charged with aggravated assault on a law enforcement officer. With a charge like that, how would it look if I released him?"

"The Commonwealth would agree to a minimal bond."

"Well, go back and sit down." Van Lear sneered. "I'll make my own decisions."

The judge winked at his bailiff. Devlin stepped forward. "The case of Commonwealth versus Thomas Cornelius Zachary. All those having interest in this matter may come forward and be heard."

Zachary and the assistant attorney stepped to the podium. Matty watched as his boss addressed the court.

"Your Honor, if I may be heard," Zachary began.

"Again, Mr. Zachary, I caution you. Anything you say may be used against you. Have you hired an attorney?"

"No, Your Honor."

"Is it a matter of cost?"

"No, sir," Zachary replied. "A matter of pride."

"You have been charged with resisting arrest, aggravated assault, criminal trespass and disturbing the peace. How do you plead?"

"I am innocent of all charges, but with an explanation."

The judge showed his open hand to Zachary. "Stop. I will hear no explanations. I will enter a plea of not guilty. Now let's turn to the matter of your pre-trial release."

Zachary turned to the prosecutor. "Can I give you my explanation?"

"No," the attorney said from the side of his mouth.

"Mr. Zachary, I do not find you to be a danger to the community or a flight risk. I will set bail at $10,000. If you make bail, then you must follow pre-trial conditions. You may not commit another crime, you may not possess dangerous drugs and you cannot leave the jurisdiction without court approval. Do you understand?"

"Yes, sir. Thank you."

"Do not thank me," Van Lear replied. "Bailiff, return Mr. Zachary to the sheriff's custody until his bond is arranged."

Matty stood to leave.

"Bailiff, call the next case," the judge ordered.

"Commonwealth of Pennsylvania versus William Herman, also known as Billy Herman."

Matty quickly returned to his seat as the injured man hobbled to the podium.

"Your Honor," the prosecutor began, "Mr. Herman was arrested by state police yesterday following an automobile accident on Route 6. He was treated and released from Kane Community this morning. He is charged with one count of driving under the influence and one count of reckless driving."

Van Lear looked at the defendant. "Do you understand the charges?"

"Yes sir," Herman answered. Matty recognized the voice.

"If you enter a plea, I'll consider your bail," the judge said.

"Not guilty, Your Honor."

"Very well," Van Lear said. "We'll do the usual $10,000 bail for this DUI case. Sir, one of the conditions of your release is turning in your driver's license. You cannot drive until this case is concluded. Do you understand?"

"Yes sir. I won't drive."

"All right. You're remanded to the custody of the McKean sheriff until your bond is arranged. Bailiff, please take Mr. Herman into custody as well."

Matty watched as Devlin led Zachary and Herman through a side door. He stood as Judge Van Lear left the bench. Matty ran to the first floor clerk's office.

"I'd like to bail out two prisoners," he said breathlessly to the criminal clerk.

"Names?"

"Zachary and Herman."

The clerk called Van Lear's chambers. She wrote information on a pad and returned to her customer.

"Two cases, each $10,000," she told Matty.

"I have one check. Can I write it for $20,000?" he asked.

"I'm sorry," she said. "I need a separate check for each case."

Matty looked at the clerk's watch. It was nearly noon. He was two hours closer to deadline. Zachary, the journalist, would surely understand.

"OK," he told the clerk. "This will be the check for Billy Herman. I'll be back later with another check."

He watched the clerk sign a receipt. "To whom should I make this out?"

"Make it out to Thomas Zachary. It's his money."

The stunned clerk did as she was told. Then she called the jail.

"How soon will Mr. Herman be released?" Matty asked.

"As soon as the sheriff's paperwork is done, maybe 15 minutes."

Matty grabbed the receipt and ran out the courthouse door. The jail was only a few minutes away by foot. He arrived in time to see Billy Herman standing before the desk sergeant. The man's arm cast was being searched for contraband.

"Who posted bond?" Herman asked the sergeant.

"I did. My name's Matthew Moore. We spoke on the phone." Matty tried to shake his hand, but Herman backed away.

"Excuse me, sergeant. I'm going." Herman lost his limp and scrambled out the jailhouse door. Matty was in hot pursuit. When they reached West Main Street, Herman stopped.

"We couldn't talk in front of the cop, so I had to get out," Herman said. "Anyway, thanks for springing me."

"Don't thank me. Just give me $10,000 worth of information. Were you with Josh Gibson when he died?"

Herman retreated a step. "Yeah, as a matter of fact, I was."

Matty swallowed. "So how did he die?"

"The stupid ass fell."

"Why was he on the bridge?"

"Listen, Jocko. The only reason I'm here, and three of my bones are broken, my nose is twisted and I'm looking at five years on a drunk driving charge is because you said the word, 'silver'. Remember that? So after driving like a maniac to get to your interview, risking life and limb, let alone Judge Ichabod Crane, some dumb kid starts asking me questions like he's a police interrogator. I want to know about the silver, period."

Matty decided to tell him. "I know where it is, all of it."

"Where?"

"I'm waiting to hear how Josh Gibson died. You know what happened."

"Maybe I do," Herman said. "But where's the silver?"

"Tell me what happened. You pushed him, didn't you?"

"Hell, no." Herman's anger was showing. "Where's the silver?"

"You thought the silver belonged to you, and he double-crossed you. So you tricked him onto the bridge and pushed him off."

"I'm not big enough to push that fat man off the bridge. He fell."

"Tell me, Mr. Herman. If you were there that night, how come your name isn't on the police reports. Why didn't you report his fall? Did you run away?"

"I don't have to answer your stupid questions. I told you what I know. Tell me about the silver."

"You're a damn liar," Matty told him. "Goodbye, Mr. Herman. Hope you can hitchhike home."

Matty pushed a button on his keychain. His Mustang lights flickered and its doors unlocked. He gave the man a few more seconds to tell the truth.

"He was dead before he fell." Herman's voice was softer, but angry. "Now, where is my silver?"

"Gibson's widow has it," Matty said. "Your turn, who killed Josh?"

Herman answered by raising his arm. His white cast crashed against the bridge of Matty's nose. The young reporter collapsed.

Chapter Sixteen
The Rescue

The pink blanket wiggled.

Jimmie held his newborn daughter tightly. A new life, light as a feather, squirmed in his arms. He watched with wonder as her little fingers poked at the air. He stroked her matted hair.

"She's beautiful," he said to no one in particular. "Welcome to the world."

Ann clutched his hand to pull him closer. "I love you, Jimmie."

They kissed above the baby's reddening face. A scream punctured the moment.

"The lungs work," the obstetrician announced, taking the baby from her father. "Let's check the heart."

Jimmie and Ann watched the physician complete his checklist. He counted her fingers and toes. He checked her spine and legs. "Here, Ann, hold her for a few minutes."

"Gladly." The baby girl rested on Ann's stomach. Little eyes began to open. The crying stopped. Was that a smile?

"This is as close as I've come to a miracle," Jimmie said.

"No," Ann said. "This is better than a miracle. And she's our child, Jimmie."

The obstetrician removed his latex gloves and patted Jimmie's back. "Well, Governor, she's a 10. A perfect child and a perfect delivery. Good job, Mom."

"Mom," Ann said. "That's a new name for me."

Jimmie watched as a nurse fixed a bracelet on his daughter and another on his wrist. Both were labeled "Baby Girl Bailey."

"Twenty-one and a half inches, eight pounds two ounces," the doctor said. "Do you have a name picked out?"

Ann looked to Jimmie for help. He nodded no.

"Good idea. Take your time," the doctor said. "We'll discharge you late tomorrow. I guarantee that after you spend a couple days with Baby Girl Bailey, a name will come to you. That happens all the time."

"Thanks, doc," Jimmie said. "That takes the pressure off now."

"The hospital is working on a press release," the doctor said. "You know, we've had a lot of media inquiries today. What should we say?"

"No problem. My chief of staff will come up with something," Jimmie said.

"Is he here at the hospital, Governor? Our community relations manager needs to speak to him as soon as possible."

Jimmie realized that he hadn't heard from Pennoyer since he left him hanging on the Kinzua Bridge trestle overnight. Certainly, Pennoyer was strong enough to climb the final 100 feet to the bridge deck, Jimmie thought.

"I'll get back to you on that, Doc."

Jimmie and Ann watched the nurse clean their baby's head and body. She gathered the baby's thin black hair into a spit-curl. "We want her to look nice for her photo," the nurse said.

Baby Girl Bailey was placed in a plastic cart. A pink card said "BAILEY" in bold black letters. "I'm taking her to the nursery for the pediatrician's visit. Once she's checked out, you can bring her back to your room for a visit. Just keep your bracelets on."

Ann tugged at Jimmie's sleeve. She whispered, "Go with her just in case."

"Just in case what?" he asked.

"They could mix up the babies. It's happened before."

"Relax, Ann. There were footprints taken and we've got these i.d. bracelets."

"Jimmie?"

"Yes."

"Do what I say." Ann turned on her side to ease her discomfort.

Jimmie kissed her on the forehead. Then he chased the nurse and his moving baby. He caught up with them at the nursery window.

"You'll have to wait here, Governor." The nurse stopped him. "You can watch today's seven babies. It's quite a show."

Jimmie kept his eyes glued to the Baby Bailey cart. His daughter was sleeping. Two other carts had blue cards and four had pink ones. Every other baby was crying. All of them were cute, but none as pretty as his.

He flipped open his cell phone. There was no signal inside the hall. Jimmie walked to the stairwell and dialed again.

"Yeah, I made it." Pennoyer answered the call. "Nice of you to think of me."

"Congratulations, Bill. You're a man. Now you can congratulate me."

"Why should I do that?"

"I'm a father."

Matty awoke under a mountain laurel bush. His head throbbed. Grass and dirt clung to his shirt as though he had been dragged to this spot.

Billy Herman was gone. So was Matty's black and gold Mustang.

No one witnessed the assault. Matty looked for help. He touched his forehead and found blood on his fingers.

Traffic was light on West Main Street. Matty crossed it as the courthouse clock struck noon. Jackie's Front Porch store was directly before him. Matty opened a screen door and found a young woman behind the counter.

"Oh, gracious," she said. "What happened? Are you all right?"

Matty emptied a napkin holder and dabbed his forehead. The clerk filled a water basin and found a wash cloth. She rubbed soap on the cloth and handed it to him.

"Thanks. I'll be OK."

"How did you hurt yourself? I can call for help."

Matty was reticent about the attack. No sense in scaring the locals, he thought.

"May I use your phone to call my sister?" he asked her.

The clerk handed him a cordless receiver and Matty punched the numbers for Megan Broward. Thankfully for him, she answered.

"Matty, where are you?"

"Across from the McKean Courthouse. Where are you?"

"At the newspaper office. I wanted to help you with the story."

"Can you pick me up? It's an emergency."

"What's wrong, Matty?"

"My car was stolen. I have to … It's an emergency."

"I'm on my way. Stay by this phone number."

The store clerk refilled the basin. "It's swelling up. What hit you?"

Matty felt she deserved some explanation. "It was a hit and run. Right here on Main Street. Did you see the car?"

"No, I didn't hear anything. You should call the sheriff. What color was the car?"

"I don't know. It happened so fast." Matty didn't want the sheriff involved yet. He had a score to settle. Swift justice was required.

The clerk rummaged through the white pages. "Here's the non-emergency number for the sheriff. I'll dial it for you."

"No," Matty said, taking the phone. "Tell me the number and I'll call."

She gave a number, but he called the News Leader office. Jessie answered.

"I'd like to report a hit and run accident," Matty said.

"Wrong number. This is the Kane News Leader. I'll get the police number for you."

"West Main Street, Smethport.   Right in front of the courthouse," Matty continued.

"Who is this?" Jessie asked. "Hey, is that you, Matty? Where's Tom. You were supposed to make bail for him."

"About ten minutes ago. I was struck by a westbound car..."

"You're delirious, Matty. You're not making sense."

"A description? No, I really didn't see the car."

"Matty, you're worrying me. What's happening with you and Tom?"

"My name?" He looked around Jackie's store. "Christmas, Roger Christmas. I know it's a funny name, but..."

"Quit goofing me, Matty. We have a paper to get out."

"Yes, I'll hold for the deputy on duty." Matty pushed the talk button and heard a dial tone. The clerk applied a gauze pad to his forehead.

In ten minutes, he watched a familiar Volkswagen park in front of the courthouse. Matty thanked his temporary nurse and dashed across the street.

"Keep driving," he told a stunned Megan. "I'll tell you where to turn."

Matty reclined his seat and held a tissue to his forehead. He recounted to Megan the morning's events, including Billy Herman's cast crashing down on his head.

"You're not thinking right," she scolded him. "This is a crime. You have to tell the police."

"I can't. Not right now, Megan. I'm chasing a news story."

"We're chasing trouble. This criminal beat you up, Matty. He'll do it again. Please call the police."

Matty raised his seat. "Can't do that. Besides we're not chasing Billy Herman."

"Then where are we going?" Megan asked.

Despite the bump on his head, Matty's thinking was clear. He recalled what he had told Herman before his lights went out. Dolores Gibson had the silver.

"Step on it, Megan."

Barely cracking 60 miles per hour, the Volkswagen rattled through a blinking light at Lantz Corners. Matty caught a glimpse of a yellowish vehicle in his side mirror.

"Stop!"

Megan braked and pulled to the shoulder. Matty saw two tractor-trailers pass to the north. When traffic cleared, he saw his Mustang parked at a convenience store.

"Wait here," he told Megan.

"No, Matty, let's just stay in the car and watch. We can follow him when he leaves."

Megan turned her Volkswagen to face the store. They waited for a few minutes before Matty became impatient.

"How long is he going to take?" Matty said.

They watched an older man fueling his pick-up and entering the store. A minute later, he returned to his truck and pulled away.

"I can't wait any longer." Matty opened his door and Megan tried to grab his arm. He crossed the highway and stared through a front window. Megan parked at the far gas pump.

"You looking for something, son?" A voice startled him from behind.

"This Mustang," Matty stammered to the stranger, "I'd like to buy it. Is the owner here?"

"Never saw you here before, son. You live around here?"

"Just for the summer. I'm temporary help at the News Leader," Matty replied.

"You work with that fella, Zachary. He fights with cops." The man smiled.

"Yeah," Matty sensed an opening. "You have Coke in bottles?"

"Sure. I'll get you one. Nice car, huh? Somebody left that Mustang here. I guess they'll pick it up later."

Matty followed him into the store. He looked around. No

Billy Herman. A young woman in a denim jumper was dispensing cappuccino from a machine. Otherwise, the place was empty.

"I thought my friend was here," Matty told the man. "About this tall with an arm in a cast. I think that Mustang is his."

"Nope. No one like that came in the store. Jenna," he hollered to the customer, "You see a man with a broken arm here?"

"No," she answered, squeezing another quarter-inch of foam into her cup.

"Well, thanks for the pop. Keep the change." Matty left the store and walked to his car. The keys were in the ignition. He waved to Megan and hopped into his car.

As he pulled to the highway, he heard the woman customer scream that her car was missing. "Somebody stoled my Chevy!" she yelled.

Matty sped away. Megan followed as closely as her engine allowed. A few miles later, he pulled into a parking space at the News Leader. Megan did the same. Matty burst into the office and found Jessie balancing the company checkbook.

"I'm not paying you this week," she told him. "You're a damn nuisance. I can't get my work done, and you haven't contributed anything since Tom got arrested."

"Jessie, dear, I'm close. Give me a few more hours. I promise."

"Mr. Zachary just called. You're in a shitload of trouble."

"I thought he was in jail. How did he call?"

"He just got released. The district attorney dropped the charges. Tom's coming after you. Why didn't you bail him out?"

"It's a long story. Promise me one thing. Hold the front page for me. OK, Jessie?"

"What happened to your face? Somebody beat you up?"

"A one-armed man. And it was his bad arm."

"That's funny," Jessie said. "A half-hour ago, a customer came in here with a broken arm."

"What d-d-did he want?" Matty stuttered.

"Said he wanted to buy last week's paper. He was standing

here reading your story about Dolores Gibson. He seemed real interested."

"Did he say where he was going?"

"No. Not really. He tucked the newspaper under his broken arm. I watched him leave. He had one of those black Chevy Tahoes with the tinted windows."

Matty leaned across the counter and kissed her cheek. "Gotta run."

As he darted out the door, Jessie wiped her face with a tissue. He's in trouble, she thought. Looking at the empty Page One display board, she sighed. "So am I."

The governor's chief of staff put final touches on the 1 p.m. news release. Nothing could be issued, he told Jimmie, until they agreed upon a name. Ann's first suggestion was the best.

Pennoyer reported the birth on the governor's website:

Governor and Mrs. Jimmie Bailey are pleased to announce the birth of their first child, Hannah Maria Bailey, at Kane Community Hospital today at 10:25 a.m. Mother and daughter are doing well. No further details were available.

"Hannah Maria?" Pennoyer had remarked to Jimmie. "Where did that name come from?"

"We wanted a name that reflected Pennsylvania," Jimmie replied.

"So, tell me."

"Well, our founder William Penn had two wives…"

"Not at the same time," Pennoyer guessed.

"After his first wife, Maria, died, he remarried a 26-year-old."

"Let me guess. That chick's name was Hannah," Pennoyer said.

"Exactly."

"That's kind of cool. Should I add that to the news release?"

"No," Jimmie said. "See if anybody figures it out."

"Where is he?" Zachary burst into the News Leader office full of rage.

Jessie cowered behind a roll of newsprint. Her mild-mannered boss had become hardened in jail, as predicted in his upcoming editorial.

"Where's Matty? He has some explaining to do." Zachary pushed the roll and it moved ominously toward his office manager. A rut in the linoleum stopped its advance.

"He's gone," Jessie told him. "He's chasing a man with a broken arm."

"Well, well," Zachary slumped into a swivel chair. "That's Matty's new friend. Do you know he used our money to bail him out of jail? Instead of me?"

"I'm sure Matty had a good reason..."

"That's ten thousand dollars from our account, Jessie. That's what Matty spent to spring a drunk driver out of the McKean County Jail."

Jessie shook her head. "Imagine that. I saw that man driving on Fraley Street in a new SUV. Judge Van Lear should have taken away his license."

Zachary clenched his teeth and shook like a bobblehead doll. "He's not allowed to drive. Holy crap! If Van Lear finds out, he'll revoke the bail and we'll never get our money back."

"Maybe that's why Matty is chasing him."

Zachary rubbed his temples. "Food. I need food. I can't think without food. Get me food!"

"Texas Hot Lunch. Is that OK?"

The editor flipped his hand as if to say, "whatever."

Jessie pulled a card from her Rolodex. "Here's the number, Dillinger. Order it yourself."

Zachary grumbled and reached for the telephone. He ordered four hot dogs with double onions and a large basket of fries, extra salt. Then he started rifling through Jessie's page layouts. She sat in the corner, waiting for him to look up.

"Did Matty talk to you in jail this morning?" Jessie asked.

"Yeah, but we were interrupted by Devlin. He dragged me to court and Matty watched from the back row. He said he had something to talk to me about. What was that?"

Jessie hated to confess her mistake while he had an empty stomach. "Let's wait for your lunch. You'll feel better."

"Why is everybody acting so weird today? Is Matty having some personal troubles? Is he homesick? He's only been here a few weeks."

"No, not that," Jessie replied. "I said something to him this morning that was… Well, I slipped up. It was an honest mistake."

"Tell me, Jessie."

"I got angry and called him a stupid rich kid." Jessie watched her boss's face turn red.

"Oh, for … What did he say?"

"Matty's smart. He picked it up right away. He now believes you chose him for this job because he's Brock Bailey's illegitimate son. Matty thinks you have an ulterior motive."

"I do. I mean, I did," Zachary said. "But he's a terrific writer and has a lot of energy. Everybody loves him. Except for me, about an hour ago."

Zachary recalled his earlier promise to Jimmie. In exchange for introducing Matty to the governor, the News Leader could publish a full story of Brock Bailey's legacy, his two sons and their very different worlds. Zachary viewed the story as his career highlight. It would put the News Leader on the map. Then he could sell the business and look for a profitable opportunity. The problem was this: to reach his goals, he had to drag a fine young man into glare of the national media. Was that fair to an 18-year-old?

Perhaps it was time to talk with Matthew Moore. The truth would be a good place to start. Zachary would own up to his promise with Jimmie Bailey. Then, if Matty wanted to be introduced to the governor, Zachary would do it. If he wanted to keep his anonymity, however, Zachary would agree. The decision would be left to his summer intern, if he ever showed up at work.

But Zachary had a more immediate task. Wednesday's edition was nearing deadline. Pages one and three were full of gaps.

"Why are you holding page one?" he asked Jessie.

"Matty has a story coming. He just needed a few more hours."

"Did he say what his story was about?" Zachary asked.

"Must have been a follow-up to the Dolores Gibson story. He didn't tell me any details, and he hasn't saved any draft on his computer."

"Well, I'm back and I'm taking charge." Zachary shimmied his chair to a computer keyboard. "Has anybody around here heard of the term, 'breaking news?' I don't think so."

Jessie watched her boss punch a 72-point headline into the system: "*First Couple Becomes First Family.*" Below it, in 36-point type, Zachary wrote: "*Pennsylvania Welcomes Baby Girl Bailey.*"

"While you and Matty were playing nice with the one-armed fugitive, I heard WLMI announce that Ann had her baby," Zachary said. "Seems like Page One news to me."

A hot dog delivery boy popped in and placed Zachary's first taste of freedom on the counter. Jessie handed her boss his lunch, a steno pad and the company camera.

"Go get your story, Tom. I'll hold the space for you. Matty can wait until next week."

Chapter Seventeen

The Casino

Monday's lunch crowd at the Golden Wheel had plenty to talk about. First, the News Leader editor was freed after all charges were dismissed. Second, Jenna Peacock's SUV was stolen in plain daylight at Lantz Corners; the thief, still at large. And, third, the baby girl, of course.

Toolie waited on every table. She joined in as much conversation as time permitted. By 1 p.m., she was exhausted. Her manager told her to lie down on the back office couch and said he would bus her tables. Reluctantly, she hung her apron and accepted his offer.

Perhaps sixty-hour work weeks were too much, she wondered. Her legs constantly ached. Her support hose irritated rather than energized. The swelling in her right knee seemed to be growing. She welcomed those few moments when she sat with familiar customers or tallied checks while resting on a bar stool. Otherwise, she worked on her feet.

Toolie closed the back office door. She reclined on the couch and pulled an afghan over her legs. She felt slight tingling down her left arm. Soon it passed. She felt much better. Just a few more minutes, she thought. She closed her eyes and relaxed. Her tables could wait.

Thoughts of the day raced through her mind. Drips of information about the Bailey baby were added by each new customer. At noon, she heard it was a girl. Minutes later, she heard that Ann and the baby were in excellent condition. Then, she heard the weight and length. Soon thereafter, local radio reported the baby's name.

None of that excited Toolie. Rather, she obsessed over the comment of a young woman at 11:30. When Toolie took her order, the woman asked her age. With great pride, Toolie answered.

"How marvelous," the woman replied. "It must be wonderful for you to be in your nineties. You are so lucky."

Toolie felt no luck, just weariness. How could she explain that without sounding old and defeated? She let the comment pass. She could vent later.

Thirty years ago, her mother passed. Her younger sister lasted until five years ago. All Toolie had left were her friends and co-workers at the Golden Wheel. That's why she tenaciously fought advances of age and fiercely guarded her job. No one worked more hours, waited on more customers or carried more food from the kitchen than Toolie. She was determined not to show any deterioration of her energy or mind. She knew that everybody watched her every move and listened to her every word. Heaven forbid if one of these young girls would take her job. What would she do?

In a few hours, her shift would end and she would climb the back stairs to her second-floor apartment. She dreaded the moment. After a day of walking and standing, Toolie found the stairs to be a challenge. Twelve steep steps between two oak handrails. A turn to the right. Then a dozen steps down a musty dark hallway to a door marked "No. 2." When Toolie moved in 50 years ago, the hotel manager advised her that even-numbered rooms were "legitimate." Odd-numbered rooms were "let by the hour," he said. She never crossed the hall.

Inside her apartment were an eat-in kitchen, a living room and a spacious bedroom. Her mother's poster bed occupied a wall opposite a 1950's tile bathroom. Everything was just so. Toolie was organized, the extreme type of organization that comes with spending decades in the same space.

Until recently, Toolie was the boarding house's only tenant. For the past two weeks, a teenage boy in the upstairs apartment both annoyed and comforted her. Hearing his footsteps late at night awoke her, but quickly made her feel safe enough to fall asleep. Whenever his music was too loud, her simple tapping on water pipes cured the problem. She found ways to signal him when he slept through his alarm and when he bounced a soccer ball against the wall.

Toolie never had a son to care for. Nor a son to look after her.

In the past two weeks, Toolie fell twice. The first happened in the bathroom. A throw rug was curled under, and she caught her foot and fell against the door. She vowed to be more observant of such things. The second occurred in her kitchen. She made a quick pivot to open the refrigerator and lost her equilibrium. Her head struck a lower cabinet handle. No one noticed the bruise under her scalp. After that scrape, she tried to move a little slower and more deliberately.

Living alone had its perils. But Toolie was too proud to seek assistance. She ate good meals with the restaurant kitchen help every day. She took over-the-counter painkillers sparingly. Her multi-vitamin was recommended by the American Medical Association. And, if something ever happened, the restaurant manager would probably come looking for her. That combination worked well for the past ten years. Why change anything?

After her 20-minute break, Toolie felt much better. She flung the blanket from her legs and stood. A few deep breaths. Big arm circles. Some ankle rotations. Fit as a fiddle, she thought. Toolie heard laughter from the dining room. She was needed there. She fixed her apron and puffed up her hair. It was show time, and she was the emcee.

Golden Wheel's veteran waitress followed sounds of clanging dishes and sizzling burgers. The main dining room was 15 steps down the hall. She teetered for a moment, catching herself by feeling a chair-rail.

"I'm OK," she reassured herself. Maybe go to bed a little earlier tonight. That would refresh her for tomorrow, she figured.

Toolie slid her fingers along the chair-rail until she reached her waitress station. She forced a smile to a table of state highway workers.

"What'll it be today, fellas?" She poised her pen and winked.

"If I wasn't married, I'd say you, Toolie," the foreman said with a chuckle.

A gleam returned to Toolie's eye. "Well, I know a good divorce attorney."

In his experience as a former city patrol officer, Billy Herman understood where thugs and punks went wrong. He investigated hundreds of car thefts. He knew the usual mistakes.

Most crooks drive too fast. Most leave fingerprints. Most travel in predictable directions. And worst of all, most are clueless about how to unload a 2,000-pound chunk of criminal evidence.

Billy vowed not to make the same mistakes.

Once Billy exited McKean County, he wanted to ditch the toxic Chevy. Unfortunately, he was in the thick of Allegheny National Forest. He could abandon the vehicle off a remote trail where it wouldn't be found for weeks, but how would he get to civilization?

There were no other cars to steal, at least ones that weren't traveling at 60 miles per hour. And if he stole a third car in his ongoing crime spree, he would risk three police reports rather than two.

A Tahoe was not a bad vehicle to steal, though. Billy envisioned ramming through a police blockade. Sawhorses would scatter. Police cruisers would bend like aluminum foil. What a great car, he thought. And, best of all, his SUV had enough cargo room for the precious metal he wanted to steal.

Billy slowed for several sharp road curves near Kinzua Dam. A gleaming motor home was parked at the visitor center. Two seniors were taking photos of each other near an overlook. Some teenagers were feeding geese. A state forestry truck drove onto the lot. Windsurfers were skimming along in the reservoir.

Too much activity here, Billy thought. He rocketed past the dam.

Route 6 followed the Allegheny River for a short distance before winding into Warren. Traffic was minor at mid-afternoon. He pulled into a gas station and filled up.

No police officer was in sight. Billy wondered if the cub newspaper reporter had regained consciousness. Maybe nobody found his body under the shrubs yet. Perhaps he killed the kid with his plaster cast. He didn't hit him that hard, did he?

Surely, someone filed a police report by now, he thought. Nearly an hour had passed since he stole the Mustang, and thirty minutes since he switched the Mustang for a Chevy. Although, if the kid were unconscious and the Chevy owner hadn't made a discovery yet, Billy's getaway was going well. His good fortune would run out at some point, he realized. Police bulletins would target a black Chevy Tahoe with a certain Pennsylvania license plate.

At least he could change the license plate.

Billy took a penny and loosened the rear plate. At the front of the vehicle, he removed the Mount Jewett Volunteer Fire Company license plate. He scoured the lot of a nearby shopping center. A Ford SUV was parked in a remote spot. So Billy switched license plates. With any luck, he thought, the driver would not notice the new plate for months.

Soon, Billy was heading south on Route 8 toward Wexford. It was time for a surprise visit with Mrs. Dolores Gibson and, hopefully, a reunion with his silver treasure.

Mr. George didn't mind being called "The Peacemaker." The role occupied most of his life as a Seneca elder. But he hadn't acted as Peacemaker for a generation. Except for his recent outings with Megan and his translation of her treasure map, Mr. George was largely forgotten in the Seneca community.

That was about to change.

Late Monday afternoon, Mr. George was visited by two thugs. They looked like thugs, although their business cards identified them as "sales associates." Mr. George recognized their company, Pathfinder Gaming Management, LLC.

They encountered him under a veranda behind his retirement home. They were dressed in white shirts and string ties – a weak attempt to appear Indian. Mr. George knew trouble when he saw it.

"Why are you looking for me?" he asked them.

The thuggier thug thrust a Bradford Era newspaper under the Peacemaker's nose. "You know anything about this?"

Mr. George mustered as much dignity as possible. He took the newspaper, fixed his reading glasses and crossed his legs. As he sipped an iced tea, he read an obituary for the shredded Professor Dulaney. All the pertinent information was there: one masticated body, two shovels and three very empty holes.

"Yeah, I heard about this. So what?" he asked.

"My boss thinks you know more than this story," the less-thuggy man said. "He'd like to talk with you."

"Now?"

"Let's check out at the front desk. It's a short drive to our business office."

The two men each took an arm and raised Mr. George to his feet. They escorted him like an indicted crime boss to a waiting limousine. Mr. George sat alone in the back, and he wondered.

Much had changed in the Seneca Nation since Mr. George held sway. Old traditions were dead, replaced by modern methods of money-changing. Slot machines, roulette wheels, and ubiquitous

Bingo parlors dominated the Seneca landscape. Visitors brought their dollar bills. Dollar bills became stacks of chips, stacks of chips became smaller stacks. And all of it ended in casino cash register drawers.

Mr. George understood the economics. American Indians had a unique legal license to peddle untaxed booze, cigarettes and gambling to a nation lacking willpower. Visitors came in droves to Indian establishments.

Money flowed in. Money dribbled out to the Indian nation. In the middle, as always, was a private management company. That's where most of the money went, although nobody could really prove it.

While the Seneca Indians grew poorer, Pathfinder Management prospered. Nobody could fix that; Pathfinder had good attorneys and an iron-clad management contract.

The limousine paused at a security gate. Words were exchanged with a guard. The gate rose, and the vehicle followed a curved driveway toward a steel and glass office building. Mr. George saw two other guards standing under a portico. When the limousine stopped, they opened his door. One guard reached in with his hand and asked Mr. George if he needed help.

He swung his legs and stood on the brick driveway. The two guards accompanied him past a front desk and to a bank of elevators. No words were spoken. Mr. George was shaken, unable to recall any magic words or curse to utter at the moment.

One guard inserted a key next to the fourth floor button and turned it. Then the guards backed out. Mr. George was alone when the elevator car began to rise.

At the fourth floor landing, he was surprised when elevator doors opened behind him. Stainless steel letters were fixed to a wall. "Pathfinder Gaming Management, Your Pathway to Fun and Profit."

"Mr. George?" A size 2 brunette took his elbow. "Please follow me."

She escorted the Peacemaker to a low black leather chair in the reception area. Mr. George lowered himself as much as possible before he let himself crash to the seat.

"Mr. Joseph will be with you shortly. May I get you a cup of coffee?" she asked.

"No, thank you. But I need to use your rest room."

She grunted a bit while pulling him to his feet. They walked around a wood-paneled corner. She pointed to the men's room door. "I'll wait for you at the front desk," she said.

Mr. George, a good five years past standing at a urinal, took the end stall. After he turned the latch and sat down, he heard two men enter. They were young enough to stand at urinals.

"I know what the contract says, but I don't agree with this new aggressive policy," one man said.

"Business is business, Jack. We're managing their assets, so we need to know where their assets are and how much. The 'reds' are stupid when it comes to money."

"Did you read the report about removing squatters from the Cornplanter Reservation? Unbelievable. The way we knocked down that one lady's cabin. What was her name?"

"Maude Thunder. I know. That was my case."

"Why couldn't we let her alone? She wasn't causing any problem."

"Listen, Jack. You need to toughen up. That land is for future development. We don't have a casino in Pennsylvania. I think Mr. Joseph is right. If Maude Thunder squatted on that land long enough, she could claim the land as hers. She could stop any development south of the Kinzua Reservoir."

"I know, Bob. It just seems so callous. The way we torched her house."

"Nobody knows that. Not even Mr. Joseph. Keep it quiet."

Mr. George heard two zips and two flushes. The men walked toward the sinks.

"So who is the senile guy that we picked up today?" one of the men asked.

"His name is Roland George. He was a tribal peacemaker about 40 years ago. Mr. Joseph thinks he has information about some Indian assets he may be hoarding."

"Like what?"

"I dunno, Jack. It has something to do with that professor who was killed by a bear last week. Mr. Joseph thinks he was a fortune hunter."

"Shit. I'm glad that's not my case. I'd hate to beat up an old man."

Mr. George stopped his flow into the toilet and raised his legs out of sight. The men laughed and exited. When the Peacemaker stood, an automatic sensor tripped, sending water gushing into the toilet. He jumped backward in fear.

When all was quiet, Mr. George sneaked to the elevator. He tapped the down button furiously. He felt a hand on his shoulder and he turned.

"Mr. George, are you all right?"

"Yes, sir," he replied to a distinguished looking gentleman. "I'm a little confused. Is this the way out?"

"Let me help you, Mr. George. Please come with me."

The two men passed a secretarial station and entered a long hallway. On either side were framed photographs of various Indian gambling houses. Above the photographs were brass picture lamps and gold lettering in the words: New York, Florida, Oklahoma and South Dakota.

"These are some of our properties, Mr. George," the man said proudly. "Pathfinder is the largest gaming management company in the world. And we're honored to be affiliated with your people."

No further introduction was needed. The tour guide was Mr. Joseph himself.

"Please sit." Mr. Joseph directed his guest to a leather side chair in his opulent corner office. Floor to ceiling windows allowed an unhealthy dose of afternoon sunshine to illuminate Mr. George.

"May I interest you in a Cuban?" Mr. Joseph asked.

"I gave up smoking years ago."

"That's why you're the only old Seneca left." Mr. Joseph fired up a cigar and blew his grayish exhaust over the Peacemaker's head. "You know where all the bodies are buried. That's why I invited you for a visit."

"The invitation must've got lost in the mail."

"That's amusing, Mr. George. I'd love to chat, but my time is valuable. So I'll get to the point. Do you know a girl named Megan Broward?"

"I've met her. She was writing a college paper about the Seneca relocation."

"Mr. George, Mr. George. Now we want you to be honest. You know more about Megan Broward, don't you? You know, for example, that she was a student of Professor Dulaney, and you know that she found an Indian treasure map."

"Yes, but..."

"And you know that Professor Dulaney was probably looking for Indian treasure when he died, right?"

Mr. George stammered. "I-I really don't know what he was doing. I never met the man."

"Stop lying, you bastard." Mr. Joseph was no longer distinguished. "Listen to me for a second, George. Nothing happens around here without me knowing. OK? We have a contract with your people. It's legal and it's binding. It runs forever unless we say so."

"I'm an old man," the Peacemaker interjected. "I know nothing about the white man's law."

"Shut up, old man. Let me put it in words that even an old Seneca can understand. Pathfinder Gaming manages all of the tribe's assets. We own a percentage of everything. Got it? If you're hiding silver, we're going to find it."

"I'm not hiding silver. I don't know what you're talking about."

Mr. Joseph pushed an intercom button. "Susie, tell the guards to return Mr. George to his nursing home. He needs his afternoon meds."

Chapter Eighteen
The Stray

Megan saw the disoriented dog before he did.

"Matty! Watch out!"

He swerved his car, narrowly missing the dog.

"Holy heck, Megan. That was Cuddles!"

Matty pulled to the shoulder and parked. They were nearly two miles from Dolores Gibson's house. How did her dog get this far away?

Megan unbuckled and caught her breath. "Cuddles? You know the dog's name?"

"This one, yeah."

"What? You could read its tag at 50 miles per hour?"

Matty watched the animal limp from the road. "No, I met this dog last week. Cuddles belongs to Mrs. Gibson. I didn't hit her, did I?"

"I don't think so. But she needs help." Megan walked behind him.

"Hi, girl. It's all right. I'll take you home." Matty approached slowly.

Cuddles appeared to be in no mood to make friends. The cocker spaniel backed away from him and gritted her teeth. For once, her tail stopped wagging.

"It's me. Matty. Come here, Cuddles. Let's go home."

When the dog heard her name, she sat. Matty and Megan walked to her. Cuddles sniffed Matty's shoes and put her paws on his jeans. He reached down and pulled her up with one hand.

"Is she OK?" Megan stroked the brown fur on the dog's back.

"She seems all right. No broken bones that I can tell. Maybe she's just tired walking this far from home."

"Hold her and I'll drive," Megan insisted. "Cuddles seems to be comfortable in your arms."

They returned to his car and Megan took the wheel. She turned the ignition and said to Matty, "This is kind of spooky, isn't it?"

"You're thinking what I'm thinking," he replied.

She pulled onto the roadway and drove well below the speed limit. "I don't want to go to Gibson's house. Something bad has happened there. I just feel it."

"I'm feeling a little of that intuition myself." Matty also felt a racing heartbeat from the dog.

"Let's call the police," she said. "We'll report a stray dog and the cops will investigate. We can watch from a distance."

The thought had occurred to Matty. But they were so close now. Maybe he could prevent something bad from happening.

"I'll make a deal with you, Megan. We'll drive to the house. If we see a Chevy Tahoe in the driveway, we'll call the police. If not, we'll investigate ourselves."

"You're braver than I am," she said.

"Or stupider."

Megan rounded the final curve at a snail's pace. She cut the ignition and shifted to neutral. The Mustang rolled to a quiet stop past a grove of maple trees.

The long driveway to the Gibson house was empty. Matty could see the front screen door open and blowing in the afternoon breeze.

"Do you suppose there's a car inside her garage?" Megan asked.

"Only one way to find out." Matty handed her the dog.

"Be careful," she called to him in a hushed voice.

Matty scampered behind a tree line and angled toward the house. He heard no sounds from inside. He could see no lights. An outdoor air conditioning unit clicked on and a loud whoosh startled him. When his courage returned, Matty stepped to a side door and peered into the garage.

He motioned to Megan that the garage was empty as well. She decided to stay in the car.

Matty then circled around to the back yard. Most of the blinds were closed. He climbed onto a rear deck and looked through partially open vertical blinds into the kitchen. Everything was in order. No dishes were on the table. The countertops were not cluttered.

In a corner, near the refrigerator, were two overturned dog bowls. Brown nuggets were scattered. A puddle of water collected near one of the bowls. Matty noticed muddy paw prints on the tile floor.

He tested the sliding doors. They were locked. A metal bar placed in the channel secured the slider. Matty rubbed his sleeve on the door handle to erase any fingerprints.

A squirrel scampered on the roof above him. Its feet loosened granules from the asphalt shingles. He heard little pings as the aggregate rolled into metal gutters. Matty's hearing was finely tuned. He would have heard any movement inside the house. Either Dolores was sleeping or, God forbid, she was...

Cuddles squirmed in Megan's arms. The dog began to whimper. Megan tried to calm her, but the whimpers were getting louder. She worried about Matty. He hadn't been visible for nearly ten minutes.

"Quiet, girl. Just hold on a little longer."

Cuddles barked. She saw her house. Megan knew the dog was thirsty. The closest water could be a place of danger, she thought.

Matty scurried from the rear yard into the maple trees. Megan watched him pick his way through the brush and return to her side window.

"Except for the front door, everything is closed up," he told her.

Cuddles barked again.

"This dog is thirsty," she said. "What should we do?"

Matty reached through the open window and pulled Cuddles from the car. "There's water on the kitchen floor. She can find it."

"No, Matty. That's too dangerous for her."

"Well, Megan, you've got a choice. It's me or the dog. One of us is going in."

She petted the dog's head. "Good luck, girl."

Matty carried Cuddles to the front sidewalk. He set her feet down and whispered, "Go on. There's water for you near the refrigerator."

He watched the dog trot to the front door landing, force open the unlatched screen door and disappear inside. Matty listened near the front door.

The dog's toenails clicked on the tile floor. Matty traced her movements. First, to the kitchen. Then to the foyer and down the hall. The dog stopped into the hall bathroom for a moment. Then the toenails clicked down the hallway. She headed toward the back study.

Cuddles seemed to pause in the study. Matty heard the dog whimpering and scratching. Minutes passed with no other sounds.

Matty grew impatient and returned to the car.

"What's happening?" Megan asked.

"The dog walked all through the house and seemed to stop in the back room. I heard some crying sounds and then everything was silent."

"Let's call the police," Megan insisted.

Matty scratched his head. "I don't think anyone's moving around inside. I would have heard something."

"They're not moving because they're dead, Matty."

"Let's not overreact. There's probably a good explanation for this." He tried to calm her. "Maybe Dolores went to the supermarket and forgot to close the front door. Cuddles escaped and…"

"And walked for two miles? I don't think so. Did you see how fast Cuddles ran back to her house? She's a cocker spaniel, not a Siberian Husky."

Matty had to agree. But he didn't concede her argument that a dead body was inside.

Megan continued with her explanation. "Everything seems obvious to me, Matty. You told Billy Herman that the silver was at Josh Gibson's house. He plunked you on the nose, stole your car and switched it with another stolen car. He drove to the News Leader office and got a copy of your article about Dolores Gibson."

"But the article didn't say where she lived," Matty said.

"Didn't you tell me that Gibson and Herman worked closely together on the Brock Bailey case years ago? Herman probably knew where Gibson lived. Maybe he even visited here."

"So you think that Billy Herman stopped here, killed Dolores and stole the silver?" Matty asked her.

"Look!" Megan pointed to the front door.

Cuddles was pushing the screen door with her nose. The dog's tail was dragging. She curled into a ball on the front step and buried her head in her body.

"I'm going in," Matty said. "You can stay here or..."

"We're this far," Megan replied. "We might as well go together."

This time, Matty walked defiantly up the driveway and onto the sidewalk. Megan followed at a close distance. Cuddles lifted her head a bit when they passed.

Matty held the screen door for Megan and they stepped into the foyer. Still no sounds. He put his index finger to her lips and pointed down the hallway. The study door was partially open – enough to allow a small dog to go in and out. Matty edged the door open with his knuckle.

No one was there, either dead or alive.

"Let's check the other rooms," Megan whispered.

"Not yet," Matty said. He leaned past her and pulled a knob

on the bi-fold closet doors.

"No dead body in there either," Megan said.

"The silver, it's gone. Somebody's taken it." Matty rubbed the floor with his hand. Bits of silver clung to his palm.

"The Indian silver?"

"Yes, Megan. What the Peacemaker told you about. The silver that got Josh Gibson killed and the professor killed and…"

"And probably Dolores killed," she added.

Matty turned and nearly stepped on Cuddles. The dog backed away quickly.

"What do you know, girl?" Matty wanted to interview the only witness, but a cocker spaniel is predominantly nonverbal. Cuddles backed from the room. Her nails clicked down the hall. She stopped and sniffed at a closed door.

"She smells something," Megan said. "Should we open this door next?"

Matty turned the knob.

"No visitors!"

The cop stationed outside Ann Bailey's hospital room was resolute.

"No visitors, and especially no visitors with cameras."

Tom Zachary tried to engage him in polite conversation. "What a wonderful moment. Should we call her the First Baby of Pennsylvania? Have you seen her?"

"No visitors, on orders of the Governor." The officer crossed his beefy arms.

Zachary would not be dissuaded. His deadline for Wednesday's edition was fast approaching. He scribbled a note on his business card.

"Here," he said, handing the note to the guard. "Tell Mrs. Bailey that her favorite newspaper editor wants just a few minutes of her time."

"You don't seem to understand, Mr. Zachary. When a police officer tells you not to do something, DON'T DO IT! Do you want another weekend in jail?"

This time, Zachary backed off. He needed a back-up plan. He could take a photo of the hospital entrance. He could take some shots of the hospital nursery. Or he could point his camera at the surly guard.

"Hey, no photos!" The officer cupped his hand over the lens. "Why, I should arrest you right here and haul your sorry ass off to Van Lear."

Before Zachary could say, "First Amendment," the governor exited an elevator and broke up the combatants.

"Tom, Tom, my friend." Jimmie put his arm around Zachary. "How nice of you to pay us a visit. Have you seen Hannah Maria?"

The guard stopped fingering his handcuffs. "Sorry, sir. You ordered no visitors."

"My apologies, Tom. That was my order."

"But you can rescind it, right? For your friend?" Zachary asked.

"Every rule has an exception, Tom. Just give me a second to make sure Ann can see you." Jimmie entered the hospital room as the guard glared at his lost prey. Zachary raised his camera for a pretend photograph. The officer stuck out his tongue.

Ann was resting in her hospital gown. Beside her was a hospital bassinet. A floor nurse was discarding a moist towelette before tugging a plastic diaper around the infant's waist. "Everything looks good, Mrs. Bailey," she announced.

Jimmie enjoyed holding his clean baby. "She smells so fresh."

"They bathed her here this morning. She loved it." Ann sat up and reached for his hand. "They're teaching me how to breast feed. The class is in a half-hour. Do you want to join me?"

Jimmie smiled. He'd had enough of the pre-natal classes. Too much detail, he'd say. Ann always reminded him that he was at least half responsible.

Meanwhile, Zachary paced the hall in anticipation of an exclusive front page photograph. His mind spun ideas for a caption. The best he could conjure was "Hannah Maria, Wowie-a!" Hopefully, Jessie had better suggestions.

In a few minutes, Jimmie opened the door and invited the editor inside. Ann had changed into a designer top. Her hair was perfect, as always. The baby was sleeping in her arms.

A photo couldn't wait. Tom asked Ann to smile and clicked several shots. Jimmie sat sidesaddle on the bed and put his arm around the new mother and child. Afternoon sunshine cast a healthy glow on the First Family. Tom couldn't wait to design Page One.

"Thank you so much for letting me share this moment." Zachary tucked his camera deep into its case.

"Don't you have any questions?" Ann asked.

He looked at his watch. "Sure, maybe a couple. When will you be released to go home?"

"The doctor wants me to rest here another day," Ann replied. "As you know, we had a high-risk pregnancy."

Tom nodded. "Is Jimmie sleeping here overnight as well?"

Ann looked at her husband. "He'd better."

"I have to watch the breast-feeding," Jimmie said.

"Don't quote him on that." Ann knew the rules of reporting.

"May I visit you at Leigh-Rose and take some family photographs there for next week's edition?" Tom asked.

"Give Pennoyer a call," Jimmie replied. "He will handle those details. And by the way…"

"Yes, Governor?"

"We have some other business to discuss as well. See if Pennoyer can schedule an appointment."

Zachary understood that Jimmie wanted to be introduced soon to his half-brother. If only Zachary could keep Matty at his newspaper desk long enough to talk about it, he thought.

"Oh," Zachary remembered. "I know where you came up with

that name, Hannah Maria. She was a famous 19th century artist. I looked it up on the Internet."

Jimmie led him from the room. "Can't get anything past you, Tom."

The door opened to Dolores Gibson's master bedroom. Matty and Megan surveyed the messy scene. Bedcovers were tossed on the floor. Two robes were flung over a post. A basket of unfolded laundry sat on a chair. Drapes were closed. An overhead fan whirred on its lowest setting.

"Looks like someone left in a hurry," Megan said.

Matty stepped over the strewn sheets. He checked out the master bath. Water droplets still clung to marble shower tiles. A curling iron plugged to a wall socket was cold. He saw whisker stubble in the sink.

Cuddles sniffed the bed sheets. The dog grasped them in her mouth and pulled them to the floor. Megan watched the dog uncover a manila envelope.

"Matty, look at this." Megan read handwriting on the outside. "Randall O'Boyd, Personal. Do you know that name?"

"Sounds familiar, maybe somebody in Pittsburgh," he said. "What's inside?"

Megan reached in. "Oh, my …"

"What is it?" Matty took the glossy photos from her hand.

"It's pornography," Megan said. "How disgusting."

"Wait." Matty examined the photographs more closely. "This is Dolores. Not bad. I guess she has a secret life."

"Let me see." Megan decided to look for investigative reasons. "She's with a man about half her age, looks like."

"That's not Billy Herman." Matty turned the photo 90 degrees. "He couldn't arch his back that far. I never saw this guy before."

"Do you think this man stole her silver?" Megan asked.

"Well, we know he was here. These photos were taken at Dolores's front door."

"Why would somebody do that – stand naked at their front door and have photos taken?"

"That's a personal question for Randall O'Boyd, Personal, I think."

Megan returned the photographs to their envelope and placed it on the bed. She pulled sheets over the envelope as Cuddles hugged her leg. Finally, the dog's tail wagged.

"It seems like we've reached the end of this investigation. There's no body, there's no silver and our only witness is drooling on my slacks," she said.

"Let's take a minute and figure out what happened here," Matty said. "I think Dolores and her boyfriend were mixing it up in bed when Billy Herman surprised them. He forced them to undress at the front door and he took their photos."

"Why would he do that?" Megan asked.

"Because he's depraved and he's a low-life. Anyway, he forces them into his car and drives them to a remote location and ..."

"Kills them, right?"

"Right. Then he cuts them into little pieces and feeds them to large-mouth bass in the Ohio River."

"So then he comes back for the silver?" Megan guessed.

"No," Matty replied. "Billy doesn't have enough time to do that. He holds them in his car while he loads silver in the back."

"So they just sit there while he steals the silver?"

"No, that wouldn't work. I know. He forces them to load the silver while he watches. He only has use of one arm. Remember?"

"That's a preposterous theory, Matty."

"Well, what's yours?"

"OK. Judging from the mess in this room, I'd say that two passionate people slept here last night. We can agree on that."

"Randall O'Boyd Personal and Dolores, correct?" Matty asked.

"They seem to get along, yes. Afterward, they left together, probably in Dolores's car."

"That makes sense," Matty said, "because her car is missing."

"Right. Now two questions remain: who took the silver and was Billy Herman here?"

Matty thought for a second. "Since Billy could only use one arm, it would take him hours to move hundreds of silver bars from this house. So I'm thinking it was Dolores and her boyfriend who took it."

"I agree," Megan said. "Now the second question, was Billy Herman here?"

The home telephone rang. A voice recorder on the nightstand clicked on. Matty and Megan waited to hear the caller's voice.

"Hello, my name is Jerome DesBois. I am an attorney representing Darla O'Boyd. This message is for Randall, if you are there. Mrs. O'Boyd will be filing divorce papers first thing tomorrow, based on your infidelity. If you wish to keep this matter from public view, please call me immediately. My secretary will provide further details."

A female voice confirmed the name and spelling of her firm and its telephone number. She closed with "Have a Good Day."

Megan jotted down the number and turned to Matty. "I guess the photographs were taken by the wife's private investigator. Maybe Darla will end up with the silver."

A light bulb went off in Matty's head. "Now, I remember. Randall and Darla O'Boyd. They advertise all the time. They're preachers from some whacked-out church in McKees Rocks. Wow, that will be some divorce case!"

Megan pointed to the door. "Let's go, Sherlock. We don't belong here."

Matty started to follow her. Cuddles clung to his ankle. "What about the dog?"

"That depends," she answered. "Is Dolores dead or alive?"

"I think she's alive."

"Then, put out some food and water. We'll leave Cuddles in

the house and close the front door."

"No," Matty said, "I can't do that."

He carried the dog under his arm, and they left the house as they found it.

Chapter Nineteen
The Motel

Most of Jessie's headline ideas were easily discarded.

"Pa. Governor is Pa Governor." Tom Zachary said no. Readers could miss the abbreviation period, he said. Visually confusing.

"That's Our Baby." Refused by the editor. Zachary thought the headline forewarned of a paternity suit.

"Commonwealth Cutie." Also turned down because such a headline violated Zachary's golden rule: the News Leader confined opinions to its editorial page.

Zachary arranged ten photographs on his desk. Most likely, he would use the best two for Wednesday's edition. He called every female employee to his computer screen for their opinions; such things cannot be decided by a man.

"This one and this one." The circulation manager chose her favorites.

"But the Governor's eyes are closed here," Zachary pointed out.

"Nobody will care about the Governor, Tom. The readers want to see the best picture of little Hannah. Look how sweet."

She was right. Zachary's photo captured the First Baby in her mother's arms. Soft sunlight. A little curl at the top of Hannah Maria's head. And a slight but adoring smile. It was the best portrait of the infant. He decided to crop out the drowsy governor.

Jessie leaned over his desk. "How's your story coming along, Tom? We have thirty-three column inches to fill."

What could he possibly write to fill thirty-three inches? Maybe if he started at the conception and worked forward, he thought. No, too much information.

"I really didn't have enough time to ask questions," he told Jessie. "Anyway, what could I ask? Natural or epidural? Did Jimmie and Ann breathe in unison? Did the baby make a doody yet?"

Jessie pointed to her Page One design sheet. "Thirty-three inches, Tom. Gotta fill it."

"Can we blow up this photo? Maybe life-size? That would fill the page."

Jessie shook her head. "Let's be tasteful. Anything wider than three columns would look sensational, like a New York tabloid. Besides, this could be the first of many babies. We'd have to devote the same amount of space to each one."

Zachary measured the remaining hole on his front page. "Looks like about twenty inches. Didn't you say that Matty had a story coming?"

"That's what he told me this morning," Jessie replied. "He said to hold the page, but he didn't tell me anything else. Can he be trusted?"

"Well, it's 4 o'clock now," Zachary said. "I'm staying late to finish my story and photo layout. If Matty shows up with something before noon tomorrow, I'll squeeze it in."

Dolores Gibson needed another little shampoo bottle. Surely, she would be taking a second shower in the morning. One shampoo wouldn't be enough for both of them.

Late that morning, Pastor Randy had driven her to his church parking lot. She retrieved her car and followed him. They drove south of Pittsburgh on Route 51. She followed his sports car past several three-star hotels. On the right was the one-star Twilight Motel.

When he signaled to turn at the Twilight sign, she anticipated a fun, cheap-hotel experience. Now that he left her for a few hours "to take care of some business," she felt cheap. He promised to return by dinner time.

Dolores had known Randy for only two days. She loved his smile and everything below it. If only he wasn't married to "DTW," his abbreviation for Darla The Witch, he said. Then his mind wouldn't wander as much as his hands did. And did his hands wander, Dolores dreamed.

The Twilight Motel offered a full range of premium movie channels. Dolores turned up the volume. Still, she was unable to tell if the bed squeaks and bathroom noises came from the units next door or the television. She checked the parking lot to make sure Randy actually left the premises rather than simply moving his car a few doors up.

Dolores was hungry. She was tired. Most of all, she was anxious to spend the night in his arms.

First, though, Pastor Randy would be seeing another woman for a few minutes that afternoon.

Randy received the woman's text message when he drove from the Twilight Motel lot. She would meet him in the church vestibule at 2 p.m. They had "details 2 discuss," the message said. Her "atty. wd not b there."

Randy couldn't wait to see her. So much had happened. So much of it good.

"Darla, Darla The Wonderful!" He swept his wife into his arms and twirled her. "This is unbelievable. Everything is working out so perfectly."

She loved his enthusiasm, especially when it was accompanied by dollar bills.

He fell onto a church pew and pulled her close. "We're rich," he whispered in her ear.

"Randy, you devil! Did she fall for it, the photos, everything?"

"Ev-er-y-thing. She believes that she is the other woman. In fact, I think she kinda likes it. That makes her feel important."

Darla pushed away. Her look said more than her question: "Do you like it?"

"Hell, no. With that old bag of bones? No way." He pushed up his sleeves. "But sometime's a man's gotta do…"

"What his wife tells him to do," Darla said.

Randy had too much energy to sit. He stood and paced before his wife.

"Do you think she'll lend you money? You know, for our divorce?" Darla asked.

"DTW, not just money. This woman has a shitload of silver bars," Randy said.

"How many?"

"About 400."

"Worth what?"

"I dunno. Maybe a few million dollars."

"Shit," Darla said. "Did you take any?"

"No. They're sitting on the floor of her freaking closet."

"Why didn't you put a few in your pockets?" Darla asked.

"No. That would be dishonest." Sincerity became him.

"OK, preacher man. How do you propose to get the silver?"

Randy had a plan. It involved a sleazy motel, a few drinks and a blank contract. He decided not to tell her the part about the motel.

"Don't get her drunk, Randy. She'll have a defense against the contract in court," Darla said. "Just use your art of persuasion. She'll sign."

"I think I know how to persuade her."

He did know. It was simple. Just unfasten her top button.

Randy returned to the Twilight Motel about twilight. He carried an envelope and pen. His two knocks on the motel door caused Dolores's heart to twitter. She flicked off "Wheel of Fortune," and unbolted the door. She let her negligee do the talking.

He softly pushed back her hair and kissed her forehead. Her

hands gripped his shoulders and pulled him toward the bed. So far so good, he thought.

"Dee Dee?"

"Yes?" Her lips were coming at him like sideways salamis.

"You're insatiable."

"Satiate me, Randy."

Maybe no unbuttoning was needed. This woman would sign her soul to the devil for a little romp, he thought. Time for business.

"I'm worried. Darla's got an attorney and she's suing me for divorce," he said. "Darla thinks I'm having an affair with you."

Dolores ripped off his belt. "Enough about Darla."

Randy had to slow her down a bit. "But I'm worried about you, Dee Dee."

"Don't worry about me, cowboy. I can handle myself. Now kick off those shoes."

"Wait a sec." He raised the envelope to block her advancing face.

"What's this?" Dolores backed away while he removed the letter.

"We have to protect your assets, Dee Dee. If we don't, Darla will come after your money and all of that silver. I know it."

"I don't see how ..."

"We need to stop her," Randy said. "So I've drafted an agreement that explains what you own and what I own. Just to be safe."

"But this says the silver will belong to the church. That's not right. Is it, Randy?"

"Oh, that. It must be a misprint. We'll fix that later." He started to untie a negligee string behind her neck.

"I can't sign something with a misprint. You'll have to fix that."

His nose nuzzled behind her ear. She could feel his warm tongue.

"You don't trust me, Dee Dee?" he whispered through her

moist ear.

"Absolutely." She cupped her hands behind him, pulling him closer.

Randy struggled to pull a pen from his shirt pocket. The pen fell when she bit his neck. He stamped his free hand on the bed to find it. No luck.

"I've waited for hours, Randy. Where were you?"

"Ah, I just stopped at the church to check on a few things. Now about this letter..."

"Screw the letter. Let's enjoy this moment." She batted the papers from his hand and bulldozed him into the worn mattress. She ripped his shirt from his trousers and tried to pull it over his head.

"Dee Dee, hold on." His plaintiveness was ignored by the aroused widow.

"Let's do something kinky, Randy." She had a wild look.

"The letter..."

"I'll sign your letter," she said. "After the fun."

"What fun?"

She pinned his shoulders to the bed. "Turn on the shower. There are shampoos and oils in the bathroom. We'll start there."

Dolores loosened her grip. He moved to the bathroom and threw his remaining clothes out to her. She smiled and wrote on the letter while Randy watched. He started the shower and stepped in. Soon steam filled the bathroom.

"Be right there, my little Randy man."

Dolores, contrary to every temptation she felt at the moment, jumped into her clothes and grabbed her purse. For added fun, she took his pants, underwear and car keys for later disposal.

Soap up really well, preacher man, she thought. Cleanliness is next to godliness.

Chief of staff Pennoyer was surprised that hooligan Billy Herman not only survived his high-speed crash, but that he was discharged from Kane Community Hospital that morning. A floor nurse told Pennoyer that Billy was released into the waiting arms of two county deputies for immediate transport to McKean County Courthouse.

Pennoyer's call to the McKean sheriff was equally distressing. Judge Van Lear arraigned the miscreant, set a modest bail and signed a release order. Billy was loose!

"How in the hell did he post bond?" Jimmie asked Pennoyer.

"According to the sheriff's office, your friend Tom Zachary paid $10,000 for his release."

Jimmie shook his head. "Thick as thieves," he muttered.

"What do you want me to do?" Pennoyer asked.

"There should be a pre-trial services officer who knows his whereabouts. Find out if he's reported to his officer. We need to know where he is."

"I have a bad feeling about this, Jimmie. Billy seems to be acting like a desperate man."

Jimmie watched Ann finish the 6 p.m. feeding. Hannah Maria started to drift asleep.

"You know I'd do anything to keep my family safe," he told Pennoyer. "Billy Herman has been threatening me for five years, and he's getting worse."

"He keeps cheating death," Pennoyer said.

"Cheaters eventually lose," Jimmie replied.

A nurse intervened. "May I take the baby back to our nursery for a few hours? Your wife could use some rest."

"Sure, ma'am." Jimmie assessed the situation. "Could I speak with the physician on call? If possible, we'd like to go home tonight."

"That's unusual, but ..." The nurse stammered.

"Tomorrow, all the media will be here," he said. "That will be very stressful for Ann. We'd like our privacy. I'm sure you understand."

"I'll speak to the doctor, sir."

Pennoyer nodded in agreement. "That's wise. We have much better security in place at Leigh-Rose Mansion.

This should be a moment of great joy, Jimmie thought. Were his fears justified, he wondered. How could he have been manipulated by such a two-bit scoundrel?

Cuddles sniffed but didn't chew Matty's extra hamburger. The dog turned up her nose, circled the back seat a few times and then fell asleep. Matty and Megan shared some fries and some theories about the missing silver.

"When I interviewed Dolores last week, she was confused. She didn't know what to do with the silver," Matty said. "Maybe she was running low on money and she sold it."

"That would explain her boyfriend," Megan said. "Maybe he's a high-priced gigolo who pretends to be a preacher."

"Megan, you don't understand Randall and Darla O'Boyd. They run a mega-church in McKees Rocks. They prey on people like Dolores. P-R-E-Y preying. My guess is that Dolores's new money makes her a very attractive parishioner for the O'Boyds."

"So you think the telephone message from Darla's attorney is a set-up?"

"Don't you?" he asked. "When you grow up in East Liberty like I did, you see all of the scams. Especially from the people who say they are doing God's work. It's only about taking money."

"Not much we can do, Matty. The silver is gone. So is your story."

He had to agree. Dolores had apparently sold out for flesh. Why bother using any more ink on her?

Matty and Megan drove onto the News Leader parking lot. Darkness was falling. The office was closed. Tomorrow he would admit to Mr. Zachary that no blockbuster story was coming. His whole week was a dud.

"Are you OK, Matty?" she asked.

"Just a little disappointed. Seems like I've screwed everything up. Billy Herman would still be in jail if I hadn't paid his bond. He wouldn't be stealing cars or messing with dogs and silver. Dolores probably would be safe at home. And I could be doing real newspaper work."

"Do you want me to stay with you for a while?" Megan asked.

"That's very nice of you, but I'll be all right," he replied. "I do have one favor to ask."

"Anything."

"I'm not allowed to have pets at the boarding house. Toolie would hear the dog shuffle around and she'd report me to the landlord in a heartbeat. So could you?"

"Oh, Matty, I can't. I live in a dorm. No pets allowed. Just explain it to Toolie. I'm sure she would understand."

No, she wouldn't, Matty realized. Toolie probably was looking for any reason to turn him in, he thought. He was hogging the hot water.

"I'm going back to Edinboro," Megan said. "It's been a long day. Call me in the morning and tell me what you're going to do about Cuddles."

She patted the dog, and then kissed Matty politely on his cheek. "Thank you for keeping me safe. You'll get your story ... someday."

"There's always next week's edition."

Matty helped her into her Volkswagen. She smiled, then turned the car to the west.

He watched her drive away.

Fraley Street was deserted at dusk. Matty decided to exhaust the dog by walking her through the business district and back to Kane Boarding House. She stayed close to his heels along the strange sidewalks. He stopped at a convenience store for some pet food and a chocolate bar for himself later.

Cuddles was full of energy. So Matty decided to take the long walk home.

Meanwhile, Megan's cell phone sounded about ten minutes into her drive. She recognized the New York State area code.

"Hello, Mr. George?"

"Miss Broward, I am so happy to reach you."

"What is it? Why are you calling so late?"

"I had a scare today. And I believe it involves you," the Peacemaker said.

"Me?"

"Two guards from the casino came into the retirement home and took me in a limousine. They drove me to the casino company's headquarters. They pushed me into an elevator and, the next thing I know, I was in the main guy's office."

"Why, Mr. George?"

"You had called them up. You asked a lot of questions. They know you have a map and that you used me to translate Indian markings on it."

"Why are they interested?" Megan asked.

"Because this company has a contract. They think they own a percentage of the Indian silver. They're coming after me and you."

"We don't have any silver. Did you tell them that, Mr. George?"

"I did, but they don't believe me."

Megan felt sorry for having involved the Peacemaker in her episode with Matty. She worried for his safety.

"Are they coming back?" she asked.

"I think so. They are goons. I overheard one of them saying I'll get beaten."

"You need to get out of there, Mr. George. Can you get on a bus tomorrow and I'll meet you at the Edinboro stop in the morning?"

"I'll find a way, Megan. I'll pack clothes for a few days if you can find me a place to stay."

"Sure. Keep my phone number handy. I'll wait for your call when you arrive here."

"Bless you, young lady."

Megan tried to call Matty, but he didn't pick up. She tried again five minutes later without success. Perhaps he was still walking the cocker spaniel. Maybe he already was sleeping.

She eased her car into the dormitory parking lot about 10 p.m. She found a space under a streetlight. If Mr. George was right, there might be someone waiting for her, a goon from the casino in New York. She tried to dismiss the thought, but couldn't.

To be safe, she called for a campus escort to her dormitory. They walked briskly across the quad. Her escort stayed until she entered the residence hall.

Megan checked her messages. No visits or calls from any goon from New York.

A slow-moving elevator cranked and carried her to the fourth floor. The hallway was empty. Only a few dorm rooms were occupied during the summer session. Her unit was at the end of the corridor.

The door was secure. She inserted her key and found everything as she had left it that morning. The twin bed was unmade. Her laptop was open on her desk. Clean laundry was folded in a plastic basket. Her room was dark except for a night-light in the bath.

Satisfied that she had completed a safe journey, Megan turned the dead-bolt lock.

The only sound was her beating heart.

Chapter Twenty
The Chase

Dolores Gibson returned home at midnight.

Horrifyingly, her house was lacking animal and mineral.

"Cuddles! Here, girl!" No dog.

"I've been robbed!" No silver.

Dolores sat and sobbed a good hour before calling the Pine Township police.

A night sergeant was dispatched to the crime scene. He arrived quickly. All the cops were familiar with the Gibson estate. Dolores had a widespread reputation, after all.

"Calm down, Mrs. Gibson. Let's start at the beginning. What did you see when you arrived at the house?"

"My landscape lighting was on, and the front door was wide open. I don't remember leaving it open when I left."

"Hmmm." The sergeant examined the door jamb. "No signs of forced entry. Mind if I look around?"

"No, but pardon the mess. I've been away all day."

The detective tested the outside doors. All were locked. The windows were secured as well.

Dolores took the opportunity to refresh her chemical intake in the hall bath.

Meanwhile, the detective entered her garage. Expensive tools hung from pegboard walls. Top of the line lawn equipment occupied one corner. Her car engine was still warm. He reached through the passenger and lifted clothes from the seat — wrinkled khaki trousers, a white dress shirt and men's underwear rolled in a ball.

He startled her in the hallway. "Did you bring anybody home with you tonight?"

"No, officer. I was alone."

He continued his search inside the house. "May I open this door?" he asked.

"If you must. That's my master bedroom. Quite a mess."

The detective noticed two robes tossed on a nightstand and the bed in disarray. "Did you sleep here last night?"

"Yes, officer."

"Alone?"

"Well, Cuddles was here."

How endearing, he thought. She has a cute name for her conquests.

"Mrs. Gibson, I'd like to take a statement from this 'Cuddles.' Where is he now?"

"HE is a SHE, officer!"

"Pardon me, ma'am. I didn't know you were..." The sergeant turned two shades of purple. "I don't mean to pry into your personal matters. What people do in their own bedrooms is their own..."

"Cuddles is my cocker spaniel," Dolores interrupted. "She's missing. Didn't your dispatcher tell you?"

"Right, right. The dog." His color returned. "Does Cuddles run away often?"

"Never," she replied. "Cuddles is scared of the outdoors. Defecation is her worst time of day. I'm really afraid she's been harmed."

"I'm not aware of any reports of found dogs. There's not much we can do about Cuddles until morning," he said. "Other than your dog, is anything missing?"

"Yes. I had some valuables in the back room. They were taken."

"Approximate value?"

"Several million dollars, I think."

The sergeant stopped writing and glared at the now-calm victim. "Exactly what kind of valuables are we talking about?"

"My husband, God bless him, was a silver collector..."

"So," the detective said, "silver plates, goblets, trays, stuff like that?"

"Oh, no," Dolores replied. "Large silver bars, hundreds of them."

"Show me where they were."

Dolores took the officer to her back study. The closet door was wide open. He bent down and saw silver fragments on the floor. The center of the floor was wiped clean, as though someone had run a hand over it.

"This is a major burglary, Mrs. Gibson. I caution you not to touch anything in this area."

"Why not?"

"Obviously, we will be dusting for fingerprints."

Toolie awoke about 4 a.m. That second glass of red wine finally reached her bladder. She tossed and turned for another few minutes. When she decided that sleep would be impossible without a bathroom break, she sat up.

She felt light-headedness. The wine was to help her circulation, but maybe the second glass slowed it. Two minutes passed. Her head cleared. She tapped at the floor for her slippers.

Toolie slowly stood. She grasped the bed post and turned to her bedroom door. A streetlight cast and orange glow to guide her. She eked past her kitchen, alternating hands on the dining room chairs. She experienced a peculiar weakness. The bathroom was steps away.

Ever since her fall in the kitchen last week, Toolie heeded advice from the restaurant manager: drink fluids before bedtime.

He convinced her that she would grow weak without hydration. She objected because she hated these dark trips to the bathroom. The nightly glass of wine was a compromise. Momentary pleasure but delayed inconvenience.

On her return trip from the bathroom, Toolie decided to double-check the lock on her apartment door. Her mind wandered. Was it morning? Did she hear noises from the restaurant below? She decided to investigate.

Toolie entered the blackened hallway. She followed the walls with her fingers, pausing slightly as the walls turned into apartment doors and then into walls again. She gained confidence and walked with more purpose. She envisioned her bedroom ahead and she was anxious to return to sleep. A few more steps, and then a turn.

In the upstairs apartment, Cuddles was sleeping in the crook of Matty's knees. The cocker spaniel's ears perked when she heard thumping noises below. She cried and licked Matty's ear.

He grumbled and turned to his side.

"Not again, Cuddles. You did your business last night. Don't you remember? We walked all over town for two hours."

The dog did not relent. Her paws dug into Matty's stomach. She pushed his nose with hers.

"Oh, for goodness... Can I just open the door and you can go out yourself? I'm too tired to walk you right now."

Cuddles barked in his ear and jumped to the door. Matty followed in a stupor. He unlatched the door and watched the dog take one step into the hallway.

"Go ahead, Cuddles. You can do it. You don't need me."

The dog sat in the hallway and barked again.

"SHUUSH. If Toolie hears you, I'm toast. Give me a second."

Matty pulled on a warm-up suit and fastened his sneakers. "OK, Cuddles. Let's go."

The dog sensed every turn in the dark hallway. She led Matty down the stairs to the second floor. They passed Toolie's apartment. The door was wide open.

"Stay here, Cuddles. I want to make sure she's all right."

Matty tip-toed into the quiet apartment. He peered into Toolie's bedroom. The sheets had been tossed to one side. No Toolie. The other rooms were empty as well.

When he returned to the door, he saw Cuddles in the shadows. "Where is she, girl?"

The dog moved to the top of the stairwell. Matty heard pained noises. He looked down the steps and saw a figure crawling toward him.

"Toolie!"

"I-I took a wrong turn and fell." A feeble voice answered him.

"Toolie, stay there! Don't move!"

Matty ran up a flight of stairs to his apartment and grabbed his cell phone. As his feet raced down two flights, he called for emergency help.

When he reached her, she was sprawled sideways on the third and fourth steps. Her hand covered an open wound on her cheek.

"You fell down all of these steps?" Matty could hardly believe she survived the fall.

"I stepped into the air. My foot went down and down, and my body just followed. I rolled. I let my body roll."

Matty tried to turn Toolie to a seated position. She had some strength left.

"Put your head back on my arm and rest," he told her. "The paramedics are on their way."

"Oh, no, Matty. I don't want to go to the hospital. I'll be all right. Help me upstairs."

She tried to stand, but the pain was too great.

"You need medical attention, Toolie. I won't let you stay here."

"Matty, I'm scared." She grasped his hand tightly and held it to her heart.

He didn't know what to say. When his grandmother took ill two years ago, Matty visited her hospital room in her last days. He had never seen such suffering. Nothing he could say would ease her pain, he thought. His mother taught him otherwise. "This is the time to talk, Matty. Grandma needs to hear your voice," his mother told him.

Now, in the dark stairwell, Matty tried to calm a very lonely woman, a woman who was in pain and fear. He could not be silent again.

"The doctors know what they're doing, Toolie. They will patch you up in no time. Don't you want to get back to work at the Golden Wheel?"

"It hurts right here." Toolie pointed toward her ribs. "I can breathe OK, but it hurts when I inhale."

Matty brushed her hair with his fingers. "You may have bruised some bones, but you're tough, Toolie. Let them take some X-rays just to make sure."

Her grip remained tight. "It could be internal bleeding, Matty. That happens in a fall. I've read that you could die from that."

Matty heard a siren getting louder. Soon, flashing blue and red lights splashed in the stairway. He heard frantic voices and the sound of a gurney being rolled over the restaurant parking lot.

"Stay with me, Matty." She winced as she turned to face him. "I need a friend right now."

"Sure, Toolie. I'll follow in my car."

He withdrew his hand from her as two paramedics evaluated her on the steps. They angled a stretcher into the stairway and eased her onto it. She was loaded quickly into the back of a Kane Community ambulance.

Before the doors closed, Toolie raised her head to make sure Matty was watching everything the paramedics were doing. She wagged her finger and called out to him, "No dogs! Read the lease!"

"OK, Toolie."

"But I won't report you this time."

The ambulance doors closed. Toolie and her attitude sped to the hospital.

Suddenly, Matty realized that he, too, was afraid.

Peggy Hoy, morning volunteer at the Steamburg retirement center, sipped coffee through a straw. She sat on the veranda with her favorite resident, Mr. George. Peggy always enjoyed talking with the old Seneca Peacemaker at the start of her shift. Today, though, Mr. George's mind seemed miles away.

"Something troubling you, Mr. George?"

"Just wish I were somewhere else," he replied.

He kicked a black tote bag deeper under the table. Peggy took another sip.

"Where would you like to be?" she asked.

"Peggy, you've known me for how long?"

"About a year."

"And all that time, I have been cooped up in this retirement center. Pinochle on Sundays. Scrabble on Tuesdays. Bingo on Fridays. I'm ready for a change."

"We've been over this before, Mr. George. You need assisted living. You would have trouble taking care of yourself. Who would cook for you? Who would clean your clothes and take you to the doctor's?"

He frowned. "I'm not talking about moving out. I just want a few days away."

Peggy reached under the table and pulled up his travel bag. "So you're packed?"

The Peacemaker grabbed the tote from her.

"Where are you going?" she asked.

"To the bus station. I wanted to ask if you'd drive me there in the van."

Peggy was amused and curious. "That's what I'm here for, Mr. George. If you need a ride in the van, I'll drive, but…"

"Thank you, dear."

"...you have to sign out at the front desk, and let them know where you're going and when you're coming home."

Mr. George knew that the front desk could screw everything up. He would be confined to his room if he told the front desk manager the real reason. He was fleeing from thugs hired by Pathfinder Gaming Management to beat him up. His destination was Megan Broward's dormitory at Edinboro State University – about 100 miles to the south.

After his visit with Megan, he didn't know where he would be.

"I'm going to visit an old friend in Pennsylvania," he told Peggy. "Will that work?"

"Probably," she replied. "As long as you leave your friend's name and number at the front desk so you can be contacted."

The old Indian hated to be treated like a child. The front desk screened his mail, monitored his telephone use and checked each night to make sure he was safe in bed. In ten years at the retirement center, he had been written up only twice. Once, for leaving an open bottle of Chianti on the pool table. The other infraction involved a dirty joke.

"What time does your bus leave, Mr. George?"

"About thirty minutes from now."

"I'll bring the van around front. You check out at the front desk, OK?"

Mr. George shuffled to the front door. He called over his shoulder to the front desk manager. "I'm taking a few things to the dry cleaners. I'll be back later."

"All right, Mr. George. See you at Scrabble tonight."

They wouldn't miss him until bed check time, he thought.

Peggy parked the retirement center van under an overhang at the main entrance. The van was freshly painted with the retirement center logo. Most of the van riders called it a mini-bus. The rear door had a wheelchair lift. The front door opened to two steep steps.

Mr. George grasped the front railing and stepped toward the

driver's chair. Peggy guided him to the first seat. She pulled a handle to close the bus doors. She adjusted the mirrors and then her lipstick.

As they pulled away, a black limousine took their space under the overhang. Mr. George turned to see two thugs from the Pathfinder company walk into the retirement center.

"Peggy, step on it!" Mr. George slapped the volunteer on her back. His skinny arm felt like a horse crop. "Faster, damn it!"

"What are you doing?" she asked, struggling to watch him and the road at the same time.

"If you can't drive faster than this, honey, get off the chair!"

"Mr. George, I always drive like this."

He wrapped his arm around her neck and dragged her to the aisle. The van swerved, nearly striking oncoming traffic. Horns blared.

"Son of a bitch!" Mr. George dumped the stupefied volunteer onto a passenger seat and clambered behind the steering wheel. He shifted lanes to avoid a truck stopped to turn left.

"What's gotten into you?" Peggy stood for a second before he downshifted and threw her forward.

"They're coming after us. Hold on!" He kept one eye glued on his side mirror.

"Who's coming after us? I think you're having an episode of some sort!"

"Keep your head down, Peggy. I'm gonna try to lose them."

He slammed the brakes and jerked the wheel. The van fishtailed onto a side street.

Peggy struggled to look out the rear window. Rounding the corner behind them was a black limousine. She couldn't see faces of the passengers through heavy tinted glass.

"It's the Mafia, isn't it? You haven't paid a gambling bet, right? Now, you're gonna get us both killed."

"It's not the Mafia, Peggy. They're mean men who think I am hiding something. They want my money and they've threatened me. That's why I need to get out of town for a few days."

Mr. George looked in his side mirror. He thought he saw a hand reaching through the limousine's side window. Something was pointing at the van.

"Stay down, I tell you," he said to Peggy. "We have to think of something, and quick!"

The limousine was gaining ground. Mr. George fishtailed again and spun back to the main road. The thugs tried to duplicate his move, but their vehicle's turning radius was too wide.

"We lost them temporarily, Peggy."

Mr. George's heart hadn't beaten this fast since his tour in Vietnam. Maybe if he had driven anything in the last thirty years he would be less excited. His last car was a 1960 Rambler. He drove it in the Seneca relocation to New York. Once he settled in the new reservation, he sold his car. When you're the Peacemaker, everyone gives you a ride.

"Come on, Peggy. Think of a plan. How can we ditch them?"

Peggy stumbled to the back of the van. She loosened two wheelchairs from their moorings. She gathered all that she could: a stretcher, first aid kits and a defibrillator device.

"There they are!" he called. "They have more speed than we do."

"I've got a plan," Peggy shouted to him. "Let them get close."

When the limousine maneuvered to within a car length, Peggy popped open the van's back door. She tossed the bulky medical equipment under the limousine's front wheels. The vehicle skidded, spun and crashed into some parked cars.

"Yeah, Peggy!" Mr. George honked the horn.

She clung to the back seat as she closed the rear door. As the van sped from Main Street's debris field, she wondered how this could be explained to the front desk.

"Mr. George," she called innocently. "Do you know this door is broken? It opens up sometimes when the van is moving."

"I've seen that happen."

"And, look, somebody stole the wheelchairs and crutches," she said.

"You should report it to the front desk."

"I think I will. Tomorrow."

Mr. George resumed normal speed. He eased into the Greyhound bus terminal lot. The Pittsburgh bus was idling at the curb.

"Looks like we got here on time, Peggy. Thank goodness traffic was light."

Mr. George pulled open the front door and gathered his things. "If I were you, I'd go back by a different route. You should take the rest of today off."

She lifted the keys from his palm.

"Who were those men, Mr. George? Why were they chasing us?"

"I can't tell you, Peggy. I don't want you to get involved."

"Involved? Are you crazy? How much more involved could I be?"

He stepped past her. She watched as he purchased a ticket and boarded the bus. He walked halfway down the aisle and found a seat beside someone's guitar. Peggy saw him wave as the bus began to roll.

She had a sickening feeling that she would never see the Peacemaker again.

Chapter Twenty-One
The Nightmare

Once the stolen Chevy was safely behind his garage door, Billy Herman could breathe.

The ride had been wild. First, he assaulted the young newspaper reporter and stole his Mustang in Smethport. Second, he parked the Mustang at a convenience store at Lantz Corners and stole a black Tahoe. Then he switched license plates with a parked Ford in Warren.

His next stop was very rewarding – Widow Gibson's house in Wexford.

Herman recalled that visit with a broad smile. He had learned from the rookie newspaper reporter that his long-sought silver treasure was there. The burglary was surprisingly easy.

When he had arrived in mid-afternoon, the house was unoccupied. Mrs. Gibson's car was gone. All he heard was high-pitched yelping from a dog inside. He circled to the rear and looked through kitchen slider doors. Only a cocker spaniel, he thought. No problem.

Herman had taken a credit card from his wallet. He slid the card between the front door latch and jamb. The door popped open. Cuddles backed from the door, but barked more loudly. If Herman only had his service revolver, Cuddles would be barking in dog heaven.

The intruder had tried to explore the house, but Cuddles was unrelenting. Fearing that barking noises would attract neighbor attention, Herman had moved to the kitchen to find the dog's food supply. He then refilled the chow bowl and water dish.

"There you go, little guy. Dig in."

As the hungry dog lapped water, Herman rushed to the master bedroom. He grabbed a sheet and stalked back to the kitchen. With a quick fling, he trapped Cuddles in the linen. The dog responded by kicking and snarling. Soon, Herman was pulled to the floor, his broken arm smashing over the bowl and dish. As chow pellets scattered over the kitchen floor, Herman pulled in the cocker spaniel like a bass fisherman at a contest.

"You're going for a little ride." Herman pulled the linen tight and circled it around the kicking dog.

Herman remembered carrying the wriggling sheet to the stolen SUV. He secured the wrapped dog in a passenger lap belt. The barking became softer.

Herman then drove five miles north. He turned onto a private dirt road.

"This is your new home, Rover. You're lucky I didn't strangle you back there."

He unlatched the belt and kicked the dog through an open passenger door. The sheet rolled a couple of times. Cuddles pawed through an opening and ran into some bushes.

Herman had returned in time to see a lawn service truck pull into Dolores Gibson's driveway. Two Hispanic men in green shirts hopped out. They unlatched the tailgate on their equipment trailer. Herman then pulled beside them.

"Hola." He had called to the older man.

"Buenas dias, Señor."

Herman walked into Gibson's house like he owned the place. He heard mowers begin to whirr outside as he closed and locked the front door.

Then his search began.

The one-story house offered few storage areas. Once Herman had finished in the garage, he started with the closets. Within 15 minutes, he discovered treasure in the back bedroom.

Four hundred silver bars. Shiny, valuable and more than a man with a broken arm could move.

"Pardon! Pardon! Señores!" Herman had flailed his good arm to stop their mowing.

"Sí?"

"I need help… ah… assistance." Herman tried to remember his Spanish I vocabulary from high school. "Asiste para mi, por favor."

"Qué?"

"Move, movar… ah… carry… movimento. Oh, crap." Herman had motioned for the two lawn workers to follow him into the house. They accompanied him to the back bedroom. Herman pointed at the silver bars.

"Steel. How do you say?" Herman searched for the word.

"PLATA! MUCHO PLATA! AAAEEE!" The lawn workers understood.

"No, no. Steel, acero, acero."

"Muy bien, Señor." The lawn workers had giggled to themselves.

"Seriously, it's steel," Herman insisted. "I want to take to recycling plant. Comprendes?"

"Sí," the older man said. "We take to recycle plant for you."

"NO PROBLEMA!" Herman had become worried that his Spanish treasure would be commandeered by two Mexicans. "I will … yo, yo do it."

"Nosotros… we." The lawn workers then pointed to each other. "No problema."

"I will pay you money, dinero, if you move it to my vehicle. Mucho dinero."

"Gracias, Señor. Mucho dinero."

The men then returned to their trailer and guided a wheelbarrow into the house. The men loaded dozens of silver bars at a time. Herman watched them place hundreds of bars into the rear compartment of his stolen SUV. It took about a half hour.

"Dinero, por favor?" The older man asked.

"Tomorrow, mañana. I will get money from the recycling plant. Come back here tomorrow. Retorno mañana." Herman then hopped into the Chevy Tahoe and began to back from the driveway.

"Mañana!" The older man had shouted. "Mucho, mucho!"

Herman then drove cautiously to his Zelienople home, mindful of the load on his rear suspension. He had pulled into his garage and closed the door.

He had two telephone calls to make.

A secretary answered on the second ring. "Pre-trial services, may I help you?"

"This is William Herman, calling in to report."

"Hold, please, Mr. Herman... Your pre-trial officer is away from his desk. Let me take your information."

"Sure. What do you need?"

"OK. Have you used any illegal drugs or alcohol since your release?"

"No."

"All right. Have you engaged in any criminal behavior."

"Ha-ha. I was released a few hours ago. How could I have time for any of this?"

"Mr. Herman, just answer the questions. I have other callers."

"I did answer your question."

"So that's a no, yes?"

"No, yes."

"Good. One more question. I see that your driver's license was revoked. Have you operated any motor vehicle since your release."

"Would that include farm tractors?"

"I don't think so, let me check... No, not farm tractors."

"Then I'm good on that question, too," Herman replied.

"So that's a no, yes?"

"Correct."

"Thank you for being so honest, Mr. Herman. Especially about the tractor. You wouldn't believe how many of our pre-trial defendants try to bend the rules."

"Just cooperating with Judge Van Lear."

"I will pass along your good report, Mr. Herman. Be sure to check back with us on Monday."

Herman ended the call and dialed another number.

"Gold and Silver Exchange. Please listen to all of our selections as our menu has changed. For current price quotations, please dial 1…"

Herman fumbled with a pen and paper. He dialed 1.

"For gold, press 1. For all other metals, press 2."

Herman pressed 2.

"For platinum, press 1. For silver, press 2. For…"

Herman pressed 2.

"For yesterday's final price, press 1. For the current day trading price, press 2. For…"

Herman pressed 2.

"For current price quotations, please dial 1, or if you wish to speak with an operator…"

Herman pressed 1.

"The current price of gold is $892.20 per ounce. If you wish to return to the main menu, press zero."

Herman clenched his teeth and pressed zero.

In his second navigation of the Gold and Silver Exchange phone system, he reached a live operator. The current price of silver was $14.39 per ounce. Not bad.

Herman figured he had about 48 hours to sell the silver and rid himself of the stolen Chevy.

Surely, by then, somebody would be coming after him.

"Jimmie, Jimmie. You're breathing so hard." Ann rubbed her husband's shoulders.

He awoke. The clock read 5 a.m.

"I'm sorry, Ann. I had an awful dream. It was so real."

"Tell me about it."

Jimmie rolled onto his side and faced her. She could see terror in his eyes.

"Tell me, Jimmie. Was I in your dream?"

They heard soft sounds from the baby intercom. Hannah Maria was stirring. Thank God she was all right, Jimmie thought.

"Let me gather my senses, Ann. We can feed our baby first."

Ann kissed him gently on his forehead. She tied her robe and headed for the nursery a few doors away. Jimmie rolled onto his back and stared at the ceiling.

As they always do, this nightmare began innocently. And he could recall every detail.

Sunshine bathed the front lawn of Leigh-Rose Mansion. Jimmie, Ann and their new daughter were enjoying their first picnic together. Hannah Maria appeared to be a year old because she was holding onto Jimmie's index fingers and walking.

Ann had spread a blanket under a magnolia. The colors seemed to be vivid. He could smell the blossoms.

He recalled no words being spoken, only laughter. The baby communicated with her eyes, bright and blue. Ann communicated with her smile and touch.

Halfway through his dream, a black sedan drove through the mansion's front gates. There was no security. No state troopers guarded the governor's mansion. All was light and innocent.

The sedan slowed. Jimmie strained to see the driver, but the sun's glare obscured his view. At times, the car seemed to stall on the long gravel path. Each time it stopped, Jimmie returned his attention to Hannah Maria. When he heard the tires crunch more gravel, he turned to see the car coming closer.

Jimmie remained complacent in his nightmare. The approaching vehicle was distracting, but not menacing. Ann didn't notice it. The baby's play was all that mattered.

Slowly and steadily, the sedan came closer. It left the driveway and started to roll over the lawn. It stopped for a few seconds. He noticed a figure walking from the mansion toward the car. It was his chief of staff, Bill Pennoyer.

Jimmie watched as Pennoyer walked around the vehicle and tapped on the driver's window. He saw the window roll down. Pennoyer appeared to be talking with the driver. He was yelling something. Then Pennoyer pointed to the front gate, as though he was ordering the driver to leave the property.

BANG, BANG! Two shots rang out. Pennoyer lurched backward. Blood streamed from his face and neck. His body was motionless on the lawn.

Jimmie tried to stand, but couldn't. The baby was across his lap. Ann stroked his face and tried to reassure him that everything was all right. The car began to move again.

"Take the baby, Ann." He tried to lift his daughter, but her little arms grasped his legs. "Take her and run!"

Ann took Hannah Maria into her arms. She cradled the baby's head and started to run.

Suddenly, the lawn was without trees. The ground was hard and hot.

The governor stood, but couldn't walk. He watched the car gaining speed. As it sped past him, Jimmie recognized the driver. He tried to yell at Ann to watch out, but his words were only loud breaths.

Before he could witness the carnage, Ann had awakened him.

The bedroom clock now read 5:25 a.m. Jimmie could hear Ann placing their daughter back into her crib. The morning feeding was over.

"She's beautiful, Jimmie." Ann bent over him and stroked his forehead. "I feel cold sweat. Are you all right?"

"It's the nightmare, Ann. I haven't yet recovered."

"Talk about it. Maybe I can ease your mind."

Jimmie described what he could recall. He couldn't move. He

couldn't yell. He couldn't stop the car from mauling his wife and child.

"First, realize that it's not real," Ann said. "Just a dream."

"I know, but something like that could happen."

"Let's interpret this," she said. "You have great feelings about protecting your family. Sometimes, I think your concerns for security are unusually strong. You've witnessed the loss of your mother and father at a young age, and that has shown you how fragile life is."

"OK. So what does the car represent?" he asked.

"The car was black. So the car represents evil and death."

"Why was Pennoyer in the dream?"

"I suppose Pennoyer represents your work, your job as governor. You have trouble separating your political career and your family obligations. So in your dream, Pennoyer's death represents the termination of your political life."

"When the car drove over you and the baby…"

"That represented the end of your family life," Ann said. "It must have been a tremendous nightmare for you."

Jimmie appreciated her insight, but her analysis lacked one fact from the dream. The driver who killed his political career and was about to kill his family life was Billy Herman.

How could he be stopped?

Greyhound's bus station was less than a mile from Megan Broward's dorm at Edinboro. She waited for the 2 p.m. arrival with a diet soda in one hand and Wednesday's News Leader edition in the other.

Matty's byline was absent. His ambitious plan to publish a story about Josh Gibson's death and his discovery of the silver treasure had to wait another week. The front page was dominated by the Bailey baby. Megan had to admit that the photographs were cute.

The bus station was largely empty. No shady characters lurked about. The Peacemaker's frantic message about thugs from the casino kept her awake most of the night. She worried that her calls to Seneca Nation created a buzz. She needed someone to translate the Indian words on an old Seneca map. Word reached the casino workers. They smelled silver.

Mr. George, the Peacemaker, warned her to be careful. Other than worry, she had no plan. Perhaps, Mr. George knew a fresh incantation to keep the goons away.

The Greyhound bus arrived on time. She waited in a customer lobby while passengers disembarked. A porter helped Mr. George with his bag. Megan called to him.

"I don't know if this was a good idea, coming here," he told her. "If they're looking for me and you, we're making it easier for them by traveling together."

"Mr. George, please relax. I can't imagine these casino guys are interested in a young girl like me and ..."

"An old man like me," he finished her thought.

"I'm sorry. I didn't mean it like that."

Mr. George took her arm. They walked to the parking lot. He placed his bag in the trunk of her Volkswagen. "Where are we going, Megan?"

"Away from here. Into the mountains, I guess."

"Look, I'm an Indian. But I'm not ready to go back to my roots. I'll need a roof over my head and some food in my belly. Do you have a room on campus?"

"Ah, I don't know if ..."

"Just for a few days?" he asked.

"We have pretty strict policies on campus, Mr. George. I have a better idea, one that will throw anybody off your trail."

After his exciting ride in the retirement center van, he was ready for peace and quiet.

"What's your idea, Megan?"

"I have a friend in Kane. Just past the Allegheny National Forest. He has an apartment in a boarding house. He won't mind company for a few days."

"Is this your newspaper reporter friend?" Mr. George asked.

"Yes. His name is Matty Moore. We can set you up in his place. He would love to interview you. He's writing a story about the silver treasure."

"Megan, that sounds fine. But what does Mr. Moore know about the silver?"

"He saw it. That is, he saw it before it was stolen."

"Goodness, Megan! Where was it? Who stole it? Where is it now?"

"Matty knows a few suspects, but he's probably waiting to see who dies next."

"You mean the curse?"

Megan checked her rear-view mirror. Nobody was following them. The afternoon sun was behind them as the Volkswagen traveled east to the mountains.

"The silver was discovered five years ago by two men, Josh Gibson and Billy Herman," she told him. "Both were police officers working on the Governor Brock Bailey disappearance. They scoured the Kinzua Valley for a gun they believed was involved in the case. They used a metal detector in their search and…"

"The metal detector lit up when they got close to the silver?"

"Right," Megan answered. "Shortly thereafter, Gibson died in a fall off the Kinzua Bridge. Herman always suspected that Gibson had returned to the treasure site alone and took all of the silver himself. But he couldn't prove it."

"Did Gibson take the silver?" Mr. George asked.

"Yes, he did. Matty visited his widow, Dolores Gibson a few weeks ago. She showed him the silver bars that Josh had stacked in their house."

"So what happened to the silver? Where is Mrs. Gibson?"

Megan shook her head. "She's missing from her house. The silver is gone. We think she's been murdered. Her front door was open and her dog was wandering around loose."

"So Josh Gibson and Dolores Gibson are dead? At least you think she's dead?"

"Yes, we do."

"Who else touched the silver?" he asked.

"Whoever stole it and, well, Matty told me he picked up a silver bar when he interviewed Mrs. Gibson, but …"

"Matty touched it?"

"Yes, but the curse only affects someone who disturbs the ground. Are you saying the curse applies to anyone who touches the silver?"

"Listen, Megan. I told you that I don't believe in witchcraft. Some Indians do, but I don't."

"Would you touch the silver?" she asked.

"Just to be on the safe side? No."

Megan realized that she had no contact with Matty for nearly a day. She left him walking the dark streets of Kane with a nervous cocker spaniel. She had tried calling him, but he didn't answer. She began to worry.

An hour later, Megan drove into the Golden Wheel Restaurant parking lot. Matty's car was missing. She escorted Mr. George to the boarding house office. No one was there.

"Wait here in the lobby," she told him. "I'll see if he's upstairs."

Megan stopped at the first floor landing. On the third step was a gauze bandage stained with blood. She bounded up the stairs and passed Toolie's open door. She peeked in, but found no one. Then she ran to the third floor. Matty's apartment door was closed but unlocked. She knocked and entered.

His bed was unmade. A cold cup of coffee was on his nightstand. Windows were open. There was no sign of Cuddles.

Megan began to panic. She called the News Leader office.

"News Leader, Pride of the Alleghenies. May I help you?"

"Jessie, have you seen Matty?" Megan asked.

"He hasn't come in today. Sorry."

"If he does, please have him call me as soon as possible."

"Sure, Megan," Jessie replied. "And if you see him..."

Tom Zachary grabbed the telephone from his office manager's hand. "You tell him that he has a lot of explaining to do!"

Chapter Twenty-Two
The Clue

Cuddles was not only safe, she was the center of attention.

Matty had tied her leash to a picnic table outside Kane Community Hospital. Every nurse and intern enjoying a lunch break stopped to pet the dog or, better yet, offer tasty human food.

About two hours had passed since orderlies wheeled Toolie from the emergency room. He overheard the ER doctor ordering a CAT scan and blood work. No one ventured an opinion as to why Toolie had awakened, became disoriented and fell down a flight of steps.

And no one would talk to Matty. Friends of the patient don't get information.

"Sir?" A clerk in blue scrubs tapped Matty's shoulder. "Please step this way. We'd like some information on the patient."

Matty followed the clerk to a cubicle adjacent to the emergency room lobby. He sat, facing the backside of a computer monitor. A framed sign to his right pronounced that all services must be paid for in advance.

"All right, sir." The clerk pulled a drawer to expose her keyboard. "Name of patient?"

"Toolie."

"OK. Last name?"

"I believe it's Toolie."

"Toolie Toolie?"

"No, just Toolie. She has a first name. I don't remember it."

"We'll just call her 'Patient Toolie.'"

Matty smiled. That's one adjective he would never ascribe to her.

"Date of birth?" the clerk asked.

"She's in her nineties. That's all I know."

"Your name?"

"Matthew Moore."

"Your relationship with the patient?"

"We're kind of off and on. She seems cool with me now."

"So you're friends?"

"At the moment, yes."

The clerk entered about a thousand keystrokes. Matty wondered how his simple answers prompted such a flurry of data.

"Does she have any family? Husband, children..."

"No. I just think she has many friends. She's a waitress at the Golden Wheel."

A light bulb lit up. "Yes, yes," the clerk said. "I thought I knew her. The waitress. She's quite a character. I'll call over to the restaurant to get more information. They'll know her date of birth and Social."

Matty pointed at the framed sign. "The Golden Wheel is a small operation. I don't believe Toolie has any medical insurance. Does that mean...?"

"We'll give her good treatment, Mr. Moore. Don't worry about that. But her lack of insurance may affect her long-term care."

"I understand."

"Is there anyone you know who can guarantee payment of her medical costs?"

"Only one person. Me."

"Mr. Moore. You're only a friend. We don't know how much care she needs. This could be extremely expensive."

"I'm prepared to take that risk."

The clerk thought Matty was ignorant of health care costs. "Thousands of dollars just for this hospital stay. Then, if she undergoes more testing, more costs. If she suffered a stroke, there will be rehabilitation expenses, including costs for a nursing facility. It's not unusual for these cases to total tens of thousands of dollars."

"Where do I sign?" he asked.

"You're a teenager. How can you afford this?"

"I've received an inheritance. Here is my account number at Carnegie Bank & Trust if you'd like to check my credit."

The clerk keyed the number into her system. She printed a page and handed him a pen.

"Kane Community Hospital Guaranty Agreement." Matty read the heading. "The undersigned agrees to be liable for all costs incurred for the necessary and reasonable medical treatment of 'Patient Toolie.' In the event 'Patient Toolie' fails to make timely payments for such costs as billed by Hospital, the undersigned hereby confesses to an entry of judgment against (him/her) in such delinquent amount in the Court of Common Pleas of McKean County."

Matty signed the agreement and handed it to the clerk.

She punched two holes in the agreement and fastened it into Toolie's file jacket.

"Thank you, Mr. Moore. You may return to the waiting area."

"Could you ask the doctor if I could speak to him about Toolie's condition?" Matty asked.

"I'm sorry, Mr. Moore. That's private information that cannot be given to you."

Dolores Gibson was aroused by an unrelenting door bell.

After a night of tossing and turning alone in her worn sheets, Dolores's flesh was weak. She estimated at most three hours of sleep. She pushed her pillow against her ear. She hoped the door bell would stop.

Being alone in a burglarized house inhibits sleeping. Dolores felt violated, and not in the way she enjoyed. Whoever took her silver was not a typical burglar, she thought. Her fine crystal had not been taken. The pearl-handled revolver remained in the glass case. Her valuable Rockwell painting still graced her living room.

Only the silver was gone. And only two people knew about it, she thought. One was the young black reporter from the Kane News Leader. The other was the wretched but sexy white preacher man. She hadn't revealed either suspect to the Pine Township detective. She was waiting for results from his fingerprint examination of her house.

The door bell stopped when the fist pounding began.

"Señor! Señor!"

Dolores removed the pillow from her ear. She gathered her robe and slippers.

"Dinero, por favor!"

Usually, Dolores heard Spanish through the din of lawn mowers. She peered through a side window and noticed the landscape service truck in her driveway.

"Un momento," she called through the front door.

She retrieved her checkbook from her study desk. She was certain that the lawn service had been paid through the month. Perhaps the check bounced. Damn that rotten insurance company, she thought. They should have paid on Josh's $2 million life policy.

"Sí?" She opened the door and found two Hispanic workers. They removed their caps and smiled.

"Pardon us, Señora, where is the man?" one of them asked.

"What man? Which man?"

"Man who take acero, acero." The worker looked at his friend for help.

"Steel. We carry his steel to his car," the other worker told Dolores.

"Did it look like silver?" Dolores asked him.

"Sí. Plata. Shiny. Nice."

"This man, hombre, what did he look like?" she asked.

"Gringo, sí." The worker held up his hand, slightly above her eye level.

"Was he white? Blanco?"

"Sí. Blanco, pálido. Él tiene un brazo roto." The older worker flexed his arm and pointed to his elbow. "Brazo roto."

"Yes, I understand. He is a muscular young man and he is brazen." Dolores recalled that Pastor Randy had tried to get her signature at the motel. He wanted her to donate silver to his mega-church. She wrote on the paper, telling Randy where he could spend eternity.

"Dinero, por favor." The worker held out his baseball cap. Dolores wrote a check and dropped it in.

"Gratias."

"My dog, perrito. Where is she?" Dolores asked. "Did gringo have perrito?"

"No, Señora. Lo siento."

"I'm sorry, too."

Matty decided to call his editor a few minutes after noon. Hopefully, Tom Zachary had left the office and was walking to Texas Hot Lunch. With any luck, Matty could leave a voice mail. He already had composed his message on a steno pad.

"At the sound of the beep, please leave a message for... (fake deep voice) Tom Zachary..."

"Mr. Z. It's Matty. There was an emergency overnight. Toolie fell down steps at the boarding house. She was conscious. The doctors are doing tests at Kane Community. Nobody else is with her, so I'll be at the hospital all day. I can work overtime later. Toolie needs me right now. Call me on my cell. Oh, by the way, I hope you can babysit my dog."

Whew! He passed all the information without Zachary yelling at him. The dog-sitting idea was an after-thought, though. How could Mr. Z turn down a cute puppy?

Matty sat in a spacious waiting area. A few older people came and went in the past few hours. Toolie apparently was the only emergency room patient for the morning. Matty leaned back in a stiff plastic chair. He angled his view away from a ceiling mounted television. He had endured about 10 cycles of CNN Headline News. Thank goodness he wrote for a newspaper rather than reading monotonous stories about Hollywood personalities.

A buzz came from his pocket. Zachary was returning his call. Matty ran outside and flipped open his phone.

"Mr. Z. How was lunch?"

"Never mind that, Matty. How is Toolie doing?"

"I haven't seen her for a few hours. They're checking her now."

"We miss you at the newspaper office," Zachary said pleasantly. "The assignments are piling up on your desk. Jessie's doing what she can, but…"

Matty understood gentle persuasion. "I can't wait to get back there. I miss writing, but I'm needed here, Mr. Z."

"You know, they caught the bear."

"The one that killed Professor Dulaney?" Matty asked.

"That's what the police say. They matched the bear's claws to Dulaney's neck."

"Pretty gross."

"Did the police shoot it?"

"Yeah. They suspect rabies. We're waiting for blood and tissue tests, too."

"I'd like to write that story, Mr. Z."

"I've started it, but you can finish it. Your deadline is Sunday, not Monday."

"I know, Mr. Z. I haven't been very reliable on my deadlines."

"You take care, Matty. Call me when you get any news on Toolie."

Matty remembered an obligation he had to pass to his editor. "Mr. Z, my dog! She's tied up to a picnic table outside the hospital. Could you?"

"What's her name?"

"Cuddles. She's trained, unless she gets excited."

"Oh, for goodness... OK." Zachary ended the call.

Matty returned to the waiting room. Someone had turned off the television.

"Mr. Moore?" A young physician sporting a 50's crew cut approached him from behind. "We've admitted your friend. She'll be assigned to a third-floor private room. I can walk you there."

"Thank you, doctor. Is Toolie going to be all right?"

"Yes. She should have a complete recovery."

"Did she have a stroke?" Matty asked.

The physician tucked a medical file under his arm. He opened a set of double-doors, leading to a patient wing of the hospital. He held an elevator door open for Matty, and they traveled to the third floor.

"I see you've signed as guarantor for Ms. Toolie? Is that correct?"

"Yes, doctor. She lives alone and she has no insurance."

"Are you her caregiver?"

"No, not really. I'm just..."

The physician interrupted. "I'll ask that question again. Are you her caregiver?"

Matty was confused. "Is there a correct answer to that question?"

"Yes, there is," the doctor said with a wink. "Especially if you want me to give you any medical information, including her diagnosis and prognosis."

"I'm not really..."

The physician reached past Matty and pulled the emergency stop button. The elevator stopped between the second and third floors.

"Listen, young man. Who are you? What do you want with Gladys Toolie?" The physician stood between Matty and the emergency switch. His eyes were piercing.

"Don't be upset, doctor. I'm trying to help a woman in need."

His answer was insufficient for the physician, so Matty gave a full explanation. Toolie was his neighbor at the boarding house. He worked as a summer intern at the newspaper. They became close friends. He found her at the foot of the steps after she fell this morning. He has money. Lots of it. She needed help. It was the right thing to do.

"I'll make a note in the file," the physician said. "You are her caregiver, right?"

"Right."

"So when she is released from the hospital in a day or two, she'll have a home and you will watch over her, correct?"

"Correct."

"You'll provide meals to her, make sure she bathes herself and gets proper exercise and rest. Do you understand?"

"Will she be able to bathe herself?" Matty asked.

"Hopefully, but if she can't..."

"OK. I will." Matty never read that part in the guarantee agreement.

The doctor turned and released the emergency stop button. The elevator car jolted and began moving upward.

"Now, I can tell you what you need to know about Toolie," he told Matty. "If you're caring for her, you must understand her condition."

"Is it terminal?"

"No. She's a physically strong woman for her age. She is mentally sound as well. But whenever we have an elderly person fall, we suspect heart disease or circulatory problems. Toolie's heart appears to function quite well, but there could be times when she moves too quickly or turns suddenly and she loses balance or awareness."

"So what you're saying is that Toolie needs to take it easy and slow down?"

"That would be good advice."

The elevator door opened. The physician paused at a nurse station and made a few notations in Toolie's file. Then he motioned for Matty to follow him to the coronary care unit.

"What else do I need to know, doc?"

"Toolie also is suffering from a condition called shingles," he answered. "It presents as a rash on her legs that is tingling and painful. We'll provide medicine to ease that condition. Also, her ribs are well bruised and it may be discomforting for Toolie to breathe deeply. That condition should resolve itself in a few months."

Matty slowed to peek into Toolie's room. A curtain had been drawn around her bed. A nurse was instructing how to operate the call button and television.

"Does Toolie know everything you told me, doctor?"

"Yes, including the part about slowing down and removing stress from her life. But she is anxious to return to work at the restaurant. You have to keep her off her feet for a while."

Matty had difficult assignments from Tom Zachary, but keeping Toolie from her customers was a doozie.

"Go on in, Mr. Moore." The physician gently pushed Matty's back. "She needs your friendship."

Matty took peepy steps into the room toward the far hospital bed. The nurse flung the curtain back to its resting place. Toolie looked ashen. She wore a hospital gown and was sitting up. Saline solution from an IV bag dripped into her arm.

"Oh, Matty. Thank you for staying. Did you talk to the doctor?"

"Yes, Toolie. He said you need rest."

"Cripes Hanna! We all need rest!"

"Simmer down, Toolie. Your heart..."

"What about my heart? Is there something wrong with my heart? Heaven's sake!"

"Toolie, if you don't relax, I'm leaving." He tried to speak firmly.

"All right. I'll behave. But you know that's almost impossible."

Matty took her free hand. It was surprisingly warm. Her color was returning.

"Did you call the Golden Wheel and tell them I'm taking the day off?"

"They know that, Gladys."

"Who the hell told you my name? If that gets out…"

"OK, let's make a deal. You don't tell the landlord about my dog and I won't say your real name."

"Deal." Toolie took back her arm and rubbed her ribs. She inhaled a shallow breath, grimaced and rolled her eyes.

"Are you eating?" Matty asked.

"Not like at the restaurant. Healthy stuff like applesauce, prunes, green tea."

"Yecch! How can you stand it?"

"I can't," Toolie replied. "Get me out of here."

Matty recalled his late grandmother telling him the same thing. In her last days in the hospital, she ordered him to call the police because she was being held against her wishes. "These nurses are evil," his grandmother told him. "Take me home."

Toolie tugged at the hospital gown as she turned to face him.

"How about that, Matty? Fell down 14 steps and no broken bones."

"You are a legend, Toolie."

"It was the cabernet, Matty. Makes you real smooth. I rolled like an angel on a cotton cloud."

"Very poetic, Toolie. I may use that sometime."

"Roses are red, Toolie is black and blue." She started to laugh, but the pain stopped it.

"I have to get back to my writing," Matty said. "I just spoke to my editor. He has several stories for me to work on. Did you know the police shot the bear that killed Professor Dulaney?"

"Goodness, no. Let's get its head and we'll mount him beside Elmer the Elk." Toolie repressed another laugh.

"So they're checking the bear for rabies," Matty said. "That would explain why it was so aggressive."

Toolie propped herself up with an elbow. Matty could sense her mind was ticking.

"I remember your news article about Professor Dulaney," Toolie said. "That whole episode, you know, the bear attack and Dulaney digging a hole in the middle of the night – a lot of that didn't make sense to me."

"What do you mean, Toolie?"

"First, the police said he was looking for soil samples. Why would you do that at night? And he didn't have any small bottles or containers. How was he going to take samples?"

Matty agreed, but he just reported the news as police described it.

"Second," Toolie continued, "Dulaney was a sociology professor. Why would soil samples interest him? Maybe he was doing archaeological digging. Maybe he found a skull or bones. Maybe he uncovered a grave. Did you ever think of that?"

Matty knew why Dulaney was digging; he was looking for the Spanish silver using Megan's treasure map. Matty was not ready to reveal that to Toolie. Not yet.

"Third, the police reported that Dulaney was using two shovels. Why would one man need two shovels?"

"Two shovels?" Matty asked. "Did I report that Dulaney had two shovels?"

"Yeah. That was in your story. One of the shovels was covered with blood. The other was dusty with dirt."

Matty tried to figure it out. "So maybe Dulaney dug with one shovel and then, when he was attacked by the bear, he fell on the second shovel. He got that one all bloody."

"My dear Matty, I would agree with your explanation if the bloody shovel was near the professor's body, but it wasn't."

Matty tried to remember what the lead detective said about the bloody shovel. So much had happened since Dulaney's death. Matty had forgotten details about the case.

"Tell me, Toolie. I forget. Where was the second shovel?"

A nurse entered the room and placed a blood pressure cuff on Toolie's arm. The nurse pumped the ball as she tried to find Toolie's pulse.

But it was Matty's heart that began to race.

Where was the second shovel? Why was Toolie so bothered by it?

"How much longer?" Matty surprised the nurse with his impatience.

"Almost done. 135 over 90, not too bad, Gladys." The nurse glared at Matty. "Is there anything you need, maybe some quiet and rest?"

"Maybe some fried food. Got any?"

The nurse smiled, recorded her patient's vitals and left. Matty pulled his chair closer to Toolie. Her impish expression said it all. Her detective skills were better than the state trooper's.

"The second shovel was found in the bushes," she said. "About 20 yards from the body."

"How did it get there, Toolie?" Matty eagerly picked her brain.

"Police said the bear dragged it to the bushes. Now, for the love of Pete, do you think a bear would carry a shovel 20 yards? In its teeth? Let me guess, the bear whacked poor Dulaney upside the head with the shovel. Then the bear decided to hide his murder weapon in some bushes? That doesn't make sense."

"No, it doesn't," Matty had to admit.

"Well, do you suppose Dulaney hit himself with the shovel and threw it into the bushes?"

"No, that doesn't make sense either."

"OK, Mr. Reporter. I have an assignment for you. Talk to the lead investigator in the Dulaney case. I'm sure they still have all of the evidence. Ask him to scrape a sample of blood from the shovel and analyze it."

"So what, Toolie?"

"Here's the deal. I'll make you a bet."

"What's the bet?"

"Ten dollars says the blood on the shovel isn't Professor Dulaney's."

Chapter Twenty-Three
The Alibi

Pastor Randy O'Boyd was numb. His upper jaw throbbed.

Various hoses sprayed water, blew air and sucked debris from his mouth. He felt a cotton ball stuffed under his lip.

Cosmetic dentistry is so irritating and so expensive. This permanent crown, to fix a tooth chipped by a jealous husband, would cost $1,200.00.

To Pastor Randy, price mattered not when the goal was lasting beauty. After all, he was a star on stage. His smile could open wallets.

The dentist raised the back of Randy's chair. "This is porcelain," he told his young patient. "So when we use the adhesive, it's there for good."

O'Boyd held a mirror and examined the crown fitted loosely in his mouth. It was pure white and blended nicely with his perfect teeth. He smiled with confidence. "Glue away, doctor," he said.

The dentist chair lowered backward. Bright lights caused the patient to close his eyes. Noisy high pressure air blew into his mouth. He could taste blood from his swollen gums. The dentist reshaped the crown with a drill, causing a burning smell. Every sense of O'Boyd was bothered. He easily missed all of the commotion behind him.

"Randy O'Boyd?" a voice called.

The dentist turned to see two burly men in casual clothes. One displayed a police badge in an open leather folder. "Pittsburgh Police."

"What is this all about? Can't you see I'm in the middle of a procedure?" The dentist pushed the glued crown onto Randy's reshaped tooth and seemingly jammed it into the pastor's sinus. Randy squirmed under the pressure.

"Is this Mr. O'Boyd?" one officer asked. "We have a few questions for him."

"If you would please wait in the lobby…" The dentist eased his fingers and directed his patient to check his bite.

"We'd prefer to keep him in our sight," the other officer said.

When the dentist finished, the cops escorted Pastor Randy to an unoccupied examination room. They directed him to sit in a dentist chair so they could extract some information.

"Do you know Dolores Gibson?"

"Yes. Dolores is a parishioner in my church. I'm the pastor."

The officers nodded at each other. So far so good. He was telling the truth, but maybe not the whole truth. Dolores Gibson had told police that Pastor Randy was the likely burglar. He knew about the silver. He seduced her. And he had a three-hour window of opportunity yesterday to steal the silver from her home in Wexford as she waited for him at a motel.

"Her home in Wexford was burglarized yesterday," one officer told him. "Did you know that?"

"No. I didn't hear about that. Why are you talking to me?"

"We're helping out with the investigation. You seem a little defensive…"

"No, I'm not," Pastor Randy interjected. "I'm a little sore right now."

"Where were you yesterday afternoon?"

"I was with my wife at the church. She will tell you that."

The officers noted his alibi witness, but they wanted to hear him confess to some other matters.

"Were you with Mrs. Gibson yesterday?" one officer asked him.

"Mrs. Gibson has some problems and I wanted to help…"

"Answer the question."

"Yes. I was with her for a few hours yesterday."

"Where?"

"Do I need an attorney?"

"I don't know," one officer said. "You tell me."

"I saw her at the Twilight Motel on Route 51. But nothing happened, I swear."

Both officers jotted down that information. "Yes or no question, Mr. O'Boyd. Have you been to Mrs. Gibson's house?" the lead officer asked.

"Yes."

"In fact, you stayed overnight there, right?"

"Yes."

"And you slept with her ... in her bed?"

"Yes, she was lonely."

"Well, that would cure her loneliness, wouldn't it, Mr. O'Boyd?"

He nodded, careful not to show his new smile.

"When you visited with Mrs. Gibson, did you find anything of value in her house? Maybe something shiny?"

Pastor Randy was guilty of many crimes, but burglary was not among them. Whoever stole Dolores's silver knew where it was and knew Dolores was not home. The only people who knew she wasn't home yesterday were himself and his wife, Darla. He remembered. He had told Darla that 400 silver bars were stacked on the floor of Dolores's closet. Then he left Darla for a few hours. But could Darla do such a thing? Sweet, sultry Darla The Wonderful?

"Mr. O'Boyd, we'd like to ask you more questions at the station." The cops stood.

"Am I under arrest?"

"No. But could you tell us where we can find your wife?"

"Gladly."

Toolie clicked off the television and squirmed in her hospital bed. About an hour had passed since Matty left her alone. He had promised to find some friends to keep her company, but no one showed. Sheets were irritating her legs. Pain from the shingles was breaking through her medication. She needed someone to talk with.

"Toolie," a voice whispered from the door. "Do you remember me? I'm Megan. Matty's friend."

Good gracious, Toolie thought. Megan stood at her bed with the oldest physician she had ever seen. Maybe the tallest, too.

"Oh, thank you for coming, Megan. I wish I had some food to serve you and…"

"This is Mr. George." Megan directed the Peacemaker to stand beside Toolie's bed. "He's my good friend from New York."

Toolie lifted herself on her elbows. She extended her hand without the IV line. "My goodness, I thought you were a doctor. There are so many here. It's good to meet you, Mr. George."

"My pleasure, young lady." He took her hand between his.

"And so polite… and dishonest." Toolie laughed without concern for her bruised ribs.

Megan sat on the edge of the bed. "I was so sorry to hear of your fall. How are you doing?"

"I'm supposed to be released tomorrow. I overheard the nurses saying that I'll be sent to a rehabilitation center, but I want to go home."

"Listen to your doctors, Toolie. They know what's best."

"Leapin Lillies! I've been around here longer than them doctors put together. They just want to get rid of me. When you're over ninety, they don't expect you to recover. I'm going home. They can't stop me. Why, I've had friends that have gone to rehabilitation centers and they turn up dead. Why I…"

Toolie felt the man's hands gently squeeze hers.

"I've lived in a nursing center for years, Ms. Toolie. People are very happy there."

"Do they die?"

"Only the sick ones." The Peacemaker tried to make light of her fears.

"Well, I don't intend to get sick. Or fall down the steps again." Toolie threw the sheet over her legs and pulled back her hand.

Megan anticipated that her visit could be contentious. Toolie was a rascal. She was perhaps so contrary that the hospital was anxious to find Toolie a place to land.

"Mr. George will be staying here a few days, Toolie. Do you suppose he could find a room at the General Kane Boarding House?"

"Not mine. I have to redd it up. Maybe Matty has an extra bed or a sofa. I think all of the other rooms are dilapidated. Did you check the Kane Manor?"

Mr. George was embarrassed to tell her that his budget was tight. His Social Security check barely covered his daily expenses. His Greyhound bus fare broke his budget this month.

"What's your business, Mr. George? Are you a retired professor?" Toolie asked.

"Oh, I'm retired all right," he replied. "For many years, I was the Peacemaker for Seneca Nation."

"So you hopped around campfires and chanted things nobody could understand, like in the movies?" Toolie could embarrass people without trying.

"More than that, Ms. Toolie. I was one of the leaders. They consulted with me on customs and beliefs. I was the tribe's historian. Quite a job."

"So you're a wise guy?" she asked.

"I used to be."

"Me too."

When Matty sneaked into the News Leader office he was greeted by a familiar yipping sound. Cuddles bolted toward him as fast as her little legs could toddle. She grabbed his leg with her two front paws. He dragged her a few steps before picking her up.

"Come on girl," he whispered. "Don't get me caught."

Jessie poked her head from the business office. "Well, look what the dog dragged in. If it isn't our star reporter and animal lover."

"Hey, Jessie. Nice edition today. Loved the baby photos."

"We had to fill the space with something, Matty. I thought you had a Page One blockbuster. What happened?"

A lot happened. Josh Gibson's widow was missing. Her home was burglarized. Matty was clunked on the nose by a fleeing felon. Thugs from a casino were chasing his new best friend. And he had signed his trust assets over to Kane Community Hospital to care for an elderly waitress.

Who has time for a summer job?

Matty looked past her and noticed an open door to the editor's private office.

"Is he...?"

"Yes, he is," Jessie answered.

"Should I...?"

"Yes, you should," she told him.

Matty handed the wriggling Cuddles to Jessie and cleared his throat. He knocked on Tom Zachary's doorjamb.

"Come in, young man," Zachary said without looking up. "How's Toolie?"

"Getting stronger. Still ornery." Matty's observations did not lighten the mood.

Zachary totaled some entries on his calculator and wrote a number in his ledger book.

Matty waited for an eternity as his boss treated him like his lowest priority.

"I'm sorry, Mr. Z." Matty broke the silence.

"Say what?"

"Sorry, with an explanation."

Zachary sighed. He dropped his calculator into an open drawer. Then he raised the News Leader's front page toward Matty's face. "Look at this."

"Yeah, I know," Matty answered. "You filled the paper with photos of the governor's baby. That's too bad. No hard news."

"Too bad?" Zachary blurted. "Are you nuts? This was the best-selling newspaper we've ever had. Babies, babies, babies. People can't get enough of this. We've had orders from outlets all over Pennsylvania. Listen. Can't you hear the presses running? We're printing a second edition."

"A money-maker, huh?"

"Oodles. I've never seen anything like this."

Suddenly, Matty felt the pressure ease. There's nothing like a happy editor, he thought. Perhaps, this was a good time to reserve front page display for Matty's unwritten story on Josh Gibson's death.

"About next week's paper..."

Zachary held up his palm and stopped Matty in mid-sentence. "Got that all planned out," Zachary said. "We're doing a follow-up about the baby, with more photos. You know, the baby in her nursery. The baby getting a bath. The baby in a stroller. The baby sleeping."

"Mr. Z, I have a story idea," Matty said.

"Hold your idea, Matty. We'll have time for your stories later. We have to ride this baby for a few more weeks. Our salaries depend on it."

Matty understood that economics sometimes controlled news judgment. But a few more weeks of baby photos?

"And as your editor," Zachary put his hand on Matty's shoulder, "I'm assigning the lead article to you. I'll help, of course."

"But then I would meet the governor?" Matty asked.

Zachary knew this day would come eventually. He had promised to arrange a meeting between the governor and his half-brother. Zachary wondered how Matty would be received by the governor. But with the baby, surely the meeting would be cordial, he thought.

"I'll be there, Matty. You have to meet Jimmie Bailey sometime. This is the perfect opportunity. You don't have to hold Hannah Maria, unless they want a family portrait."

"Very funny, Mr. Z."

"Well, what do you say? Will you write the story?"

"On one condition," Matty replied. "Take me to the Kane police barracks this afternoon. Introduce me to the lead detective in Professor Dulaney's bear attack."

"The cop I wrestled with? The one who put me into jail? Why?"

Matty reminded Zachary of his story about the rabid bear being captured. "There are some inconsistencies in the evidence, Mr. Z. I need to follow up with a few questions."

"Seems simple to me, Matty. Bear attacks. Man dies. Bear shot by police. End of story."

"Maybe you're right, Mr. Z. But Toolie said something very interesting to me..."

"Toolie? She's always starting rumors. Don't go on a wild goose chase, Matty. Newspaper reporters don't have time to waste on crazy leads from crazy sources."

Perhaps Zachary only had babies and dollar signs in his eyes. This was not the editor who defended his First Amendment rights, challenged legal authority and sacrificed his liberty in the McKean County Jail, depriving himself of carrot cake and Milky Way bars.

"Haven't you ever investigated a story that seemed preposterous, Mr. Z?"

Zachary was caught on that question. Years ago, he doubted whether Governor Brock Bailey was killed when his limousine plunged into the Monongahela River in Pittsburgh. Zachary interviewed dozens of witnesses who were unable to place Bailey in the limousine, learned that Bailey's blood was not present in the fallen vehicle and challenged state police commissioner Josh

Gibson to confirm the old governor's death. Now, the editor could not deprive his summer intern of similar investigative curiosity.

"OK, Matty." Zachary shut down his computer and took his car keys. "We'll drive to the barracks. But you have one hour to show me this story is worth pursuing. If not, it's baby time!"

The Pine Township police car idled in Dolores Gibson's driveway. Two plainclothes detectives kept the engine running because their visit would be short.

Dolores knew they were coming, so she left open her front door. Her favorite appliance, a blender on her bar stand, chewed through a batch of ice cubes. Triple-sec and orange juice splashed in the canister. She was moments from delirium.

"Mrs. Gibson!" a voice called from the front step. Dolores took a swig, fluffed her hair and answered the call. She always delighted in meeting police officers, especially in the privacy of her home.

"Please come in." She directed the officers to her living room. "How about a drink?"

"No, ma'am," one detective said. "Official business, you know."

Her tongue followed a drop down the side of her martini glass. The detectives watched her lick it as it dangled on the base. "It's very good. Smoothes out the day."

"Mrs. Gibson, we're here to complete our investigation of your burglary complaint, and had a few questions, if you don't mind."

Dolores chased an olive with a swizzle stick. She stabbed it several times before balancing it between her teeth. The detectives watched the olive pop into her mouth. She smiled and licked her lips.

"The suspect you named, Randall O'Boyd, denied taking anything from your house. He has an alibi witness. We interviewed her, and she confirmed that her husband was with her."

"Darla The Witch? He was with Darla? That's impossible.

They're going through a divorce. I got a call from her attorney."

"She verified that she was with Mr. O'Boyd for about two hours yesterday afternoon. They used the church computer. She told police they printed out a form for you to sign."

Dolores was livid. That scoundrel left her at a motel and went to see his wife. How depraved was that?

"Mrs. O'Boyd told police that you signed the form. Is that true?"

"I wrote on it, but I didn't sign it." Dolores stabbed an ice cube and broke the swizzler.

"Mrs. O'Boyd showed us a copy of the form. You agreed to donate your silver to the Church of Higher Science. The form looked to be legal."

"So he took the silver?" Dolores asked.

"Mrs. Gibson, he didn't steal it. But he says you gave it to him. He wants to know where it is."

"Well, you tell that son-of-a ..."

One of the detectives stood and motioned his partner toward the door. "Mrs. Gibson, this seems to be a civil matter. There is a dispute between you and the O'Boyds over the ownership of this silver. Our department cannot get involved in a civil case."

"There's no dispute, officer. The silver belongs to me."

One of the detectives turned to her at the front door. "My advice to you Mrs. Gibson is to get an attorney. Don't involve the police department in your private matters."

"What do you mean, 'private matters?' I was robbed..."

"You slept with the preacher. You nearly wrecked his marriage. Look at you – a middle-aged woman having an affair with a married man half your age. You were asking for trouble. And now you want us to get mixed up in this mess? Grow up. Goodbye, Mrs. Gibson."

The other detective shook his head and pointed to her. "Very messy."

Dolores threw back the rest of her drink and watched them

back from her driveway. She could tolerate insults by township cops, but she couldn't let Pastor Randy escape unscathed.

She slapped her face with cold water. A plan hatched in her mind. It was brilliant.

"Hello, Church of Higher Science. How may we help you find peace today?" a cheery voice answered the office telephone.

"This is the North Side Photo Lab." Dolores spoke through a handkerchief into the receiver. "The color slides Pastor Randy ordered for Sunday's service are ready."

"I'll be sure to tell him," the cheery voice replied.

"No need for that. We deliver," Dolores answered. "Just give me the name of the individual who operates the slide projector."

"That would be Hank. He needs them by Sunday at 9 a.m."

"I'll be there by 9." Dolores balanced the envelope containing 8 x 10 glossies of her and the preacher man in the palm of her hand.

"One more question," the receptionist said. "Are these slides for his sermon on sin or his sermon on love?"

"Either one."

Chapter Twenty-Four
The Shovel

Kane's state police barracks were barely large enough to house a dispatcher, a commander's office and a coffee room. So a wooden crate bearing the killer bear rested on cinder blocks outside a rear exit door.

Game Commission regulations required that the bear be preserved for 60 days after Professor Dulaney's death case was closed. State troopers had carried the crate behind the building before sunrise. No sense in attracting flies inside.

Lead investigator, Sergeant Cal Heinrich completed a five-page report before closing the Dulaney file. After about a dozen references to "Subject Bear," the sergeant decided to call it "Einstein." He told his commander that the bear had a wild look, had messy fur and "obviously was smarter than a college professor."

Einstein had been cornered in Kinzua Valley by three police marksmen two evenings ago. When the bear charged at one, the other two fired. One round to the head, another to the throat and Einstein dropped. Blood loss was minimal. The troopers immediately wrapped the bear in a body bag and transported it to the Game Commission office. A tissue sample tested positive for rabies.

Sgt. Heinrich relied on medical examiner findings to verify that Einstein killed Professor Dulaney. Every wound was "induced by Subject Bear," according to Heinrich's report. Claw marks and bite marks on the victim's body were consistent with a bear attack. "There was no other perpetrator, human or animal," the report concluded.

Tom Zachary's call to the barracks was routed to Heinrich. "Sure the evidence is still here," he told the editor. "We're done with the investigation, so you can look at it."

Why was the newspaper interested? Heinrich worried that his investigation may have been too hurried. Police work requires an open mind, but everyone called this a bear attack from the start. Could Einstein have had an accomplice?

Zachary and Matty arrived at the Kane barracks shortly before an afternoon shift change. Heinrich met them at the front counter. He held the thin Dulaney file under his arm. Heinrich hadn't seen Zachary since the sergeant had him arrested for disturbing the peace at Kinzua Bridge.

"Mr. Zachary, I understand you've paid your debt to society," Heinrich said. "So you're back on the street?"

"Look, Cal. Judge Van Lear dismissed the charges. Why don't you save your sarcasm for real criminals – that is, if you can find any." Zachary stiffened to a taller height. Matty stepped between the two men. He didn't have time for machismo.

"Here's the report, Zachary." Heinrich stood on tip-toes to talk over Matty. "I made a copy for you. No charge. If you don't mind, I'm done for the day and I want to go home."

Matty took the report and paged through it. All of the proper conclusions were made, but Heinrich did not mention a second shovel in the bushes.

"We want to see the physical evidence, sergeant," Matty said. "Do you have an evidence room?"

"Sure. Out back. Look in the box," Heinrich replied. "But hold your nose, bears can smell pretty bad after a few days."

Matty resisted the urge to tell Heinrich to drop the attitude. Matty needed his help.

"I'm not interested in the bear," he said. "I'm sure state police gathered up other evidence at the scene. That would be standard procedure for a death case, right?"

"Of course, young man," Heinrich said. "And you are…?"

"Matthew Moore, summer intern working at the News Leader."

"Well, Matthew Moore, summer intern, let me tell you a little about police work. Your boss here probably knows as much about police work as Einstein."

"Thank you," Zachary said. "Finally, some respect."

Sgt. Heinrich stifled a laugh. He found Zachary to be obnoxious, but the kid seemed genuinely interested.

"Every time we investigate a suspicious death, we do an inventory of property collected at the scene. We list the property on an evidence log. Some of the evidence we retain for a certain period."

"What about the other evidence?" Matty asked.

"We dispose of it, either by returning it to the property owner or destroying it. We don't have the storage to keep evidence forever."

"Did you keep an evidence log in the Dulaney case?" Matty asked.

"Sure," Heinrich replied. "Let me find it."

When the sergeant entered a back room, Zachary turned to Matty and asked, "Are you looking for something in particular? Everything seems cut and dried to me."

"I have a hunch," Matty answered. "And it has nothing to do with Dulaney."

Heinrich returned with a single sheet of paper. "Evidence Log" was the heading. Underneath were six entries – "Dulaney wallet and contents, Dulaney shirt, Dulaney blood sample, shovel 1, shovel 2 and drawing of unknown origin."

Matty re-read Heinrich's final report. No mention was made of any drawing.

"Sergeant, have you kept all of this evidence?" he asked.

"Not everything. Look at the check marks. We returned the wallet to the professor's family. The family directed us to destroy the shirt. The blood sample is preserved. And the shovels we have out back with the crate."

"What about the drawing?" Matty asked. "Did you preserve that?"

Heinrich recalled finding a folded paper near Dulaney's body. He showed it to the Kinzua Park ranger. That's when it left police custody.

"No, we didn't keep that," Heinrich told Matty. "Upon examination, we determined that the drawing was not relevant to the investigation."

"What did the drawing look like?" Matty asked.

"The park ranger showed it to Governor Bailey when he visited the death scene. The governor said the drawing was an Indian relic that belonged in a museum."

"But what did it look like?" Matty pressed him.

"It looked like a freaking map to me, but I ain't no Indian."

"So there were Indian words on the map?"

"Indian words? Yeah, maybe."

"In what color?"

"Red, I believe," Heinrich answered. "Why is this important?"

Matty made notes on his legal pad – map, red words, governor takes it for museum. Now he had some good questions for his upcoming story about Jimmie Bailey and his famous baby.

"I can show you the shovels, if you like. Other than the bear, that's all we have here." Heinrich motioned for them to follow into a back room. He returned a few minutes later with a long plastic bag in each hand. He placed them on a conference table and unzipped them, exposing two shovels. Shovel 1 was about three feet long and appeared to be lightly used. Shovel 2 had a long wooden handle and was stained and rusty.

Zachary reached over to touch them, but Matty swatted away his arm.

"Where was each found, sergeant?" Matty asked.

"Shovel 1 was found next to the body. It appeared pretty much like it looks now, only with loose dirt and sand. Most of that has fallen off as we handled it."

"Did the dirt and sand match the area where Dulaney was digging?"

"Ah, we didn't do a soil comparison, no. But I'd say that would be a logical conclusion." Heinrich wondered whether the young reporter was smarter than Einstein.

"What about Shovel 2? Where did you find that?"

"The bear dragged that shovel away from the scene, maybe about 20 yards." Heinrich was proud of his empirical reasoning. After all, how else could the shovel be so far removed from the body?

"Shovel 2 is about five feet long," Zachary observed. "Are you telling me that a bear would carry this shovel..."

"Well, not in his hands, er, paws. He couldn't grip it," Heinrich said. "Probably in his mouth. That would be my guess."

"Guess?" Zachary's journalistic juices started to flow. "So after the bear had a tasty human neck in his teeth, he decided to chew on a wooden shovel?"

"Well, maybe he chewed on the shovel before he chewed on Dulaney's neck," Heinrich stammered. "That's a possibility, right?"

"No, sergeant," Matty replied. "That's not possible. There's blood on the blade, so it happened after the bear attack."

"OK, you're right, Mr. Moore." Heinrich was fidgeting in his seat. "If you're done, can I go home now?"

"Wait a second, Matty." Zachary grabbed his intern's arm and stood for a better view of Shovel 2. "If the bear took this shovel in its mouth after the attack on Dulaney, we'd see teeth marks and Dulaney's blood on the handle. I don't see anything."

"That's right, Mr. Z. No teeth marks. No blood."

"So you're telling me what, guys?" Heinrich was about ready to rip up his report.

"This shovel had nothing to do with Dulaney's death. It was just an old shovel you found in the bushes," Zachary said.

"With a blood stain…" Matty waited for Heinrich's reaction. Heinrich stood and zipped the two evidence bags.

"The report on Dulaney is accurate. Nothing you have told me changes my mind. Dulaney was killed by the bear in the box outside. End of case. Now if you gentlemen will excuse me, there are some trout waiting for me."

"Sergeant, please," Matty pleaded. "You have a blood-stained shovel. Aren't you curious whose blood it is? You have a sample of Dulaney's blood. It would be easy."

"OK, Mr. Moore. If I order a blood comparison would you go away?"

"Depends. How fast could we get the results?"

"Tomorrow morning, noon at the latest," the sergeant replied.

"Good enough for me," Zachary told his intern. "That will give you some time to work on the Bailey baby story."

"Yippee," Matty muttered under his breath.

Toolie was awakened by deep coughing.

She turned to see a patient in the adjacent bed. Her room was no longer private.

"Mercy sakes, woman," Toolie called to her. "You got the whooping cough or something?"

The woman answered with a wheeze and a smoker's hack. She looked ashen. Her hands trembled between outbursts. Her white hair was matted down, as though she had taken off a wig. She couldn't speak. Her phlegm was rearranging violently in her throat.

"You contagious?" Toolie covered her nose and mouth with a sheet. She faced away from the convulsing woman while jamming the nurse call button like a maniac.

After a minute under her sheet, Toolie heard voices. Maybe the nurse came to save her, she thought.

"Aunt Evelyn, here, drink some water."

Toolie peeked. A younger woman in a denim jumpsuit was leaning over the patient. She held a plastic cup. The patient took a drink. Her coughing subsided.

Evelyn? Could it be Evelyn Reilly? Toolie took another look. Wow, Toolie thought, she looks awful. Just last week, Evelyn and her bridge partners had lunch at the restaurant. She appeared to be marvelous then – trim, bright-eyed and perky. And a good appetite for red meat. Evelyn couldn't be more than 70 years old. How can someone twenty years younger than Toolie seem so close to death?

"Now you lean back and close your eyes. Let the medicine work." The visitor placed the water cup on a hospital tray.

Toolie lifted herself on one elbow. Her natural curiosity took control.

"Miss, I know Evelyn," Toolie said. "She is one of my customers at the Golden Wheel. If you don't mind, could you tell me what's wrong?"

"Aunt Evelyn had a bad night. She fell in the bathroom between the toilet and sink."

"Oh, I understand," Toolie said. "That can happen."

"Well, the doctors say she broke her hip, so she will be here at least a week."

"But the cough, why the cough? It sounds terrible."

"Aunt Evelyn lives alone. Nobody found her in the bathroom for six hours. She may have pneumonia from that."

Toolie raised the sheet over her mouth again. Her friend Evelyn fell, broke her hip and contracted pneumonia – probably about the same time Toolie tumbled down the staircase. Thank goodness Toolie took her vitamins and calcium. But was she strong enough to survive the germs now breeding in her hospital room?

"Aunt Evelyn's on antibiotics and we think she's not contagious," the woman said. "No need to worry."

But worry Toolie did well.

"It's a real shame," the visitor said. "We tried to have a caregiver come to Aunt Evelyn's house every day. But she wouldn't listen. She said she could take care of herself. And now this."

Toolie always believed that only other people got older, that other people needed assistance, that other people required daily companionship.

It is a real shame, Toolie grudgingly agreed. It took a fall down the stairs for Toolie to realize that she needed somebody else in her life.

Matty fed and walked Cuddles before their drive. For the dog, it was a ride home.

Dolores Gibson waited at the end of her driveway. When Matty called her an hour earlier to tell her that Cuddles was safe in his care, she cried. Her cocker spaniel was too passive to survive in the wild, she believed.

Matty had not explained his earlier visit to her house. He only told her that Cuddles was wandering on the road and that, as a kind gesture, he would drive her home. He mentioned nothing about searching her house with Megan and definitely nothing about the missing silver.

Cuddles hopped from seat to seat when she recognized her old neighborhood. When Matty turned into the driveway, Dolores instinctively reached for her pet through a moving car window.

"Cuddles, girl!" Dolores hugged the dog like her only friend. "Mommy missed you so much."

Matty stood to the side and watched the happy reunion.

"Thank you, Mr. Moore. How did you ever find her?"

"It was the strangest thing. I will just passing through and I saw her stumbling on the side of the road. She looked familiar. When I read the tag, I said, 'Heck, that's Mrs. Gibson's dog.' So I called you and here we are."

Dolores kissed the dog's mouth and detected the smell of

wieners. For the past few days, Zachary had shared his lunch with Cuddles.

"Please stay for a while," she said, taking Matty's arm. "There's so much to tell you."

Matty had hoped for an invitation. He had some information for her as well.

"I was robbed this week," Dolores told him. "All that silver you saw, it's gone."

"Did you call the police? Do you know who did it?" Matty asked.

"I have a good idea, but the police say it's a civil matter and they won't investigate."

"Who was it?"

"This man from Pittsburgh," Dolores replied. "He forced me to sleep with him, and the police say they don't want to get involved in a lover's quarrel."

Dolores and Billy Herman? In bed? That was one repulsive thought for Matty.

"Can you describe him for me?" Matty asked.

"He's fairly short, stubby with a peach fuzz face. I'd say about 25 years old."

Probably not Herman, Matty thought. Could this woman be mistaken?

"Does he have a broken arm?" Matty asked.

"No. His arms are very strong," Dolores replied. "He's in great shape. I bet he exercises all the time."

Definitely not Herman, Matty realized.

"His name is Randy O'Boyd," Dolores said. "He runs a church in McKees Rocks."

"I think I've seen some photographs of him," Matty said.

"Yeah, I've seen some, too."

Matty sat beside her on the couch and took her hand. "Look, Mrs. Gibson, I don't think O'Boyd took your silver. I think it was taken by the man who murdered Josh."

"What?" Dolores gasped.

"I can't prove it yet, but I'm getting close."

"Who is he?"

"Before I tell you, I need your help," Matty said.

"Anything."

"First, I need to prove that Josh was murdered. The state police have recovered a shovel near the spot where Josh's body was found. There's a blood stain on the shovel. It could be the murder weapon. Police are doing tests right now, but they have nothing to compare the blood stains with."

"What can I do?" Dolores asked.

"I need a tissue sample from Josh. That way we can match the blood on the shovel."

"Josh has been dead for five years. How can we get a tissue sample?"

"Where's his body, Mrs. Gibson?"

"Oh, Mr. Moore. We cannot disturb the dead. Josh is at rest now. I cannot violate the sacred peace between Josh and his Maker."

Matty understood, but also was driven to learn the truth. "Mrs. Gibson, if the tissue sample matches with the shovel, Josh was murdered and you get $2 million in insurance money!"

"Twin Oaks Cemetery, about fifteen minutes from here."

Daylight ebbed as Matty drove Dolores through the Twin Oaks gate. They slowly passed rows of tombstones, many decayed and bent by extremes of summers and winters. Religious statues dotted the landscape. They seemed to move with shadows from his headlights. The scene was eerie at this hour. Most disturbing was the absolute silence.

Dolores pointed to the right. Matty steered his Mustang down a gravel path. The headstones here seemed to be newer and the shrubbery, more nicely trimmed. He slowed for a sharp bend. Dolores opened a pill box and swallowed two tablets without water.

"This is only the second time I've visited Josh since his fall. The first time was his funeral. I had to be here."

Matty tried to understand her, but couldn't. At first, she appeared to be a grieving widow. Now, he viewed her as a fighter, ready to reclaim her silver and insurance money. He would help her if he could, especially for a page one story.

"Park the car, Mr. Moore. We can walk from here."

Matty opened the trunk and collected the ax and shovel he borrowed from the Gibson garage. Together, they walked through the graves toward a small rise.

"There, Mr. Moore. That's where Josh is."

Fifty feet in front of Matty was a marble building. Drawers were stacked six high and about 50 long.

"Shit, Mrs. Gibson! That's a mausoleum! Are you telling me Josh was buried inside a mausoleum?"

"Why, yes. That's what he wanted. His spot is Number 57. It's under the bug zapper."

Matty dropped his tools.

"What's wrong?" she asked.

"I can't break into a mausoleum. I'd need a jackhammer."

"I'm sorry, Mr. Moore. I didn't realize..."

"It was probably a stupid idea anyway. You know, digging up a grave just to take a piece of skin or a patch of hair..."

Dolores began to laugh. "Is that what you want? You should have told me."

"Why?" Matty asked.

"You can have all the hair you want. His old brush is under my sink."

Chapter Twenty-Five
The Threat

"This will work for a day or two. I could sleep on the sofa tonight."

Mr. George removed a bag of tortilla chips and Matty's gym shorts before sitting down. The accommodations were less antiseptic than his retirement home in New York. On the bright side, though, Matty's apartment at General Kane Boarding House would be free of senior citizen noise – loud televisions, squeaky walkers and "Smoky" Bernie's oxygen compressor.

"I'm sure Matty won't mind having some company," Megan told the Seneca Peacemaker. "He likes stories, and you like to tell them."

Mr. George used a napkin to remove French fries from a coffee table. He opened his overnight bag and retrieved a tattered scrapbook.

"I never leave home without this." He handed his book to Megan. She slowly coursed through the pages.

"Is this you?" She pointed to a black and white photograph. A young man in American Indian garb stood proudly behind a split rail fence. Behind him were a deep forest and a pink painted sky.

"Turn it over," he said. "What's the date?"

"Nineteen sixty-four," she replied.

"Seneca Nation had just selected me as Peacemaker. That was a very important time in my life."

"So handsome," Megan said. She flipped over more pages. Many photographs showed Mr. George posing with other Seneca leaders. Some photographs showed construction of new homes and community centers for the Pennsylvania Indians relocated to New York. What the scrapbook did not reveal was Mr. George's personal life.

"Was there a Mrs. George? Did you have anyone special in your life?" she asked.

He opened his wallet and removed a small photograph from a pocket. "Just one. Her name was Karen. We met in high school. I had such a crush on her…"

"You've kept her in your wallet all of these years? Why?"

"I don't know," he said. "I take out her photo, look at her, and dream about how life could have turned out differently. Karen died suddenly. She was 18."

"Oh, I'm sorry," Megan said.

"You'd think after 50 years…" Mr. George looked at the ceiling.

Megan felt awkward. Perhaps no one had spoken to the Peacemaker on a personal level for years, especially if he had no family.

"Let me clean up a bit," she said, breaking the silence. "Matty needs a housekeeper. Look at this bedroom. Maybe we should do his laundry."

She began shuffling about the apartment, gathering clothes and putting everything in its place. After a dizzying few minutes, Mr. George motioned for her to sit beside him.

"That can wait," he told her. "You haven't finished the scrapbook. There's more I want you to see."

Megan dropped a laundry hamper near the door and returned to him. Mr. George flipped to the back of the scrapbook and placed it on her lap.

"What's this?" she asked.

"We Indians can do some bad things, like gambling, alcohol and tobacco. But we do some things well. Genealogy is one thing Senecas do extremely well."

Megan examined a chart of names she did not recognize. The first name, Sky of Morning, was listed with the dates of 1798-1859. Below Sky of Morning were two names, James Searcy and Effie Hardy. Below them were six pairs of names. Dozens of names flowed from the six pairs and filled the page. None looked familiar to Megan.

"Is this what you do, Mr. George? People ask you to trace their Indian history and you prepare these charts?" Megan asked.

He smiled. "No, this is much too complicated. I asked the Seneca clerk's office to prepare this one for me. Look at the detail. The dates of birth and death. The full names of each offspring – all written in the finest calligraphy. This is painstaking work. The ladies at the clerk's office spend days looking through volumes. But when they're done and they certify the result..."

"You know you're a certified Seneca Indian," Megan said.

"No doubt," he said.

"How proud you must be, Mr. George. You know your ancestors' names. You know where you came from. Nobody can take that heritage from you."

"Thank you, Megan. I am proud. But please, this family chart continues on the back side of the paper."

She turned the page. Names were written in a smaller print. Families were larger. This tree was fruitful, she thought. Some names seemed to ring a bell. Henry Byrnes and his wife, Catherine. They had a son, Cyril. Megan remembered her uncle, Cyril. Everyone called him "Scoop." She looked at the chart and saw Cyril's two brothers, Daniel and David. Quite a coincidence, she thought. She had two uncles by those names. Both had been killed in Vietnam.

On the chart, Daniel and David had death dates of 1968.

Then she saw the names of her parents and, below them, "Megan Elizabeth." She touched the Peacemaker's hand. Tears welled in her eyes.

"You did this for me, Mr. George," she said. "I am so touched."

"The seventh generation, Megan. You never knew this?"

"Nobody in my family bothered looking at our history," she said. "When we were kids, we heard rumors. Mom always referred to us as her little Indians, but we didn't take it literally."

"Well, you can take it literally. This is proof you are a Seneca Indian."

"May I keep this paper?" Megan asked.

"It is for you," Mr. George replied. "But I've done more research."

"About Sky of Morning?"

"Yes. She was quite a character. She was raised on the Cornplanter Reservation along the Allegheny River. She operated a school for Indian girls. Rather than teaching them how to cook and make clothes, Sky of Morning taught the girls to speak and read English. This caused great distress to others in the Nation. She was ostracized from her people. Our records indicate that she befriended an American pioneer and gave birth out of wedlock. She was a rare Indian feminist, I suppose."

"That's very interesting," Megan said. "Are any of my other ancestors Indian?"

"Here's how we look at that. If you descend from a Seneca woman, then you are a Seneca Indian."

"So you're saying…"

"All of your ancestors and you, Megan, are Senecas. Welcome to the tribe!"

Bill Pennoyer curled into a ball. He pulled a wool blanket to his neck. Another sleepless night in the governor's guest house. Another night alone with his thoughts.

Being chief-of-staff to Jimmie Bailey had its perks, for sure. Travel, expense accounts, and satisfactions of public service he didn't experience as a private attorney and sports agent. But it was the dark side of the job that kept Pennoyer awake.

Jimmie Bailey grabbed power five years ago when his father, Governor Brock Bailey, disappeared. Pennoyer, like everyone else, assumed that Brock had perished when his limousine disappeared into the Monongahela River in Pittsburgh. When Brock's body was pulled downstream from the crash site four months later, he suspected no foul play. And certainly he suspected no foul play by his best friend, Jimmie.

Pennoyer became Jimmie's campaign manager for the gubernatorial race. Together, they toured Pennsylvania. They spent nearly every day side-by-side. Every day except for one – the day Brock returned to Kinzua Valley unexpectedly, the day Brock and Jimmie fought on the railroad bridge, the day Brock fell to his death.

Jimmie kept the secret from his friend for about a year. Then bizarre letters started to appear at the governor's office. Pennoyer could not understand the cryptic messages from a writer identified only as "the governor's friend." He showed them to Jimmie, but he laughed them off. "Just some kook," Jimmie said.

Then phone calls started. The "kook" left messages on the governor's personal phone line. "I know what you did," the messages would say. "We need to talk or things will get out of control." Pennoyer was disturbed, but the governor told him to ignore the threats.

Soon thereafter, a visitor appeared at the governor's Capitol office. He told a receptionist in the outer office that, if he did not meet the governor, he would have him arrested. He pushed past the receptionist, who hurriedly called for security.

Pennoyer stopped the strange man in the governor's private waiting room. He asked for the visitor's name. The man said it was Billy Herman. When Pennoyer asked what business he had with the governor, Herman said it was personal. Pennoyer told him to leave, and then he told Jimmie about the incident.

At that moment, Jimmie told his story to Pennoyer. He had

THE THREAT 291

struck his father on the bridge, a storm brewed from the east and Brock was thrown 300 feet into Kinzua Valley. Fearful that he would be charged with killing his father, Jimmie transported the body to Pittsburgh's West End Bridge. He dumped his father over the railing. The dead governor was found in the Ohio River shortly thereafter.

Jimmie told Pennoyer that Josh Gibson learned those details when he confronted the new governor at Leigh-Rose Mansion. Josh agreed to keep the matter quiet; in return, the governor re-appointed him as state police commissioner. Two other men had learned the secret as well: Kane News Leader editor Tom Zachary and a Pittsburgh police detective, Billy Herman.

Zachary chose not to print the story after Jimmie promised him a bigger scoop. Herman, however, could be kept quiet only with money.

Pennoyer's role was to protect Jimmie. He did that by paying Herman whenever he needed money. But as years passed, Herman became more threatening. Last week, Herman unleashed his most dangerous threat upon the governor.

Only hours before the speeding Herman was chased by state police through the Allegheny National Forest and was injured in a car crash, he telephoned Pennoyer. Herman repeated his belief that Gibson paid off Jimmie with silver. Herman demanded $100,000 from the governor or else.

"Or else what?" Pennoyer had asked.

"Or else the baby dies!"

Such a threat was unspeakable, Pennoyer thought. The governor could never be told. Instead, he reported to Jimmie that Herman wanted more money and that he was driving to McKean County to get it. Jimmie told Pennoyer to alert the state police and have the man tailed.

Pennoyer now tossed in bed. Wind-blown pine branches scratched the guest house roof with a quickening tempo. He could see an upstairs bedroom light flicker on at the governor's mansion.

He heard soft cries from Hannah Maria through a screened window. The cries were not comforting; he knew that Billy Herman was on the loose.

Certainly the Bailey family was safe in their mansion. And certainly, the governor's state police protection detail would stop any intruder.

Pennoyer struggled with his decision not to tell Jimmie of Herman's threat. If he did, Jimmie might take matters into his own hands.

And he knew Jimmie slept with a loaded handgun close at hand.

Matty returned to General Kane Boarding House with a headache and a zippered plastic bag filled with Josh Gibson's hair. By habit, he sneaked past Toolie's darkened apartment. He momentarily forgot that his neighbor was spending the night at Kane Community Hospital. Matty reached the third floor landing. He saw light filtering under his closed apartment door.

Perhaps his lamp was on when he responded to Toolie's fall that morning. Maybe he forgot to turn it off when he returned to the apartment after following her to the hospital. He couldn't remember details of the day. So much had happened since.

Matty tested the door knob. It was unlocked. With a creak, the door opened. The apartment was not as he had left it. The floor was free of clothes and clutter. No dirty dishes were stacked in the kitchen. And the place had a disinfectant smell.

He soon observed that he was not alone. Megan was curled in his recliner. She was wrapped in his bedspread. On his sofa was a long old man. His feet were stretched beyond the cushions. His head was bent backward. His mouth was wide open.

Matty knelt beside the recliner. "Megan, Megan." He pushed his friend lightly on her shoulder. She turned and was startled.

"You're home," Megan said hoarsely. "We wondered where you were."

Matty glanced at the strange man on his couch. "Who is 'we,' Megan?"

"He is Mr. George, the Seneca Peacemaker I was telling you about. He needed a place to stay tonight and I volunteered your apartment. Is that OK?"

Matty was too exhausted to answer. He merely nodded.

"Do you want your bedspread?" she whispered.

"No, you can have it," Matty said. "I'm going to get a bite to eat, hit the shower and get some sleep. What time is it anyway?"

"About 1 a.m."

Matty opened a kitchen cabinet. "Megan," he whispered. "Have you seen my tortilla chips and French fries?"

"Sorry, Matty. We cleaned up the place a bit and ..."

"You threw out my food?"

Megan stood and joined him in the kitchen. "Let me make you some soup or a sandwich. What do you have here?"

He opened his pantry door. It was empty.

"Come on, let's go downstairs," he told her. "Toolie's apartment is well stocked."

Matty and Megan crept through the dark hallway and down a flight of steps. Toolie's door was unlocked, just as Matty had left it 20 hours earlier. The waitress's kitchen was immaculate; her pantry, bounteous.

"Let's find perishable food, something Toolie wouldn't mind us eating," Megan said. "How about a turkey sandwich on rye?"

"Great." Matty watched his friend rummage through Toolie's cabinets to find mustard. "Megan, look at this, Toolie actually has fresh fruit. I have to eat these blackberries before they go bad."

Megan assembled two sandwiches and arranged them on paper plates. She set two places at Toolie's dining table. Matty devoured his meal. Megan watched him with amusement and sympathy.

"We visited Toolie at the hospital this afternoon, me and Mr.

George," Megan said. "She's doing very well at her age. Imagine, falling down a flight of stairs. She was lucky that you came to her rescue."

"Anybody could have helped her, Megan. I just happened to be there."

Megan paused while he drank Toolie's orange juice. "Don't be so modest, Matty. You were very kind to Toolie, even though she has been difficult with you."

"She needed a friend at the moment, that's all."

"Toolie told me about the other thing you did. You agreed to pay for her hospital expenses. That's very generous. But, Matty, why would you agree to such a thing? Your pay at the newspaper cannot be that great."

"I have some money back at home, Megan. Toolie needs it more than I do."

Megan reached across the table and took his hand. "Your act of kindness says a lot about you, Matty. You've only lived in McKean County for a few weeks, and you've touched so many lives."

"Just Toolie's, a little bit. I don't know of anyone else's life …"

"How about mine?"

Megan leaned toward him. She closed her eyes and kissed him tenderly. Her lips were softer than he'd imagined. And he had imagined, several times.

"Do you think Toolie would mind if we sat together on her sofa?" Matty asked.

He took Megan's hand and led her across the room. Toolie's sofa was circa 1950. Large red flowers had been woven into a seafoam-colored background. The headrests were covered with knitted doilies. A hand-crocheted afghan blanket was draped over one cushion. Matty sat against an armrest covered with plastic. Megan cozied beside him.

They faced an unshaded double window. A soft breeze cooled the room. Sheer ivory curtains brushed the floor. The summer air was dense and warm. At that hour, Fraley Street was quiet and its sidewalks, deserted. Matty pulled a chain to turn off Toolie's lamp.

Megan broke the silence. "Where are you going to college next year, Matty?"

"I've been accepted to Pitt. I'd like to go into pre-med, but this summer job has me interested in journalism."

"You write well. I don't see you as a doctor, not office-bound enough."

"Thanks, I think," Matty replied. "Whatever I do, I'm going to own the business, whether it's a newspaper or a hospital. I can't see myself working for someone else."

"Like Tom Zachary?" Megan asked.

Matty laughed. "Mr. Z is a good man, a little eccentric, but good. If I bought his newspaper, I'd keep him as my editor. And I'd pay him well."

Megan seemed to be deep in thought. Matty adjusted a pillow behind her back and waited for her to break the silence.

"Pitt and Edinboro, they're only a few hours apart," Megan said. "We could even meet halfway."

"That would be great, if you're not too busy."

He stroked her hair and kissed her forehead. She snuggled closer. They watched the star-filled sky. A few silent minutes passed.

"Matty, what did you bring home in the plastic bag?"

"Josh Gibson's hair."

"Oh."

More silence and more star-gazing.

"Megan, why is the Peacemaker sleeping in my apartment?"

"Two goons from a casino are trying to beat him up."

"Oh."

A whippoorwill called in the distance. Toolie's sheer curtains hung listlessly as breezes calmed. The sky seemed to darken.

"I was walking in a cemetery tonight," Matty whispered to her. "I was carrying a pick and a shovel. Ask me why."

Megan did not answer. Her head bobbed toward his chest. Her body was warm and relaxed. He felt her easy heartbeat. He rubbed his fingers along her arm and under her chin. Her skin was bronze, a touch lighter than his. He marveled at the soft features of her face, now only inches from his. She was a beautiful young lady, he thought. And she seemed to be interested in him.

A wonderful new emotion stirred in him.

Matty reached behind her head and lifted Toolie's afghan. He spread it over Megan's legs. She didn't react. She had fallen asleep in his arms.

He kissed her again and tried to relax beside her.

In about an hour, his pulse slowed. Then he slept.

Chapter Twenty-Six
The Curse

The ceiling creaked above him. Matty was awakened by sounds of shuffling feet moving from his bathroom to his kitchen. A minute later, his microwave buzzed. He heard the clang of spoons and forks, followed by the squeal of a chair being dragged over his linoleum floor.

So this is what Toolie endured for the past few weeks, he thought. No wonder she was cranky.

Matty and Megan had left the Peacemaker asleep on the upstairs sofa about midnight. Now, the old Indian was stirring, no doubt energized by sharp morning sunshine. Daylight was streaming into Toolie's apartment as well. But not sharp enough to awaken Megan.

Still clad in yesterday's dress shirt and jeans, Matty took the stairs to his apartment. He was greeted by the smell of cinnamon and coffee. He watched the Peacemaker spooning instant oatmeal into his mouth and chasing it with a bite of toast.

"Good morning, sir." Matty nodded as he entered.

"You must be Mr. Moore." The Peacemaker wadded a napkin and wiped crumbs from his hands. "I hope you don't mind. Miss Megan offered your apartment for a night. But she seems to be missing."

"Megan is safe downstairs. She told me, though, that you were being chased by some bad characters."

"I suppose she explained to you that a casino management company thinks we have the missing Seneca silver. These goons were following me, so I had to get out of town."

Matty extended his hand. "Matthew Moore."

"Roland George." They shook.

"What's the name of the management company, Mr. George?"

"Pathfinder. They're located in Steamburg, New York."

Matty dialed directory assistance. "Do you have a contact name there?"

"The man I spoke with was Mr. Joseph. I think he runs the company."

Matty was transferred to a company receptionist. "Mr. Joseph, please. ... Tell him that Matthew Moore of the Kane News Leader wanted to get a comment about the Seneca silver treasure. ... No, it's not missing. The silver has been found. ... Sure, I'll hold."

The Peacemaker's mouth was agape. What was this young man doing?

"Mr. Joseph, I'm so sorry to bother you. But I'm on deadline and a need a response from Pathfinder. ... Yes, the Spanish silver. ... Ha-ha. You're way off the mark. That old Peacemaker has nothing to do with it. You scared the crap out of that poor man. ... Let me give you the name, Billy Herman. You know him? ... No, 'H'-E-R-M-A-N. 'H' as in Henry. ... Yeah, right. ... He has the silver at his house in Zelienople. ... No, I don't have his address. So, Mr. Joseph, how about a comment for my story?"

Click. Matty put down the phone and smiled.

"That should take care of your problem, Mr. George."

"Yes. I suppose that it's Mr. Herman's problem now."

Matty excused himself to take a shower and shave. Tom Zachary was to pick him up at any moment. His 10 a.m. interview with the Baileys at Leigh-Rose Mansion was rapidly approaching. He anticipated that Zachary would be at least 30 minutes early. After all, the editor was chasing two stories that would sell out his newspaper for weeks. The first would be a mushy profile of the new parents and celebrity baby at home. The second would be a blockbuster exposé detailed a meeting between the two half-brothers, the long separated heirs of Brock Bailey's mammoth estate.

An excited Zachary pulled into the General Kane Boarding House lot 40 minutes early. Matty heard his editor's obnoxious horn.

"Let's go, Matty. We want to catch little Hannah Maria between her feedings."

"All right. But one stop first." Matty tossed his steno pad in the back seat. He held a plastic bag in his teeth as he tucked in his shirttail.

"What's in there?" Zachary asked. "Looks like dust balls."

"While you were sleeping last night, Mr. Z, I was doing some investigating at the Twin Oaks Cemetery," Matty told his stunned editor. "This is Josh Gibson's hair."

"You – you – you dug up the commissioner? Jeez, Matty, you could get time for that."

"Take me to the state police barracks. Sgt. Heinrich has a forensic pathologist on standby."

"So you think the blood on the shovel is ..."

"Gibson's," Matty answered. "We know it's not Professor Dulaney's."

Zachary drove in silence. In ten minutes, he pulled into the barracks parking lot. Matty bounced from the car and met Heinrich and a German-looking young woman at the door. She took the bag and disappeared inside. Matty and Heinrich spoke a bit. Then Heinrich handed him a paper. Matty gave Zachary a thumbs-up.

"What was that all about?" Zachary asked.

"Just as we thought, Mr. Z. There is blood on the shovel and it's not Dulaney's."

"And the woman?"

"That was Dr. Greta from Harrisburg. She was anxious to compare the hair sample."

"Did you tell her whose hair it was?" Zachary asked.

"Are you nuts? I mean, why should she find out for free? She can buy the News Leader and read my story like everyone else will. If it turns out to be Gibson's blood, do you realize..."

Zachary realized the value of a good reporter with a sharp mind. He had hired Matty as a favor to the governor, but later realized that Matty could be enticed into buying the struggling News Leader. He never dreamed the young man possessed such news gathering skills.

Their car turned off Route 6 and onto Sowers Road. The Leigh-Rose Mansion was a few minutes to the north.

"So what did he look like?" Zachary asked.

"Who?"

"Josh Gibson. Did he still have a nose and eyeballs?"

"That's what I wondered when I opened the coffin lid. It was dark and really spooky, Mr. Z. I brushed away some dirt that fell on his face. A worm was crawling from his ear. His eyes were rolled back into his head and the whites of his eyes..."

"Yes?"

"Were charcoal gray. But I tried not to look when I snipped off some of his hair. I'll never forget his mouth, though. It was open. His teeth were rotten and, when the wind blew, well I'll never forget what I heard."

"What did you hear?" Zachary inched closer as Matty's voice softened.

"It was a faint, whistling sound. Almost like he was speaking. I heard words, Mr. Z, and you'll never convince me otherwise."

"Gosh! What were the words?"

"It was very soft, but it sounded like: 'I'll get you, Tom Zachary!'"

Matty slapped his boss on the back and let out a hearty laugh. Zachary was not amused.

"You're full of crap, Matty. You're funny, but full of crap."

They were waved through security at the mansion gate. The beautiful stone house stood in full grandeur before Matty. Here is where his father, Brock Bailey, was born. And here is where his mother worked as a housekeeper.

Matty did not feel welcome.

"Dolores Gibson, please."

A voice on the other end of her telephone sounded familiar and menacing. But she loved the soft baritone.

"This is she."

"I am Jerome DesBois. I'll say it again more slowly, Daay Bwaaah. Accent on the Bwaah. I am an attorney representing Mr. Randall O'Boyd."

"Well, good morning, Mister Day Bra. I remember your voice mail. Didn't you say you represented Darla O'Boyd?"

"The O'Boyds have reconciled. I represent them both."

"That's so sweet, Day Bra. They deserve each other."

"I have before me an agreement, signed by you, that pledges about $4 million worth of silver to the Church of Higher Science," the attorney declared. "This contract is ironclad."

"You need to adjust your straps, Bra Man. I didn't sign your contract. Besides, I don't have any silver. It was stolen."

"Don't fiddle with Attorney DesBois. I graduated in the upper half of my law school class. I have the resources to crush you with endless lawsuits. By the time we're done, you won't have two pennies to scratch together!"

"And don't you mess with the Widow Geeb-sone! Accent on the Geeeeb!" Dolores shot back. "If Pastor Randy wants to steal my silver, tell him to track down my thief. His name is Billy Herman. He lives in Zelienople. Go get him, counselor."

Dolores could hear him muttering on the line, "H-E-R-M-A-N."

"Do you know his address or phone number?" the attorney asked.

"No, but I could call the Pine Township Police and let them know you're interested," Dolores offered.

"Oh, please don't do that. The DesBois Law Firm has people. We can find him."

Matty fidgeted on the governor's leather sofa while Tom Zachary set up his tripod. From down the hall, the clicks of high heels and dress shoes grew louder. Zachary motioned for Matty to stand. Zachary then swept the sofa with his hand as though Matty had soiled it.

"Governor, Mrs. Bailey," Zachary said. "I'd like to introduce my summer intern, Matthew Moore."

Matty extended his hand confidently. Jimmie Bailey took a step forward and grasped it. Ann followed.

"Please, let's sit," Jimmie said. "Hannah Maria is being dressed by the nanny, so we can have our family portrait in a few minutes."

The Baileys sat on a sofa, across a coffee table from Matty and Zachary. Nobody said anything for a few seconds.

"This is kind of clumsy," Jimmie started. "Come here, Matty."

The two men stood. Jimmie sidestepped the table and hugged his half-brother. Matty tried to show affection for his editor's sake, but felt no attachment to this stranger.

"I apologize for not finding you sooner," Jimmie said, breaking his hold. "I wanted to wait until you were 18. There was enough turmoil in your life."

What turmoil? Matty thought. He had a stable family, a loving mother, a supporting step-father and about $25 million in a trust, thanks to the infidelity of Jimmie's father and a ruling by Judge Van Lear. But if the Governor of Pennsylvania wanted to be his buddy, that was OK, too.

Jimmie observed his half-brother's face. The eyes and cheekbones were familiar. Matty was tall and angular, as was his father. The young man had the same confident smile and charm that Brock Bailey had used to woo voters.

"It's an honor to meet you, sir," was all Matty could think to say.

"Tom, Ann, if you could excuse us for a few minutes, I'd like to offer Matty a tour of Leigh-Rose."

Zachary collected his camera and tripod. "Perhaps we could take solo shots of the baby while we're waiting," he suggested to Ann.

"This way, Tom." Ann led Zachary through double doors to a formal living room. A nanny carried a wiggly Hannah Maria to her mother's arms. Zachary closed the double doors and winked at his intern.

Matty followed Jimmie through a mahogany-lined corridor and into the governor's study. Jimmie directed Matty to sit in his wingback chair. Jimmie sat in an opposite rocker.

"We come from very different backgrounds, don't we?" the governor asked.

"My birth was an accident, or so I'm told," Matty answered.

"No accident. No accident at all, Matty. My father loved your mother. If there's love, there is no accident."

"With all due respect, Governor, Brock Bailey was 'our' father. Has this been bothering you all these years? That our father loved two women at the same time?"

"Our father was incapable of loving two women at the same time, Matty. I knew him. I lived with him for more years than you've been alive. Brock Bailey existed for Brock Bailey. Whatever pleased him at the moment, he did. When he stopped loving my mother, he began loving yours. It's that simple."

"Governor?"

"Please call me Jimmie, we're brothers."

"OK, Jimmie. To be honest with you, I don't really care about 'our' father. He abandoned me when I needed a dad. He kept my mother away from me for years. I didn't know who my father was until he died. So I don't share in your neuroses about Brock Bailey's love life or love lives."

"I'm not neurotic about this. Is there something wrong with wanting to meet my father's other son?"

"No, but you need to take advice from a teenager who's visited just about every guidance counselor in the Pittsburgh school district. The advice is: let it go. Stop fixating on Brock Bailey. I did for about a month until my grandmother smacked me. I have realized that I am not defined by what my father did. You should realize that, too."

"So why did you call yourself an accident?" Jimmie asked.

"We're all accidents," Matty answered.

But Jimmie had not thought of himself as an accident. He was the product of loving parents, at least when he was born. And those whimpering sounds from his daughter down the hall, certainly Hannah Maria was not an accident. Didn't he love Ann? But was he wired like his scoundrel father? Was Jimmie doomed to repeat the mistakes of his father, he wondered.

"Why did you want to meet me, Jimmie? Why did you set me up with Mr. Zachary? You could have sent a letter or, better yet, ignored me altogether. What's your plan?"

Jimmie had no plan. He wanted to meet the man who ended up with half of Brock Bailey's inheritance. Beyond that, he questioned whether they would cross paths again.

"I didn't know anything about you," Jimmie said. "Perhaps you needed a hand. Maybe there was something I could do to help you. My family has become very small and I …"

"I don't need a government job, Governor," Matty interrupted. "I'm very happy at the News Leader this summer. And I have enough money…"

"Don't remind me." Jimmie interrupted. "All I'm saying is, if you ever need anything, call me."

Matty remembered one little thing.

"I'm supposed to do this 'baby' story for the newspaper and to be honest, Jimmie, I don't have the time. I'm working on an in-depth piece about Josh Gibson's death. So could you help me?"

Jimmie looked puzzled. "I don't know much about Gibson's death. That was a long time ago and it didn't involve me."

"Oh, no, Governor. What I need is someone to write the baby story. Can someone on your staff ghost-write it for me? Don't tell Mr. Z."

"Ah, sure. I'll have Pennoyer do it. How many words?"

"Three pages, double-spaced. E-mail it to me by 5 p.m. Here's my card."

"No problem," Jimmie said. "So, what have you learned about Josh Gibson's death?"

"Plenty. I really can't tell you now. I have one more interview to do."

"Who? Anybody I know?" Jimmie asked.

"Probably not. His name is Billy Herman. I think he was with Gibson the night he fell to his death."

Matty touched a raw nerve. Jimmie's reaction was quick and extreme.

"Herman is a creep and a liar! Don't believe a word he tells you, Matty."

"You know him?" Matty was surprised.

Jimmie knew Billy Herman, all right. The reprobate had been extorting money from him for the past five years. Herman was a constant threat to Jimmie and his family.

"Only by reputation," Jimmie answered. "He and Josh worked on the investigation when my, I mean our, father disappeared. He, ah … he was arrested for driving under the influence a few days ago, but Van Lear set bail."

"I know," Matty said. "I paid to spring him from jail."

"Why the hell would you do that?" Jimmie couldn't mask his anger.

"For my story. The sheriff stopped me from questioning him in jail because I wasn't his attorney or his family. So I had to get him on the outside."

"What did he say?" Jimmie cooled a bit.

"He said Gibson died before he hit the ground, and then he smashed me with the cast on his broken arm. The lights went out for me. And he stole my car."

"So you called the police?"

"No," Matty explained. "If the police arrested Herman before I could talk to him, I'd never get my story. His attorney would tell him to shut up. So my best chance is to corner him and try to get a confession."

"You think he murdered Gibson?"

"No comment. Buy the newspaper."

So Billy Herman could be a murderer, Jimmie thought. And if he murdered once, why not again?

"This seems far-fetched to me, Matty. Gibson and Herman were both cops. They worked together for years. What possible motive would there be for murder?"

Matty had the conversation right where he wanted it.

"That's a question you can answer, Governor."

"Why me?"

"Just yesterday, I saw the state police evidence log on Professor Dulaney's case. You were on the scene there with the state police." Matty remembered Jimmie ducking him and sprinting down the valley path as Matty and Zachary approached the Kinzua lookout.

"Well, yes. That was a few yards from our house."

"Whatever, Jimmie. I took photographs of you in the valley talking to the troopers. I watched one of them hand you a paper. What was that paper?"

"I don't know, Matty. Maybe just some notes."

"Come on, Jimmie. I know what the paper was. It was described on the police evidence log. It was a map, right?"

"OK. It was a map. Some kind of Indian map. So what?"

"You told the trooper that the map had nothing to do with Dulaney's death and you said the map should be given to the County Historical Society."

How did this kid find out, Jimmie wondered.

"But you didn't give the map away, did you? Because it was a treasure map, correct?"

"Listen, Matty. I've been busy. I haven't turned it over yet."

"Where is it, Governor?"

Jimmie keyed open a desk drawer. He unfolded the paper and handed it over. Matty recognized the map as a color copy of Megan's original.

"Thank God you still have this," he told Jimmie. "Because if anybody tried to dig up the treasure, well, they would be cursed."

Jimmie laughed. "Cursed? Now your story really is far-fetched."

Matty pointed at the red letters. "This is an Indian curse. It says that great harm will come to any white man who disturbs the peace of this land. So anyone who tried to dig up this treasure would be cursed."

"I don't believe in curses," Jimmie said.

"Dulaney had this map. He dug the earth. He died."

"That was a bear, Matty. An unfortunate accident."

"Josh Gibson dug the earth. He died."

"Gibson? When?"

"Jimmie, Josh Gibson found the treasure by accident. If you read the police reports, he was looking for a gun in the Kinzua Valley when his metal detector landed on this spot. Billy Herman was with him when they found a mother lode of Spanish silver. Gibson came back a few days later, dug it up himself, and kept all of the silver in his house. Herman was so angry that, I believe, he killed Gibson."

"So whoever digs there…" Jimmie pointed at a spot on the map.

"Dies," Matty replied.

Jimmie still didn't believe in curses. But Gibson and Dulaney seemed to prove otherwise. He and Pennoyer shoveled dirt at the silver burial site a week ago, and they were still living. But the

Indian curse did not say harm would come immediately.

Matty's cell phone vibrated on his belt. He checked the caller's number and excused himself from the room.

"Hello. This is Matty."

"Mr. Moore, this is Kane Community Hospital. We're letting you know that Gladys Toolie is being discharged at noon. I understand that you are her caregiver and you will come to take her home."

"That's correct."

"Please report to the main reception desk as soon as possible. You will be directed to the attending physician who will provide you with discharge instructions."

"Thank you, ma'am. This is great news," he said.

Matty returned to the governor's study. Jimmie was pacing the floor. Pennoyer had joined him.

"Sorry, Governor, I can't stay," Matty said.

"This is my chief of staff, Matty. Tell him what you told me about this Indian curse," Jimmie directed.

"Pretty simple. Don't dig up the earth here and nothing bad will happen to you."

The governor looked anxious. "Didn't Billy Herman dig around here? That's what you said. That was five years ago. He didn't die."

Matty's response only fueled Jimmie's anxiety.

"Not yet."

Chapter Twenty-Seven
The Romance

"You want me to sit in that? You can't be serious."

Toolie pointed to Matty's flashy Mustang. His bucket seats were too low for her bucket.

Matty positioned her at the open passenger door and lifted her from the hospital's courtesy wheelchair. She seemed a tad weak and uncertain as she pivoted her backside toward the seat.

"Ease on down, Toolie," he said.

She huffed, closed her eyes and plunked. She reached behind her back and pulled out a half-eaten granola bar. "I'll thank my lucky stars if I survive this," Toolie said.

Matty closed her door, scrambled around the car and hopped behind the wheel. He turned the ignition. A growling rumble vibrated the vehicle.

"Land sakes, is this car gonna explode?" Toolie held her seat belt in both hands, not quite ready to click it and commit to the ride home.

"Explode? If we're lucky. I can rev this baby up to 60 miles per hour in three seconds. It's a Shelby GT 500KR."

"I'd rather ride a sheltie. Just get me home ... within the speed limit."

Matty obeyed, at least for a mile or two. He made an unexpected detour to the Kane state police barracks. When he stopped, Toolie's carping became intolerable.

"Why the hell did you pull in here?" She started to rub her legs. "My shingles, my shingles are flaring up again. Take me home,

Matty."

"I have your discharge papers, Toolie. The doctor did not limit any physical activity." Matty slammed shut his car door while Toolie was comparing her doctor to a limp pickle.

"Just cool it," he scolded her through his open window. "We'll be back at the boarding house in a few minutes. Wait here. There's someone here I need to see."

Matty bolted into the station and encountered Sgt. Heinrich at the front counter.

"Here's Dr. Greta's preliminary report on the samples." The sergeant handed Matty a manila envelope. "You may be pleased."

Matty flipped to the conclusion page and smiled. Dr. Greta confirmed that the stain on the shovel blade was blood, but she found two distinct blood types. Neither type matched Professor Dulaney's sample. Her DNA testing showed a match of one blood type with the hair sample Matty provided.

"Who's hair was it, Mr. Moore?" the trooper asked.

"You won't believe this, sergeant. Josh Gibson's."

Heinrich appeared to be dumbfounded. "What does that mean?"

"Josh Gibson was murdered. And the shovel is the murder weapon," Matty replied.

"But who did it?"

"My guess would be the same person whose blood is also on the shovel," Matty said.

"How could we figure that out?" the trooper asked.

"I'll get you another sample of hair," Matty said. "Maybe tonight."

Dolores Gibson was relaxing with her third Xanex when her telephone rang.

"Please hold for Judge Van Lear," a voice said.

A judge calling her?   Does Xanex cause hallucinations? Perhaps she needed to dial back her meds.

"Mrs. Gibson, this is Horace Van Lear. I was the judge in your insurance case.   Do you remember?"

Yes, that was a clear memory.   The judge had denied her $2 million in insurance because he determined that Josh committed suicide. That was a clear memory, but a bad one.   Uh-oh, depression coming on.   Maybe she needed to dial up her meds.

"Mrs. Gibson, I understand that the Pennsylvania State Police have opened a murder investigation for Josh.   Apparently, some new evidence has come to light."

"Your Honor, I knew Josh didn't take his life. I told you that, but you didn't believe me."

"My ruling can be overturned, Mrs. Gibson.   You have to act quickly."

"I'll do what I can."

"Call the County district attorney.   Don't tell him about this call.   I have to be neutral."

"Gotcha."

"Get details about a certain shovel from him and then have your attorney petition the Superior Court to remand the matter to me in light of newly discovered evidence.   Got it?"

"Got it."

"Then there's a ruling I can make. A certain insurance company may be very unhappy."

"Would I be happy?" Dolores asked.

"Very.   Oh and another thing.   Despite what you said in the newspaper article, my wife and I are having normal relations."

"That's good."

"You know, I mean, all of my equipment is functioning properly."

"Good for you."

"I don't mean office equipment, I mean, you know..."

"I know," Dolores said.   "You're keeping the misses satisfied."

"Exactly."

Toolie batted away Matty's hand.

"I can do this myself!" She grasped the railing and climbed the first step. Then the second step, and third. She stopped to look behind. Matty was two steps below her with his arms outstretched, just in case she lost her balance.

"Oh, for goodness … Matty, you can't be following me up the steps every day. I have to do this by myself."

"Just today, I promise. Then you're on your own. Now turn around and look where you're going."

Toolie snorted and turned to face eleven more steps. When she reached the eighth, she gained confidence and speed. On the top step, she loosened her grip from the railing and did a slow-motion pirouette.

Matty reached to keep her balanced.

"Get your hands away from me, you cad! Have you no manners?" Toolie sneered, but Matty detected a twinkle in her eye.

She turned a corner and began hobbling down her second floor hallway. Her apartment door was open. Helium balloons bobbed from the doorknob.

"Welcome home, Toolie!" Megan and Mr. George shouted as she peeked in the doorway. Her apartment was spotless. Her dining table was dressed with a freshly-pressed flowered tablecloth. Pink roses were gathered in a glass vase. She could smell a roasting chicken.

"Saints preserve us, Miss Megan! What a beautiful welcome! And Mr. George, what a pleasant surprise. You've extended your stay in Pennsylvania."

The elderly Indian took Toolie's arm and guided her to her recliner.

Matty whispered to Megan, "She didn't want me to touch her. Look at this."

"May I get you a cup of tea?" the Peacemaker asked her. "You must be exhausted from your hospital stay."

"Thank you, Mr. George," Toolie cooed. "A cup of tea would be delightful."

"A cup of tea would be delightful," Matty mocked her. "Megan, I've never seen Toolie so sickeningly sweet."

"Shhh," Megan said. "Let's just watch."

Mr. George assembled a tray with two china teacups and saucers, a silver bowl with sugar and the best two spoons from the kitchen drawer. He warmed a Pyrex cup with water in Toolie's microwave and whistled as the timer neared zero. Toolie hopped to the sofa and fluffed a pillow beside her.

"Matty, I have an idea," Megan whispered. "It was nice of you to sign papers to be Toolie's guardian, but you're only here for the summer. Who will care for Toolie when you're gone?"

They watched Mr. George return to the sofa and softly place his tray on a coffee table. He sat beside Toolie. They exchanged smiles. Obviously, she was charmed by the Peacemaker.

"Do you suppose Mr. George would stay a few more weeks, or months?" Matty asked.

"I'll ask," Megan replied.

Toolie and her new best friend were laughing. She didn't complain about her bruised ribs. She momentarily forgot about pain from the shingles. And she was so smitten that she probably didn't hear Matty recite his new poem:

"Roses are red, violets are bluey.

"That old Indian sure looks good with Toolie."

Tom Zachary opened the unmarked envelope on his desk. Inside were three typewritten pages. No strikeouts, no transpositions, no scribbles in the margins. And the most amazing thing, the story was delivered well before deadline.

"Jessie," he called to his office manager. "Look. Matty's story

314   WOODS ON FIRE

about the Bailey baby. I can't believe it. It looks perfect."

"Are you sure?" she asked, reading the copy over his shoulder.

"Little Hannah Maria must have really inspired him," Zachary said. "This is good stuff."

An ivory chiffon blanket framed her angelic face. A small curl entwining golden strands of hair peeked from the fabric like strings gathered from a celestial harp. The baby's lips, soft and dewy, parted slightly, and a sweet gurgle sound warmed our hearts.

"Our readers are going to eat this up," Zachary said. "Another sell-out on its way!"

Jessie read all three pages of pabulum. Either Matty's story was ghost-written or he intended the piece to be satire. But the editor liked it, and he was the final say.

"Slap Matty's byline on it and send it to production, Jessie."

Zachary had a self-satisfied grin. His investment in Matty was finally paying off.

"Mark my words, Jessie. That young man has a bright future."

Chapter Twenty-Seven
The Intruder

Nothing can focus the senses quite like a brick crashing through your bedroom window.

Billy Herman instinctively grabbed his handgun from a nightstand. He took cover behind an armoire and took aim at the broken window. Minutes passed. No hand reached in to open the lock. Billy stepped carefully amidst the broken glass. He ventured toward the window. His backyard was empty. Just some damn kid, he thought.

The brick had worked. It distracted Billy. He didn't notice the tiny sound – the pop of his front door lock.

Midnight had passed in downtown Zelienople. Streets were empty. Miles to the north, Billy's ranch house occupied a remote tract along Connoquenessing Creek. Signs were posted against hunting. Except for an occasional doe or buck feeding in the open fields, Billy had no nighttime visitors.

Until tonight.

The intruder paused, waiting to hear any movement. Billy obliged, opening his bedroom door and inching down the dark hallway. When Billy came into the intruder's view, his hands appeared to be empty. Billy peered into the black living room, and then reached for the light switch.

"Don't touch that!" the intruder ordered him.

Billy raised his hands like a captured criminal. "Who is it? What do you want?"

"Sit," the voice commanded.

Billy dropped to the nearest chair. The intruder stepped closer. Billy squinted, trying to recognize a face in the darkness.

"Have you come for the silver?" Billy asked.

There was no answer.

"Because the silver is gone. Went out this afternoon to a broker. No money here, either. It's supposed to be wired to my account. So you might as well go."

Billy could distinguish the metal object now shaking in the hand a few yards away.

"Don't be upset about the silver," Billy said. "It was mine. I found it. Josh Gibson stole it from me."

The hand waved more erratically. "Tell me more," the voice said.

"Gibson was a stupid ass," Billy said. "He didn't think I had the guts to stand up to him, the state police commissioner. Well, I did. And he learned a hard lesson."

"More!" the voice commanded.

Billy squirmed in his seat. The bulge in his back pocket was uncomfortable.

"I'll never forget the night Josh died. I called him at home and acted real friendly. I told him I knew that he dug up the silver. We were supposed to share it, but it took it himself. When I said that I forgave him, he was surprised. I told him on the phone that I needed his help. I said that I returned to Kinzua Valley because I believed there was more treasure. I told him that I found a lot more. And this time, it wasn't silver, it was gold!

"I told him there was so much gold that I couldn't dig it up alone, and that he was the only person who could help me and keep quiet about it. So he started mumbling something on the phone. It sounded like he was frothing at the mouth. He agreed to meet me in the valley at midnight.

"I spent the next few hours setting up my trap. I'd brought a few gold coins that I purchased at a dealer in Pittsburgh. They looked old and authentic. Then I took a shovel and dug a few test holes under the bridge. I waited until I saw headlights from his car pulling into Kinzua Park. I shined my flashlight toward him as he made his way down the valley path. I could see that he was wearing a shoulder holster, but a gun means nothing if you have the element of surprise.

"I showed Gibson the gold coins that I had roughed up. 'There's a chest full of them over there about a hundred yards,' I said, pointing toward the last remaining bridge trestle. I shined the flashlight and he led the way. We passed my test holes and he remarked that I had done a good job finding more treasure.

"His next words to me made me angry. He admitted that he double-crossed me and that he had taken the silver. I asked him what he had done with it and he said, 'I gave it all to Jimmie Bailey.' I said, 'What?' And he said that he had to give up the silver because he took it from state park property. He said he didn't want to be arrested. I said, 'That's ridiculous. What's the truth, Josh?'

"Gibson stuck to that story for a while, and then he admitted that he gave up the silver to 'buy' another term as police commissioner. I didn't believe that either. Not totally. "

Billy stared at the intruder and asked, "What do you think?"

The hand shook again. The intruder's face partially emerged from the shadow. "Tell me about Gibson's death."

"It was quick," Billy replied. "Not particularly painless, though.

"When we reached a spot near the last bridge trestle, I whacked the back of his head with a shovel. He was dazed, but he managed to grab the shovel and try to wrestle it from me. The shovel cut a gash in my shoulder. I kicked him and he stumbled backwards. I drove the shovel into his neck. He landed against the concrete base of the bridge. Blood was everywhere. Soon, he lost consciousness and collapsed.

"Gibson's body was just where I wanted it, at the foot of Kinzua Bridge. There was one problem, though. It wasn't smashed up enough to look like he fell from the bridge.

"So I took a heavy rock and smashed his skull. No matter, I

thought. The man was already dead. Then I kicked him in the ribs to break as many bones as possible. I was careful not to touch his service revolver. I figured if his gun were intact, nobody would suspect a murder.

"Then I threw the shovel and rock away into some bushes about a hundred feet away. I took off my shoes and kicked dirt into the little holes that I dug. And I tried to erase all of our footprints so it would appear that Gibson fell from the sky.

"Do I feel sorry for the man? Hell, no. It took me five years to get my silver. And you, my friend, were five hours too late. I sold it, and it's gone."

The intruder stepped forward into clearer light.

"You son of a bitch," the voice said.

"Put the damn gun away," Billy ordered. "You'll regret..."

A blast ended the conversation.

One body slumped to the floor.

One heart stopped beating.

The End

Author's Note

The only authentic character name in *Woods on Fire* is Woods on Fire. Little is known about this 18th Century Seneca Indian leader, other than his signature to the Treaty of Canandaigua of 1794. The Treaty allocated tens of thousands of acres along the Allegheny River Valley to the Seneca tribe. George Washington approved the Treaty, which was signed by his representative, Colonel Timothy Pickering. According to Article 3 of the Treaty:

"Now, the United States acknowledge all the land within the aforementioned boundaries, to be the property of the Seneka nation; and the United States will never claim the same, nor disturb the Seneka Nation, nor any of the Six Nations, or of their Indian friends residing thereon and united with them, in the free use and enjoyment thereof; but it shall remain theirs, until they choose to sell the same to the people of the United States, who have the right to purchase."

Despite the clear language of this Treaty, the U.S. Government took back about one-third of the Treaty lands, approximately 10,000 acres, by eminent domain. In the 1950's, Congress funded a Corps of Engineers project to construct a dam on the Allegheny River near Warren. The dam's purpose was flood water control downstream in Pittsburgh, although political leaders were intrigued by the recreational opportunities offered by the resulting reservoir. (In fact, the former Seneca reservation is now called "the Allegheny National Recreation Area.") Protests and lawsuits by Seneca leaders fell on the deaf ears of politicians and judges. In researching Seneca history for this book, I was surprised to learn of the callousness with which federal leaders treated the Seneca Nation. Major civil rights leaders of the day, including renowned civil libertarians on the Warren Supreme Court, President John Kennedy, Pittsburgh Mayor David Lawrence and civil rights proponent Thurgood Marshall, supported moves to take Seneca land without regard to any Treaty rights. In fact, these leaders, who touted their sympathy toward the nation's oppressed, refused to consider an engineering alternative to the Kinzua Dam project that would have protected the Treaty land.

On June 2, 1965, six months before the Kinzua Dam was completed, the Great Relocation began with a solemn ceremony by the Six Nations of the Iroquois. As author Joy A. Bilharz recounted in her excellent book, *The Allegany Senecas and Kinzua Dam: Forced Relocation Through Two Generations*, University of Nebraska Press, 1998, p.62:

"Corbett Sundown, a prominent chief at Tonawanda, led the ceremony, which began at 10:30 a.m. and lasted for nine hours. It ended with the Great Feather Dance at the old Longhouse and a cavalcade to the new one at Steamburg. ... The "moving of the fire" showed the continuing religious cohesiveness of the followers of Handsome Lake, a reaffirmation of Iroquois religious identity. Additionally, the composition of the ceremony incorporated basic elements of other ceremonies sanctioned by Handsome Lake, such as wampum, the Thanksgiving Speech, and tobacco burning. Several current Longhouse leaders recalled with awe the emotion generated by the final Great Feather Dance at the old Longhouse."

Many of the anecdotes described in *Woods on Fire* were initially published by Author Bilharz, including the exhumation of Seneca graves, the torching of homes and businesses by federal agents and the emotional "Relocation Day" in September 1965. I am grateful for her objective account of the trauma endured by Pennsylvania Senecas and especially by their children. (The story about a Seneca student spearing a goldfish with a pencil in protest of a classroom model of the Kinzua Dam is true and was first reported by Author

Bilharz.)

Additionally, I thank the following authors for their research, which offered me a more complete understanding of Seneca history: Thomas G. Smith, *Green Republican, John Saylor and the Preservation of America's Wilderness*, University of Pittsburgh Press, 2006; Barbara Graymont, *Iroquois: Indians of North America*, Chelsea House, 1988, and Tebbel and Jennison, *The American Indian Wars*, Castle Books, 2003.

The Seneca Nation of Indians operates a splendid website, which contains much information on its history and culture – *www.sni.org*. There you can find a complete text of the Treaty of Canandaigua, as well as a list of all signatories. Any of the signatories could have been a title for this book, including "Heap of Dogs," "Broxen Axe" and "Stinking Fish." I chose "Woods on Fire" as a more appropriate title for a mystery.

Works by the Nobel Prize winning poet, Czeslaw Milosz, are scattered in this book. Tom Zachary's jailhouse lament in Chapter 10, "Here I sit, a sly and angry journalist...," is derived from my favorite poem, "The Poor Poet," Czeslaw Milosz, *Collected Poems*, HarperCollins, 2003. Milosz was born in Poland and wrote about Nazi and Soviet occupation of his country, topics infinitely more profound than Zachary's weekend incarceration in the McKean County Jail.

Again, I thank my wife, Louann, for her editing skills and unending encouragement. Tom Costello earns my respect for generating interest in the publishing community for the Rivers of Pittsburgh Mystery Trilogy series. Tom is one of few remaining publishers in today's economy who is not afraid to take a calculated risk on new talent. I also congratulate Pittsburgh's most creative illustrator, Taylor Callery, for his intriguing cover art and design.

I am deeply indebted to my new friends in Kane and Smethport, whose eagerness to share interesting stories and legends of northwestern Pennsylvania contributed greatly to the Rivers of Pittsburgh Mystery Trilogy. I thank Amber Hancharick, the Kane

322   WOODS ON FIRE

Chamber of Commerce, Kane Mayor Doug Caldwell, Dave Krieg, Deborah Lunden, Dale Delong, Bill Kilmer, Earl Kilmer, Joan Yeckley and Jackie Taylor. I also thank the world's finest nature photographer, Rocky Holland, for his blue jay photograph, which inspired the surly attitude drawn for Toolie the waitress.

Not having spent my youth in and around Kinzua State Park, I relied on memories and experiences of McKean County natives. Apparently, when the Kinzua Bridge was intact and somewhat structurally sound, teenage boys climbed up the 300-foot-high steel trestles at night. It was a foolish "rite of passage," one reader told me. Hence, Jimmie Bailey and Bill Pennoyer copied the stunt to prove their manhood in Chapter 14. Another McKean County native, currently residing in Washington State, advised me to visit Kinzua Park after dark because "I've been there to see the black bears in the dumpsters at night far more times than I've been up to look at the bridge in the daylight." Hence, the appearance of Einstein the Bear in four chapters.

Other readers related to me the myth that treasure was buried in Kinzua Valley. The most popular story involves "Blackbeard's silver." A complete account of this legend was written by Francis X. Scully, "Pennsylvania's Lost Silver Treasure." See *www.coudy.com*. Mr. Scully's account is similar to Megan Broward's description of Captain Blackbeard's harrowing voyage in Chapter 13. A key difference is the alleged location of Blackbeard's treasure. Rather than in the shadow of Kinzua Bridge, the treasure is rumored to be buried in Gardeau, a tiny village in the southeastern corner of McKean County. In today's dollars, Mr. Scully estimates the value of the lost treasure at $3 million.

McKean County offers "a rare opportunity for an enterprising treasure hunter," he writes.

Nobody knows, however, whether the treasure comes with an Indian curse.

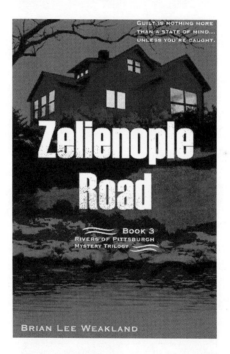

WA